D0256588

Red Mist

Also by Geoff Thompson:

Watch My Back
The Elephant and the Twig
The Great Escape
A Book for the Seriously Stressed
Fear - The Friend of Exceptional People
The Throws & Take-downs of Judo
The Throws & Take-downs of Sombo
The Throws & Take-downs of Free-Style Wrestling
The Throws & Take-downs of Greco-Roman Wrestling
Animal Day
The Art of Fighting Without Fighting
Dead Or Alive - The Choice Is Yours
The Fence
The Pavement Arena
Real Head, Knees and Elbows
Real Grappling
Real Kicking
Real Punching
Three Second Fighter
Weight Training for the Martial Artist
Pins: the Bedrock
The Escapes
Chokes and Strangles
Fighting from your Back
Fighting from your Knees
Arm Bars and Joint Locks

RED MIST

by

GEOFF THOMPSON

summersdale

Summersdale Publishers Ltd
46 West Street
Chichester
West Sussex
PO19 1RP
UK

www.summersdale.com
www.geoffthompson.com

Printed and bound in Great Britain.

ISBN: 184024 370 8

Acknowledgements

To Rachael Osborne, my lovely editor, with much appreciation for her kind words of advice and encouragement.

To Stewart and Alastair for having ten years' worth of faith in me and for massive encouragement with my first novel.

To Ros for making such a big difference.

To Vicky for her fantastic promotion.

To Liz, Kelly and all the beautiful staff at Summersdale Publishers for their love and support.

To Derek Searle and all the great people at Derek Searle Associates for doing such a fabulous job selling *Red Mist*.

Dedicated to my late friend Peter Robins,
a great martial artist and a true gentleman.
He is sadly missed.

To Sharon
– as always –
because I love her bones.

Prologue

There's a story I heard once, about a king in a faraway land who was determined to own a fighting rooster of repute, a bird that could beat all others. He summoned one of his many subjects to him and commanded the man, known throughout the kingdom for his skill at schooling roosters in the art of fighting, to train one for him. The man agreed. He began by teaching the rooster all the techniques of combat.

After ten days the king summoned him. 'Is the bird ready?' he asked. 'Can I organise a fight for him yet?'

'Not yet, sir,' said the man. 'He is powerful but his strength is empty, he is full of hot air. He wants to fight all the time; he is overexcited and he has no endurance.'

Ten days later the king called the trainer again, impatient now. Again he asked, 'Is he ready yet? Can I organise a fight?'

'No, no, no!' The trainer was adamant. 'He is not ready. Not yet. He is still too fierce, he is still looking to fight all the time. Whenever he hears another rooster crowing, even in the next village, he flies into a rage and wants to fight. He's nowhere near ready.'

Another ten days of training went by. The king made his request a third time. 'Now is it possible? Is he ready yet?'

The trainer replied, 'Well, he has stopped flying into a rage now and he manages to keep calm when he hears another rooster crowing. His posture is good, and he has a lot of power in reserve. He has stopped losing his temper all the time. Looking at him, you are not aware of his energy and strength.'

'Can we go ahead with the fight?' asked the king.

The trainer thought for a moment then nodded. 'Yes.'

So a great many fighting roosters were assembled for the long-awaited fight and the tournament began.

However, no bird would come near the king's rooster. They all ran away, terrified, the moment they saw him.

The fighting rooster had become a rooster of wood. He had gone beyond his technical training. He possessed enormous energy but it was all inside, he never showed it. His power stayed within himself, and the other birds had no choice but to bow before his tranquil assurance and undisplayed strength.

- Adapted from the writings of Master Taisen Deshimaru.

After

He's a mysterious fucker is God. Mysterious. He moves in *mysterious* ways. And what he gives he can take away. I should know, the Fucker (capital 'F' just in case) has been giving and taking from me all my life. For instance: one minute he gives me the girl of my dreams and the possibility of a blissful life, the next I'm stuck in a police cell facing life in prison on the back of a murder charge.

Eighteen years behind bars. Can you imagine that? That's nine if I keep a clean nose, seven after spending eighteen months on remand awaiting trial. Nine Christmases, nine birthdays, a tenth of my life (if I live to be anywhere near a hundred). From the outside looking in, it might not sound like much, but when you're living in a grey brick cage locked behind a steel door with nothing for company but your own thoughts (and your right fist) it's a fucking eternity. They couldn't punish you more if they strapped you naked to a post and gave you a hundred lashes with the cat-o'-nine-tails.

Life? You'd come out a different man. Parts of you broken beyond repair. Your woman, if she isn't already shacked up with someone else, will have plenty of broken bits too. When you finally do get out, leashed to a curfew tag, you'll be a veritable stranger to her. You'll have to start all over again, with a backpack of old regrets that will get heavier the longer you carry them.

I couldn't believe I was facing an eighteen. And all because I let myself get dragged into a domestic in some greasy spoon café...

Chapter One

Café

I love cafés. Love them. I am a connoisseur. And this one, The Bacon Butty, was one of the best. It was a real place with real people and real food: greasy, buttery, artery-thickening grub that sends you to the coffin with a big fuck-off smile on your face. I'd decided to take a two-week annual holiday from work as a brickie and I intended to enjoy every minute of it.

The girl that served my tea was as thick as a butcher's block. She had a face like a boxing trainer but her manner was sweet and attentive.

'Anyfin' else, bab?'

'No, that's great, thanks.' I tried not to talk to her teeth, which were stained the same shitty brown as the chrome two-cup teapot. The butter, slapped on with a trowel, dripped from my toast on to a chipped plate, which had a withered flower motif that looked like a sauce stain. I might as well have plastered the butter right on to my belly.

The waitress picked up a used cup from the next table and the heavy flesh of her upper arm swung dangerously; I instinctively wanted to duck for cover. I tried to visualise her as a young girl, before the nicotine had stained her fingers autumnal brown and dyed her hair an unfortunate yellow. Before life had dragged her down to a nine-to-five in a dirty, greasy spoon café. It was difficult. I wondered how lives ended this bare. Stripped to the metal. Horribly sparse. I wondered why my life mirrored hers (except for the floppy arms and Hallowe'en teeth). I watched in fascination as the ladder in her tights expanded and contracted as she walked away. She had a tear at the heel where her ill-fitting shoes had rubbed. Calves like Spanish wine bottles.

The girls in the café were homely. They smiled and made tea for you like they made for their old man at home. Who cared if their floppy arms knocked cups off tables? Who cared if they failed their 11-plus and got pregnant at 15, divorced with two children at 19, disillusioned and fat by 25, and wiping tables at a small café in a shitty part of an even shittier city at 30? You still got the feeling that when they smiled it was genuine, and when they called you 'love' they meant it.

As the waitress walked past the next table she spoke to a girl who was sat alone with a cup of tea. I hadn't seen her here before, and I'd remember: she was gorgeous. Her angelic face was proof of a god. She had long ginger hair that curled pleasingly around the shoulders and teasingly off the eyes, and a body to die for; there was an innocence about her that I liked. I got the feeling that if she knew just how beautiful she was you wouldn't get near her without a healthy wad and a Porsche Boxter. As it was, she seemed too naive to recognise what was obvious to anyone with two eyes and a libido. She was a stunner. I couldn't lift my eyes off her.

I caught her eye. She smiled shyly. I looked back at my chipped plate and then again looked surreptitiously across at Ginger (already named in my mind because of her beautiful mane). She seemed to be looking straight at me. I looked behind to see who the freckled beauty was smiling at. It *couldn't* be me. I was the wrong type for a start. Thirty-five and dishevelled, nice but plain, a charmer but under-confident, heavy on the sides but light on the crown. A good man, but an ordinary man, and certainly the beast to this beauty.

There was no one behind me other than a 90-year-old lady with a walnut face and a neck like a gathered sock. I looked back at Ginger, the smile still on her face, then behind again, double-checking. I raised my eyebrows in a question. Her teasing smile said, 'Yes, you.' I half committed myself and smiled back.

I didn't talk to her in case she wasn't smiling at me after all and I embarrassed myself. So no words, just a smile that I could pass off if she returned one of those 'what the fuck are you smiling at?' looks. When I realised that she *was* actually smiling at me I nearly fell off my chair.

Before I had the chance to think, her eyes went blank. Oh fuck, she wasn't smiling at me after all. There is nothing more humiliating than returning a greeting that was meant for someone else, some good-looking clothes-horse behind you.

Her eyes locked firmly on the café door behind me. The smile dropped from her face, to be replaced by a look of terror; eyes colonised by fear, skin clammy and pale. I scrunched up my eyes, confused. I felt the draught on my back. The atmosphere hit January. The cheerful banter from behind the counter stopped. I turned around.

He stood in the doorway, a saloon cowboy looking for a shoot-out. His eyes had an angry, bulbous look that said 'crazy fucker'. He was not a big man physically (the really dangerous types rarely are), eleven stone at the most, but he was agitated. One of those guys that could kill you with half a reason and a very sharp pencil. It was a look I had seen before. Another bully, another piece of shit. A dark cloud on an otherwise sunny day. Life is full of them. In school they stalk the playground seeking prey; the kid with the briefcase instead of a rucksack, the lad with the glasses and freckles and the nice accent. You get them at the factory, blisters looking for an easy target. The apprentice entering a new world. The baggy-skinned labourer frightened to argue back.

My toast suddenly looked like a carpet tile, my appetite wilted. As the cloud stormed through the café, people ducked for cover under shadows of fear. The cowboy's eyes dropped challengingly on each person in turn. From the old man slurping loudly on his third tea to the pubescent lovers two tables across, eating more face than fry-up, then to the staff behind the counter. Even old sock-neck got a challenging glare. He locked in on me. Fair enough. I was probably the only legitimate threat in the room. He looked me up and down. A small grin lifted the corner of his mouth. It said: 'You're no threat at all.' I was happy with his assessment; I hoped it meant that I could avoid a fight. I looked away; I didn't want trouble. I'd had a lifetime of the stuff. I wasn't about to court more. I'd taken enough drunken beatings from my dad when I was a kid to know that it wasn't the place to be if you had even a modicum of sense.

I had learned to avoid eye contact with violent people like you would wild dogs. Eye contact is a challenge to fight. Whether you hold the gaze or not is your choice not theirs. Holding eye contact is the acceptance of a challenge. It's not John Wayne. It's not an old black-and-white Western. It's not *Star Wars* or Bruce Lee – that stuff is testicles. That's no more real than Father Christmas. In this arena and with these babies it's real-time, life-changing danger that might leave you with anything from a plum eye to a toe tag and your own slot at the local cemetery. And that's their choice, not yours.

Violence in this arena, the pavement arena, is a serious business where the wrong look or a glance held too long could get you a glass ashtray in the teeth and enough post-knock-out boots in the head to send your blood spitting and pumping into the carpet. If you like your face in place, and not crushed under the boot of some brain-shy, then stay at home and enjoy it on DVD where you can hide behind the fast-forward button or the pillow if things get a little too real.

I didn't even know this crazy fucker so I had no intention of trading knuckle with him. Not while I had a choice in the matter.

The cowboy strode over to Ginger and leaned on the edge of her table. He stared her into submission. She quivered. It hurt just to watch. I knew the script. It was predictable and ugly. She would make a feeble attempt to stand her ground in the hope that someone might step in and fight her corner. If anyone did, the chances were that this man of violence would dispatch them very quickly, which meant she'd get a perfunctory beating anyway, just to let her know not to argue in future. It was just a domestic, a lovers' tiff. He'll give her a bit of heavy, she'll have a cry in public, and they'll kiss and make up. Seen it happen a million times. I did not get involved in domestics. I'd got my own baggage. I was pretty fucked up myself, and I don't remember anyone coming to my rescue when life dealt me a cruel blow.

'Get up. Now!' He delivered the statement with venom. Even I wanted to obey him. The menace in his voice came out in chunks.

Ginger's reply was brave but shaky. 'You can't keep doing this to me, Mick.'

So he was a Mick. I was not far out when I thought 'prick'.

'I'm not fucking asking you, I'm telling you.' He delivered his words in a forced whisper, angry and embarrassed at having to ask twice. 'You're coming with me. Fucking move. Now!'

He leaned forward, the palms of his hands on the table. He was nose to nose with Ginger. Close enough to shoot the words right into her skin. She leaned back into the bench. Her face flinched involuntarily, as though she was expecting a dig at any minute. She'd obviously been here before. She shook her head and screwed up her eyes, waiting for the attack that her defiance would surely bring.

'I said you're fucking coming back with me now.' The expletive spat venomously from his lips. Ginger backed further into her seat.

By now the whole café was a graveyard. Teacups hung suspended between saucer and mouth. Conversations paused mid-gossip. All eyes locked on to the real-life soap to see if strong words would spill into hard violence. The cowboy was a table away from me; I could smell his sweaty armpits and the stale breath of last night's beer. His face was sharp, brimming with hate. Every dent in his skin, every scar reeked of malevolence. I looked him up and down, measuring and assessing the potential threat, something I had learned to do as a nightclub doorman, something I'd done off and on for years when bad weather made building work impossible and money tight. He was a scrawny bastard with sinewy muscles and a prominent Adam's apple. His squeezy-bottle neck looked ripe for the wringing.

Fast bobsleigh adrenalin raced around my veins, burrowing into my fighting muscles. My mouth felt dry and pasty. My thighs were heavy and trembling. Bats raced around in my belly, ready for the ruck. Neck hair stood to attention. Internal dialogue – that cowering voice in the back of your mind that seems to step forward every time confrontation is imminent – looking for a way out; I wished that I was anywhere but stuck in this domestic quandary. I felt vulnerable. Alone. Conflicted.

If I walked and left the girl to face a bashing, I would not be able to live with myself. If I stayed and made pizza out of her threat, I was opening myself up to unknown complications. If this was on celluloid, on TV or at the pictures where the hero saves the damsel from the dressed-in-black baddie and everyone lives happily ever after (except for the baddie who, by then, is fertiliser), it would have been fine. Dandy. Tomato ketchup blood. A handful of tit. That was all that was needed to get spontaneous applause from people who'd be traumatised if they got within a mile of the real thing. Off screen, actions have consequences that change lives, and not often for the better. Violence stinks. It's ugly.

There was no way out. No movie director to stop the action with a shout of 'Cut!' I knew I would have to do something, and soon, before this piece of shit found his violent feet and used them to trample on the heads of innocents.

Why was I worried? Why the fuck was I worried? What did it have to do with me? It had nothing to do with me. I didn't even know this girl. And I didn't know the goon hovering over her, a drooling beast about to eat. See, my problem was the fact that whenever I witnessed abuse I wanted to stop it there and then. I made it my problem. It could have been anyone – not just some gorgeous face on an hourglass – I always felt as though it was down to me. But this was not my problem. This was not my world, it was not where I wanted to be. I decided to make my exit before I was forced into a sticky altercation.

'Well?' It was Mick again, in Ginger's face and wanting an answer. He'd slid into the seat opposite her.

I stood up to leave. Ginger's eyes lifted from the table to meet mine. Her lips trembled as she smiled hopefully. Mick looked at me too. A challenging glare that said 'fuck off, it's a domestic'. Ginger must have thought I was standing to fight her corner. She did everything but wave a white hanky. The look of expectation on her face placed a lump in my throat. It was only surpassed by the look of disappointment when I got up and started walking to the door. I could feel Mick following me with his eyes as I walked. Smug. Smarmy. Grinning across his face.

I had no obligations to an imaginary girlfriend.

My eyes dropped to the cracked floor tiles. As I walked towards the door I caught my reflection in the mirror above the tables. I looked how I felt. A fat coward leaving the scene of a beating. And there would be a beating. If not there in the café, then certainly later. You can kid yourself all day long that it's a domestic and that it is none of your business, but the bottom line is that you're walking away and you shouldn't be. My reflection was not kind: thinning on top, a broken nose (but handsomely so I liked to think), a pouch of fat hanging over my jeans and a fat arse. A fat arse walking away from a fight.

It was none of my business.

'I'm not coming back, Mick. I'm never coming back.' I heard Ginger's voice behind me, trembling with fear.

'I don't fucking remember making it an option, you cunt.' This Mick was a charmer. Had a real way with women.

It was fuck-all to do with me. I opened the door to leave. I was halfway out. Halfway to freedom; normality almost within my grasp. Suddenly the sound of punched face echoed off the walls. A cold tremble went from my arse to my neck. My legs felt hollow.

I turned back to confirm what I already knew: he had punched her. I looked at Ginger. Her face was flushed red. A trickle of blood dripped from her nose and dribbled over her pale lips. A look of sad acceptance was on her face as she wiped the blood away with the back of her hand. Eyes switched off.

In my mind's eye I saw my mum, post-beating. That same look of surrender. Of inevitability. She wore it every Sunday when the old man came back from the pub with a skin full of strong ale and a different personality.

Ginger looked at the table. Mick never lifted his eyes from her.

'Listen, Mick.' It was one of the waitresses, she'd come from behind the counter. A short, brave doughnut of a girl with red hair and a farmer's face. Her words were pleading. 'She don't need this no more. You've been split up for six months, she ain't never comin' back, she –'

'Listen, twat.' Mick placed venom behind the word 'twat'. He picked up an egg-stained menu. 'When I want somethin' from you,' he told her, 'I'll look at the fucking menu. Now keep your cunt out of it.'

He put a full stop on his verbal assault by skimming the menu across the counter like a discus. Everyone ducked instinctively.

The doughnut backed off, suitably reprimanded. I lined up Mick as I walked back into the café. My mind was in the pre-fight tremble that makes runners out of most would-be fighters. I gripped my fear and made myself step forward, even though everything inside me wanted to retreat. I was angry that he had not allowed me to exit, that he had not allowed me to butt out. Now I was forced to do something. I caught the eye of the doughnut. She gave a look that said 'Do something you worthless, ball-less bastard.'

Mick was poking Ginger in the chest now.

'You don't fucking listen, do ya?' he snarled at her, each word punctuated by a sharp finger poke.

I could hear her involuntary sobs as his fingers pushed the air from her lungs. It caught the fear as it left her throat. I couldn't stand it any more. I stood over the table, inches away from him.

Ginger looked up at me and then immediately looked away again. My presence might complicate things for her. No complications for me. Just a matter of controlling the fear. Not the fear of having a fight. Not the fear of fisticuffs, that was the easy bit. It could be dealt with. Not that the thought of a fight was nerve-wracking, although you'd be a fool to enter an affray too cocky, but I'd spent most of my youth studying pragmatic fighting arts in a bid to fight off invasions and fears that demanded a strong arm and a sinewy mentality. I had wrestled with enough broken noses and cauliflower ears on the door to know my way around a physical fight, but it had been a while since my last fracas. It was the fear of consequence that was threatening to fill my nappy. This situation was more than physical. You don't just twat a maniac like Mick and neatly put the situation to bed. It doesn't store away. It don't do neat. If Mick was still coming back for Ginger six months after they'd broken up, what would be in store for me? You do not take on a man like this in a three-second fight; you take the fucker on for life. Forever.

Mick's eyes darted to the corners of their sockets as if they were being worked by a stick at the back of his head. He looked crazy, like he was laced with Class A. His eyes locked on to me but his head remained facing Ginger. Then his eyes swivelled back to her.

'Unless your friend is looking for a bit of contact, he'd better fuck off,' he said.

She didn't speak. She was mute with fear. I don't know who was more scared, her or me.

This was my chance to fuck off. He had offered me a window. And believe me, I felt like climbing through it. I wanted to be far away from this shit hole. Everything inside me was screaming 'Run you fucker, run!' Sometimes running is the right thing to do. Sometimes you should listen to natural instinct, the survival mechanism, and run like the wind blows. But at other times, running is not appropriate. It is not the right response, despite what your arsehole is telling you. Sometimes you should stay. This was one of those times. Over the years swapping leather in boxing gyms and wrestling with the pros I'd developed the willpower to stand and fight even when my kneecaps were doing an involuntary bossanova.

The fight was already on. It starts with the interview, the dialogue; his leading technique was verbal. Fights are often won and lost this way. His way of trying to psych me out was to direct his verbal at me through a third party; Ginger in this case. It's the game. It's supposed to say that he rates me so little he doesn't even need to look at me. I had played the game before, and with better players than this. I'd already made up my mind to smash his sneaky, greasy little head right in. So for me the preliminaries were just a warm-up, my chance to find an opening for the first shot. I played the game right back. I pitched my voice up above the adrenal tremor that had the vocals doing a riverdance in my throat and held my voice firm. I looked straight at Ginger.

'You all right, mate? You need any help?'

This was my way of playing the psych game right back. I ignored his threat as if it had failed to reach my ears. Instead of talking directly to him I spoke to Ginger. And anyway, I needed to know that she did actually want my help. Domestics are funny. Very unpredictable. I had a mate who got his bicep slashed by a bird with a Stanley knife because he had tried to stop her boyfriend from flattening the world with her head. As soon as my mate stepped in they both turned on him. As he lay bleeding into a drain, the couple – after kicking his head until their feet hurt – kissed and made up. You can never be sure. So I asked.

It was Mick who answered. He spoke without moving his eyes from Ginger's face. Everyone in the shop looked on in stunned silence. I heard pins dropping.

'She's got all the fucking help she needs right here.' He lifted his bony left fist and placed it by her nose to underline what he meant by 'here'. Her face trembled against his hard fist. My right fingers bunched lightly, ready to break his jaw just under the ear.

If you want to knock them out you hit them low on the jaw. It jars the head and causes unconsciousness. And normally that's what I'd have been looking for. Fuck the restraints and wrist locks. Unconsciousness is the only safe restraint. When they're sleeping they're no longer a danger.

As it was, the angle never offered me the end of the jaw, but it did offer me a clean shot where the jawbone met with the skull. The jaw gives very little at this point. A good shot snaps the bone like a Twiglet.

'Do you want some help, bab?'

It was the second time I'd asked her. She looked up at me. Eyes pleading. Words unnecessary.

I was hoping to do this without being physical – even though I knew that with men of this ilk there was little chance. I had to exhaust negotiation before sending in the troops.

'Listen, mate.' I spoke to him in a soft voice, so as not to trigger a Neanderthal rage. 'She don't want any of it. Leave it out, eh?' It was worth a try.

Bang! Before I could stop him, and completely to my surprise, he thrust his tattooed right hand – 'Hate' across the fingers, dead original, with 'Love' on the left knuckles no doubt – across the table and grabbed Ginger by the throat. She looked up in startled terror. She grabbed his hand and tried to peel his taut fingers from her neck. The pubescent lovers looked on in shocked silence, gripping each other's hands so hard the knuckles were white. The sock-neck lady trembled in her seat, trapped by the violence.

I have to tell you that this was not in my game-plan; I did not expect such a blatant and immediate reaction to my presence. It took me by surprise. No more dialogue. No more over-the-table negotiations. My attempts at a peace treaty had failed abysmally. Time for a little physical.

Ginger was choking and spluttering and watering at the eyes. The girls behind the counter had become ice statues. Mick was salivating with anger and shouting obscenities.

'Who the fuck do you think you're talking to?' he shouted at me, oblivious now to the rest of the people in the café. This was a man who was used to enacting violence in public places and relying on his violent reputation to stop people from becoming involved. 'You think I'm some kind of cunt, hey? I got "cunt" written across me fucking swede or summut?'

He didn't have 'cunt' written across his swede, but he fucking should have. Written in bold Las Vegas neon. The lad was as big a fanny as I'd ever seen.

Everyone else in the café pushed back into their seats as far as possible and looked on in startled, fascinated terror. Those that could backed towards the door or a wall or the counter. None left the premises. The waitresses – used to the violence of a back street café with its drunks and druggies and single mums and unemployable youths – were frozen to the spot. Bacon fizzed on a spitting griddle. If there had been a juke-box I am sure that the music would have stopped dead, mid-record.

'Get the fuck off her!' I shouted, already knowing that my voice would not pierce his adrenal deafness – and even if it did I knew that this yoke would listen to nothing less than a heavy dose of pain. I was ready to give it to him. I whipped my right arm around his throat as I shouted. I made a strangle, cutting off the blood supply to the lad's brain. A good strangle can start brain death in seconds: it cuts the blood off via the carotid arteries at the base of the neck, killing the oxygen supply to the brain. No danger here. For this fucker, brain death had obviously occurred at birth. He immediately released his grip on Ginger who made a swallowed-fish-bone cough and gasped for breath. He tried to prise my arm from his scrawny neck. He was a lifetime too late. Too fucking late; it was on and going nowhere. He was already mine. There was not a lot he could do other than wriggle and splutter and die; he was trapped between the table and bench.

As I tightened my strangle he exploded out of the chair with a strength that surprised me. His pubic bone smashed into the lip of the table. A half-full teapot catapulted off the surface and onto the floor with a loud clatter. The tea splashed across the chipped tiles. Ginger jumped in her seat in fright.

When I get a strangle on I normally get them out very quickly. Keep it for a few seconds and it gives them a little slice of death. Hold it on for a minute or more and they get to meet their maker. This bastard was hardy; he wasn't going down without a fight. But he was going down. I would make sure of that. He was fighting, scratching, gargling (they always gargle when you cut their life off from the neck) and spitting. His fingers were reaching behind him trying to poke and scratch at my eyes. I tucked my face into the back of his head to protect them. I pulled him back tightly into the chair, which creaked and strained and trapped him between it and the table. He was still struggling like a fish on a hook, flipping and thrashing. He suddenly forced himself out between the chair and the table in an attempt to escape. We staggered backwards into the aisle. Screams from the captive audience pierced my adrenal deafness.

As we struggled he lurched backwards and we smashed into the glass counter and fell to the floor. I was still holding on to the strangle. Mick's back was tightly wedged against my belly. I wrapped my legs around his torso as we fell and tightened my thighs into a scissor so that he couldn't turn out of the hold.

A couple of mugs and a cream bun fell from the glass display cabinet onto my head. One shattered across the floor. All the girls behind the counter screamed in unison; backing singers at a punk concert. Mick thrashed around, rolling onto his belly, right on top of the two mugs – one in sharp broken pieces – and the cake, with me still stuck to his back like I was riding rodeo. It was the worst thing he could have done. But it is the first thing most people do when they have no knowledge of fighting on the ground. They roll onto their belly in the mistaken belief that they can push up and get back on their feet. In reality, all they do is trap their one means of escape – their hands – under their own body weight. Once on his belly the game was over for Mick.

My breathing was laboured – I was not in the right shape to be rolling around café floors with bastards like this. I tightened my legs around his waist and forced my pubic bone into his back so that all his remaining breath (and whatever he might have eaten for breakfast) was forced up through his diaphragm like a reverse suffocation. I squashed his face so hard into the floor that bits of broken china punctured his cheek and stuck to his face like hideous party glitter. My face was forced tightly against the back of his head. Sweat dripped from my brow into his greasy hair. Every gap closed until we were as one. I was so tight that even his pores were choking. The fear pulsed out from his eyes and panicky girly whimpers escaped his throat.

It was a good feeling, knowing that I had won, knowing that he was nearly finished. As his struggles became weaker I knew that he was seconds from unconsciousness so I sent him to sleep with a little message.

‘I’m gonna hold this on,’ I whispered, ‘until you’re dead, you piece of shit.’

This was just part of the psych-out. It sent him to sleep full of terror thinking that he might never wake up again. When – if – he did wake, my words would still be fresh in his mind. It would tell him two things: firstly, that I was capable of killing him, and secondly, that he was still alive, but only because I had been merciful and given him a reprieve. That made him mine forever. Sounds gratuitous I know, but it does the job. Stops the fuckers coming back for a return match – well, usually.

I watched as his colour turned to blue. His eyes stayed open when he went out – sometimes they do – but I could tell he’d gone because the struggle had left his limbs and small branches of blood started to creep along his eyeballs as they swelled out of their sockets.

Recognising that Mick was no longer a threat, the girls behind the till burst into a volley of spontaneous chatter and raced around the counter to console Ginger. She was sobbing uncontrollably. The little red-haired doughnut kicked one of the mugs that had fallen in the struggle into Mick’s face as she stepped over us. She gave him an evil glare as she did so. The mug clanged off his brow, producing an immediate mouse over his eye. Mick did not respond. Well, they don’t when they’re unconscious. He was unconscious! So why was I still holding on to him?

His body convulsed below me in a death shudder, but I still held on. This was the bit that I didn’t like about me. I could see that he was out there with Pluto and I knew that the job was done and that I should let go, but I didn’t. I couldn’t. This was the dark part of me that scared me most. The red mist that came over me every time I entered an affray. I wanted to hold on to the strangle until I drained every last beat out of his heart, until the blue on his skin was a permanent fixture and the last bit of black had left those shark eyes. Until he was proper dead. And he almost was when I finally realised that everyone in the café had stopped talking and sobbing and consoling and all eyes were firmly locked on me. My space.

I was still lying on Mick's back, arms tight around his neck in a death hug. There was fear in their eyes. For a second I felt confused. Why were they scared? Hadn't I taken away the threat? Then the realisation hit me. They were frightened of me! No one moved. As they continued the death-watch and I continued to strangle I caught a glance from Ginger. She looked sad. That made me feel sad.

There was a stain deep below my skin that I couldn't seem to lose, even though I keep trying to choke it out of other people, like Mick. I wasn't sad because this piece of shit was unconscious and blue and dying. I was sad because I realised that when I entered the darkness I became the darkness. Looking at Mick was like looking into a mirror. I still didn't stop. I couldn't. It was like this other person had taken over. I had lost all sense of who I was. I could feel myself almost enjoying it. And he was dying.

Chapter Two

Runner

I have a recurring dream. I am sitting on top of a dead body, strangling a faceless, lifeless foe. Dread fills me. In my dream I jump off the body with a startled jerk. I lift the dead skull by the hair to look for any sign of life. There is none. When I release the hair, the floppy head thumps on to the concrete with a hollow thud. The veins in my temples start to pulsate and a sob that doesn't belong to me bursts from my throat. I try to hold it in, but I have been holding it in for too long and it is big enough now to come out despite my best efforts to stop it. A seed that I locked in so many years ago is now an oak forcing its thick branches and trunk out of my throat. My body convulses as the second sob leaves and then the third and then so many that my shoulders become piston rods and tears coat my face. In my dream I cover my face, ashamed. Real men don't cry.

Where I come from you learned not to cry from an early age. In a family of tough men – my dad was an Irish road digger and labourer and my brother carried a hod – crying was attacked with the same venom as intimacy. If you had a problem, you went down to the pub and drowned it under a gallon of strong ale or displaced it in a fight outside the chip shop. Real men! They never cried. Not in our house, not in my world. When things got shadowy, you filled yourself to the throat with beer.

The dream is always the same one. I choke with chunky, violent tears. I can't breathe. I'm gasping to get some air back into my lungs. I'm dizzy with the effort, dizzy, my head spinning and floating. I feel like I am dying, like the reaper has come and I am desperately trying to avoid the appointment.

Then I wake. My day-to-day life flashes before me. It's not much of a show. Twelve hours a day on the buildings shovelling concrete, laying bricks and developing a very strong back and just enough black humour to get me through until Friday. Friday afternoon to Sunday night an oblivion of drink and takeaway food. The occasional shag from some faceless, bra-less moose who looked great in the nightclub shadows and felt good in the bed but turned into an unspeakable troll by the time sobriety and light returned with the morning. Every beer-princess turned into a frog in my bed. It was probably just as bad for them. Many of the girls I picked up were gone by the morning. And those that weren't never stayed for breakfast. They hovered around in embarrassed silence looking for last night's tights and the soiled pants of promiscuity. Then I never saw them again, sometimes because I didn't want to, but usually because they just disappeared. It was almost as though they never existed outside the nightclub where I wooed them with promises of exotic food (a curry) and travel (a taxi to my flat).

The nightmarish sobs turn into one long shudder as years of tears force themselves from a self-imposed captivity. No time to get my breath in between. My hands wrestle with the blankets, the claustrophobia closes in, my face contorts as the pain creases me. Faces are ugly when they cry. That's what my dad told me when I was little. I couldn't help crying one day because he came back from the pub drunk and vile and staggering. It was like I had two dads. One was an honest, hard-working dad that came home from the buildings smelling of fresh air and sweat. The other was an unpredictable ogre, one minute slobbering over you, the next a monster shouting words I'd never heard before, words that always made Mum cry; the dad who would drag Mum by the hair, like a sack of coal, from the front room to the kitchen because his dinner wasn't hot enough.

'Not in front of the kids!' she'd cry, thinking about us even in the middle of a beating. I remember running after him crying, hanging on to the back of his jacket and begging him to leave her alone. He swiped me away with a heavy arm. When he'd finished with my mum, when she was bleeding from the mouth and propped over the cooker like a crash-test dummy, he'd grabbed me by the cheek with his thumb and finger and thrust my crying face into the mirror so hard that my nose bled into the glass. The blood and tears and breath mixed into a steamy crimson stain.

'See that?' he said with a force that turned me mute. 'That's how you look when you cry, you slimy little cunt. Ugly.'

I looked up from the café floor and realised that I had let go of Mick. He was flopped unconscious on the floor in an impossibly grotesque shape, like he had fallen from a great height. Ginger was standing above me, right hand extended, smiling nervously and crying. I took her hand, and she helped me up and led me away from Mick. Warmth rushed through me at her touch. She was still trembling with the shock of everything.

'Are you all right?' I asked.

'Yeah. Yeah,' she replied. Her voice held a nervy quiver. It made me feel protective immediately.

I inhaled deeply, catching a whiff of Ginger's perfume, which cleared my head like a cool breeze. Suddenly life came back into perspective. All the café girls, the young courting couple and old sock-neck were hovering round in a ring of death looking down at Mick. He was still out on his belly and looking very ill. Reality kicked in. I parted the circle like a paramedic at a crash scene, grabbed the unconscious Mick by the shirt and hauled him onto his side, placing him in the recovery position – something I had been taught in Health and Safety on the building site. I checked his pulse. There was none. It didn't take a genius to see that he wasn't breathing. I looked down at him. What to do?

I lay him on his back. It was like moving a slab of meat. I started mouth-to-mouth. The taste of stale cigarettes and beer stuck in my throat as I tried to breathe life into an empty chest cavity. Then I did CPR on his chest. One, two, three, four, five. Ginger stopped me. For a moment I thought that she wanted me to let Mick die. Who could have blamed her? The lad was a violent headbanger, a menace, and the morgue would be a fitting place to send him. She gently moved me over and started chest compressions on him. I gave him mouth-to-mouth in between her chest compressions. Nothing. Not a ripple. Fuck. Don't die on me.

We kept trying, but to no avail. I was starting to panic inside. I looked around the room and my eyes snagged on a glass of pop sat unfinished on a table. I grabbed it and threw the contents over Mick's face. I did it on the doors occasionally, and it worked sometimes. But not with Mick.

Come on, mate, I said in my mind. *Live. For fuck's sake, live. Fucking live. Please.*

'He's breathing.' It was Ginger. Her flat voice had elevated. 'He's breathing, turn him onto his side.'

I turned him quickly and relief raced through my veins. He was alive. Alive. I looked at Ginger, the most beautiful woman I had ever set my weary eyes on. He was alive and I was thanking fuck for it.

When I left the café, Mick was sitting up and conscious. The pot of cold tea in the face, courtesy of the waitress, had helped. I didn't envy him. When you put them out for that long they often don't know who the fuck they are when they come around. I was just grateful that he wasn't brown bread. As much as I despised Mick and men of his ilk, I still didn't want to be responsible for sending him to his Maker. Part of me could not see beyond the red mist that descended every time I entered an affray, but I also had a real fear of killing. A dread that invaded my nightmares and woke me with cold sweats and fears too big to control. Maybe it was a Catholic thing, you know, Hell and damnation if you break a commandment. It's the thought of being cooked in a devil's kitchen with a spit up your arse and an apple in your mouth until your skin crackles and your bollocks pop. It's the thought of being Sunday roast for eternity. Yet at the same time, when I was throttling Mick, I felt I couldn't let go. I wanted to see him disappear from the face of the earth. Men like him represented all that was dark in the world, and I had this insatiable urge to stamp on him like a cockroach. The fuckers seem to make their employ mugging old ladies in the street and robbing nice people of their peace of mind. You can't switch on the TV or read the local rag these days without stumbling across yet another unsolicited, late night, cowardly attack. Two things that piss me right off: one, they pick on the weak and the vulnerable, like a tiger hunting an antelope, always on the prowl for the young or very old, the infirm or those that get detached from the herd. And two, the jammy fuckers never seem to get caught. Plod are so busy working their paper or playing Twister with rolls of red tape that wankers like Mick have free rein to bash the vulnerable and frighten the horses. But this time he'd underestimated the threat and he'd got a little of what he deserved.

Ginger told me not to hang around at the café. The police were bound to get a sniff and arrive looking for a lift. She knew the crack, I could tell that. What I couldn't get my swede around was how a classy girl like her had ended up on the arm (later on the fist) of a cokehead like Mick, a fucking scrotum of the first order.

'He wasn't like that when I met him,' she told me sadly before I left. 'I was only a babby when I met him. He was older, had a car, bought me flowers; he was dead nice, really nice. Even my mum loved him.' Her eyes dropped to the floor. 'He changed, that's all. People do.' There was a sad inevitability about her words. *That's how it is and that's how it always will be*. That's what she seemed to be saying. She lifted her eyes from the floor and looked directly into my eyes, almost challenging me to be different.

I nodded. I think I knew what she meant. Mick had once been attentive and loving, but a concoction of familiarity, drugs and maniacal jealousy had turned a once-caring man into a possessive bag of sick. Her existence had become unbearable, one where the key in the door at midnight triggered terror because Mick's mood might bring a takeaway curry, a drunken fuck or an unprovoked beating, or sometimes all three and not necessarily in that order.

The pub was pretty near empty. Just me and a flopping beer skeleton nodding over a flat pint at the end of the bar. He was legless and dishevelled, with hair that might have been combed over from his arse. His nappy-rash face looked as though it had seen enough alcohol to shrink even the hardiest liver. His nose looked like a boil about to burst.

This was a real spit-and-sawdust pub. The beer was cheap and the company sparse but hospitable.

The girl behind the bar was wide and busty. 'What can I get you, duck?'

She had a lovely invite-you-in voice that didn't match her bloated frame.

'Pint of straight lager please.'

The barmaid poured my beer with impressive ease. She purred in my direction. The eye-fluttering was getting thicker by the second. On any other night (after a few more beers) there might have been a shared taxi and some energetic sex. But tonight, all I could think about was Ginger. Why hadn't I taken her number? I was so full of the fight that I'd walked home in a daze. It was only when I put the key in the lock that it hit me: I would probably never see her again. The reality hit me in the pit of my stomach and I felt sick. I felt that I had lost something dear to me, even though I still didn't know her real name. So I was following in my father's footsteps: filling the void inside with drink.

I reached into my trousers for some loose change to pay for the pint. My hand brushed against a heavy weight in the pit of my pocket. My knuckleduster. I always carried it after a fight. It was personal security, an equaliser should I encounter any aftermath from the café. It was a habit that I had picked up from the doors, bouncing in the violent city clubs. It was wise to carry a small appendage to counter any possible come-backs from the punters you threw out or beat up.

I thought it was unlikely that Mick would come back on me. I didn't know him and he didn't know me; the chances of a return bout were minimal.

The barmaid interrupted my reverie.

'Someone let you down, lover?' There was sympathy in her voice, and it was welcome.

I shrugged. 'Don't they all?'

'Not all,' she replied, placing her hand close to mine on the bar. The pause was awkward so I took a long swig of my beer and scanned the room as I swallowed.

'You look like you're no stranger to the gym,' she said, looking me up and down with a bed in her eye. She was being kind. I was stocky, and there was a bit of weight in my shoulders and thick arms but my waist was embarrassingly flaccid. She was extending the conversation and offering a little invitation but my mind was full of another woman, a sweet girl with flame-coloured hair and innocence in her eyes.

'I'm a runner, me,' the barmaid said proudly, perhaps to endear herself to me. I hid my disbelief behind another gulp from the pint of piss-weak lager. I squinted my eyes and stared, looking for any semblance of an athlete behind the layers of lard, vacuum-packed under tight denims. The Viking blonde, shoulder-length hair held together by smoke and hairspray was candyfloss on her head. Her make-up was rendering that had not quite covered all the cracks. A bumper of fat sat on her belt and her bust spread across the bar like liquid as she leaned in my direction. Unkindly, I had the feeling that once her bra came off you'd have trouble keeping track of them. I had bedded a few fleshy barmaids in my time. In the back of the car, up the side of a chip shop wall. I did it once on a stone-tiled kitchen floor back at hers. Both of us naked, her fleshy tits flopping round her back with no bra to hold them in place, the clammy hands pulling at my arse and the wine-and-cigarette tongue thrusting into my throat. It's no fun bedding a lass who weighs twice as much as you do, I have to say.

I looked as deep as I could, but there was no runner behind this bar. Unless she'd swallowed one. My beer was mid-swallow when the beer skeleton at the end of the bar piped up.

'The only thing you ever ran for was the fucking ice-cream van,' he told her.

I nearly choked as a spontaneous and violent laugh shot from my belly and tried to leave my mouth past a throat full of beer. I coughed and spluttered as the beer and the laugh left my face. Her eyes darted from the skeleton to me, then back to the skeleton again, unsure of whom to be angry with first. I know I shouldn't have laughed, I know it was cruel and unkind, but I had no choice. I laughed so much that tears started to dribble down my cheeks and my body rocked. It was one of those silent laughs that was intense enough to stop the breath in your chest. In between the sobbing laughter I tried to apologise to the barmaid and at the same time reprimand the beer philosopher at the end of the bar. It all came out as a hysterical nothing. I replaced my pint on the bar – most of it was either down my shirt or over the counter by now – and backed out of the pub trying to apologise in between the fits of laughter.

A plume of smoke and the smell of beer followed me into the street and the door closed behind me. Outside in the cold, sobering air, the street was dark and empty. I was still laughing hysterically. It felt mean laughing into an empty street at a nice bird with a Pillsbury belly and pudding thighs. A woman, someone's daughter, someone's mum. Someone. It felt cruel laughing at a nice someone who was probably just trying to get through life, looking for a little bit of human contact, even if it was just for the one night.

I realised with a sudden jolt that she was like me. Getting through life on a diet of one-night stands and takeaways. Never quite knowing where the next fuck might come from, but pretty sure that it would be burger and not sirloin. So many lonely people in this world, starving for a bit of love. I thought about the barmaid, and I thought about me, and I thought about Ginger. I thought about the dark, empty street and how it reflected my life. I wondered what the fuck it was all about.

Why had God let me lose the closest thing to perfection I had ever seen in my life? He did move in mysterious ways. I've never trusted God. Never. God was for the posh kids. I knew that much. He didn't come to houses where mums had faces permanently bent from too many drunken beatings, and dads who had crippled minds, and kids who wore plimsolls through winter and summer because the family allowance was fighting on too many fronts. I remember those white pumps and how ashamed I was to wear them to school because all the other kids had proper shoes and mine let in water when it rained and bubbled at the seams. And by the summer the toe of the right shoe was always gaping and flapping like a slobbering dog's tongue. My mum glued it back together so it lasted another term.

I was one of those boys the other kids called 'tramp'. One of those snotty-nosed kids living a hand-me-down existence, wearing jackets three sizes too big because my brother was two years older and broader at the shoulders. I was one of those kids who got the free dinners and deliberately missed my lunch because I was ashamed to go down the queue with a ticket to hand over for my meal. Everyone knew that you couldn't afford dinners. That you were a tramp. The other kids didn't mind letting you know about it either. Kids can be cruel. My mum said they didn't know what they were doing and I should try and forgive them. That word. Forgive. Like my mum forgave my dad for the violence and each time she forgave him he would come back and hit her twice as hard. Re-break a nose that looked so out of place on the face of a mum, like a lump of plasticine.

I did go to church; I was made to. My dad hated God, that much was sure, but my mum held on to her faith by an end-of-tether thread. And she made sure that me and my brother visited Jesus every Sunday and sat our bony arses on the hard benches of Christianity. But I knew, I innately felt, that the God they preached about was not for the likes of me. You daren't mention God in our house, not while the old man was in drunken residence anyway. If you did he'd shake his fist and shout 'Cunt!' at the sky. It was a funny thing that. He didn't believe in God, yet he blamed Him for his sad life. He was an atheist who 'cunted' the sky and cursed at the mention of His name.

'What kind of God,' he would shout, 'preaches unconditional love and humility and then fucks you with eternal hellfire if you don't place a fucking capital letter in front of his name? What kind of God gives you free will then cunts you off if you do something he don't like? He's a fucking hypocrite. A queer. Any man that hangs around sea-ports with a bunch of fishermen has to be chasing the wrong hole.'

His mum, my nan, was a raging alcoholic. Anger and bitterness displaced itself from one generation to the next. And there was I continuing the tradition, taking the angry-baton and running with it like a good 'un. My dad didn't know what he was doing. There was at least a little innocence in his madness. He was working within his knowledge, or within his ignorance.

He was from Carrickfergus in Northern Ireland and as crazy as the sectioned cousin of a mad March hare. Harry-from-Carry they called him at the club. On the sites where his prowess with a shovel was legendary, it was Harry-from-Carry, the mad Irishman, who worked all day on two cans of breakfast breaker and four pints of heavy as a liquid lunch.

Outside the pub, I sat on the cold pavement with the dark world spinning around me, feeling sorry for myself and thinking about Ginger and the look we shared and the promises I sensed in her touch. And her sadness. You couldn't miss the sadness; it was on her skin. I thought about the promise that my life had shown, just for a split-second, in that dingy café when, above the chips and egg and tea and toast and fry-ups and lost old people looking for solace in a hot brew and a kind word, above the tabloid shit and the crap soaps on the telly, and despite being surrounded by the ugly that was in all things, I saw what could have been. I didn't have to be a nobody moving brick and block and muck around a hundred construction sites that built structures and broke men. I didn't have to live the nine-to-five, hand-me-down, second-hand, shopsoiled, third-rate, bog-paper life that I was told to be grateful for at the comprehensive.

I saw so much promise in those few seconds that my life had lit up and glowed. I felt an excitement that had never been a part of my life before. The girl in that café was the girl of my dreams, and, amazingly, there was no feeling that she would be horrified by the likes of me with my bad mouth, calloused fingers, fat arse and my hard, hard life. I felt that she had completely accepted me, an ordinary, plain, unremarkable man. It felt unconditional. Something I had not sensed in church in my youth where the fat-fingered priest placed himself above you in his pulpit and attacked you in front of the whole congregation if you so much as missed a mass or didn't place a coin in the collection basket. And who betrayed me when I went to him looking for God.

I leaned against the pub wall and the cold of the cobbles below me started to hurt the bones of my fat arse. It penetrated into my skin and the darkness pervaded me. The streetlights swelled and streaked into fuzzy stars. I looked up into the sky and shook my head.

'What the fuck is this all about?' I asked out loud. I had found something and lost it almost in the same breath. I got to my feet.

No sense in screaming into an empty sky.

I decided to do what I always did when life shat on me from above: make for the chippy. It did nothing for my waistline but it was reliable. The chip shop was not a beautiful girl, it was not a good fuck or a BJ under the duvet. But you could depend on it. Our chip shop even opened on Christmas Day: now that's reliable. I wanted to bury my woes under a meat pie and a heavy portion of sliced potato saturated in good, wholesome fat. I'd spent many an evening with my dinner wrapped in last night's news on my lap, burning my thighs, watching telly and wondering 'Is this it?' and fucking hoping not.

I walked down the street with a heavy heart. I wondered whether I should have taken the offer of a shag from the would-be athlete from behind the bar. But Ginger filled my senses, and nothing could take my mind off her.

Suddenly the screech of car tyres startled me. I looked behind to see a two-door BMW 3-series racing down the road and heading in my direction.

Chapter Three

Demolition Man

I ran up the pavement, the car at my heels and fire in my boots. My wind felt all right until I stopped at a lamp-post, the only chance I had of them not running me over. I was breathing out of my intestines, my lungs trying to suck in oxygen and my fighting brain kicking into gear, racing and analysing, trying to make sense of what was happening. Then I spotted Mick the Prick in the back of the car, bat in hand, a face full of retribution, and I knew. Revenge, they say, is sweet. And it can also be very fucking fast. From my experience in these matters, come-backs happen quickly, usually the next night or a week to the night. Any longer than that and it tends to go away. Most people lose their anger after a few days so if it hasn't happened by then the chances are it never will. I really wasn't expecting a come-back from Mick, he didn't know me and how the fuck did he know where to find me? He must have been driving around all afternoon asking questions. And his anger was as fresh as it could be.

The car screeched to a halt right next to the lamp-post: two men in the back, two in the front, all carrying weapons, all salivating for a fight. I knew I was dead the moment I saw four men and their bats. My chest was heaving; heart looking for extra oxygen and finding dust. I felt like I was going to shit my pants. All this bullshit about one man taking on four, all carrying; I have to tell you that it's a fucking myth. Two men with bad intention will kill you dead. Four – unless you have luck on your side and an eye for an opportunity – and your arse is already grass. Luckily fate did favour me on this occasion. When the car skidded within inches of my ankles, it got so close to the lamp-post that the passenger door was wedged against it. The front passenger tried to thrust open his door for a fast exit. *Crunch!* It smashed against the metal of the post, putting a dent in the door that'd cost a grand to mend. He tried again. *Bang!* Another dent. He panicked. *Bang! Bang! Bang!* I think he thought that the post might somehow move if he kept hitting it.

The driver, a barrel of a man with a seventies' ponytail and a silver baseball bat, jumped out of the driver's door, not realising that he had trapped his mates, and raced around the bonnet towards me. His angry jowls shuddered with each step. His mates were stuck in the car, desperately trying to clamber over the seats to get out. I knew from my days on the door that when fear is on the agenda and blood is pumping to all the major muscles ready for a little fight or flight, the fine motor actions (like fiddling with a seat release) take a back seat (if you'll forgive the pun) and the gross motor actions (swinging baseball bats at heads) come to the fore. So the three were temporarily stuck in the car – two of them trying to force the driver's seat down, the third still smashing his door against the lamp-post. They were all making a meal of it and getting in each other's way. This was an opportunity, my only one.

I slipped my duster over my fingers, let out a fearsome scream and ran around the back of the car to their only exit, the front driver's door, punching in the window. The driver, temporarily stunned by my explosion, was frozen to the spot. Fear had glued him to the floor and his moral fibre was already starting to leak out of his flapping arsehole. I was punching glass when I could have been punching flesh because I knew that when dealing with undisciplined men of violence, fight psychology is your greatest weapon. So you attack their minds rather than their bodies. I knew that the very act of screaming and smashing glass would trigger adrenal dump in these wankers and that their immediate instinct would be to either freeze or retreat. Or, at the very least, hesitate. That was all I needed. Hesitation begets defeat. And they did hesitate. It was as if someone had pressed the pause button and locked them into a freeze-frame of violence.

I slammed the driver's door shut and kicked the wing mirror off. Then I smashed the rear passenger window. Diamonds littered the floor like it had been raining window. A slush of glass formed on the ground. When the glass imploded, I saw Mick cowering in the back seat and I leaned in and tried to smash the very teeth out of his head. He covered his face and took my blows on his arms. I let the spit and snot hang from my face – it all added to the act. Only now the act had become real and I was actually trying to kill him.

As I pulled out of the back window of the car, I instinctively lurched to my left just as a baseball bat swung at my head. It clattered on the roof of the car, leaving another expensive dent. I managed to get out of the way just in time. It was Ponytail, the driver.

'Come on you wanker, you cocksucker, you, you … look at me fucking motor!' he screamed, inviting me forward. He was panting with fear and anger, his eyes darting from me to his smashed vehicle, obviously his pride and joy. He was not happy and he wanted to let me know about it.

I stepped away from the car, into the arena, arms splayed, instinctively trying to make myself look bigger.

'Let's go then, cunt! Come on! Come on!'

I sent the invite right back at him, all part of the set-up. I had a gap to negotiate and was using attacking dialogue to bridge it. I was about to make his bad day considerably worse. We circled each other for a second like contemporary gladiators, him with his bat, me with my duster, both looking for the right time to move. I knew that the right time for me to move would be when he lifted his bat to strike. I waited and beckoned to him but despite his anger he wasn't taking the bait. I could sense the other three behind me trying to edge out of the car. I turned on them.

'Stay where you are, cunts!' I shouted. The three of them froze again. When men are afraid they have a tendency to obey simple commands, like dogs do.

'First one of you fuckers to get out of that car's gonna get this fucker in the teeth!' I lifted my steel fist to underline the threat. I looked back at Ponytail.

'So you gonna use that bat you fat, ponytailed cunt?'

He still didn't react. I thought the 'ponytail' attack was a work of genius. I've pulled many a man into a fight with a follicle attack. I thought it might have moved him; middle-aged men are very tetchy about their hair. He didn't buy it. He knew the crack, he was waiting for me to rush forward so that he could take my head off with the practised swing of his bat. I needed something – and in a hurry – to provoke him.

Bang! I booted off his wing mirror – it was still hanging by a few wires from my first kick – and it clattered to the floor by his feet. If attacking the hair don't do the job then go for the next best thing: the car. It's sure to work. Some men have their heads in the car mags more than they thumb the porn.

He looked down at the wing mirror, then back at the car. His baby. Fuck me, that did the trick. Anyone would have thought I'd killed his mum and stuck her head on a spike.

'Bastard!' he cried as he raised his bat and ran at me. It took me a bit by surprise to be honest. I had expected a reaction but not one as immediate as this. The lad obviously thought a lot about his car. I back-peddled a few steps and my back hit the car right behind me. I'd run out of room in a heartbeat and in doing so lost the use of my hands; the distance had been gobbled up by Ponytail, hungry to avenge the death of his wing mirror. I gave him the only thing I had left. My head. Just as his bat was at its furthest retraction, mid-swing, I smashed my nut and every ounce of my body weight into his jowly face. It's the best way to take out a guy with a long weapon. The power of the bat comes from the swing, and to get a good swing there needs to be a little retraction. But that makes it a slow weapon and your one chance at keeping your head attached to your shoulders is to enter his space when the weapon is at its furthest retraction. It all happens in a second so there is no time for hesitation. It's a spontaneous thing. You can't really plan it, you either go or you don't, and if you don't then your head is dead.

My entire body weight landed behind my nut. It was as if he had been hit in the face by a bowling ball. His nose splattered. The dull, hollow thud of contact as head and nose met echoed up the street and off the walls. As he staggered backwards, he dropped the bat like it was on fire. I stumbled over with the momentum of my attack, leaving the knees of my best grey trousers (and about half an inch of skin) on the gravel. I jumped back to my feet and quickly lunged in to finish the driver with a practised right hand. I caught him, but the contact was weak and the punch slipped off the side of his head. He fell into me, grabbing my green fleece jumper with a panic grip that only a pair of pliers was likely to break. I was forced into a vertical grapple. Not the best place to be in a fight that involves more than one opponent. Grappling is a great art, one of the best, but fuck me, when you are facing men that have murder in mind, you'd better give it a very wide berth. I like to be in and out within three seconds. Any longer than that and a fight is bound to go to the floor where the four *b*'s are your greatest enemy: biting (a desperate man will bite the nose off your face without even thinking about it); butting (it can be over in one if you catch a good cranium in the face); blinding (a thumb in the eye might not be fair play, but in the game of maim it comes with the territory – and even a novice can stick a thumb in your eye); and buddies (you can be rolling around the floor with a guy and think that he's on his own only to find that three of his mates have just left the chip shop and are about to kick you till their feet hurt).

I didn't want to be there, and even as I gripped him I could sense the others in the car seeing their opportunity, scrambling to get out and at me. I smashed my head into his face again, rammed my knee into his pubic bone and dragged him by the shoulders of his leather bomber jacket head first into the front alloy wheel of his own car. His skull made a dull clang, and then he was out there, lying in a slowly expanding pool of his own blood.

Mick had managed to climb out of the shattered rear window and was holding his bat looking venomous. His right eye was purple and so swollen it was almost closed. His face was covered in fresh scabs from where I had ground his face into the broken crockery on the floor that afternoon. His left wrist was bandaged and I swear he was stooping slightly, probably trying to stand up straight with a few cracked ribs. Served the fucker right.

'You fucking piece of shit!' I said, still angry, still raring to go, still reacting to the fact that these fuckers would have killed me but for their shit parking. A picture of Ginger, her face recoiling from Mick's blows, flashed into my mind with a powerful clarity. 'You want to go again, cunt? Step over here with your bat and I'll bury it up your clay-hole. Come on!' He hesitated, looking around for support that was non-existent as the other two dicks were stuck in the car, glued to their seats by a mixture of perverse fascination and gut-wrenching fear. He was alone and the full realisation of his predicament hit him hard. The bat fell out of his fingers and clunked to the floor, benign without the gripping fingers of bad intention.

'Fuck off out of my face, you wanker, before I level you! Go on, fuck off!' It was my final word on the matter, his final chance to leave without a fight.

His eyes hit the floor like marbles. He scanned the debris. He looked into the car and the two other flaccid penises shrugged their shoulders. He scuttled away, leaving something that he might never find again: his courage.

'This ain't over!' he snarled over his shoulder.

I calmly placed my knuckleduster in my pocket and picked up the silver bat from the floor, the one that the driver tried to marry with my head. I spent what was left of my energy, and about twenty years of bottled aggression, into the bodywork of the car.

'If you want to play with me, you bunch of cunts,' I shouted, 'don't come to the game in your best car!'

I took out the front headlights with a double swing of the bat; it felt light in my hands, comfortable. I would probably be shit at hitting baseballs in parks but I was ace when it came to heads, headlights and car bonnets. When I had finished refiguring the shape of the car, I dashed the bat in through the cracked windscreen, glass imploding across the neat leather interior. The two inhabitants, still frozen to their seats, reeled backwards to avoid the shards of broken window and the bat.

I turned to leave and caught the driver in my peripheral vision. He was still out and the pool of blood had spread a good foot around his head. Even though he was no longer a threat, there was still an angry part of me that wanted to kick the head off his shoulders, kick him again and again so that his jelly-body shifted along the floor. I was so angry, crimson clouded my vision. My right leg twitched as though it was about to fly out all on its own. It was not gratuitous, it was not sadistic, not animalistic: it was fear. It was survival. I wanted to kick him again to make sure that he was no longer a threat to me, that he was no longer capable of attack. It was my fear of nearly dying at the hands of this man that made me want to end him. Fuck, I was angry.

I stood over the driver. He was as pale as a Russian swimmer. A large expanse of damp appeared at the crotch of his trousers. Steam started rising. He looked dead. I moved closer to him. I could hear snores leaving his mouth as the air on the way out of his throat met the blood on the way in.

Fuck him, I thought, trying to stop the panic from welling up inside me. *The cunt tried to run me over. He deserves an alloy in the head.*

Then I thought about the consequences of death, the reality of murder and the time I could spend in the big house if I took this life – even if it was in self-defence. Even the hereafter is no safe harbour when you have broken one of the big Ten Commandments and killed, and I'd be fucked if I was going to spend eternity with Lucifer in the burning fires of Hell. I harboured a swelling fear of murder; I already had a full quota of bad conscience. My horror-film nightmares were bad enough as it was without adding a fat ponytail to the cast list. I grabbed my unconscious friend by the neck of his leather jacket and turned him onto his side. His friends looked on from inside the car. As I lifted his head out of the crimson puddle, the congealed blood hung from him like goo. I dragged him away from the car. The toes of his shoes scuffed along the floor. I placed him in the recovery position on the pavement to stop him from choking. I didn't want him to die. Not because I had any regard for him; as far as I could see he was just a piece of shit. I just didn't want to go to jail, that was the bottom line. And I wanted to sleep nights.

I left him to find his own consciousness and strode off into the night, the endorphins running around my veins in a celebratory lap of honour. But I'd learned my lesson. I never thought for a second that it was over. You never think that. The old samurai had a saying: 'After the battle tighten your helmet straps.'

My breath was coming back to normal and I felt high. Not because I had damaged, not because I had smashed and hurt, rather, I felt high because I had survived, and against odds that should have left me on a cold slab.

At the first sight of a drain, I dropped my duster into the sewers. The first rule of survival after a fight is to recognise that the law is the second enemy. Especially if you've used a weapon and even more especially if you leave your first enemy knee deep in the red stuff. So I had to lose the evidence. It was hard to let it go; it held memories and a feeling of safety that I didn't want to lose. Never mind, I still had my baseball bat at home. The evidence was gone. I was on my way home.

I didn't even make the chippy before a police car pulled up alongside me and two PCs raced towards me.

Chapter Four

Manhandled

Arrested. Can you believe it? I was attacked by four men with two tons of metal and hand weapons; four men who might have killed me given even half a chance, and *I* was arrested. Mick weighed me in with the police.

Now I don't usually fuck with the police. I make a habit of not doing so. They have a hard job to do, and I am happy to leave them to it. And when the two rookie PCs arrested me up the road not far from the BMW I tried to go quietly. But they wouldn't have any of it. Actually, it was one in particular. The second PC, the fat one, was reluctantly pulled into the affray when his mate kicked off. This wanker was taking it all personal, like he had a chip on his shoulder or an old score to settle. I couldn't quite figure out which. He was a stranger to me, and – as far as I knew – me to him. Some coppers are just like that though, they take it all very personal, like they're on a kind of judge-jury-executioner mission. Either that or they've seen the heavy arrest on *The Bill* and fancied a little go at it themselves. Wouldn't be the first policemen to mistake fiction for real life.

Even though I'd put my hands up and done the whole 'it's a fair cop, guv' routine, they insisted on manhandling me, trying to rough me up. It was comical. I didn't mind being arrested, goes with the territory, but manhandled? I don't think so.

The first copper, who had a shiny bald head like a Cox's Red Delicious, pushed me hard against the wall while he frisked me, slapping my body rather than feeling for weapons. Then he spun me round and started pushing me, giving me the whole 'you're going down, son' routine. Son? You can fuck right off, you hairy testicle. Not having any of that. They were doing my swede right in. It was when Apple put his hand on my face – the sad bastard actually slapped me – that I lost the plot. Fatty was the first to get it. When he stepped forward I punched him in the belly, not hard, and more out of frustration than badness, and left him sat on the kerb, gasping for air. Then I lunged at PC Apple, and held him above my head in a fireman's carry. He'd run at me flailing like a bird; I had to do something. I span him around and around, WWF-style, until he was dizzy and shouting for me to put him down. I dropped him into a pile of dustbin bags abandoned on the side of the road (I didn't want to go as far as slamming him on the pavement on his back) and got into the police car. PC Apple and his winded mate straightened their clothes and tried to recover their dignity.

'Animals like you should be kept in a cage,' PC Apple snarled, leaning into the car and snapping handcuffs on my wrists. Fucking knob. He'd got less idea about policing than I had about nuclear physics. He slid into the passenger seat.

'How the fuck did you get through Hendon?' I asked. 'Were they looking for a token dunce?'

I'm an expert at taking the piss. I learned it on the building sites where black humour was the only thing that got you through impossible workloads and bitter winters where your fingers froze before you even got out of the van in the morning. The piss was ripped from everyone who set foot on site. Those that bit would be slaughtered mercilessly before breakfast (if they lasted that long). You quickly learned in that game how cruel people could be when lower backs were locked in footings laying 1,500 bricks a day and muscles screamed for rest, when the hod could not keep up with two fast trowels. I learned from the best. I could take it at a hundred miles an hour and as personal as you like. But I could give it back just as quickly. So some nonsense-case PC still working out his two-year probation, still got the umbilical cord hanging out of his pristine jacket, was no threat to me, no threat at all.

I was too lippy for my own good most of the time. I knew that. But I couldn't help myself. My comment obviously hit a nerve because his apple-shiny head lit up like neon. His upper lip twitched involuntarily. When PC Fatty, who was driving, failed to suppress a giggle Apple got even worse.

'Keep it up,' he said, taking a snap at the bait. 'It'll be just me and you back at the station. See how brave you are then.'

'I'm scared,' I said, a mock tremble in my voice. He smiled, not realising that there was a little bit of piss to be taken here and I was about to do the extraction. 'Scared that if we're left alone for too long I might fucking kill you.'

I looked out of the window at the passing streets and thought about Ginger. I could tell he was getting annoyed because his shot at intimidation had fallen short.

'We have stairs at the station.' He said it with a knowing wink. He aimed a 'trying to impress' smile across at the driver. Bless him. He was trying hard. I guessed the intimation was that, in the very near future, I might be having an accident whilst negotiating those stairs. I'm sure that I wouldn't be the first or last.

'And who's gonna stop me kicking you up and down the fuckers if we're left on our own?' I asked cheekily, still looking out of the window,

Apple's head did a 90-degree in my direction, and then he shot a look over to Fatty who failed for the second time to stop a giggle from bursting free. He was trying to suppress the laugh but his shoulders were rocking up and down as if he was doing a silent Tommy Cooper impression.

'We'll see how smart your mouth is when we get back to the station and you're eating fucking truncheon.' Now Apple was really angry.

'Ain't you going to buy me dinner first?' I said. 'I hardly know you.'

I really should have shut my mouth while I was ahead. It's not professional to back-chat the police. If you're smart you say nothing because 'nothing' cannot be misheard or misinterpreted and used against you later, perhaps in a court of law. Normally I would have adhered to this rule. But this guy was trying to bully and intimidate me. And anyway, I was fucked off: four men had tried to kill me with a smart car, I'd been roughed up by these losers, and I had missed my pie-and-chip supper. Besides that, I was fucked off with life. I had nothing to lose. I was just giving this doughnut a bit of what he had given me.

Well that was it: I'd hit the latent-homosexual-phallic-truncheon jackpot. The driver burst into tears of laughter, and Apple went red-at-head and made a grab for me.

'Whoa, whoa,' Fatty panicked. This wasn't supposed to happen, this wasn't how they did it at Hendon. He screeched the car over to the kerb. I used the chain of my handcuffs to try and push

Apple's choking fingers away from my neck. Fatty jumped out of the car still shouting 'whoa' at Apple like he was trying to stop a stampeding horse, and opened the passenger door. He dragged the out-of-control PC from the car.

'Leave it out, Paul,' he said. 'He's not worth it. Leave it, you daft prick, he'll press charges and then we'll both be in the shit.'

'That's a good idea,' I said, rubbing my sore throat.

They got back into the car. Apple was breathing heavily, panting, a sprinter after the race. Snorting a little too, like he was using his breath to hold back his anger. We drove on through the dark streets.

'I'll fuck you,' he said without looking back.

'You're not fit enough,' I replied, fuelling his anger. 'But if you fancy a bit of a pull I could always send me sister round.'

Fatty cracked up again. He couldn't help himself. He'd got the giggles now and they were working all by themselves. Within seconds the tears were rolling down his face. He tried to apologise to his mate Apple, but he had lost the plot. The ability to speak coherently had deserted him. His laughter was infectious and in seconds I was laughing too. This didn't help the situation at all. Apple's head lit up like a stop sign. His temples throbbed. His shoulders hunched. He was a pulsating mass of stress.

Some people, I thought, *are just too easy*.

Apple was seething. His chest was in and out like an old accordion. I could hear the wheeze as his rusted lungs (probably hadn't been stretched since Hendon) tried to expand to take in the extra workload.

I really should have left well alone but I was on a roll. It was just like being back on the building sites. I couldn't stop myself. Apple was lined up and just waiting to be shot down. I had to go for the kill.

'Are you always this rough with your dates?' I asked.

As soon as Fatty started to laugh again – against his own will and angry at me now for making him betray his mate – Apple lost it.

'ARGHHHH!' He was up and trying to climb over the back seat to get at me again, arms thrashing and murder in his eyes. Fatty hung on to his coat, swerving the car across the road, and screaming for restraint. It took him several seconds and repeated pleas for calm to cool his mate down.

'That's enough, now,' Fatty said to me from the front, eyes back on the road again and Apple finally calmed. 'Enough!' He pointed his cigarette-stained finger at me to add authority to his command. He drove on silently.

Apple tidied himself in the front of the car. He was still dishevelled from the fight and the bins. He obviously wanted to brush away any evidence of the debacle before we made the station. As he straightened the sleeves of his police-issue jacket he suddenly jerked up his left sleeve. There was panic in his actions. He looked at his right wrist, pulled up his right sleeve, then he started to search through his jacket pockets, and on the floor. Something was missing and his panic had become tangible. Fatty noticed.

'What's up?'

Apple didn't answer, just kept searching around. He leaned over to the back of the car and looked around on the floor by my feet.

'If you're looking for your dignity I think you left it back at the chippy with your bottle,' I offered coolly.

Apple glared at me. If looks were bullets then I'd just been machine-gunned.

Fatty again. 'What you lost?'

Apple looked at his wrist for a second time. 'Stop the car. Stop, stop the car!' He was panicking.

'What?'

'Fucking stop!'

'For what? Stop for what?' Fatty pulled over to the kerb. 'Fuck's sake! What you lost?'

Apple didn't answer, he just got out of the car and took his jacket off. He shook it. Nothing. He was pale as a doughboy and cursing under his breath. He went through the pockets urgently. Whatever he'd lost wasn't there. He threw the jacket on the floor. He knelt on the kerb and began searching around the passenger seat and the floor. Nothing.

'For fuck's sake, what you lost?'

'Me Cartier, me fucking clock. I 'ad it on, I know I did.' Still searching fruitlessly. Fatty got out of the car and helped him.

'Two grand's worth of fucking clock that,' I could hear Apple complaining. 'Two fucking grand. Fucking gone. I 'ad it on, I definitely 'ad it on.'

'You sure? Check your jacket again.' Fatty thought for a second. 'What the fuck you doin' with a two-grand watch?'

'Must have fell off when I was wrestling with that cunt near the chippy. Cunt.' Apple yanked open the back door of the car. 'Get out. Get the fuck out!'

I eased my way out. Apple leaned into the back of the car as I stood on the pavement. He searched all around the floor in the back of the car. Nothing. He was seething now.

'You sure you had it on?' Fatty asked.

'It'll be back near the fucking chip shop. Course I 'ad it on. I know I did.' He paused, though. Retraced his steps in his head. 'Yeah, yeah, I remember, I had it on when I came out the house, definitely. Definitely had the fucker on. It'll be back by the chip shop. Get back in,' he barked at me.

I stayed still. 'Say "please",' I said. It was not a lot to ask.

'Please,' said Fatty, anything for a quiet life.

I did as I was asked.

Within minutes we were back near the chippy, me in the back of the car looking out and smiling. The two policemen rummaged around the black bags looking for a very expensive Cartier watch. I wondered how a PC on a flat rate could afford a watch worth six weeks' wages. Maybe he'd been selling his arsehole over the Internet. I didn't ask – I don't think he would have appreciated it.

By the time we got to the station, Apple had found his breath, even though he hadn't managed to find his watch.

'It's insured, innit?' Fatty was desperately trying to placate his mate. Apple shot him a look that said 'don't be so fucking naive'.

'Report it when we get back, eh?' Fatty tried again. 'Have a word with the Sarge about –'

'No!' Apple's interruption was a bit too hasty. He tried to retreat. Obviously hadn't meant to snap like that. 'No, it's all right, don't bother. I ain't even sure I had it on. It'll turn up at home, I'm sure of it.'

'Well, it won't hurt to mention it.'

Apple dragged Fatty over to one side by the sleeve, just out of my earshot. He whispered urgently to him. I couldn't quite hear what he said, but I got the impression that if the Sarge heard about Apple's expensive watch he might be asking a few questions. Didn't take a genius to work out that he'd appropriated the watch by less than legal means. I could see that Fatty was not happy; he looked suspiciously at Apple out of the corner of his eye.

In the station, the two PCs took me straight to the booking-in sergeant, a veteran policeman with a wealth of experience in his seen-it-done-it-used-the-T-shirt-for-dusters face. He looked like a good sort. A fit man with a rugger-ball face and yards of hands. The Sarge looked at the rookie policemen. They were red-faced and dishevelled. Apple had a Müller Light yogurt lid stuck to the seat of his trousers. Sarge could tell that something was amiss.

'What's up with you pair?'

'Nothing, Sarge.' It was Apple. He turned to look at Fatty for back up. As Apple turned, the Sarge took in the stains and creases on his jacket. Dust all over his trousers. The yogurt lid. The Sarge gave him a searching look. He pointed to his dishevelled apparel, the dirt, the creases, the disarray.

Apple and Fatty went crimson and looked shifty.

'I've got a complaint,' I said to the Sarge, breaking the embarrassing impasse and saving the men from further inquisition.

'Oh yeah?' he replied seriously. 'And what would that be?'

The two policemen looked at me with a mixture of hate and disbelief. Their pensions were on the carpet.

'Well,' I said slowly, stretching the agony for them, 'these handcuffs are dead tight.' The relief in the room was palpable. Sarge smiled sardonically. I liked him already. I waited for a second, just until the men thought that they were in the clear, and then added, 'And I want to press charges against him.' I pointed to Apple. His face contorted into an angry mass. He went to speak, to defend himself, but the Sergeant put his hand up to stop him.

'We'll talk about this later,' said the Sarge.

Apple and Fatty retreated to the corner of the room. I watched them as they talked in hushed whispers, every now and then looking over at me and nodding.

I was searched by the Sarge and my possessions bagged and logged. He called Fatty over to take me to a holding cell. He also called Apple over. Wanted a word he said. As Fatty led me away, I turned to Apple.

'Oi!' I called. Apple looked at me. 'You ain't got the right time, 'ave you?' I asked.

He was so angry I thought he might pop. He took two steps forward and then stopped himself, aware that the Sarge was watching his every move. Apple's chest ballooned as he took a sharp intake of breath.

I smiled and let Fatty lead me away. I turned again as I was led through the door into the cells just in time to see Apple getting a finger wagging from the Sergeant. I heard the words 'Get yourself cleaned up, you greenhorn' as I was led to my room for the night. My eyes met Apple's. I winked. He hated me to pieces. I had made another enemy that night.

My room was a shitty little affair with a bench and a loo (built into the end of the bench) and no outside window. You just can't get the accommodation these days. After the door clanged behind me and the lock turned, I lay on the hard bench (no blanket, no pillow, no goodnight kiss, just the promise of some fellatio with a copper's truncheon) and thought about Ginger and the opportunity that had slipped through my fingers. I made up my mind to go back to the café and ask the waitresses if they knew where she lived. I wanted to do everything in my power to try and find her again.

After only a couple of seconds the flap on the door slid open. Apple looked in and smiled.

'The driver of that BMW's in a bad way. Might not last the night. Even if he lives you'll do a five on an eighteen. I'll make sure of it.' He winked. And before he closed the hatch he added maliciously, 'Oh, and don't think this cell's gonna protect you. I got mates outside the law.' That wink again. 'You know what I'm saying?' The hatch slammed shut.

Chapter Five

Interview

I was left to sleep. Not much chance of that. The thought of a five on the back of an eighteen – five years in jail for a Section 18: Wounding with Intent – scared me shitless. That bastard Apple must have known that the thought of five years in prison would rob me of a night's sleep. My peace of mind was fucked. What if Ponytail did die? I'd be up to my knees in the brown stuff. The adrenalin was on permanent alert. It was hard not to think about the consequences. I thought about Ginger instead. Every time I closed my eyes a picture of her appeared in front of me. I allowed myself to daydream about what might have been. Let my mind drift to the possible tomorrows that I had envisioned for a fleeting moment in the café. When you are immersed in pain and discomfort, or in a police cell looking at five on the back of an eighteen, it does you good to take your mind to another place. A nicer place. Helps you to cope with the stress and the fear, helps to stop your mind from running away with itself.

The mind is its own place. I knew that much, and I knew it could be a heaven or it could be a hell. It's all to do with perspective. Control. Not allowing negative thoughts to colonise you. One thing I had learned from my years of facing down adversity was that you have to make your thoughts work for you when shit and fan meet. It would have been easy to let my mind become drowned in thoughts of doom. Most people do. They have no control over their thoughts.

I concentrated hard on Ginger. Forced my mind away from the grey of my cell and the possibility of prison. I placed myself in her world, in her arms. I imagined her smile, her voice, her smell, those freckles. I talked to her and she talked back to me. I concentrated so hard that in the end I felt as if she was there in the cell with me; I could almost touch her. Me inside her world, her arms, her confidence. I visualised us laughing and joking. I felt her tracing her fingers across my face, kissing my lips, touching me ...

In the middle of the night Apple and Fatty took me from my cell to a small interview room somewhere at the back of the police station. They wanted a statement and the best time for them to get one, the time when I was most likely to incriminate myself, was when I was very tired.

'Reckon he ain't gonna make it.' PC Apple started the proceedings with a veiled attempt at psyching me out, weakening me, priming me for a full confession. He was talking about Ponytail, the guy whose head I smashed into the alloy of his own car.

It was 3 a.m. and the interview had started. I had the right to a duty solicitor, of course, or I could have called my own, but I knew my way around the judicial system (experience-based knowledge) and could handle myself.

Post-assault is a vulnerable time, and the police are often guilty of rushing statements and using subtle intimidation techniques to prize incriminating words from innocent lips: leaving you alone for long periods so that your own mind goes to work on you; planting negative seeds into your head ('You're going to jail, son, for a very long time'); even the good cop, bad cop routine. However, when you know the rules the game is a little easier to play, but it is still tricky, and there are lots of places to trip yourself up if you aren't careful.

'He might not pull through,' Apple said.

He smiled, knowing what the implication would do to me. There were many tricks they could employ in their bid to elicit a full 'I did it and I'm really sorry' confession that would lock me up for several birthdays. Between three and four in the morning is a good time to work because it is your tired time. The time when being awake physically hurts and it takes all your willpower just to stop your eyes from closing and your lips from betraying you. It is a weak time as far as the mind is concerned, and a good time to plant negative seeds that can turn men from hard to lard.

I knew the crack though, and I had expected no less, especially from rookie PCs wanting to try their techniques on real people. Even though I was ready for the tricks, this one still got me, and *whoosh!* my belly filled with butterflies. Inadvertently he had hit a hole in one; he had accidentally stumbled upon my deepest fear: my fear of killing someone. I breathed in deeply through my nose, careful to hide the intake of breath. Wouldn't like them to see that they'd got to me, that would not do at all. Show them a chink and they will go in for the kill.

My head raced. The thought of having to wait long months for the inevitable court case where my liberty would be left in the judging hands of twelve good men was overwhelming. I quickly reminded myself of the facts so far: I was in this position because four men had tried to kill me with a car. If that hadn't worked, they were tooled up and well oiled to finish the job. What I did was self-defence. Sometimes, when the judicial system has you over the barrel, you do have to blag it, you do have to stretch the truth a little to make it fit the law. But in this case it *was* self-defence. There was no unprovoked violence in my actions. When I was attacked I had feared for my life; I was fighting for survival. And if the guy I chinned died, then fuck it. He was the one who aimed his car at my knees, he was the one who had initiated the attack, so his current situation – in hospital breathing through a machine – was his own fault. What was I supposed to do, stand there and let them play ball with my head? I don't think so.

I shrugged my shoulders nonchalantly, internal dialogue under control, adrenalin slowed, calm, cool, sunglasses. My indifference upset Apple. He had expected a reaction, he had expected cheap suits to fall apart and livers to turn yellow; he expected more than I gave because I was playing the game. That's how you play when you're in a police station, isolated from the world, intimidated by the hired-help (don't we pay their wages?), looking at prison, looking at a severe loss of liberty. It is a game. And they play it hard. They want you to write the kind of hassle-free statement that leaves them with a clear road from the station to the courts and from the courts to prison. I was going to do my best to complicate things, to fill their path with problems and paperwork and mess. You have to look after yourself. No one else is going to do it.

'You know that you're looking at an eighteen, don't you? An eighteen with intent?' Apple had another stab.

'There'll be a definite five on the back of it,' Fatty butted in. They were obviously working as a double act.

'And that's if he lives. If he croaks ...' added Apple.

Fatty interrupted, 'And he looks like he might. They're still prising chunks of alloy out of his head with pliers and disinfectant.'

'Fucking right,' Apple agreed. 'You're looking at a fifteen, the big house, down the steps, the four greys.' He certainly knew the terminology.

'It was self-defence.' My answer was blunt, rehearsed, and much practised. I knew the law, I had dealt with it on more occasions that I cared to remember – working as a bouncer you get to deal with the police on a nightly basis. People are convicted for what they say and not for what they do. I knew what to say. Knew my right to self-defence.

'Self-de-fucking-fence.' Apple was indignant. Incredulous even. 'Self-de-fucking-fence.'

'Is there an echo in here?' I asked, looking at Fatty.

'Self-defence?' he continued, forcing his point home. 'You've got more chance of shagging the Queen, you prick.'

'It was self-defence, your honour,' I said, talking in my very best courtroom voice as if I was already in the dock and giving my speech to a judge. 'Four men tried to run me over in a car. One of the men got out of the car and tried to attack me with a baseball bat. He missed a few times and hit his own car. I feared for my life so I did the only thing I could. I attacked him in my own defence. He fell to the floor and hit his head on the alloy wheel, knocking himself unconscious. I was so worried about his welfare that I placed him in the recovery position and then ran for my life.' I looked at Apple. I smiled. 'How was I?' I asked. His jaw fell open like a cartoon cash register. 'It *was* self-defence,' I repeated and added one of those patronising winks that drive young policemen fucking crazy.

Apple leaned across the small table and glared at me menacingly, his top lip twitching. And it wasn't a bad try, the yellowing tombstone teeth, gaps lined with tartar, had me worried for a while, and the nostril hair that hung from his nose like spiders' legs; well, they were quite scary. And then there was the halitosis. That would have cracked many a man.

But I had seen hard, and this was not it. The silence was palpable. Fatty and Apple shared a 'what the fuck do we do now?' look. I knew I had them.

'Is this the part where I eat truncheon?' I asked innocently. Apple twitched angrily but did not reply. 'Oh, one more thing,' I added almost as an afterthought. 'I want to press charges myself, against the blokes in that car.' Apple looked at me as if to say 'you cheeky bastard'. I left a deliberate gap before I added, looking straight at Apple, 'And I still want to press charges against you. Don't forget, you assaulted me in the car, and you' – I pointed to Fatty – 'you were witness to it.'

Fatty actually took a step back, as though trying to separate himself from it all. Apple nearly fell over with the shock. Two can play the 3 a.m. trick, I thought; hit them when they are at their lowest. If I was tired and feeling fragile, these guys – especially Apple who had attacked me in the police car – would be feeling just the same.

Apple panicked and his words came out spontaneously, before he had a chance to prepare.

'You assaulted us, you prick! You'll never make that fucker stick,' he said. 'It's our word against yours.'

He looked over to Fatty as if to say 'isn't it?' Fatty, getting closer and closer to the door, gave a non-committal shrug.

'I'm not bothered whether it sticks or not, you lardy cunt. If you two want to get yourselves in the shit with fucking lies – because you did attack me, in fact, the fingerprints are probably still on my neck – if you want to lie, that's up to you.' I said it casually, as if it was a matter of fact. In reality, I was not bothered in the least whether the charges stuck or not, in fact, I had no intention of pressing charges. I just wanted to complicate things for them as much as they were trying to complicate them for me. It seemed to be doing the trick.

'Did you even bother to look in the car?' I asked them. 'All four of them scroats were tooled up. It was a fucking set-up. Did you even bother to check? Four men with bats in a BMW. Give us a fucking Kit-Kat.'

Fatty looked at Apple as if to say 'he's right, he is right'. Apple stormed out. Fatty followed.

I was taken back to my cell. I slumped onto the bench. I had spent my energy in the interview, trying hard not to show my fear. The grey that I had managed to drown out raced back towards me with a vengeance. I thought about the men in the BMW again. Those cunts were not looking for directions when they wheel-spun their car at me. But I didn't have a mark on me, I was uninjured; but one of them was in intensive care and his car was at the body shop (stable but unlikely to pull through). If the driver didn't make it, it could send me away for a long time. My obvious innocence guaranteed nothing.

Real fighting is not like those kung fu films, which lack the fear of a real encounter and are full of action but totally lacking in emotional content. They fail to convey that 'I'm gonna die' feeling that a real encounter triggers. No credibility. Written by yokes whose only experience of a ruck has patently been from the safety of a crime novel. On celluloid the attackers strike one at a time, in order and with a formulaic, learned-in-the-dojo, unrealistic assault that totally lacks credibility. In real life they come at you mobbed up, team handed, en masse, as one, like fucking flies around shit. They are like piranha going in for the kill: the instant one of them takes a bite, the others attack in one big lump – and in a fucking hurry. Real violence is random, frenzied, fast and right in your fucking face. It's more Jerry Springer than Jacky Chan; think *Saving Private Ryan*, forget *Star Wars*, and fuck the force (especially the police force). And you can forget the honour and the camaraderie and the respect; think abyss, think darkness, think sore feet from kicking heads, broken hands from punching teeth, and socks soaked in blood from where you've kicked the nose right off someone's swede. And you can definitely forget the swooning damsels; I never saw a swooner that didn't have a face like a horse. The romance that cinema promises will come with the violence is a lie. All you elicit when you enter the arena is fear and loathing and disgust and the odd fuck from some dysfunctional junkie or drunk who'd fuck a frog if she could stop it hopping for long enough. Forget the frame-by-frame, close up, slow-mo action shots that are the mainstay of action movies: the real stuff explodes in your face like a dodgy banger on bonfire night.

A million 'how to' books on the mysterious fighting arts and none of the fuckers have ever had it outside the chip shop. They're too busy pushing their heads up the arse of some Eastern master, some chip-fryer from Bolton with an Asian dad and a great memory for fortune-cookie philosophy. That stuff only works in the James Bond films (and on police self-defence courses). Makes me fucking laugh, makes me fucking smile.

It is a lonely place to be I have to tell you, in a police cell at 4 a.m. and on the wrong side of a very sticky judicial system. I had made my statement before they brought me back to the cell. *It was self-defence*, I wrote. *I was in fear for my life, and I had the honest belief that these men were going to kill me so I attacked first. I used reasonable force*. I said all the things you should say and left out anything that might incriminate me. The words 'honest belief' and 'reasonable force' were the mainstay of my statement. They were taken right out of the police bible: *Butterworth Police Law*. I think it's only right when entering an enemy's lair (and in cases like this the police were the enemy; they were trying to take away my liberty after all) that you know the layout of their world. You need to know how they work, how they think and the game-plans they employ. You need to know the books they work from, and in this case I did. I knew that *reasonable force* (the key words used by the police and the courts in cases of self-defence) was a vague anomaly, an intangible something that no one seemed to be able to fully measure. What the fuck is 'reasonable'?

I had learned that this subjective term was whatever you believed it was. *You* determine reasonable force (of course, you might have to defend your version of the term in a court of law). If you think that only a severe blow will stop your assailant, then that is reasonable force; if you have to kill him to stop him from killing you, then that is also reasonable in the circumstances. However, if it is to be deemed reasonable in the eyes of the law, then you need to know the right words to say in your statement. These words are only two in number: honest belief. Even a pre-emptive attack can be acceptable in law if in your statement you say 'I had the honest belief that he was going to attack me so I attacked first in self-defence.' If, however, you do a flamenco on his head when he is on the floor you may be stretching the law (and your luck). Might sound like I'm a right clever fucker but believe me, when you work a nightclub door you learn about the police and their ways very fucking heartbeat fast. You either learn the law or you go to the big house.

It was 5 a.m. when I got the news, when I thought my world had ended. PC Apple delivered the bad tidings. He slid open the peephole in my door. He was so happy I thought he was going to get his cock out and have a wank.

'Oi, shit-head. Your man is dead.'

I lay still, not wanting to give him the pleasure of a reaction. Any reaction.

'You do know you're looking at life on this baby?' he continued, disappointed that the moment did not leave me whimpering like a fool. 'How do you feel knowing that you're gonna be away for eighteen years? Hey? Tell me. How do you feel?'

'I feel hungry. Any chance of some tea and toast?' I asked, not looking up. Made him believe that I didn't give a fuck. But he must have known how hard the news had hit me, even if I did hide it like a pirate's treasure, because as I glanced at him he suddenly smiled. One of those fuck-off smiles that peels right back over your teeth and sticks there uncomfortably. He held the smile for a long moment and then slid the latch shut with a resounding clang. I could hear him laughing all the way down the alley of cells.

I lay still, my body numb, my mind in utter disarray. Voices and images and feelings colonised me, eating me; I was unable to control a single thought. I gave up. What was the use? I was fucked. Jail was all I could see. If I thought that God was out of my reach before then I was definitely lost now. There was no room for me in any of His many mansions now that I had committed the gravest of sins. I had been told this a million times on rainy Sundays when angry, preachy, pulpit priests warned us not to fuck with the All Powerful. He was loving and benevolent they told us, but if you fuck with Him, He will know and you will pay. The word 'pay' was spat out and poked home with the jab of a priestly finger. It was as if he was saying 'You fuckers think you are getting away with all your sins, but you will pay and I'll be there to see it.' *Yeah, course you will*, I used to think, *with a judgmental plank in your eye that size you'll be in the firing line with us*.

So there I was. Paying. Sat in a grey world no bigger than a bedsit kitchen with just the karmic consequences of my own actions for company. I was fucked; it was over. And suddenly the realisation of what I had done hit me. The guy I smashed into the wheel of an expensive motor was a man, a human being, someone's son, a brother, probably a husband, maybe even a father. When you're kicking the life out of them you don't see them like that. You just see aggression and body weight and targets and survival. You don't think of them as someone's daddy, someone's son. When you use your feet to break their bones a lot of dehumanisation takes place. It has to or you wouldn't be able to do it. Sat in a cell looking at life through the eyes of regret and retrospect you re-humanise them. And you start thinking about the consequences of death. Who it will affect. The number of people the ripples will touch. The far-reaching consequences of your actions suddenly become clear and you wish with every fibre of your being that you could press rewind on time and wake up yesterday. Change all the things that involved hurt, get back the person that you lost somewhere in the murk of yesteryear.

I wished that I could have cancelled my meeting with fate by never setting foot in that fateful fucking bastard café, or at the very least that I'd made my exit when the first smell of trouble hit my nostrils. I thought about my life, my shit life, my dank existence and how beautiful it was, how lucky I was to have had liberty to do whatever the fuck I wanted with it. I realised that the only reason my life stank was because I did nothing to change it. I was in a job I hated because I didn't have the testicles to try anything else. My flat was a kennel because that was the way I chose to live. Moreover, I realised that all those people that I blamed for my shit life – and I did blame everyone – well, it wasn't their fault. The fault was entirely mine. I realised all too late that I had been in nirvana all along and didn't even know it. Now that I had lost it I knew it all too well; loss has that annoying habit of showing you what you had. Isn't retrospect a bastard?

I was too traumatised to cry, my tears were frozen, just like the rest of me.

When I awoke from a fitful sleep I didn't know what day it was. For the first couple of seconds I felt great: I remembered that I was off work for two weeks and that I still had ages left before I had to go back. I thought of Ginger and how beautiful she was, and that smile.

Then my nightmare became real. The realisation hit me so suddenly that I said 'No!' out loud.

It couldn't be true. Yesterday I was living a normal life; today I was looking at life in prison. My body flooded with anxiety and my mind raced at a speed I could not control.

'Calm yourself, Martin,' I said quietly, urgently. 'Breathe deeply. Breathe.' I took a long, slow intake of breath through my nose and held it for three seconds. Deep diaphragmatic breathing slows down the fear. I got up from the bench, feet apart, and stretched my arms up to the ceiling and breathed deeply again. On the out-breath I bent forward so that my hands rested on the floor in front of me. The aches from two fights in one day racked my body. I stretched out and breathed deeper.

As I breathed and stretched, my internal dialogue went to work. I had learned through the years to talk firmly to myself when thoughts and fears tried to colonise my head. 'You can handle this. You can handle this. Breathe deeply, breathe deeply, stretch, stretch, breathe.' At the back of my positive internal dialogue another voice was trying to crack through.

'I don't like this,' it was crying and whimpering. 'I don't like this. I can't handle it. I want to go home, I want to go home.'

I got firm with myself. 'Shut the fuck up and breathe. You can handle it, and you can't go home. You are in charge, you can deal with anything, *anything*. You are strong.'

Then the coward in me again, wanting space. 'I can't handle it! I can't, I can't, I can't.'

Fuck me, I needed help, I needed it. I got on my knees by the bench, clenched my hands together tightly and looked up to the sky.

'Listen, mate,' I said to the God of the posh kids, sure that he would not help me. 'I need Your help. If You are there, if You are really there, please help me out here. I'm drowning.'

I didn't know why I was asking. I had asked before, in my childhood, when I was a vulnerable boy. It hadn't worked then. The opposite in fact. I asked for an angel, but a devil in a dog collar turned up.

I got to my feet and decided to do what I always did when circumstances turned against me. Deal with it myself.

I heard the rattle of my cell door as it opened. I quickly sat back on my bench and waited for the inevitable. I was bursting for a shit and every muscle in my body ached.

'Time to go.' It was the Sarge. He was a pleasant sight. I had been dreading that fucking Apple. I didn't want to see him again for as long as I lived. The Sarge was silent as he led me through the hall of cells and up the stairs. I presumed I was being taken to a local jail on remand while awaiting a court date. There was no way that they were going to let me out on bail, not on a murder charge. At the booking-in desk the Sarge handed me an envelope with all my possessions: a sovereign ring, my wallet and some keys. A Cartier watch. Two grand's worth, easy. He asked me to sign for them. I signed and he gave me the envelope.

'Expensive watch,' said the Sarge. Everyone knows a Cartier.

I nodded. 'I'm keeping it warm for someone.' As I put it on I noticed that Apple had inscribed his name, Paul Burns, on the back. Thank fuck that the Sarge didn't take a closer look. I'd have been right in the shit.

Sarge again, stern now. 'You wanted to press charges against one of my officers?'

I shook my head. 'I just said that to wind him up. I don't want to press any charges.'

He smiled. 'We'll be in touch,' he said, nodding to the exit.

'Pardon?' I was confused.

'The driver of the car was released from hospital last night. He's got a hole in his head the size of Brighton but he didn't want to press charges either.'

'What do you mean, "released from hospital"? He's dead.'

'Dead?'

'Yeah, your man told me last night.'

The Sarge laughed. 'No, he's not dead.' He thought for a second, then smiled. 'Probably just said that to wind you up.'

'Touché.'

The Sergeant laughed again, and as I left the station my body flooded with relief. I looked up at the sky. Was God on my side again? I gave out an involuntary whoop.

Ponytail's alive! I told myself. *He's alive. He's fucking alive!*

I headed home.

Chapter Six

Cap

Let me describe my flat. Two damp rooms where I sleep and eat. That's it. No need to spend time and money making it look like anything other than what it is. A shit hole. I'm a single man with simple tastes and a lazy streak that does not extend to decorating or cleaning. Anyway, I had no one to share it with, so why bother? It was a little place, the ground floor of an old two-up, two-down terraced dump in a cheaper part of the city. But when I got out of the taxi after my night of hell it was the sweetest little haven I had ever seen. It was beautiful, even with the chipped red front door and the neighbours who looked like serial killers. It was a shit hole but it was home and it was freedom.

In the flat above me lived a strange character called 'Who-the-fuck-is-Dennis' (so-called because people kept asking me 'Who the fuck is he?'). Strange name I know, but he was a strange man, with strange habits and a cat called One Eye, for obvious reasons. Never seen him shaved, ever, but he never seemed to grow a beard either. He came and went, did Dennis. Sometimes he was gone for days on end, no one knew where or why. Dennis hardly ever smiled, but he'd nod and chat politely for ages whenever he saw me, and he'd stroke his cat until it purred, and he was pleasant enough to strangers. He claimed to be a writer, and that he'd been asked on to *Parkinson* to talk about his new book deal with some big fuck-off publisher. I didn't believe for one second that he was a writer. If he was, then certainly not a successful one, what with the rented flat he lived in, the ten-year-old Ford he drove, and the fact that I rarely saw him dressed in anything other than an egg-stained string vest, flat-at-the-heel chequered slippers, and the type of pyjama bottoms you tie at the waist with a cord. He said he wanted to live in a shit hole to research his latest novel. It reflected the lifestyle of his main character. I told him that I wanted to live in a shit hole because it reflected the lifestyle I had come to expect. 'Nothing novel about that,' I added.

He smiled and made a note of my philosophical quip in a little black notepad that he took from the back pocket of his pyjamas. So I might end up in a novel! Perhaps get my name mentioned on Parky.

Yeah, that'd be right, me living below a novelist. It was not so much that I didn't believe him, which I didn't if I am being completely honest, it's just that he gave me no reason to. Most of the people I knew were through-their-teeth liars. It was a part of their social fabric; they lied as though their very lives depended on it. The untruths varied from the traditional white variety: 'Sorry I'm late for work, I'm having problems with my back' (problems getting the fucker off the bed in the morning), to the very black variety: 'I was nowhere near the scene of the crime, on my mother's life' (she's five years dead already), 'I have five witnesses to prove it' (three secured, two more yet to convince). So when Who-the-fuck-is-Dennis told me about his house in the country and the six-figure publishing deal and the slot on Parky (when he could find the time – in between novels, he was very busy), I didn't mind. It made him feel better, and while he was spinning the yarn it made me feel good too because for a little while it lit my dull existence. I let myself believe it because it injected a bit of hope (or should I say soap) into my otherwise dank, colourless world. I liked the guy despite his rampant abuse of the truth. Maybe it was just me, maybe I was an old cynic, maybe he really was a literary giant penning the next *Catcher in the Rye* above my very ceiling, and if I ever saw him on Parky, or in the top ten at Smiths, believe me, I would be the first to put my hands up and there would definitely be hats for dinner.

Lying is important. I learned that at an early age from my mum. She was the best, the very best, liar. Her life demanded no less. When the concerned neighbours asked about the broken teeth and lumpy plum mouth, it was easier to reply, 'I walked into a door,' than 'My husband came home drunk and boxed the fucking head off me and tried to drown me in a bath of cold water for no particular reason'. It lets everyone off. The neighbours don't have the problem of whether they should report the abuse, and my mum gets away with minimal embarrassment. One white lie and a blanket is drawn over the unsightly. My mum was an expert at butting doors and stair tumbling. And lying through her beautiful cracked teeth. Fuck me, I loved her. I loved her very bones. There was something about her that I had seen in Ginger the previous afternoon in the café. An innocence, a loyalty.

I'd hardly been home long enough to boil a kettle when there it was. A definite knock at my door. I had no friends that liked me enough to want to knock on my door for a social chat and a cup of tea, and it was too late in the day for the post. I walked to the door, making a mental note of the baseball bat standing sentry in the hall. I looked through the curtain. The net was stuck to the glass with condensation. There were two men on my front mat, both creepy-looking fuckers with darting eyes and an air of bad intention. I didn't know them. What the fuck did they want?

One of them was wearing a baseball cap, with a long ginger ponytail hanging down from under the cap to his Fila tracksuit jacket. Heavy, show-of-wealth gold jewellery swung from his wrists. His face was pretty, almost womanly, but then I checked out his hands. I always check out the hands; they give a window to the man who owns them. The hands, specifically the knuckles, tell their own story. I look for scars from past wars. Bulbous knuckles hint at hard karate sessions where makiwari punching and hard contact temper indomitable spirits. Knuckles out of place tell me that they have been used to punch something very hard – probably someone's head – and bent fingers with knuckles pushed back into the hands tell the same story. Big, heavy hand and wrist veins hint at hard, manual workloads (road diggers are harder work than trained fighters if they get a hold on you), fat middle knuckles are the weapons of gi-grapplers, judo players.

Cap's knuckles were bent and scarred. I knew he was a fighter. The other fellow was a heavyset built-like-a-box type with a blond handlebar moustache and a stern red face. High blood pressure or a long beach sleep was my guess. I didn't need to look at his hands, his eyes said it all: head-the-ball and best avoided. His arms were splayed from their sides, hands turned inwards so that I couldn't see the palms, like he was still going through the Darwinian transition. Not a good sign. If you can't see the palms then you have to assume that they are carrying.

I opened the door a crack and poked my head out, aware of the bat to my right should the situation get saucy.

'All right?' I kept it genial, but firm. The game has to start right from the off, even when you are not sure that a game is even on the agenda.

'Martin?' It was Baseball Cap.

He'd got my name right. Sunburn, his back up, fidgeted and stared.

'What can I do for you?'

The hair was already standing up on the back of my neck, and my hand was stretching for the bat but I couldn't quite reach it without making it obvious.

'Can we have a minute?' Cap nodded to the door, intimating that he wanted to come inside. My adrenalin hit the ceiling as I tried to work out what was going on.

'A minute for what?' Let the dog see the rabbit.

'Just need a minute.' Cap again. 'It's private.' His eyes flicked from left to right for prying eyes.

'Have your minute, but have it from there.' I was firmer now. My flat might be bombsite scruffy, but it was my flat and no one got past the door without a personal invite or an impersonal bat in the head.

Cap looked at Sunburn, then back to me. 'You did a right job on Mick in the café,' he said, taking off his cap. 'The lad's still walking with a limp.'

At the mention of the café my adrenalin shot through the roof and I felt an instant urge to shit my nappy. I clenched my bum cheeks and held on for dear life. Fuck me, I didn't need this, not at my house, not with these fucking goons. The internal dialogue shot off on a panicky tangent and I had to grip it firmly and quickly. The inner opponent, that little voice in your head that seems to be attached to your arsehole, is the maker or the breaker of courage. Let it race away and your arsehole goes manhole in a heartbeat. If you can grip hold of that inner voice and instruct it well, it will take you through any adversity that life, even death has to offer. But fuck me it was hard; all I wanted to do was let it go and crumble and beg and say 'Listen lads, I don't need this.

Can't we talk about it? Can't we come to some arrangement? I'm sorry about your mate, I didn't really want to hurt him, I ...'

Shut the fuck up you quivering twat! It was my positive internal voice clicking in. *Now listen to me. These brain-shy pieces of shite are at your door and looking for a little contact. They will be as scared as you, probably more so due to the fact that you have already turned their mate into a vegetable. They won't want to be at your door any more than you want them there. And the minute they see a chink in your armour they will manipulate it and drive a fucking tank through the hole. You'll be fucked within seconds if you let them see even a flicker of fear. This is the consequence of your actions in the café. Your consequence. Something that is not going to go away unless you send it away. So get a grip of yourself and fucking deal with it. Answer them; say something clever, say something smart, say something Clint Eastwood.*

'And?' It was all I could come up with.

They both looked at each other again. Sunburn twitched his right eye and the man with the golden wrists fiddled with his cap, a sure sign that he was preparing to 'go'. I'd learned to read the body language of bad intention: fidgeting, stripping of jewellery, closing range, narrowing of eyes, dropping of jaw, splaying of arms. It's my trigger to let the first one go, and I always hit the most dangerous one first. And he's not necessarily the one with the mouth. He might be the one closing in on the edge of your tunnel vision or the one moving round to your flank. You have seconds to decide, no time for deliberation or morals or contemplation on your right-to-fight in the eyes of the law or your place in the hereafter should your maim end the game. No grapple with morality, just get in first and then get the fuck out, and don't wait for the police because they'll shag you if you so much as drop an 'h' on your statement. So do the job and melt into the background before plod can appear and take you to jail (do not pass Go).

I was ready. Determined, in charge. The minute the conversation turned offensive, I was going to reach for the bat and bury it in the big fucker's mouth. Leave a gap in his teeth that you could park a small car in – work experience for some spotty apprentice at the dental surgery. That would leave me with only one to deal with, and he'd be on the back foot with his dinner trying to force its way south. More than one is one too many, and it is always scary.

I couldn't reach the bat without being obvious and giving away my game-plan and that was bothering me. With men of violent intention, especially when facing two or more, you need an appendage, something to even up the numbers a little. A bat usually does the job right enough. When it is within reach. Baseball Cap moved forward.

'Get the fuck off my doorstep, you piece of shit,' I said as I thrust my left hand out and pulled the door wide open. I allowed a little saliva to spit from my mouth. Hits them right in the mid-brain, makes them think that they are dinner for a sabre-toothed tiger. He shot backwards and his itchy-trigger-fingered-gunslinger mate splayed at the arms. His lips puckered into a pre-fight kiss. His jowly face shuddered in anticipation. His eyes locked on to mine like we were attached. I picked up my bat from beside the door with my right hand and tapped the head of the bat into my left palm. I stepped forward, they stepped back.

'Unless you want to be wearing this fucker you'd better get the fuck out of my world.' I pointed the bat in the general direction that I wanted them to go.

'Hold up, hold up.' It was Cap and he was flapping like a baggy vagina, his heavy bracelets jangling as he waved his hands in front of him, a gospel singer preaching the word.

'Steady tiger,' he continued, taking yet another step away, right out of bat range. 'Friend not foe. Fuck's sake, put the bat down.

We don't want to play, no grief man, we're here to party not fight. We're on your side.'

'What the fuck are you on about, you spaceman?' A legitimate question I felt. He'd turned up at my door with Herman Munster and arms full of drug-dealer jewellery, asking for a little private time in my own abode and only hours after I'd choked the life out of a local face, and thought I should automatically be OK with it.

'Give me a good reason for being on my doorstep or start running from my bat you druggy fucker.'

'Julie! I'm Julie's brother,' said Cap.

Sunburn still hadn't spoken. I was beginning to wonder if he was a mute.

I scrunched my eyes up and made one of those 'who the fuck?' faces.

'Who the fuck's Julie?' I asked in case he didn't do faces.

'Julie,' he repeated emphatically. 'Julie! The girl you saved at the café, man. You heroed my sister.' He pointed to his ginger ponytail as validation that she was in fact his sister.

He stuck out his hand to give me five, but I didn't trust him so I kept my hands on the bat where they would better serve me should the situation turn physical.

'That's what I've come to talk to you about.'

The penny suddenly dropped. 'Oh, Ginger,' I said without thinking.

'Ginger?' Cap didn't know what the fuck I was talking about.

'Julie.' I thought I was making perfect sense.

'Julie?' He was more confused than ever now.

Oh fuck. 'You'd better come in.'

I stood back and beckoned them forward. Cap walked past me but Sunburn stood back, still rooted to the spot. He was ready for some contact. I held out my hand in a gesture of friendship and the kiss on his lips disappeared; a small smile appeared, we shook hands and he entered my flat.

Cap looked around at the bleak room.

'Wow, what happened here?' His question was innocent enough.

'I moved in.'

Cap sat down on my ageing leather settee, while Sunburn parked himself on my seventies' beanbag, old and worn, where he sank to an undignified floor level. He looked comical.

'How did you find me?' I asked.

'We know your mate, Gary,' replied Cap. Ah, good old Gary. He used to work with me on the doors. He was as thick as fuck; the lad could row some but was not big on complicated things like thinking and talking in long sentences. It would never occur to him that someone asking questions about me might not have good intentions.

'So, what's the story?' I directed my question to Cap.

'Story?'

'With Ginger.'

'Ginger?'

'Ginger. Ginger,' I said rather testily. *Fuck me*, I thought, *don't you know your own sister?*

'Who's this Ginger you keep on about, man?'

Fuck me, here we go again. 'Julie. I mean Julie, your sister.'

'Oh, yeah, Julie.' His eyes dropped to the floor. I could tell that this was going to be bad news.

Cap said that before coming to find me, Mick had forced his way into Ginger's flat and taken revenge for his humiliation in the café. I felt terrible, responsible. I had disappeared before the police came sniffing, not thinking that Ginger would be in any more danger. He also told me that Mick had placed a contract on my kneecaps. A head-the-ball called Bilko had been paid to do a proper job. I knew of this Bilko. I had heard his name on many occasions and never in a good light. Descriptions of him varied from 'dirty, greasy ball-bag' to 'fat cunt' (that already included half my neighbourhood). When I worked the doors he was feared, even by the bouncers. Not just because he could have a fight – and there was no doubt that he could, he put three good men away one night in a pub car park using just his head – but also because he was known as a come-back merchant. He had no qualms about bringing the fight to your home. Or to your mother's home, or to the home of anyone that might know you. Rumour had it that he'd topped a Rasta named Kelvin in The Pig and Whistle, a local bar full of in-breds and career criminals. He'd stamped on Kelvin's head until he was unconscious. Then dropped a pool table on the lad's throat. They reckoned you could hear the snap of cartilage from across the street. He got away with it too, Bilko. By the time the police got to the scene of the crime he was already in Ireland 'with relatives'. All the police found was a dead body, a carpet sopped in red and a bar full of witnesses who saw and heard fuck all.

With murder added to his CV, Bilko's reputation rocketed. People started to offer him money to do their dirty work. And it *was* dirty. By all accounts he would do anyone at any time for the right price. His reputation for come-back preceded him. Most people would not enter an affray with him – even if they knew they could beat him in a three-second fight – because they knew, win or lose, he would come back and there would be blood.

I only ever saw Bilko the once. He came to The Lion when I was working on the door. A big man. Fat. Actually, fat don't do him justice. The guy had postcodes on each cheek of his arse. Put his belt on with a boomerang. You know the type. As it turned out, he knew the gaffer so nothing untoward happened. But he filled the room with fear when he entered and the atmosphere stayed clammy and cold until he moved his fat arse to another club a mile down the road.

No one wants an enemy for life. It appeared that I had just found one.

I was filled with a mixture of joy (I could get in touch with Ginger again), anger (because Mick the Prick had set me up for a kneecapping), and fear (because Bilko was not to be taken on lightly). All these feelings raced around my head, a cocktail that left me with a heavy-beat background noise of dread. I was lost in the middle of a thousand thoughts all vying for the front of my consciousness. Cap broke the spell.

'So what you gonna do?'

'First thing I'm going to do,' I said, 'is go and see Ginger.'

Cap thrust his arms into the air. 'Who the fuck is Ginger?'

Chapter Seven

Bilko

I've never liked hospitals. I spent too many hours in there as a youngster, surrounded by the smells and the sounds of pain and hurt and suffering and abuse. I did not like them. Maybe my fear was that I might end up in one myself some day, attached to a robot to keep me breathing and a tube for food. Like my mum did so many times on the end of my dad's heavy hands. Like my dad did all those times when he left his liver down the working men's club and had to be carried to Casualty by his same ilk mates. Bloated in the belly and Yoda-yellow from his top to his toes. Yellow. I have to say that the colour suited him.

Mum always said the drink would kill him eventually anyway. I never made my peace with him. Never learned to forgive because to me forgiving was like letting him off. I couldn't do that.

I didn't like him very much by the end, but I still loved him. When all's said and done he was still my dad. But watching his body melt into the quicksand of that hospital bed – nurses feeding tubes up his prick and down his throat – with a look of terror on a face that had aged overnight, it was hard not to feel a little compassion. It was worse for my mum. She was quivering in her skin, unsure whether to be happy or sad. I was all indifferent on the outside but inside I squirmed uncomfortably because it is hard to watch the man that produced you and abused you in the same lifetime falling away in every way except his eyes. Even when he was all but gone he still seemed to be climbing out of those eyes. And you know the hardest thing, for my mum especially, after all her years of sticking by him, of standing his corner, of backing him even after the abuse, it was his drunken mate he cried out for when the throes of death finally took him. His fucking mate. Slaughtered my mum it did, slaughtered her. I had to sit and watch him abuse her one more time. Not with his fists this time, but with his thoughtlessness. One last time. Even as he died, he still had the capacity to hurt her, to take one last crushing swipe. And then him dead and buried and problem free, where do you think we held the wake? At his fucking local with his fucking drunks-for-friends staggering round like circus clowns talking about what a great man my dad was and how lucky me, my mum and my brother were to have had him. Yeah, that'd be right enough. We were lucky; lucky the bastard never killed one of us.

My mum sat there agreeing with them, using words that had no semblance of truth in them. You only had to look at her eyes to see that she was lying. As I said, the lady was an expert. And they were honourable lies; she was protecting my dad's reputation with the people that mattered to him most: his drinking pals. My mum said that they didn't need to know the truth because it didn't matter. To them he was the best bloke in the pub and that's how it should remain because (and this was the way my mum reasoned) it was true. When I argued, she snaked her arm through mine and gently but very firmly pointed out that my dad had been a good friend to these men, the best. So when they said he was a great bloke they meant it. To them he was. I told my mum that it was a pity he never brought any of that 'great bloke' stuff back to us. He might have been the best bloke in the pub but he was the worst bloke in our house. That's where the conversation ended because my mum said that she would not hear ill of the dead and whilst my father had his faults he was a good provider. A good man spoiled by the drink.

A good provider? The cunt bounced her nut off every sharp edge in our house and she was there at the wake bigging him up like everyone else. And I loved her for it. She was so much stronger than me.

So I didn't like hospitals, and yet there I was again visiting with flowers and chocolates and trepidation and fear and loathing. I wondered what the fuck I was doing there. My life seemed to be on an endless loop that started and finished at a hospital bed.

I made my way through Casualty, down the whitewashed halls of ill, the sounds of busy in my ears and the smells of disinfectant and decay in my nose. I passed a row of small emergency cubicles on my left. There was a disembodied commotion coming from one of them.

'Leave me, leave me alone! Get away from me you bastards! I want to go home, you can't keep me here …'

It was the sound of hurt and pain, the sound of a woman. I could hear the nurses shushing and trying to calm her down.

'Hush now, Sarah,' I heard them saying. 'We just want to help you.'

The familiarity in their voices told me that their patient was a regular. Then suddenly Sarah came rushing out of the room in one of those backless paper gowns that showed your arse and raped your dignity. The nurses were on her trail.

'Come on now, Sarah,' one of the nurses called, mid-chase. 'We have to wash you, love. The doctors won't see you while you're in this mess.'

Sarah, a skeleton of a woman, dashed down the corridor while three nurses gave chase. She was probably thirty but looked sixty. Face deflated and grey with cheekbones like headstones. Hair matted with vomit and dirt. She was obviously a down-and-out, one of the invisible people that sit on our streets in oversized army coats selling begs for bucks. The smell of shit got to me first. It was like muck-laying day on the farm. As she passed me, the nurses still in hot pursuit, my eyes automatically followed. I could see where the smell was coming from. Sarah was naked below the paper dressing gown, which was flapping open at the back. Her naked arse was covered in shit, caked on like mud-pie from the cheeks to the backs of her knees. The stench was horrendous. The nurses caught her and, after an initial struggle, she calmed down. They ushered her back to the cubicle. From inside I heard a kindly matron say, 'Now Sarah, you must let us treat you or you might die.'

A pause. Then Sarah said, 'I'm dead anyway.'

I hurried through to the wards. Nurses were toing and froing, tending to the needy and the dying on a tight budget that was so stretched it barely paid the carer to care. Angels would be about right.

I came to Ward B2 and tentatively peeped through the double doors to see if Ginger was there. Four beds, one hidden by curtains, the other three filled with the ill. An old guy with death on his face was surrounded by his doting family; a lady with a bandaged head looked up at the telly, which was perched in the corner of the room. The third bed contained a young girl with a wired jaw and a look of lost. She was holding hands with a young man, probably her boyfriend, but the grip was strained. I guessed that she was holding hands with her attacker. I entered the room through the squeaky swing doors, soft carpet tiles underfoot, fearful of what I might find. The nerves kicked in. I didn't know what to expect, what the damage might be. I didn't know if I should be there at all. What kind of reception would I get? Would she blame me for what had happened to her?

As I approached the curtains around the fourth bed a small nurse with a strawberry face and spotty nose pulled them back. Seeing me, she stopped and threw a look that could cut steel. I was confused for a second, wondering why she had hate on her face, but then it dawned on me. She thought that I'd done the damage to her patient, and I felt that I had in a way. She looked back to the girl in the bed, as if to ask 'Is this the bastard that closed your eyes with the toe of his boot?' But there was nothing in her patient's eyes but a smile. The nurse nodded, almost apologetically, her unspoken question answered, and made her exit.

For a second I was rooted to the spot with horror and a hundred bloody images of my mum raced through my mind. Ginger was a mass of bandages, dried, caked blood and lumps that looked like growths. Her left eye was almost completely closed and swollen, and her mouth was lumpy and torn and full of bloody eggs. Her left cheek was a red and yellow balloon. She looked at me and even through the bloodshot eyes I could see the beauty from the café.

'I'm sorry,' she said, each word a painful effort.

She was sorry. She'd been battered, and it was my fault, and she was sorry. A ball of sadness was growing in my chest and rising. I couldn't help seeing my mum on the kitchen floor, face in a pool of her own blood, looking up at me and saying the same thing: 'Sorry, son. Sorry.'

I tried to speak but the words were jammed in my throat. I was afraid to force them out because I knew that they'd bring the ball of hurt with it and my voice would tremble with emotion and vulnerability. I managed one word, and it was laced with sadness.

'Sorry?'

She tried to smile but I could see that every movement brought pain. I lifted my arm to stop her from making the effort but it trembled in the air. I could feel my bottom lip quiver and my eyes fill with water. I brought my hand back to my face to try and disguise the features that were going to jelly. There was no way I was going to let myself cry. Crying was weak. Men didn't cry.

Ginger beckoned me over to her. I stood by her bed, unable to speak. She leaned over and lifted a jug of water to pour me a drink. Her hand and arm shuddered in pain. I took the jug from her and poured the drink myself, even though I didn't want it. She brushed her blood-hard ginger hair back.

'If I'd known you were coming I'd have done something with my hair.'

Her body rocked with a forced laugh but no noise left her lips. I laughed with her but the laugh was in danger of becoming a sob, and there was a danger that if I let it go it might never stop. I couldn't do that. I took a deep breath to try and stop the tears that were welling up behind my eyes. My face was still quivering at the lip. *Fuck*, I thought, *what's happening to me? I can't cry. Can't. I don't do crying*. I took a deep breath and held it.

'What happened?' I asked, even though I knew the answer.

She shrugged nonchalantly like she'd been asked the question a million times before. 'Oh, you know.'

'Yeah,' I said. And I did know too. Seen it a million times.

I sat down on the side of the bed. I held her hand, caressing her fingers. I took another deep breath. 'I'm dead sorry. Dead,

dead sorry. If it wasn't for me, none of this would have happened. I feel awful about it. I'm so sorry.'

'What you did for me in the café … I really appreciate it. No one's ever stood up to Mick before. Everyone's scared of him.' Her voice was childlike, her eyes filled as she spoke and a tear ran down her cheek. I wiped it away. As I did she noticed the cuts on my hand from my fight. She looked sad. 'I knew he'd come back. He always does. Are you all right? Did he …?'

'No,' I interrupted, shaking my head as though it was nothing to worry about. 'No, they tried, but …' I didn't really want to tell her; she had enough on her plate. 'Well, they weren't up to the job.' I smiled and spared her the details.

The nurse walked to the bed. 'Can I get you anything, love?' she asked Ginger.

Ginger shook her head, and the nurse walked over to the other beds. Ginger leaned forward and spoke into my ear, quietly, like she was passing on a secret.

'If I wanted to see you again …' She hesitated. 'Would you want to see me?'

She asked it with such insecurity, with such an attractive naivety that I wanted to hug her to pieces. Would I want to see her again? That's what she asked. I smiled, so happy, so delighted, so privileged. She wanted *me* to see her again. Me. Ugly, fat, a builder with absolutely nothing going for him. This beauty, this gorgeous lady, was asking me for a date. I was overwhelmed. I didn't know what to say.

I nodded. 'I would. Very much. Be great,' I said. 'Be dead good.'

I couldn't understand why she might think, even for a nanosecond, that I wouldn't want to see her again. She was blindingly beautiful.

'You're gorgeous,' I said honestly. 'Why would anyone not want to go out with a girl like you? They'd have to be out there with Pluto if they said anything other than "Yes, please".'

She laughed and blushed. 'You'd be surprised,' she said, looking down nervously at the bed. 'Everyone knows who Mick is. That's enough to put most people off. Not that there's been many,' she added quickly, looking embarrassed. 'I don't blame them either. It isn't fair on them.' She looked up at me. 'He doesn't like me seeing anyone.' She said it with a seriousness that sounded like a warning. Then she looked down at the bed again sadly. 'I'm a fucking liability.'

The moment she said it I burst out laughing. If I didn't laugh I would have definitely cried. It was the way she said it, so matter of fact, so honest, and the swearword sounded so funny coming from the lips of someone so feminine. She looked up and smiled, and then laughed with me, holding her ribs again to stop them from hurting.

'Hey, let me tell you,' I said, grinning all over my face, 'you're just the kind of liability a bloke like me needs.'

When the laughing stopped she leaned forward and hugged me closely to her. I held her gently and waited for her to release the grip. She didn't. It had been an age since I had felt the warmth of a hug that wasn't attached to some loveless sex. I stayed in that embrace for a long time. Even the nurses left us to it, pulling the curtains around the bed and letting us be.

In those hours in the hospital I shared my life with Ginger. I told her things that had never before left my lips, and she shared things back. We merged and touched and kissed. She told me about her life, about Mick and how his insecurity and jealousy turned a fine relationship from loving to threatening.

'When we first got together,' she told me, 'I quite liked his jealousy. It was sort of quirky, like a small insecurity. I thought it showed that he cared.' Then her face dropped as she continued. 'Didn't take long for that to change. He got really possessive, so possessive. Started pushing me around a bit, not too hard at first, but hard enough. Then it grew to the odd slap because he thought I was looking at other blokes. I wasn't – I wasn't even interested in other men, I just loved him. I did love him then,' she added sadly. 'The slaps became hits, the hits became thumps. In the end I was like a punch-bag. I was terrified of him. I couldn't even leave the house without him interrogating or accusing me.' Her eyes welled with tears again as she remembered the bad old days with Mick. I sat and listened.

'When I went shopping he'd check my parking tickets when he thought I wasn't looking, to make sure I'd been where I said I'd been. I even caught him checking my knickers in the laundry basket while he thought I was in the shower.' She looked at me as she spoke, unsure about whether or not she should be sharing such private thoughts with me; it was only the second time we'd met. But she trusted me. I also think it was her way of saying 'Have a good look at what you're taking on before you make up your mind.' As far as I was concerned my mind had been made up the very first time I set eyes on her that fateful day in the café.

'He was checking my knickers …' she carried on incredulously, embarrassed by what she was about to reveal. 'He was checking for traffic. Spunk.'

I lifted my eyebrows, shocked. Wasn't quite sure I heard her correctly.

'What?' Now it was my turn to be incredulous.

'It wasn't enough that he quizzed me about where I'd been and who I'd spoken to. He didn't believe a word I said. He checked my pants for spunk. For the mark of other men, for signs of …' she hesitated. 'The worst betrayal.' She looked me firmly in the eye. 'There was no betrayal, Martin. It was all in his warped mind.'

She shook her head. 'I can't believe how normal that became. I actually found myself leaving my knickers out one night before I went to bed in case he wanted to inspect them before I put them through the washer.'

'That is bad,' I said.

She went on to tell me that the less evidence he found the more convinced he became that she was having an affair and hiding it well. Her life turned into a nightmare where she was frightened of even changing the TV channel for fear that it might trigger a rage, or a beating. Her mood became almost symbiotically linked to his; if he came home under a cloud her shoulders would hunch and she'd become a fearful wreck, frightened of making even the simplest error, not even sure what an error might be. One day his dinner would be too cold, another day too hot; the central heating in the house would be up too high or not enough; the clothes she wore were either old fashioned or too revealing. If she used make-up to cheer herself up, he accused her of wearing it for another man, if she wore no make-up at all she was letting herself go. His moods were unpredictable and ugly.

His last beating had left her in a hospital bed and, despite the harassment and the threats that followed, she never went back to him again. She found herself a job, sorted out a flat, tried to leave her old life behind. But Mick had pursued her for six months, waiting outside her flat, stalking her to work, calling her so often that she'd changed her number countless times. Then there was that fateful meeting in the café where I beat him a new head. She told me how worried she was because Mick had promised her, while kicking her around the floor at her flat, that I would be dealt with. I told her not to worry. I could look after myself.

Eventually she fell asleep holding my hand. I sat in a chair by her bed for the entire night.

What she told me about Mick and his warped mind brought back memories that I had long suppressed. I knew about warped minds. Mine had been dangerously close to overload as a younger man. My memories were of my first love. I hadn't experienced intimacy since Janie beyond drunken one-night fucks. It was an early relationship after my dad had died and left me with a legacy of imbalance that I could not seem to shake. At times I felt I was going mad. Later I learned to ignore the thoughts that entered my mind like squatters, but as a younger man I made the mistake of feeding them with my attention and allowing them to become real. They destroyed everything I loved.

I would see violence in everything, in everyone. When I spoke with people, nice people, these thoughts of violence would leap into my consciousness and go to work. Mid-conversation I would see myself – in my warped mind's eye – headbutting them to the floor and stamping on them for no reason. The thoughts would trigger massive anxiety, and the anxiety would trigger more thoughts of violence. It was a downward spiral that I could not seem to escape. At the time I thought I was becoming my dad, that I would be another him, and that any girl I managed to get would eventually find the end of my fist, like my mum ended up on the end of his. I thought that when my dad died my freedom would be liberating: no more fear of how his mood might affect my world; no more fear of arriving home to find my mum in a bloody heap on the kitchen floor or propped over the kitchen sink covered in bruises and crying because it had happened again. But it wasn't liberating because although he had left us, dying in that hospital bed with his yellow skin and scared eyes and shrunken liver, he still hadn't left my head.

I felt trapped in my own body. Sometimes when I think back I can feel it all over again. Trapped in my own skin like a giant squeezed into a dwarf. Trapped in a flesh and bone jail, screaming to get out, clawing at my own face, my fingers trying to tear an exit. It scared me. Often when we were sat in the comfort of a darkened room, Janie lying in my arms on the settee watching TV, the thoughts would come and my mind's eye would enact the worst atrocities on her. A red mist would blur my vision. My limbs would freeze, and I would have to get out of the room for fear my thoughts might manifest themselves. She would look at me, startled, and ask me what was wrong. But how could I tell her? How can you share your innermost thoughts when they are all so ugly?

I kept getting the urge to punch her in the face for no reason. Punch her unconscious. That sickly crack of knuckle on teeth, her on the floor looking up at me, dazed and confused and sad and bleeding saying, 'What's up love? What did I do?' I imagined how I would feel trying to explain that there was no reason for it. She had done nothing wrong.

I didn't want a phantom hand that shook with rage and threatened to strike out against my will at any minute. I had carried these thoughts for an age, not daring to share them with a soul. It was because of my dad. I'd read enough psychology when I was on the doors to know that much. I'd wanted to know what was going on inside the minds of all the head-the-balls who walked through the doors. I learned a lot about myself in the process. I had developed what they called a schema, like an internal scar that had the tendency to turn child victims into adult abusers. My fucking legacy. It was as though I had this other entity inside me. Another, younger me. An eleven-year-old boy who was so traumatised by his abuse that he was frozen in the moment, stuck as a child living in the body of an adult, only to emerge when fear came to the fore. It was like this little kid was frozen in a permanent state of anxiety, just waiting, terrified, to be abused all over again.

Now he had the body and muscle of a grown man he knew he could lash out and hurt someone, not be the victim any more. I knew he was there, in his own little prison; I just didn't quite know how to let him out, how to set him free, liberate him and hug him and tell him 'Look mate, you're a man now, a tough man, a hard man, a man to be respected, a bloke that won't be abused, who won't be attacked, who won't take shit from any man, not ever again. But you have to leave, let go.'

Maybe he was stuck beneath my darkest secret, smothered beneath my father's shadow, the secret that weighed down on me most, the one that I made the mistake of sharing with Janie. I had shared it with only one person before her and he had abused my trust and destroyed my faith in the world. I vowed never to do it again. But I did tell her because I thought she would understand. I finally told her, but I regretted it the minute the words left my lips. But I thought she might have understood. We were lying in bed after having sex. She was touching my chest, drawing circles with her very soft fingers and smiling, a face full of love. I loved that smile.

She said, 'Sometimes you look so lost, like a little boy. I wish you'd let me in.'

It was as if she knew my mind. As she stroked her fingers across my lips she said, 'Tell me what's weighing on you.'

I looked at her quizzically and she must have known that she was close to getting the truth from me, because a look of sympathy fell across her face and her mouth pouted. 'You can tell me. I love you, all of you, even your darkest parts.'

That's when I told her. I trusted her, see. That was my mistake. I trusted her to understand something that even I could not come to terms with. She was so young and so new and so vulnerable. I made a mistake. As soon as I told her, I knew it. Her face took on a distant look. Then she laughed, only her mouth didn't move, as though the laugh had been thrown out of her throat before her lips were ready. My secret was a burden beyond her capacity to bear. It had sucked her out of my reach. She went rigid and slid away from me as if she'd just woken up and found herself in bed with a complete stranger.

'I didn't want to do it,' I said, already wishing that I had kept the secret under wraps. Then she started crying. I tried to hold her but she backed away, repelled by me. She had gone. She hovered on the periphery of my world for a couple of weeks like a haunting spirit. But I knew that she was gone.

I couldn't believe that I'd lost her. I loved her bones but she was no longer mine, I couldn't touch her. She used to say that I was quiet and deep; she liked that. At school if you were quiet and deep you got the fuck beaten out of you. At home it was even worse. My dad attacked it, like it was a personal affront to his manhood. But she liked it. She was the first woman who really cared about me, and I loved her for that. I can't tell you how exciting it was to realise that even I could be loved.

So I lost her, and I learned to hide the few thoughts that I couldn't control and if the thoughts got too bad I'd take it out on the punch-bag.

Anyway, that was past and gone; the thoughts were pretty much under control most of the time, the secret buried deep inside. I'd learned to keep it under lock and key.

In the morning when Ginger awoke, I was still by her side. She gripped my hand tightly, and I leaned over. I kissed her gently on the face and hugged her. She let out a soft moan where her ribs were sore and my touch had awakened the pain.

'Sorry,' I said, pulling back.

She smiled crookedly, her lips unable to follow the command of her emotions because they were pumped like bike tyres after a puncture fix.

'It's OK.' She gripped my hand.

The nurse, smiling and sprightly, arrived by the bed with tea and toast.

'How are we this morning?' Her voice was full of concern. I liked the fact that within the space of one night Ginger and I had become a 'we'.

'Good,' Ginger replied.

The nurse left. Ginger handed the tea to me.

'You have it,' I said. She shook her head and insisted that I drink first. I took a sip and handed it back. Ginger lifted the teacup to her mouth and sipped, careful not to burn her cut lips. She handed me a slice of toast. Again I declined and again she insisted. I ate a slice of toast and watched as she struggled to swallow the small mouthfuls that she'd taken. Her hand was permanently on mine, rubbing my fingers and squeezing. I was tired. I had hardly slept a wink and it was starting to catch up with me.

'Go home now and get some sleep,' she said. 'You look tired.'

'I'm all right.' I yawned, then cursed myself for not being able to stop it. 'I want to stay here. With you.'

She smiled. 'I need to rest,' she said, giving me a way out. 'Come back soon though, yeah?'

'I'm all right. Honest.' I didn't want to go, didn't want to leave her. I was frightened to leave her.

'Go,' she said gently. 'Come back soon.' She rubbed my fingers again. 'Honestly, I'll be all right. I'll still be here when you get back.'

She was right of course. I did need sleep, and there were a couple of other things that needed tending to.

'I won't be long,' I said, still gripping her fingers.

She squeezed my hand and then let it go. I smiled and stood to leave.

'Promise me you won't do anything dangerous,' she said as I bent to kiss her goodbye.

I smiled and nodded. I looked behind me as I left, and she waved.

When I left the hospital, it was with the full intention of keeping my promise. I had spent enough of my young life in strife; I had lost love and liberty to violence and was not about to make the same mistakes again. I told myself that I would let the law deal with Mick; he was no longer my problem. It was out of my hands. And after all, a promise is a promise.

I'd forgotten all about Bilko and the contract on my knees.

Chapter Eight

A Monkey on My Back

When I arrived back at my flat it was with weary limbs and tired eyes on the verge of closing. The taxi dropped me off outside, and I was surprised to see Dennis standing by my front door, which was wide open. The adrenalin shot straight into my stomach and my legs suddenly felt hollow.

'Oh fuck,' I said aloud.

My mind was racing and throbbing and buzzing. I couldn't believe it. They'd done a home visit, a house call. You know it's bad when they come to your home. Even as I was stepping out of the taxi I was killing people and kicking their heads around pub car parks in my mind's eye. What bothered me most was not so much that my front door was kicked in – that could easily be repaired – it was the fact that Mick had organised another return visit, and so quickly. This situation was not going to go away easily. That was hard to get my head around. The fact that I had a life-threatening situation and it was never going to go away was evident. Any fucker can have a fight in the car park at the pub and shake hands over a drink afterwards, but taking on an enemy for the rest of your natural is another matter.

'What's happened, Dennis? What's going on?'

My door was open, there were splinters of wood on the floor and a heavy boot mark just below the letterbox. I knew what had happened. Of course I did. I don't know why I even asked, I think I just wanted him to tell me that my worst suspicions were not true.

'Happened about four in the morning, love. Woke me with quite a start. It was a good moment before I was able to access my notepad.' Dennis had a lovely middle-class, posh-school accent, and usually I would have been happy to indulge him, but not today. I wanted information and fast.

'Dennis! Get to the point!' I started to get irritable. If it was bad news, and I knew it would be, I wanted to know immediately so that I could kill the wait before the waiting killed me. I can deal with adversity, fuck knows I've had enough of it in my life, and I could have a fight with just about anyone that cared to step into my world. As long as I didn't have to wait. When I was at school I'd fight anyone in a spontaneous playground battle, but if they ever did the whole 'meet me after school' scenario I'd cack my khakis and run for the hills. It made me a terrible boxer. All that waiting around for weeks on end for match night with the drip-drip of adrenalin eating into my will until I thought I might explode.

Dennis recoiled, offended by my outburst.

'Sorry, Dennis. I'm tense. I haven't slept all night. Please, what's the story?'

My apology did the trick.

'It's a rather short narrative and I suspect that the ending is still unwritten …'

I gave him one of those 'get the fuck on with it' looks. He continued. 'A rather big gentleman pulled up in a Shogun motorcar – one of those four-wheel drive jobbies – nice vehicle actually, little rusty around the wheel arches, but besides that ...'

I closed my eyes, exasperated, and shook my head.

'Yes. Quite.' Dennis got the message. 'A rather large gent got out of the vehicle and proceeded to kick your door down. Of course, you weren't there so he left almost as quickly as he arrived.'

'A big fat cunt you say?'

I already knew who it was – Bilko – but I wanted it repeated and underlined. Dennis took out his pad and began to write.

'Yes,' he said as he wrote, 'that's quite a graphic description, and very accurate. "A big fat cunt." Sounds like the beginning of a limerick. One big fat cunt kicking down a door, one big fat cunt settling a score, one –'

'Save it for Parky, eh Dennis?'

Dennis stopped mid-rhyme.

I walked past him into my home, my mind break-dancing inside my head. What to do, what to do? Inside, the place was virtually untouched, though all the doors were wide open. It was a 4 a.m. job. Typical of men like Bilko. They come when the night is blackest and sleep is deepest. They kick down doors and smash sleeping bodies before the victims have a chance to react. It does two things: firstly, it makes the target easy to beat because they are still only half awake and totally unaware. Secondly, it steals peace of mind because those who were attacked will never feel safe again. Some never get over it. It was a dirty trick because cunts like that don't even bother to find out if women and children are in the house, and even when they do, it still doesn't stop them.

My breathing was heavy. I needed to use the toilet. The cooked breakfast that I had intended to purchase suddenly lost its appeal as fear colonised my whole body. This Bilko needed to be stopped and in a hurry before things got right out of hand, and the best way to do that was to stop hanging around waiting for night-callers and start doing a little calling myself.

I was full of trepidation and it was hurting my day, so the first thing I needed to do was get to a gym – hadn't been to one in a while – and take the top off the anxiety. If you don't bleed it, it can overwhelm you. The best way to do that is to train it out until you are ready to use it for real.

Before I left I made a phone call to a friend from my past.

'Hello you old fucker.' I hadn't spoken to Kevin in months. Talking to him now, it seemed as though it'd only been days. We'd worked the doors together.

'How are you then?' I asked, a big fuck-off smile on my face. I had made few friends over the years; it was not in my nature to add to a Christmas card list that did not even extend to my own brother. But I liked this guy. I'd seconded for him in a car park match fight with a local boxer called Smithy, and although Kevin lost the bout, his bravery had left an indelible mark on me. He was the bravest fucker I ever saw. One of those guys that couldn't fight the tide in the bath, but would never back down from anyone. Smithy had boxed him a new head, and, after a ten-minute fight at the local park, I'd had to throw in the towel for Kevin. He was semi-conscious and battered and bleeding but wouldn't give up. He lost the fight but he won my respect with his indomitable spirit.

Kevin's specialities were names and faces. He could spot a scroat at half a mile. On the door he was a diplomat, the man we sent in when things needed a little over the table negotiation. He knew everyone who was worth knowing and everyone who was best avoided. He would know about Bilko, where I could find him and what I should expect when I did.

I filled him in on everything that had happened.

'You sure you know what you're doing, mate?' There was fear in Kevin's voice.

I smiled. 'Yeah, I think so.' Then there was a pause over the phone, one of those long pauses that makes you think that the person on the other end of the line has hung up.

'You want a bit of help?' Kevin asked.

The smile lit my whole face. 'You mad fucker,' I said jokingly, 'what you gonna do, send your sister down?'

We both laughed.

'Listen,' he continued, 'even if I just fall over and trip someone up it's got to be better than you going in alone,' he said.

'Knowing you, y'cunt, it'd be me you tripped up!'

We were in full flow now, laughing like we were back on the door, like the old days.

There was relief in his voice now because he knew that even though he'd offered and the offer was genuine and appreciated, he wasn't going to be taken up on it. 'You know where Bilko hangs out, don't you? The Border Working Men's Club? It's like fucking Middle-earth down there. It's full of potato heads. Listen, they're blaming the outbreak of foot-and-mouth on some of the Dorises down there. Fucking drastic! Last time I was there some Doris – horrible piece she was – comes up, listen Martin, you'll like this, comes up to me, Scottish bird she was, Billy Connolly in a dress, she goes, "Buy me a wee drinky, will ya?" Never seen the fucker before in me life. I go, "Who the fuck are you?" She goes, "They call me the Beasty." Martin, I never saw anyone with a better nickname in my entire fucking life. She was a scarer. The Beasty!'

I was crying with laughter, the tears streaming down my face.

He became serious. 'You sure you don't want me to come? I could ring a few of the lads, give you a hand. They'd come out for you, I know they would.'

'Nah. Thanks bud but, well, you know how it is. It's personal, one on one. I need to do the park with this fucker, let everyone else know not to fuck.'

'You do know who he is, don't you? You know his cred?'

I nodded to myself. 'Yeah, I've heard.'

We said our goodbyes. Kevin had given me what I needed, and we promised – as you do – not to leave it so long the next time.

I left the flat and made my way up the street. I didn't bother trying to fix the door; the chances were that it would be kicked in again that night unless I could find this Bilko cunt first. And anyway, there was nothing in my flat worth stealing; if someone did break in they'd probably end up decorating the kitchen and leaving a donation.

All I needed to do now was make the visit and give Bilko the bad news.

Ginger was on my mind. The night in the hospital had been bliss, and I couldn't wait to see her again. The images of her smashed face still haunted me. That was another score that I had to settle and the minute I had got Bilko off my 'to do' list I would make Mick a priority. This time I would not be so soft on him. He needed to know that if he wanted to fuck about in my world it would cost him.

I needed to train. Needed it. I had to get this dynamite out of me before it exploded into my underpants. There was a job to do and I needed to be sharp. I could not and would not underestimate Bilko. He might be a fat cunt, I told myself, he might have ten chins and leave a trail like a slug, but that didn't mean that the old lad couldn't have a fight. If he was being paid to damage people then you could safely assume that he was good at it. But he wouldn't be fit. Not carrying that amount of surplus fat. That would be the chink in his very obese armour. He might be good for thirty seconds, a minute max – an eternity when the arena is the street. So all I had to do was last a little longer than him and the fight was mine. Either that or get the first one in and eclipse him before the fight hit the pavement.

These guys are killers until their wind goes, then they're punch-bags. And anyway, I knew that the physical fight wasn't going to be the problem: it would be the pre-fight, the adrenal build-up that would be hard to control; it was already trying to eat into my will. Very few people have the fortitude to handle anticipation, especially when the thing you anticipate wants to use your head for a football. Anticipation hurts. But pain could be managed and fear could be relegated to background noise if you had the training.

On the door you got all the training you wanted. You had to deal with anticipation every night of the week. There was nowhere to run, nowhere to hide, and the source of your fear wore a different mask every night. So you learned to avoid conflict when you could; the stuff that couldn't be avoided you dealt with as soon as. And if it couldn't be dealt with in a hurry then you learned to put it in the back of your mind until an opportunity presented itself.

It's a matter of survival. You suck in the air through your nose and fill your lungs to slow the fear down a little; you swill saliva around your gums, that also helps. A dry mouth is one of the first signs of fear and swilling saliva around the gums fools the brain into thinking that the threat has gone, thus slowing down the flow of adrenalin. You sit in the fear so it melts around you and you become one with it until you no longer know where you start and the fear ends. It becomes so normal after a while that you stop minding. If the fear gets too much then it's the gym that provides salvation.

This situation had taken me by surprise and the adrenalin had got in before I'd had time to stop it. The gym was not just the right place to be: it was the only place. I needed to be sharp, roadworthy. I had taken Mick out easily enough but I'd felt it in my breath. It was heavier than I'd have liked. You are only as good as your conditioning: you can have the best right cross in the world – and having a main artillery attack is vital – but it doesn't help if you don't have the fuel to deliver it.

This was my first time at this particular gym. Even though it was in my area I had not frequented it before. Never had a reason to. I suppose that I could have gone to Reg's old place, but, well, you know how it is; didn't really want to bump into any of the old faces. It was a shitty little gym not unlike the shitty little café and the shitty little pub; I knew I'd have to break this habit I had of frequenting shitty little establishments if I ever wanted to get away from shitty little people. Maybe it was my shitty little mentality that didn't think I was good enough for anything better. The gym was in the corner of an old industrial estate just off the city centre. A tin shack of iron and testosterone, straining muscles and stretching, girning faces.

I made my way up the stone stairs to the second-floor gym. I was met by the smell of damp carpet and sweating meat. It was an old-fashioned gym where you were allowed to sweat on the machines without getting a letter from the gym committee. It was full of large men with square jaws and gunslinger arms. Some of them were shouting at the bar-bells and loose weights. A muscle-man in the corner was hitting a cracked leather punch-bag held together with sweat and masking tape that hung from a naked metal beam in the ceiling by chains. The chains clunked with every punch. As I walked in I was greeted by a hard face and a small vest that didn't even cover the nipples of the man wearing it. He looked me up and down. His gaze lingered on my belly for an uncomfortable moment. He smiled. Sardonic.

'What you after, mate?'

He said it like it was a challenge to fight. His chest was in a permanent state of flex as if he was holding his breath. It looked as though it had been inflated with a bike pump and coated in beaten egg. I waited for him to exhale. He never did. His chest remained skin-stretchingly taut.

'I just need a little conditioning,' I said.

'Yeah, I can see that.' His eyes dropped back to my belly. I ignored him. My belly might have been big but I could punch elephants to death with my hands – and every time he opened his big mouth he started to look more and more like an elephant.

'Can I work out?' I indicated the gym with a nod of my head. That sardonic smile was now a permanent fixture, and I had the urge to knock the fucker right off his steroid head. But that was not why I was there.

'Four quid,' he said, without me even having to ask. His social grace left a little to be desired; not the best way to bring punters and revenue into the gym. The statement was stuffed with challenge. But I didn't want challenge. Didn't need it. Had enough in my life as it was, thank you very much. All I wanted was a workout, the use of a few loose weights and a punch-bag. I was tired of entering establishments and finding threat.

'Four quid?' I replied scornfully, not able to control myself any more. I took out my wallet and extracted a five-pound note.

'I only want to train, mate, I'm not looking to buy you out.' I threw the fiver on the counter, where it landed in a puddle of spilled tea. I smiled as I said it but my shot at a joke was lost to this brain-shy. He scrunched his face up into a confused ball. His melon-biceps flexed involuntarily and the veins pumped to attention. His pecs rippled across the front of his vest in response. I think I was meant to be impressed. Muscle this prominent was no more than a visual, a giant's robe on a dwarfish thief. If you fight a colossus like this baby you don't worry about chest measurements and bench poundage because they have no relation to being able to fight. The muscle is usually just a shell, an armour hiding a ten-stone cerebral weakling.

The bloke looked at the money lying on the counter and then back at me.

'Keep the change,' I said, smiling. I could feel his eyes boring into me as I walked into the gym, and I knew that he would still be flexing with no one left to see.

A few eyes turned to me as I made my way through benches and machines. I did my best not to make eye contact with any of the natives. It was a serious gym where people who pushed heavy weight posed as people that could have a fight. Most of them had probably come here in search of some self-esteem and found arrogance, aggression and bad company at the heavy end of a barbell and the sharp end of a hypodermic needle.

The floor was covered by bits of old carpet, just enough to take the chill off the concrete. Above me the frosted glass ceiling was apexed and rusting at the frame. Elvis Presley was crooning 'Are You Lonesome Tonight?' on a dusty LP spinning on an old stereo propped precariously behind the squatting station. The record jumped every time some grunter dropped a weight. I approached the punch-bag in the corner, waiting for a little attention.

It's a funny thing. When you go on the bag in a gym like this one everyone likes to watch, corner-of-the-eye slyly. It's a kind of assessment. If you can hit the bag or push heavy weight, you might be accepted. If you can't do either then the chances are you will be treated accordingly. No matter if you are a great guy, a brain surgeon or a fucking millionaire, if you wanted to be in this club then you'd have to have a little physicality about you. But the looks when you hit the bag are always surreptitious. It's not cool in the world of iron to openly show that you are interested or impressed.

The brick wall behind the bag was covered in flaking paint. A sign squeezed between a myriad of posters of posing men and semi-naked supermodels and pop divas read: *Do Not Kick The Bag*. It didn't say anything about biting or butting or kneeing.

I dropped my weathered training bag and took in the sights and smells of the gym. It brought back memories of times gone by. As I carefully wrapped my hands in blood- and sweat-stained boxing bandages (got to protect the bones, I still relied on these hands to earn my crust on the sites), my mind revisited gymnasiums of the past. Places not unlike this one where the decor was shit, the showers dirty and dilapidated, and the people unwelcoming and aggressive. But at least you got a proper work-out. No time for socialising in a place like this. If you stood and talked for too long it would elicit challenging looks from posturing men with pain on their mind. I'd spent my youth in similar places where the old wrestlers and boxers had a back room with a ring, some sparring gloves and focus pads, and you could get tuition from masters who would hold good on a nightclub dancefloor or outside the chippy where your arena was the pavement and fighting techniques either worked or you went to A&E.

I learned from people with broken noses and cauliflower ears. They spared you the bullshit and sparred you till you dropped. No syllabus or gradings or belts – other than those that you got in the gob; just boxing gloves and bollocks. And there were no hiding places in those gyms; they had you in the ring from day one, fighting for your very life. You learned pretty fucking quick when your mistakes left you on the canvas with blood and stars. My trainer Reg was a grizzly old fighter. A spit, snot and sawdust type who had wrestled the great Billy Riley from Bolton at the Snake Pit Gym and sparred with Randolph Turpin when he took the title from Sugar Ray. He was a hardy fucker and no mistake. His face was like chewed toffee, a history of scars and breaks and bruises, a reminder of every knock-down and eight-count from 193 fights, both amateur and pro. And for every contest round he did there were another fifty in training halls where the fighting often turned to brawling when club egos got the better of good sense.

There was a hard life in that face, weathered by long hours in the ring and late nights in the clubs where managers paid good money and free pints to protect the licence, the punters and the property from the criminal underbelly and the weekend fighters out to displace a bad week in a good night. He once went thirty minutes with the British heavyweight champ in the underground bar of the Ton Up Club. Thirty minutes swapping blow for blow. Smashed the jukebox to pieces when they fell on it. They went through tables and chairs, down the cellar steps and eventually wrestled in a pool of beer on the stone cellar floor where Reg took a choke and ended the affray. Fucking legendary. They still talk about it now, thirty years on. And so when Reg walked, when this man walked you could see his worth, his pedigree, his stature in every step. He had presence. An energy that made you look on in awe. That made you want to be just like him. And even though his hands were clawed by arthritis and his speech was like a growl, people still cowered when he lifted those hands to fight and they still listened when he raised his voice to speak. When this man opened his mouth it was like fucking thunder. I loved the old guy. He was the dad I never had.

He was sixty when I found him. I got him for ten good years before time and too many bangs on the head caught up with him. His funeral was something to behold, processions of fighting men, dangerous people who had their character moulded in the most unforgiving forge.

He skilfully combined the hook wrestling, the old catch-as-catch-can with the skills of the pugilist. A vicious combination of grabbing and ripping and striking that has never let me down. He was never one for kicking. 'Your feet are for balance,' he'd say, 'and when you take one of them off the floor to kick, your balance is impaired. Use your feet to plant your punch or for running away. And running away should always be your first option. The only time you kick,' he'd tell me, 'is when they fall over. If you've ever kicked a football across a park then you already know enough technique to kill a man dead. No need to add to that.'

He'd say to me, 'Look for the scruffy stuff, kid, the stuff that don't look nice in a photo. That's the stuff that's gonna work for you when fate gives you three goons looking for a pull and you've only got half a foot to work with.' He wasn't interested in talk; he was never impressed by the bag punchers and the posers; he wouldn't swap techniques in the pub or talk hypothesis over a beer. His answer to the bag punchers was: 'If you've got something to say, get in the ring and say it proper; if you can't say it in there then you ain't got nothing to say.'

He was a good old sort, a proper fighter. I went to him when I was fifteen to learn how to fight. It was when my dad was at his worst and I was at my most scared. Reg didn't want to know; said I was too young for his type of fighting and that I should come back when I'd got hairs on my bollocks. But I kept turning up and watching and eventually he threw me a pair of foul, stinking gloves and said, 'Get in the ring and show me what you've got.' He put me in with this young bloke who proceeded to tear me a new arsehole. Every time I went down I got back up; every time I got back up I was knocked back down. Eventually, when my lips were as thick as car tyres and I was looking out of one eye, he'd said, 'Come back next week and I'll show you some skills.'

So I did. And twenty years later the skills were still with me. When you train them in that well they never leave you; they're as much a part of you as your arms and legs. The only thing that goes is the edge, the conditioning, and that's what I was here to try and find.

I slipped the Lonsdale's over my bandaged hands. Started to move around the bag. Dropped the odd shot into the belly, just to warm my limbs up. I moved the bag around, pushing it with my left elbow to set up with a right cross then catching a left hook as it swung back to me followed by a little head-butt and another elbow. It felt good to be back on the leather.

As I moved around I noticed a physique to the left of the bag, about ten feet back. He was standing almost to attention like a meercat, his weights abandoned at his feet. His face was indignant, elbows splayed out from his sides like he was going to burst into the funky chicken at any minute. His eyes were glued to my space. He was a dark-skinned fellow and looked as thick as porridge. I can't say that I was surprised at his attention, or even disappointed: I was new blood in the gym and this was obviously his shitting ground. It was a territorial thing. I understood that. He had an impressive shape though, all sinewy and raw and cut. And big. Fuck me. Fucker looked as if he'd fallen asleep in a grow-bag. Woke up on the set of *Land of the Giants*, and he was the giant. Stretch marks ran across his shoulder muscles, hinting at fast weight increase and anabolic steroids. When he turned to look over at the counter – probably looking for a little back-up – I noticed the Braille-board acne across his back. It confirmed my suspicions: definitely injecting. Stretch marks on the shoulders and back, acne and aggression by the truckload are sure indications of someone looking for a fast track to a big back (and the by-products of bitch-tits and shrinking testicles).

As he looked back at me I let out a football-type kick to the base of the bag. I was just testing. I could see that my new friend was looking for an excuse, any excuse, to step into my world. And he was going to, sooner or later, so I was just making it sooner and on my terms. If he wanted it then the sooner he came and got it the better; then I could get back on with my work-out in peace. Get the monkey off your back, bring on the clowns. As my kick landed, his eyes nearly popped out of his head. He stepped forward, then stopped just as quickly as if halted by some unseen force. He looked over to the counter again for a little 'watch my back'. His oppo was busy looking down the cleavage of a Barbie doll in full make-up and an aerobics leotard, perhaps on her way to the tan bed. His eyes locked back on to me and he bumped forward to give me a piece of his mind (which wouldn't have left a lot for him). I couldn't stop a smile from spreading across my mouth. *Fucking nipple*, I thought. You can control these fuckers like they're on strings. One little gesture and the hard of thinking are reacting. I slipped behind the bag as he approached. My heart was racing, blood bursting at the veins. But I'd trained my will to override this natural instinct, and to handle the caustic feel of fear. It can be a mind-killer if you let it take over, but if you merge with it, let it in, ride it like a big wave, it can lift your game to the level of the gods. Reg had always told me that the only time to worry was when you didn't feel fear because that meant you were over-confident and unprepared. When I entered the ring he'd always ask me, 'Scared, kid?' And my pale face would nod and I'd bite hard into my gumshield. 'Good,' he'd say. 'Then you're in the arena.'

He always maintained that the only way to prepare for a real fight was to recreate it right down to the tiniest detail. That's why he combined the hook wrestling and the boxing. He said that if you could survive the fights in his gym, you could survive anything. He had this theory that you should make the training in the gym harder and more frightening than the real thing, so when it came to having it outside the chip shop it was easy by comparison. No matter what they did in the street, it couldn't be as bad as what his boys gave you in the ring.

Just as the physique was about to open his mouth to tell me off for kicking the bag, close enough for me to smell him, I let go with a three-punch combination that sent dust flying from the leather and shrieks from the chains.

'ARRGGGHHHHHHHHHH!'

As the third punch connected, I let out a fuck-off scream to underline the aggression, gobbed a cupful of saliva at the bag, head-butted it and finished the combination by sinking my teeth into it, ripping a section of masking tape and leather clean off. The taste of sweat in my mouth made me grimace. I spat it onto the floor and glared at my visitor. Spit rolled down my chin. Violence was in my eyes. The red mist descended again. It wasn't hard to be angry. I was full of the stuff: right up to the brim and overflowing. Bilko on my mind. And Mick. And a backpack of grudges and wounds that I'd been carrying since my youth. So this small-minded, bullying, baggy-trousered-clown behemoth was all the excuse I needed to displace a little fury. The lad was doing me a huge favour by stepping into my world with his acre of muscle and very limited intellect.

Well, fuck me, that did the job. I knew it would.

The physique froze on the spot. Mouth open. Eyes locked on to the ripped leather on the floor. The scream and the bite would have jolted his heart rate into hyperdrive.

He was frozen. His face was a picture, a photo-booth snapshot caught before he was ready. He was clown-pale. His aggression was trying to find an exit through the back of his baggy squat pants. Fucking cock-hole. I drilled him with a hard look that said 'fuck off'. He did. He wandered back to his station by the dumb-bells and fiddled with an inanimate enemy that didn't fight back. The rest of the gym, also frozen by the screams and bites and spits of the strange maniac on the bag, were suitably scared and, whilst the odd glance was sneaked in my direction, none met my gaze. For the rest of the session I was left alone. Even the muscle-rippler at the counter seemed to have grown a healthy respect for me in the hour I spent in his establishment. By the time I'd finished my ten twos on the bag and a little weight moving he was very friendly. Who was I? Where was I from? Did I want a cup of tea and would I be coming to the gym again?

Fuck off.

After I left the gym I made straight for the café across the road. My appetite was back and I needed some fuel. The first thing that goes when fear is on the agenda is the appetite; the last thing you want to do when your life is being threatened is eat. And yet it is the first thing you should do. You can't fight a war without supplies: you need the food. In fact you are burning up so much energy just coping with the stress that you need more of it than usual. So in times of stress I would eat, even if I didn't feel like it (especially if I didn't feel like it), and even if it meant force-feeding the stuff down my neck. The minute you let the food go you begin a downward spiral. Your bottle soon goes if you don't give the body and brain any sustenance.

As it was I'd just trained and had cleared the backlog of unused adrenalin from my system so I had an appetite. I made for the café and ate a hearty breakfast followed by a banana and a mug of honeyed tea. Then I made my way back to my flat to get a little shut-eye. Sleep and meditation are your mainstays when you have strife in your life. Without them you can easily become a snivelling wreck. It's a way of taking your mind off the worry and giving your brain some vital energy. I needed to be fit in every respect. I suspected that Bilko would be hard work, and I knew that my problems would not end with him. It wasn't that simple. But he would be a start. After the sleep, I decided, I would go and see him. Get this thing sorted once and for all.

CHAPTER NINE

MIDDLE-EARTH

I had a short sleep. When I opened my eyes I felt fine until the realisation of what I was facing hit me and fear was back on the agenda. When you first wake it's a vulnerable time for the mind: your mental guard is down and all the fears that you managed to block out in sleep are sat waiting for you to open your eyes, fatter than ever. The dread that met my waking mind was almost overwhelming. I remember the sad, sad feeling that engrossed me. For a second I couldn't move from the bed. *What's the fucking point?* I thought.

I wanted to shrivel up under the blankets and die. I pulled them over my face. I tried to hide from the feelings but they were inside my head. I'd thought I would never be in this position again. I rarely worked on the doors any more, and, while I had few real trusted friends, I didn't have any enemies either. Until now. And here I was, in the thick of it with no way out. Negative thoughts ravaged my mind and old wounds reopened. To say that my head was swimming would be an understatement; I felt as though I was in the deep end and drowning. Like most people I clung to my own comfort like a suckle blanket. I was safe in my own shitty little comfort zone, and when a situation – any situation – threatened to force me out of it I became stressed and anxious. I suppose that's what keeps most people in shitty relationships, crap jobs, tiny houses, small minds; it's why we are not driving the cars that we want to drive or living the lives we want to live. We're frightened of change. We run away from it like it's the Beast of Bodmin Moor. Reg always told me that our biggest stressor as a species, the thing that hurt more people than it healed, was our inability to adapt to change. And it was all because we are frightened of what we don't know, so we cling by our fingernails to what we do.

I found myself in a situation where my comfort was not only threatened, it was being raped and pillaged. I was propelled from the mellow levels of ease to the higher echelons of violence in one fell swoop. Quite a leap, I have to tell you. A leap that I did not want to take. But there was a monkey on my back – and there was very little I could do about that now – and these monkeys have a habit of getting fat. I could feel the familiar tingle of melancholy trying to grip me. I quickly stopped it in its tracks. I got my internal dialogue up and running. I took over the situation, reminded myself that I was in this position for honourable reasons. You do not stand by and watch nice people get hurt by clay-holes, you stand up and get amongst the head count.

And that's what you did, I told myself. *So stop being hard on yourself, stop feeling sorry for yourself and get out of bed. You're doing this for Ginger. Think of her.*

I jumped to attention. I got out of bed. I washed. I dressed. I ate. I got myself busy. When the feelings came over me I didn't try to fight them. I invited them in. Sat in them. Let them wash over me like a wave, reminded myself that these feelings could not hurt me and that they were there to help. Fear is man's natural survival mechanism. It is only when we panic that the feelings multiply and overwhelm us.

So I didn't panic. I talked to myself. I encouraged myself. I reminded myself that this situation would be a memory before long. You can't stop time. Everything passes sooner or later. Then I sat and watched the negative feelings as they drifted by.

It hadn't taken me long to find out where Bilko hung out. Kevin had given me all the information I needed. Bilko, Kevin had informed me in between the laughter, spent most of his time at the local working men's club. What Bilko liked to call his office and Kevin liked to call Middle-earth on account of the fact that it was filled with orc-like characters from *The Lord of the Rings*.

On the way to the club I convinced myself that going to see Bilko was a good idea. Like a parachute jump for charity is a good idea until you are 2,000 feet up, waiting to jump, and looking at death. But by the time the taxi dropped me outside the club doors I was having second thoughts. My feet felt glued to the floor: when I tried to move, some unseen force held me back.

What the fuck was I doing there? I could have been back at home, I could have been at the hospital with Ginger, I could have been anywhere I wanted and it would surely have been better than this. I turned to go. After walking only a few steps I stopped and walked back. Anyone looking on must have wondered what the fuck was going on. I was walking back and forward and muttering to myself like a maniacal line-dancer. It didn't take me long to realise that my home was not safe. This man had violated it. The hospital was no sanctuary either. Even though every single part of me wanted to be there I knew that I couldn't rest until I'd dealt with the threat and eradicated my fear.

There are only two things you can do with fear: you can take away the thing that is causing it, or you can learn to live with it. This was a fear that I could not live with. It was a physical threat to my well-being that was unlikely to go away unless I found it and faced it. And if you face it then best do it sooner rather than later. The longer you leave it the fatter it will grow. I felt that I had no choice: this thing needed to be dealt with.

So I decided to enter the club and start looking for Bilko. Looking, but not really wanting to find, if I am being honest. But if I didn't find him, he would definitely find me. That would give him the upper hand. Besides that, the wait would have killed me. Problems are easier and more quickly solved if you go out and confront them while they are still relatively small. Better than hanging from the ceiling by your fingernails while time slows to the pace of a snail with a bad leg, waiting for death to rap on your door with a reaper's scythe. I had made it there but I was scared. Nothing new there; fear had been my companion for as long as I could remember. Fear of change, fear of abandonment, fear of living in that fucking flat for the rest of my life, fear of leaving that fucking flat. I had a fear of life. But it wasn't going to stop me from facing my fear; it wasn't going to stop me from doing the things that needed doing. I guess that's what you could call authentic power; the ability to feel the fear, and do the fucker anyway.

It was half-past seven on Friday night and the place was just starting to fill. I walked through the bar where the beer-sticky carpet was five years past its refurb date. The run of leather seating at the side of the small bar was worn and ripped. The place looked more like a work canteen than a drinking establishment. The bar was right in front of me and the queue for drinks was ten people long. I didn't join it, the last thing I needed now was drink; I'd been for a shit and three pisses already as the adrenalin was playing havoc with my digestion.

I scanned the room looking for the guy with my kneecaps on his agenda. A cheap hit-man, not a proper one that kills SAS style, rather a home-grown lad who can have a proper fight and doesn't mind lending his skills – if the price was right – to break a few bones. My kneecaps were precious to me; I didn't want them crumbled by some fucking Neanderthal with a baseball bat and a heavy swing. That's why I was there, at the club. No other reason. And afterwards I had every intention of finding Mick the Prick and giving him some more bad news. Can't have low-lifes fucking with my incarnation, messing with my knees. I needed to send a big fuck-off message out to the world that said 'Fuck with me and I'll make it personal. I'll come around when you're having tea with your mum and bite the fucking nose off your face.'

Sometimes you have to slaughter a chicken to train a monkey. It's how the Chinese dealt with monkeys that were resistant to domestication. They would fetch a chicken and cut its head off in full view of the difficult primate. Afterwards – not surprisingly – the monkey was pretty keen to do the bidding of its master.

The smoke filled the room like cloud cover. The banter over the tabletops was lively. In the background I could hear the fast rattle of a football commentator on the TV.

The girls were in their Friday frocks and the men polished up and clean-shaven for the weekend. This was the kind of fuel stop that my dad used when he was alive. Walk in straight from the sites. A few pints. Then a few more until he felt like a new man. Then the new man wanted a drink and that's how it went until his words came out like he was speaking a different language and Dad Number Two appeared, made for the chippy and then home. Sometimes that meant a bag of chips for me and my brother from a sloppy but amicable drunk; he'd get us out of our beds and make us come down the stairs to eat with him. Other times it meant lying in bed listening as he told our mum how he could cut her up into tiny pieces and bury her under the floorboards and no one would ever know; in which case he would wake us from our beds and make us watch the humiliation. Either way we were woken up and either way we were on a knife's edge until he fell asleep, never knowing which way the drink might take him, never knowing if it was going to be drunken philosophy or drunken abuse. When the sleep finally did take him, a cigarette dangling from his face like it had grown there, we all sat there, frozen and goose-pimpled, until Mum would give us the nod to go back to bed. Two dads. One fucker that I hardly ever saw, the other a bullying cunt.

I always found it easier to psych myself up for a fight when I thought about my dad. I was about to bring him back to life now, at the club. Bring every bad memory of the old man to the front of my mind – and there had been a few I have to say – and cannon them into Bilko. I would make the knee-capper from Wood Green the walking manifestation of my father. Every blow I landed and every bit of pain I inflicted would be recompense for the hurt that bastard brought to my youth. When I kicked Bilko's head around the club floor like a Coke can it would be my dad's head I'd be kicking. I remembered all the terrible things he'd done so that I could displace my rage and turn it on to Bilko, and then on to Mick, who was treating Ginger like my dad treated my mum. I was powerless to stop it then, but I sure as hell was going to stop it now. I wasn't going to sit and watch another beautiful, wonderful woman have her life destroyed by some wanker.

I remembered the time when my dad punched the teeth right out of Mum's face and left her in a hospital bed for a week, eating lunch through a straw. My brother and I had to pick the broken teeth from puddles of congealed blood, thick as pork jelly. Then we had to stay with relatives and lie to the police about how Mum was more of a stair tumbler than she was a victim of domestic violence. I remembered the time when Dad brought three of his same-ilk mates back from the pub at three in the morning with the promise of a hot meal. He dragged Mum – who had declined the offer of being a late-night cook, thank you very much – by the hair into our room and kicked her till she bled from her fanny to her face. Made quite an impression on us kids that one I have to say, waking up to screaming and blood and Mum out on the floor, and himself still kicking her like he's converting a football.

Then I brought to mind the worst thing of all that my dad ever did to me, the thing that made my whole body clench in rage and shame. I knew that when I hit Bilko, all my anger, all my bitterness and all the twisted, shattered shards of my broken childhood would be behind that punch. The time when (pissed again, no surprises there), Dad shoved his fatty into his eleven-year-old's mouth and forced him to swallow and not tell a soul if he wanted to avoid the hiding of his young life. A fucking psychiatrist with a JCB couldn't help me out with that one.

I scanned the room for Bilko but I couldn't see him.

'Excuse me, mate.' I leaned over a table of card players. A skinny man with a yellowing dress shirt opened to reveal a bony chest, a cigarette dangling from blue lips looked up at me. His egg yolk eyes searched for a clue as to who the fuck I was. He nodded.

'Sorry to interrupt your game of cards. I'm looking for a big, fat, ugly cunt called Bilko.'

The guy's right eye squinted; he was unsure whether I was making a legitimate funny or walking around with a death wish dangling from my dialogue. The rest of the table looked at me warily and then got right back into their game.

'Bilko? Try the bagatelle room.' He nodded his head towards an open door at the other end of the bar. Ash fell from his cigarette onto his hand of cards. He flicked it off and turned his eyes back to the game.

I made my way to the other side of the bar through the lower working classes in the shittiest district in the city where dogs roamed in gangs (it was safer that way) and the police spoke with batons.

By the time I got to the door, all eyes were on me; the word had spread as fast as I could walk. Which was good enough; it was how I wanted it. If you are going to slaughter a chicken to train a monkey, the more monkeys that watched, the better. I entered the bagatelle room. Tattoos and broken noses were in abundance. Some of the men looked rough too. A couple of dozen men and around six women were hovering over or sitting close to the semi-circular bagatelle table. They watched as the resident expert shot billiard balls around the pristine cloth. I scanned the room quickly. No sight of the fat cunt I was looking for. I turned to look behind me, back into the bar. Couldn't see him. It would be hard to miss him: he was so big that no matter where he sat in the room he would be sat next to you. Big man. Fat man. Should I leave and come back another day? Maybe I wasn't meant to be there and fate was smiling down on me.

I was wrong.

I was on the way out of the bagatelle room when –

'You looking for me?'

It was Bilko. Standing in front of me. Looking for a fight.

For a second I wished that I was back at the hospital, sitting on the bed and talking to Ginger. Or better still that I had taken Kevin's offer of a little assistance. A team would have been nice at that moment. I knew that neither option was right. I needed to deal with this situation on my own. Just me. So that when I fucked Bilko – *if* I fucked him – no one could accuse me of coming team-handed or tooled up. To really humiliate this man I needed to meet him and beat him man to man. One on one. And with witnesses. That way he'd have nowhere to hide when Chinese whispers spread his defeat, his vulnerability, like a dose. But doing it on your own is lonely. Shows you who you are. Anyone can turn up with three mates and have a bit of a fight. It's dead easy. There is comfort in numbers, a hiding place for anyone lacking guts. Doing it on your own, now that is a different matter. Lonely. But lonely is not so bad if you face it. It is just another disguise for fear. The fear of being alone. By sitting in it, facing it, challenging it, you realise that there is no poison in its tail. It is an empty threat that has nothing to blackmail you with other than more of itself. If you are not frightened of fear you are invincible.

That's the theory anyway.

'If you can't do it on your own,' my trainer Reg'd tell me, 'then don't do it at all.'

Very few men have the bottle for a match fight. That's why I liked to turn up on my own. Frightens the living crap out of people.

Bilko had proffered a question that demanded an answer and as soon as I could force my heart back out of my mouth I was going to reply. He stood before me. A big man at six four. Larger than life and staring down at me. He must have weighed 300 pounds, most of it hung over the top of his trousers. His face was in a permanent frown; it was enough to send dinners through digestive systems at record-breaking speeds. I'd describe him as a piece of shit, a turd meister, but that'd be prettying him up. He was a captain of ugly, on the wrong side of heinous, rancid made manifest. I didn't like him. I didn't like his eyes (especially the one that was looking at me), I didn't like his whole fat-bastard-blocking-the-light persona.

He placed his jacket on the floor. The fight was already on, that much I knew. Jackets off and shirt collars loosened; the signs of imminent violence do not come any clearer than this. Sometimes you can talk them down, hammer out some kind of compromise over the negotiation table, beg for mercy or run for your life. With men of his ilk none of that was going to work, not even in theory. He was a fighter. He spoke with physical acts of violence. And it didn't matter to him whether you were male or female, old or young. If you stepped into this guy's world you paid in broken bones. Kevin had told me how Bilko had used a craft knife on his first wife. Turned her face into a jigsaw with bits missing. All because she talked when she should have been listening. Slaughtered her face. Looked like a patchwork quilt when he finished his bloody slicing; they stopped counting the stitches at the hospital.

Me. 'You Bilko?'

Him. 'Who's asking?'

Me, you fat cunt, are you fucking deaf as well as fat? I thought.

As I spoke we went through the pre-fight ritual, like two cats down an alley ready for a tear-up. We sized each other up, arching our backs and sharpening our claws. It was an unspoken dialogue that you learned when the pavement was your arena. Fights were won and lost with this silent discourse. Those that did not, could not or would not understand normally got taken out of the game before they even realised they were in it. In this arena the loser is lucky to get home without the aid of an ambulance; some are taken home in a box.

I was an unknown entity to Bilko, so all he could do was assess me on three things: how I looked, how I sounded, and my actions. The fact that I had entered his world looking for him was a one-up for me. I had taken the initiative and come to him so, he would figure I'd got testicles if nothing else. I knew this would have thrown him, even unnerved him a little. That's one of the reasons I did it. He was used to calling the shots, setting the time and the date and letting people know how and when the job was going to be done. It was his way of rubbing down and priming his victims before the paint job. A week of expecting the knee-capper is enough to turn even the hardy lardy. A week of waiting for this fat fuck to knock on your door with the bad news is enough to place your life on hold and your arsehole on permanent evacuation. That is why I was there. Calling the shots. Trembling so much at my knees that you could almost hear them rattle.

The best way to win a battle is to take the fight to a terrain that the enemy does not expect and at a time that inconveniences them. Gives them no chance to prepare, no time to make plans. You just turn up and plant yourself before them. *Bang!* Just like that. It works. It takes bollocks, of course; you need gonads the size of pineapples. And there is always that little bit of you that thinks, 'If I leave it, it might go away.'

People of his ilk are herpes. They don't go away, not ever, and unless you do a proper job on them – kill the germ as it were – then they will keep coming back. Your only hope is to accept the fact that your life is going to be uncomfortable for a short while and get on with it. Either that or you can call in plod. But they are about as useful as a tin sun-hat. All they do is exacerbate the problem, drive it underground and delay the inevitable.

'I heard my name was on your job sheet.' I controlled my voice to hide the quiver as I spoke.

'Who the fuck are you?' He spat a gob of spit the size of a dinner plate into my face when he said 'fuck'. I pretended not to notice, but it was hard because it weighed as much as a small child and hung from my cheek like a rock climber. He hovered over me as he spoke. By the way he was bearing forward I could tell that he had made his assessment of me and that it was somewhere down there in the 'no real threat' category. I liked being down there. Especially with a big, capable yoke like this one. When they underestimate you it gives you the first free shot, and when you train for the one-punch kill that is all you need.

I surreptitiously placed my hands in front of me as a fence to stop him from closing the gap and stealing my space. The fight was on. In my eyes it was already over. I'm not being arrogant, not even for a minute. I just know when it's mine. When they look down on me like the fight is already won it's the biggest indication of impending victory for me. It is like an omen, a sign from the gods. The moment they underestimate me they've lost. All I had to do now was hold my nerve and give myself the first shot. If it didn't comatose him it would definitely guarantee me the next three.

Another question needed answering. He had underestimated me, so I decided the best way to set up my first shot was to play on that. Allow a little fear to tremble in my words. If he had already underestimated me a drop of fear in the dialogue would confirm his belief that I was out of my league.

'I had a little trouble with a guy called Mick. I heard that he'd cut a deal with you to equal things out.' My voice sounded scared, just how I wanted it to.

'And you've come down here to do what?' Bilko again. He splayed his arms.

My ploy had worked. The arrogance rose in his voice. He had taken the bait. His voice was laced with contempt; he even started to take his watch off in readiness for the slaughter. As he was fiddling with the watch strap – the amateur was taking his attention away from me – I asked, allowing even more tremor into my voice, 'Can we talk about this?'

As he lifted his eyes from the watch, a smile spread across his fat face. He was just about to tell me, 'No, actually you little cunt, talking is not on the agenda.' He was about to earn his money easier than he thought when *bang!* I hit him with a mighty right hand. It landed directly on the end of his jaw. His head spun around, cartoonesque, his watch fired off his wrist and landed several feet away. The Sasquatch hit the deck, taking two tables and a chair out in the fall. Everyone in the room oohed in unison and took two steps back.

'Anyone else want a bit?' I snarled, glaring at everyone. They all took another step back, answering with their feet. This was a perfunctory part of the post-fight. When the monkeys are suitably scared you anchor that feeling by turning the threat on them, just in case they might be thinking of entering the arena. I walked over to my unconscious adversary, pushing tables and chairs out of my way. I looked down on the sleeping piece of shit. I lifted my right knee high in the air and stamped on his ankle very hard. The sickly crack echoed around the room, raising a murmur from the onlookers.

'Don't you ever,' I hissed as I stamped again, '*ever* come to my fucking place again, you piece of shit.' I was on autopilot and doing enough damage to prevent come-backs. You only want to fight a man like this once, and the techniques that I had used – mental disarmament (feeding his confidence by allowing him to see my fear) and brain engagement (asking a question to engage the brain before attacking with a reliable, road-tested right cross) – were unlikely to work a second time. So you break small bones that heal slowly. Leave them in no physical condition to come back for a straightner. By the time the bones heal the anger has usually gone, taking with it the threat of reprisals.

I stamped again, this time on the other leg, same crack, same murmur from the crowd. Stamping, kicking and breaking bones on a body that shifts along the floor and shudders but does not cry out in pain or try to defend itself. I felt the humanity leaving me. A red mist clouded my vision. A compelling darkness enveloped me as I moved another chair to kick his face. I lifted my knee high for the next break.

A voice penetrated the adrenal deafness and stopped me in my tracks.

'Martin!'

I knew the voice. I loved the voice. I didn't dare turn around. I couldn't face her. The voice did not sound judgemental. It wasn't condemning – it wasn't even horrified. It was just a voice laced with concern and love. I heard love and that was the only thing powerful enough to stop me. I placed my foot on the floor and felt the anger leaving my spent body. The emotion welled up inside me and the red mist dissipated.

Chapter Ten

Forgiveness

We were lying in bed, after sex. Ginger was dozing in my arms. It was as if she was the missing piece of me. She was wrapped around me, afraid I might disappear. I held her tight and felt just as scared. The intimacy of new love, the closeness, the oneness. I had felt warmth before, on other days and with other women, but none as complete and right as this. The other women all turned sour after the honeymoon period had passed and the chase long forgotten. How soon the soft contented breath turns to snores of boredom. How quickly the intimacy needs new spice in bed. Sex becomes a listless merging of two loveless bodies, the minds sleeping with someone else. She is fucking your mate in her mind's eye, or some impossible-to-reach pop idol off the TV, and you can only come if you've thumbed the porn mags as foreplay.

'The lust is lost with the shine,' my mum always used to say. 'When the shine goes your eye starts to wander.'

'So why don't people keep the shine, Mum?' I would ask.

She'd look at me with a mixture of love and sorrow. 'People don't have the discipline, son. It's easier to start looking outside than it is to look in.'

She said it like she'd lived it. When she woke in the morning it was obviously with a different man to the one she'd married all those years before. The one who couldn't touch her enough, who couldn't love her more and who swore allegiance and devotion and undying love. Ten years and two kids later the metamorphosis had already occurred. The young smoothy, my dad, who looked like Sacha Distel when they first met, had turned into a hairy-backed, farting doughnut who showered twice a week and only fucked after eyeing the *Playboy* centrefold.

People don't have the discipline! So, is that it? Is that all that stands between a honeymoon and a hard place?

I looked at Ginger and vowed to never let that happen to us. I stroked her face with my fingers, brushing across the bruised skin as light as smoke. Her face was still a mass of lumps and contusions and hurt, a rainbow of colours. I wanted to make it better. I stroked her hair rhythmically. Her breathing was even. Every couple of minutes she opened her eyes as though checking that I was still there, that I was still real. When she saw that I was, she smiled sleepily and closed them again.

The curtains in the bedroom shut out the world. It was a moment of nirvana, one of those times that you wished you could stay in for ever. I held the feeling for as long as I could. I breathed slowly and deeply and even held my breath to try and slow time. I promised myself that I would have the discipline and that I would not let the shine dull. But I reminded myself *That's what they all say*. The cynical me took over for a moment; the preening and the posturing, my negative self pointed out, are a part of the ritual, the catch. It is a human thing. It is about procreation, keeping the species alive. Once the catch is caught and the seed planted, the art of attraction becomes a redundant commodity. No need for a shiny float or a juicy worm once the fish has already done its death dance on a grassy knoll.

This was a part of my problem. I always thought weird shit like that. My head seemed to manufacture problems before they even arose. It took pleasure in ruining great moments. My mum always said I was deep. Deep? It was a word she used when she really meant weird. I was a weird fucker with weird ideas and notions. I was the kid that said he didn't want to work in a factory; I wanted to do something special with my life. My teacher at school – 'Conc' we called him, because he had a nose like Concord, a nose big enough to slide off – was one of those teachers that hated kids, and he said that I should keep my feet on the ground and concentrate on something a little more achievable. A steady job at the local car factory perhaps. Many ordinary folk (he emphasised the word *ordinary*) had done very well for themselves at the factory. Yeah. I knew a few of them. They lived on the council estate by us. 'The Friday People' I called them, because that was all they lived for. Friday afternoon when the shift ended for the week and they could dunk their woes under a gallon of beer until they quietened. They never drowned. Just choked a little and went quiet until the Monday. You don't drown your problems in ale, you feed them. Like my dad; first sign of trouble and he headed for the pub. The Friday People. Living for the weekend and two weeks in a caravan at a holiday camp every July.

I was the one who said I wanted more. Conc did everything but laugh out loud. I suppose my mistake was sharing a confidence with a man who had never left school himself. A man who had never realised his own dreams. I made the mistake of sharing a grand ambition with someone who had covered his own ambitions with blankets of security; I shared it only to see it decapitated by a maths teacher who seconded as a careers adviser at the end of every school year. You don't ask a drowning man for advice on breaststroke.

I kissed Ginger's head through a clump of red hair. Her hair had exploded on impact with the bed. Her make-up, an unsuccessful attempt at covering the memories of Mick's last visit, was on cotton wool in the bedside bin. She looked all the more beautiful without it: a natural beauty that astounded me. Her hair hung teasingly. It curtained bright hazel eyes, a small neat nose surrounded by a brush-flick of freckles, full smiling lips and beautiful white teeth. She had a simple beauty that I could almost taste. And she was mine. She was mine, and I couldn't believe my good fortune.

As I combed my fingers through her locks she stirred again and her eyes peeped through half-mast lids. I kissed her face gently, then her lips, then her eyes. The left one was still half-closed with swelling. I really couldn't believe I was there, that I was sharing space with this lady. The feeling of being inside her was still fresh in my mind. The climactic surrender had frightened me.

After another couple of hours, Ginger stirred. We sat in the kitchen talking over a hot, sweet tea. It was a homely room with a small table and chairs in the centre on a white ceramic floor. The decor was plain and clean, neutral colours, white cupboards with silver handles. Neat, tidy and organised with a hint of modesty, just like Ginger. I was still pinching myself to make sure that it was all real, that I was actually there.

'How did you know I was at the club?' I asked.

I had used Bilko to redecorate the working men's club. If it wasn't for her I might have gone too far. Again.

'Your mate Kevin told my brother. When you go looking for a man like Bilko, word carries.'

I nodded.

'Steve came to the hospital. He told me. He was worried.'

'Who's Steve?'

'Steve, my brother.'

'Oh, Cap.'

'Cap?'

'Cap. Your brother Steve.' *Oh fuck, here we go again.* 'It's just a nickname I made up for him,' I laughed. 'When he came to my flat he was wearing a baseball cap. It's a habit I've got. I make up nicknames for people. He was wearing a cap, so he became "Cap".' It sounded obvious to me.

Ginger smiled mischievously. 'So what's my nickname?'

I couldn't resist. 'You were "Fat Arse",' I said, teasing. She immediately turned in horror to look at her bottom.

'In fact,' I continued, knowing that she was on the hook, 'when I look at you now it's hard to see a Julie; I just see a fat arse.'

I was teasing, of course, but she was wounded.

'Really?' Again she looked at her bottom, the tightest little job I ever had the pleasure of laying my hands on. The kind of bum that could drive a guy crazy. I regretted it as quickly as I said it. She had bitten: she thought I was being serious.

'Really?' she repeated, feeling her bottom for fat now.

I tried to retreat. 'No, no, I'm joking! I'm just winding your key, honestly. You've got a lovely bum. Honest. The best.'

I could tell she didn't believe me.

'Honest, I'm joking,' I continued, trying to convince her. 'Your nickname was, well, still is "Ginger". Because of your hair. Ginger. Honest.'

She rose from the chair and walked round the table to me, squinting her eyes as if she didn't know if she could believe me. I turned my chair and opened my legs. She stood between them and put her hands on my head and stroked.

'Are you sure?' she asked. I put my arms around her and squeezed her bum, pulling her closely to me. I could feel every curve as she moulded into my body. I could smell the musky warmth of her perfume and feel the firmness of her breasts. I felt a stirring in my loins.

'I'm sure.' I buried my head into her warm, tight belly and she stroked my head.

'That's good,' she replied, with a touch of fun in her voice. 'Because if I thought for one second you were being serious I'd have to tell you what nickname I had for you when we first met in the café.'

I pulled back from the embrace and looked up at her. 'What was that, then?' I had taken the bait. I was sure that it would be Baldy or Fatso or Lard Arse.

'I'd rather not say,' she said, smiling, knowing that she'd got me right back. She pulled away from me and walked over to the sink and started to wash her cup. 'I wouldn't want to upset you.'

Now it was my turn to be paranoid. She was built like a swimwear model, all the curves and bumps in the right places. The only thing I could have modelled for was wanted posters.

I jumped from the water, a fish on a hook. 'So what was it?' I said, sure that it would not be complimentary. I held her shoulders gently and begged.

'Oh please, tell us.'

When she turned around, she had a huge grin on her face and I realised I had been shot down in flames.

'See how it feels?' she said as she put her arms around my neck and kissed me. I kissed her back and she flinched. Her mouth was still badly swollen and sore. I kissed her again, in the same place, very gently this time.

'You are a bad person,' I said, smiling. Then I added, remembering that I had started it, 'I'm sorry.'

'So you should be. Fat Arse indeed!' She kissed me and looked mischievous. 'You're in big trouble, mister.'

'I was only joking. You're gorgeous,' I said between kisses and then added, 'now, if I'd have said Old Double Chin you'd have known I was serious.'

She leaned out of the embrace and slapped me playfully on the shoulder and we both laughed. Another kiss. It lingered.

We headed for the bedroom where I stood Ginger by the bed and gently undressed her again. Her body, covered in fading bruises, was the most beautiful thing I'd ever set eyes on. She was perfectly proportioned: curves in all the right places, with long, smooth thighs. I sat on the bed with her in front of me. She looked down at me shyly, her hair falling over her shoulders in soft waves. I ran my hands over her, feeling her tremble with pleasure. I kissed her soft, taut belly and ran my fingers over her breasts. I pulled her towards me and kissed them, pushing the nipples between my lips and feeling them harden against my tongue. I breathed in the scent of her; warm and feminine. It was like a drug – I needed it more and more. I couldn't get enough of her. She whispered my name, and then called it louder and louder as she allowed herself to lose control.

Afterwards, we lay on the bed, breathless. She snuggled against me, her arm over my chest. I loved her as I never thought I could love anyone.

We started talking, long-buried secrets coming out of both of us, bobbing to the surface like corks in water.

I asked her about Mick again. I still found it hard to comprehend how she could have lived with a man so obviously below her standard.

'I met him when I was in my teens,' she said, sipping on a post-sex cup of sweet tea. 'He was eight years older than me. I was smitten. Actually I idolised him. He was nice then. Not the bloke you saw in the café. That was what he turned into. Nasty.' She spoke about him like he was a repugnant smell. As far as I could ascertain that was exactly what he was. I wanted to know, and I guessed that she wanted to tell. Gets it out of your system to share.

'My dad died when I was little,' she said sadly. 'My mum brought us up on her own.'

'What happened to him? Your dad?'

'Accident at work. Sad.' Then she smiled as she remembered something nice from way back then. 'Him and my mum were really tight. One of those proper couples, you know, that are meant to be together. Like me and you.' As she said it, my heart leaped. 'They were so happy,' she continued. 'My mum used to meet him every day from work for lunch, me and Steve in the double pushchair. They couldn't even go the day without seeing each other. They used to go to a local café. My dad'd have his usual bacon and eggs and toast and tea, the whole thing, and me and Steve would have jam on toast. My mum'd just have a cup of tea. They used to talk and talk and talk. They were so in love.' Tears were already streaming down her face.

'So what happened?' I asked, wiping away her tears. I had to know.

'She rang him up at the factory, same as usual, to let him know that she was on her way. He was fine, "See you soon," he said. When she got there he was being carried into an ambulance. A pallet had fallen from a fork-lift and hit him. Dead. Like that. Freak accident they reckon.' She looked at me, her eyes full of tears. 'Dead. Just like that. Gone.'

I didn't know what to say. I held her and she wept. She cried easily, but there was something endearing about it. I never cried, ever, but now there was a feeling of weakness about me because I couldn't let the tears flow.

'Don't mind me,' she said, wiping her face with a tissue from the bedside drawer. 'I cry if the weather changes.' She laughed. 'My mum always said that emotions moved easiest when first felt and hurt most when held in.'

She didn't know how true and how close to home that statement was.

'I suppose Mick was my father figure. Sounds corny but it's true. I think I was always looking for what they had, my mum and dad. They were perfect together. I always wanted it. And I thought Mick was up for the job. Shows how wrong you can be, doesn't it? What a wanker he turned out to be.'

I laughed bitterly. Women usually wear an expletive like a Hallowe'en mask, but with her, with Ginger, it was almost sweet.

'I was a housewife at seventeen. I quite liked it at first, felt like I was all grown up, responsible, capable of looking after a man. Crazy kid. I was just a baby.' She looked at me. 'I had no idea. Didn't even know how to cook a chicken when I first moved in with him. Had to ring my mum up the first Sunday to ask her how to switch the cooker on. Even then I cooked the chicken with the giblets still pushed up its bum.'

'Sounds painful.'

'Me and Mick or the chicken?'

This time we both laughed.

'I soon grew up. Too soon. You do, don't you?'

I nodded. I knew all about growing up too fast. I knew all about lost innocence and a childhood missing, presumed dead. My mind wandered back to those melancholy times. The sadness. The isolation. Knowing that in the space of one night a part of me had been slaughtered and left without a pulse. That little eleven-year-old inside me came to the surface looking for an exit. I could feel him trying to get out, crying to get out, the quiver on my lower lip, a coating of tears welling at the back of my eyes. I held him back. Too raw Too much hurt. Too much trust. You can't let him out again, just in case. You need to protect the little lad. The memories still raw in my mind. Waking up the morning after the first abuse a different boy from the day before. And knowing it too. Knowing that when I climbed out of bed it would be as a different person. One that would not, could not, ever trust again. The day before I had been a normal boy. Running through the summer days playing tig, hide-and-seek, kiss chase. Writing girls' names on the thigh of my jeans in biro. Getting love letters through my back door that made me tingle to my toes. Innocence. Fucking innocence and bliss and heaven. That all went. I woke up a dull boy. A sad and lonely boy. I woke up knowing that life as I knew it was over and not having any fucking idea whatsoever about what to do about it or where to turn or how to cope now that I was no longer normal. I was hurt beyond my capacity to cope, but I had to all the same. Who do you tell? Couldn't tell my mum. Couldn't pass the gauntlet to that lovely lady. What would she do with it other than confront the beast and get battered for her troubles. No, I didn't know a lot but I knew enough to make it my secret and bear the burden myself. A different boy. The old one locked into a freeze-frame of abuse.

'Where did you drift off to then?' Ginger asked. She was full of concern. Smiling and touching my face, aware that I was holding back and that I was lost.

I shrugged my shoulders. I couldn't share it. You can't. Too risky.

'OK?' She was gentle, asking without asking.

I nodded. No words. They were attached to a tap at the back of my eyes that would overflow the moment I spoke. She wrapped her warm arms around my neck. Kissed me. Dabbed at my eyes with the corner of her dressing gown. Kissed my nose. Brushed her lips over mine.

'So much pain,' she said, as if she could read my thoughts.

I inhaled sharply.

'You don't have to tell me, love. Still hurts, doesn't it?'

I nodded. Deep intake of breath. Holding it back. Controlling it. More deep breathing. Got it under control. In charge again.

She leaned out of the embrace and held my face between her warm hands. She looked me in the eyes. Sincere. 'Know what?' she said. 'I love you.'

I nodded. I knew it but it was incredible to hear it out loud. I believed her. She did love me.

'And I'm here for you. I am. Not just saying it. This is coming from my boots. It's as real as this room.'

I smiled. I loved this girl. She had lined me up lovely, then she said something that knocked my socks off.

'And I am never – listen to me when I say this because if you don't you're in big trouble,' she smiled mischievously, 'I am never ever, ever going to let you down. Never. Never, never, never, never. Right?'

I nodded. She hugged me close. I felt safe. All of me felt safe. Even the little wounded bits that were stuck inside me like chewing gum. And that was when I knew I could tell her. I felt no risk. I just knew. I spoke but kept my face turned away from her.

'Woke up one night. It was dead warm, you know how it used to get in the summers, roasting?' I began, unsure if I really wanted to go where I knew this was taking me. I was back there, it was real again, and I was terrified. 'It was really hot, just had me 'jama bottoms on, it was so roasting. Woke up, there was a hand on me bits, you know ...' My voice was almost a whisper. I could feel the growing lump in my throat and the fear in my voice and the beat of my heart as my mind went back to that small bedroom. 'Thought I was dreaming at first, a nightmare. Then I realised it was real, that someone was actually feeling me ... It was a big hand, an adult's, rough skin, heavy, but ...' I felt my words choking in my throat and my voice becoming high-pitched, skidding out of control. I coughed quickly to try and hide it, took a sharp breath, tried all the things I'd learned to stop myself from losing it. 'Just one of those things. Happens. I'm not the only kid with wounds. Nothing compared to what you've gone through.' I tried to play it down. Ginger was already sliding closer to me in the bed, aware that what was coming out was virgin, never shared before, never seen the light of day. Her hot arms wrapped around my neck, her lips were on mine, gently kissing away the pain.

'I'm so sorry,' she said, pulling me tightly to her.

'It wasn't so much the sexual thing, you know ...' I needed to get it out now, to let it free, it was so close and the trust and the warmth made me feel safe. 'It's the betrayal ...' Again, my words stuttered and an involuntary sob found its way through my mouth, it came from somewhere deep, like it didn't belong to me. 'You know that feeling that you can never ever trust anyone ever again. I mean, if you can't trust your own dad ...'

At the word 'dad', Ginger gasped.

'No, no, no.' She held my face gently, shocked at the revelation. She started crying then, and hugging me so close that I thought I might stop breathing. The crying was infectious. I couldn't hold back any longer. First it came as a small shudder, almost as if I was testing the waters, making sure that the territory was safe and that I was not going to get my ugly face smashed into a mirror. Once I realised it wasn't, the shudder grew into a fully fledged, large as you like sob. A dam had burst and the more I cried, the more Ginger cried, and the more she cried, the more I did until we were both blarting like nippers. I cried and cried and cried, my head tucked into her shoulder so that she couldn't see my face. There was a lot of shame in that cry, but it was a massive relief to finally get it out.

Ginger gently gripped my face and pulled it away from her shoulder. Looked at me. I tried to hide. I didn't want her to see me like this. She kissed my nose, that broken lump that carried the scars of a thousand fights. She kissed my hard, hard face and told me that I was beautiful. And I felt that to her I was.

'Sorry,' I said, feeling ashamed and embarrassed as the tears continued to flow. I felt like such a wanker, like a little tart. I could almost hear my dad's voice echoing in the background, 'You slimy little cunt'.

'Sorry for what?' she asked, genuinely puzzled. My crying wouldn't stop. My shoulders rocked. I tried to get up and leave the bed, to run away, to find a small space where I could hide until I was decent again. Ginger pulled me back, into the bed, into her arms; she cuddled me and rocked me until all the tears had gone.

I must have fallen asleep like that, wrapped in her warmth. When I awoke she was beside me with a hot, sweet tea, jam on toast and a smile. I turned my face away at first, still feeling embarrassed, a little ashamed.

She got back in bed and looked at me. She could sense I didn't want to talk about myself any more. She began telling me more about Mick.

'I started to outgrow Mick, Martin. I wanted to get a job, you know, a proper job, earn my own money. I wanted to live. He hated it. At first he was dead subtle about it. He fed my ego, told me that he needed me at home and that I did an important job. He couldn't do without me, stuff like that. All rubbish. But I was young. I was flattered. "You don't need your own money," he said. "I can give you whatever you want." It kept me quiet for a bit, but not for long. I wanted out. That's when he started to kick off. I was trapped. Unhappy. But too scared to do anything about it. The irony was, I did love him. I didn't actually want to be away from him, I just needed a little room to stretch. Been six months now. Still chasing me. I can't even leave the flat without checking in case he's lying in wait. But I still don't regret being with him, you know. In fact, I'm glad. I'm glad it happened.'

'Glad?' It seemed an odd thing to say about an abusive relationship.

'If Mick hadn't have been a right wanker he'd have never been at that café, he'd have never hit me in front of you and ...' She paused, seeing if I was getting it, allowing me to catch up. 'If it weren't for him, I'd never have met you.'

We ate toast and drank tea in bed. We couldn't stop talking. I told her about my life and how my self-esteem was down there with the worms. I talked about my dad. I talked a lot about my dad. It was cathartic. Like the crying had released something. Now that it was out I felt free to talk about it, more for me than for her if I am being honest. It was good to get it out. I felt dead light. The monkey was off my back for the first time in years, and it felt fine. And I talked about my sweet, lovely mum and how she had suffered, and my brother too. I also talked about my own violence, about how I could not let it go when the red mist blurred my vision and how I distrusted myself. I knew where it had come from: I knew it was to do with my dad and my anger; my dad was gone but the anger remained. Ginger said that it had remained because I had kept it alive.

'The only way to kill it,' she said, 'is to forgive.'

I nearly fell over with the shock. 'Forgive him?' I felt the anger racing along the words and Ginger recoiled, scared. It upset me. I wound my neck in quickly. 'Sorry, sorry, it's just ... I can't forgive,

I can't let him get away with it. That'd be like saying that it was OK for him to abuse me.'

Then she said something that changed me. It changed my world. She said that I didn't need to hold the grudge any more because my dad was dead. She said it gently, and with empathy.

'It's time for you to give it over.'

Give it over. That was the phrase she used. To forgive, she said, was to give it over to God, the universe, whatever it was that spun the planets.

'The moment you forgive,' she said as she brushed my lips with her fingers, 'is the moment you set yourself free.' She explained it to me in a way that I understood, in a way that made sense.

I'd heard about forgiveness before. Of course I had – it was at the very core of Catholicism. But the way it had been sold to me was down right insulting, delivered from the mouths of vengeful and hypocritical priests who all but attacked you if you didn't get to church once a week.

'Turn the other cheek,' they'd say, and in the same breath they'd condemn all us sinners with self-righteous, salivating anger.

That stuff did not resonate with me, in fact it insulted my intelligence. Forgiving people, as far as I could see, was like giving them a licence to do it all the more. Fuck that. But Ginger had come in from a different angle. She said that forgiveness was good for the person doing the forgiving – it was almost a selfish thing.

'You don't let people off when you forgive them. They've got their own karma to work out. This is about you. When you forgive them, you let yourself off. How long's your dad been dead?'

'Ten years.'

'But he's still abusing you because you rerun it in your head every day of your life. And when you do he hurts you all over again. The man that abused you ten years ago is still abusing you today, and you're letting him. You've got to let it go.'

I suddenly smiled. I knew she was right. It made perfect sense.

Ginger continued. 'My mum always said – she liked her philosophy, my mum – she used to say that if you stood by the riverbank for long enough, you would see the bodies of all your enemies float by.' It was the great and universal law of causation, the karmic boomerang. Everything that went out eventually came back; no one could escape providence and destiny was cast by one's deeds. You can't bury your sins or run from the consequences of your actions.

It was so true. I really got it. I knew she was right. I knew it. There was nothing I could do to change what happened before, but I could change what was happening now by letting it go, by forgiving, by setting myself free. Ginger said that once you learned to forgive, all the poison leaves your body and makes room for the love. Fucking *love*!

My anger was back. That word. Love. It triggered things from long ago that I did not want to remember, a time when I had tried to share my abuse with someone, looking for a little balm, some help, only to have my young confidence shattered and my trust clubbed like a seal pup.

Before that day, talking about love had been another flower-power load of bollocks that I had heard and just as quickly dismissed because it was preached by people who wouldn't know real love if it marched up to them in the street and hit them in the eye. People without integrity.

Priests! Fucking hypocritical priests. Perhaps I could find forgiveness for my dad. But some people were surely beyond forgiveness. Even if I couldn't forgive everyone all at once, I did understand. Forgiveness is letting yourself off. Ginger said that once you learned to forgive and you understood that what others did to you always came back to haunt them, you even started to feel compassion for your abusers because you knew that they, in their turn, would suffer for their sins.

'It's a karmic thing,' she said matter-of-factly, like it was the simplest thing in the world. 'What you give out must come back. It's like a boomerang. Everyone has to face the consequences of their own actions.'

She leaned over and pulled me on top of her, then opened her dressing gown. I could feel the warmth of her naked body beneath the soft towelling. She kissed my face.

'So, mister, you can let it go,' she said. 'Let it go and start again.'

And I did. In that moment, I let it go and I was flying. I was alive. I was free.

We talked for hours until Ginger fell asleep. I lay and watched her. She was mine. Not only did I have my whole life in front of me, but I had also escaped my past.

Well, most of it. Some things take time.

Chapter Eleven

The Spark

I promised Ginger that I wouldn't tear Mick a new arsehole. She made me.

'I mean it,' she said, like she was my mum giving me a friendly telling off. 'You'll be in big trouble.'

I agreed and smiled, but every time I looked at her broken face and heard her whimpers of pain when she turned over in the night I knew that I would have to break my promise. The problem was, after leaving that prison cell and getting away with murder, almost literally, my attitude had changed. I now realised for the very first time that I actually had a life, and a great one at that. Sitting in that cell and looking at the world through the eyes of a lifer allowed me to see what I could lose. Liberty is a fantastic thing, fantastic, but the problem is we often don't appreciate it until some fucker tries to take it away from us.

PC Apple was a cunt, but I really did appreciate the lesson he'd inadvertently taught me. I didn't want to lose my liberty. So far I'd dealt with hardy men. Ugly men. Men you wouldn't want to introduce to your family, but hardy and honest in their own way. They were not the type of men to enter into a fight and then run to the police if tits started pointing to the ceiling. There was some honour. And that's why, up until this point, I had managed to evade police involvement beyond station level. However, that kind of luck could only be stretched so far. Once you start killing the fuckers – and let's be straight here, you could do that without even trying – things go into a different league. The crack of skull on pavement, one kick in the head too many, a stamp beyond the call of duty, it's easily done; once you kill there is no more honour, no more criminal camaraderie. Your liberty is confiscated, and for long enough to fuck up your life. So I was in no hurry to face that baby again. No hurry at all. Now that I had Ginger, my liberty was worth a vault of gold. But this Mick fellow still needed looking at. I couldn't have him visiting every time he felt like leaving his mark on my lady. The moment he heard that I had taken his place in her life and her bed the lad would be cabbaged. He would visit. He wouldn't be able to stop himself. He'd already stamped my card by involving his connections – albeit local and amateur – in my world. I had coped OK thus far but I was in no shape to be taking it any further. I was still hurting from the bag session at the scrapyard gym.

Ginger was adamant. 'Can't you just leave it, Martin? He'll go away.'

'From my experience,' I told her, 'some things never go away unless you make them.'

It'd been a week since she'd left hospital and her wounds were healing nicely. A week of lazing around, drinking tea, making love. Ginger had phoned in sick at her shop job. I'd booked another week off work so that I could be with her, help her to heal. I didn't want to be away from her for a second if I could help it.

That beautiful face was starting to shine through again. I tried to convince her about Mick.

'He won't go away, Ginger.' She had become Ginger for real now, her new life came with a new name. 'You know what he's like. He don't know how to go away. Listen, I ain't gonna hit the guy, I just want to warn him off. I just want to make sure that he keeps out of our life. I'm worried about you.'

'I'm worried about *you*,' she replied.

I took her gently in my arms and held her. I stroked her long auburn locks.

'You don't need to worry about me.'

'But I do.' She paused. 'Let's just leave it, hey? See what happens. He might stay away.' Her voice was pleading and it upset me.

'But look what he did to you! Look.' I touched her fading, multicoloured bruises. Her face was a rainbow of hurt.

'They're just bruises. They'll disappear.' She kissed me. 'Please.' Another kiss; she knew how to win a guy over. 'My face'll come back,' she continued, knowing that she was winning me over, knowing how pliable I was in her deft hands. 'I'm worried that if you go and see Mick you might not come back.'

She was right of course. The thought was unbearable. I wasn't worried about getting physically hurt. I was more worried about me getting locked up for a very long time and only seeing Ginger from behind bars. Deep down I knew that she was on the bull's-eye about the danger of me not coming back if I went to see Mick, but I also knew in my heart that Mick would not stay out of our lives. People like that never do. They don't know when to quit; someone has to teach them.

This was confirmed one day when we heard the sound of a key in the lock. Ginger glanced at me, her eyes wide with apprehension. I was by the door in an instant.

'Who's there?'

'Hey, man, cool down! It's me!'

Cap let himself in.

'Steve!' Ginger said, relief in her voice but still annoyed with him. 'Knock, can't you?'

'You gave me a key!'

'Knock anyway.'

'All right. Wind your neck in. Listen, there's something you should know ...'

Cap told us that Mick was salivating with anger because I had strangled him on the café floor in front of 'all them slags' and beat his mate Bilko a new head. And the word was that he was going to do something about it. Bilko was keeping quiet at least. That was expected. The fat cunt was embarrassed about being ragged around the floor like the cleaner's mop. Might even have to pay his wages back now since the job he had been paid to do did him instead. Like a mouse killing the cat – and a fucking fat cat at that. I'd done enough damage to make sure that he kept out of my life for a while. It's hard to fight when you're wearing Paris plaster ankle warmers. Generally I take little notice of grapevine threats; they are usually just the Chinese whispers of drunken cowards desperately trying to regain a little face. But in the case of Mick I believed the rumours. Ordinarily I wouldn't have been talking this through with anyone; I'd have done a home visit and dealt with it. Job done. The consequences would be mine and I'd be prepared to deal with them. Now things had changed. The consequences didn't just affect me, they also affected Ginger, and I had to take that into consideration. My actions from that moment on could and probably would have a direct effect on her. I couldn't bear to see her hurt again.

'All right,' I conceded. 'I'll leave it, but if he starts making noises ...'

She gave me a big hug and kissed my face a dozen times, stopping me from speaking with each kiss. She said, 'Thank you, thank you, thank you,' then she banged the kettle on for a celebratory cup of tea. I liked it when she did that. Life – I have to tell you – does not get any better than this. A cup of tea, maybe a bit of honey in it, and the girl of your dreams.

I kissed her and we headed for the bedroom. Something to do while the kettle boiled.

I went back to my own flat later to collect a few things. I was excited. I was moving in with Ginger. Of course I was worried that it might all be happening a bit too quickly, but as she said, life is short, and when something felt right you didn't need to wait for permission or for a respectable time-lapse to move in together. Living was for now, not for tomorrow or next week or next year. She said that too many people lived their lives on permanent hold, too scared to take a chance. For the first time in my life I felt that luck was on my side.

'There is no luck,' Ginger told me, 'other than the stuff you make yourself.'

I was also scared, I have to admit. I was fearful of what might or might not happen, but my desire to be with her far outweighed my fear of it not working.

My door was still broken and flapping in the breeze when I arrived back. Who-the-fuck-is-Dennis was peeping through his upstairs window as I made for the door. I looked up. His face was one big question mark. I nodded and winked, then I smiled. My way of saying 'All is well'. He nodded back, a look of relief on his face. He opened his window and shouted down.

'Parky. Next week, dear boy. My new novel. Look out for me!'

I smiled and entered my flat thinking, *Yeah, course you will. I'll set the video on record*. Perhaps it was unkind, but then he had been saying it for a while.

Entering the flat was like revisiting the past. I half expected the old me – and there can be no doubt that there was a new me now – to walk out of the kitchen with a baseball bat and a growl saying, 'Who the fuck are you?' It was a strange feeling.

I looked around the front room. It was spartan. Woodchip being pushed off the wall by the damp, an old rented telly on a single leg stand that wobbled when you walked across the floor. A brick fireplace that looked as though it was built from the instructions in a DIY book. And a threadbare blue carpet that was dirty brown in all the places I'd walked most and cleaned least. There was no life in the place. After staying for a week in Ginger's spit-and-polish luxury, I wondered how I had ever laid my head down in this dump. It looked as though it hadn't been lived in for years. The bed was unmade and dirty mugs sat on every surface that could hold a cup. I only used to wash up when I'd run out of clean stuff, and even then I cleaned only what I needed and nothing more.

The place had fallen into disrepair with my discipline right after my dad had died. Up until then I was military in my regime. Everything was in order, cleaned and polished, and I was a training fanatic – at the gym every day, never missing it, not once. I needed to be ordered. I needed conditioning. Shape. Routine. I was still that kid of eleven waiting for the creak of my bedroom door in the night and the abuse that had become a regular occurrence until I was old enough to do something about it. The training saved me. It was my salvation. As long as I trained I felt safe. When he was free of the drink the old man would brag about me to his friends and tell them what a great boxer I was and how I wrestled with the pros and how proud he was. And he was too. But when the drink was in him I was a slimy little cunt again.

'You think you're somethin' now your doing a bit of fighting at the gym, do ya? Think you're someone? Your gym fighting won't help you if I ever lift my hand to you.' He'd raise his fist to underline his power. But the power was waning. I could see that. The drink was taking the last bit of him. The big-backed builder was losing his power to his addiction. At fifteen years of age I was fighting in the ring with grown men who forced my strength and technique to grow beyond my years. When I pushed him away in those dark moments he could feel my growing strength and he could tell that my resistance was no longer futile. Before the training he would just crush my arms as I placed them between us in a wasted attempt to protect my space and my young body. But after only six months of moving sweaty hard bodies on the wrestling-ring floor my arms had developed muscularity and when I pushed, things moved.

I was still only slight, maybe nine stone, but my trainer Reg showed me how to use every ounce of that weight and more. He said that if I threw my weight behind a punch I would be using all nine stone plus momentum. He showed me how to punch from my stomach, just below my belly button.

'Most people punch with their arms, son,' he had said on numerous occasions. 'The better punchers use their shoulders and torso, but the best punchers, the knock-out merchants, punch from their hara, their centre. Here.' He'd tap his belly to show me exactly where 'here' was.

'When you punch from here people fall over.'

Once I got the hang of 'here' he got me to speed up the process. The speed gave the punch impact. Even a piece of straw can pierce a telegraph pole if it hits it fast enough. Then, once the speed was in order, Reg added what he called 'travel'. Travel, he told me, is when you add your weight to the momentum of the punch. As you threw the shot you propelled your body behind the punch so that when it landed it had all your body weight plus the projection behind it. Then he taught me to add 'bounce'. If you bounced at the knees just before you threw the punch, it gave you a kind of kick-start, like a runner from a starter's block. Then, as if that wasn't enough, he added 'double hip'. He learned it from a martial arts powerhouse called Consterdine (who punched opponents so hard in the chest that they bled from their ears), who'd learned it from the legendary Japanese karateka Kimura when he was training in the Orient. This was the penultimate piece of the jigsaw. When most people throw a punch they throw it so that the hip and the arm land at the same time, but the best way to throw a punch is not hip and arm together, but hip and arm apart, the same way that you would throw a stone or a javelin. You throw your hip forward very fast and then allow the arm to whiplash right behind it. Reg always told me that you could get power with some of these elements missing – and lots of people did, boxers and karate men were powerful just using one or two of these elements – but you could never reach your full potential unless you had it all.

'There's one last thing that I can tell you about but can't give you, son,' Reg had said at the end of a particularly gruelling session. 'The spark.'

'The spark?' I was perplexed.

With thumb and forefinger together he reached up as if trying to pick 'the spark' from out of the air. His eyes disappeared into a furrow of skin folds that threatened to engulf his entire face. His mind drifted off. I don't know where he went but whenever he talked about those little somethings that no teacher could give you his mind went somewhere else. It was as if he was accessing a state of nirvana where intangibles could be located but only by those who had stayed the course. One day I hoped I would be privvy to the same halls.

After a few seconds he said, 'Yes, the spark. There is a certain something that has to happen at the end of the punch to make it complete. A spark, a small explosion, a feeling.' He stretched the word 'feeling' as though it were made of elastic. He was struggling to capture it in words. 'I can't give it to you,' he said matter-of-factly. 'No one can. But you can get it.' Then he laughed as if an unseen someone had just whispered a joke in his ear. He shared the nature of his mirth. 'Any fifteen-year-old with twenty years of experience can get it.' And that was how he left it. 'A thousand repetitions to get the technique,' he told me. 'Ten thousand to make it yours.'

I guessed he was saying that that was the price I would have to pay to find the spark. And over the years I did pay the price, I did my 10,000-rep apprenticeship and much more. I would wrap a bicycle inner tube around a metal post on the wall and grip one end with either hand to simulate gripping a jacket then drill the footwork for my throws until my hands bled. I would crawl out of the gym on my hands and knees, too tired even to swallow my food. I would face the biggest monsters in the gym even though every single part of me wanted to retreat to the corner with the bag punchers and hide from my fear.

I found the spark. But I fucking earned it. And when I tried to explain it to people, I too found myself struggling for the words to define it, accessing the far corners of my mind's eye to find the right phrases and never succeeding. And that's one of the things that I liked about this game. There were certain things that you paid for in blood and sweat and some tears too. You couldn't get it from a book or a video; you wouldn't find it on a course or a two-week trip to Japan looking for mysteries. A million pounds couldn't buy you the spark, the feeling, the certain something that the Japanese called *ki*. It was almost like a gift that you received when you pushed yourself beyond your own limits, a tempered blade that could not be cast without going through the most unforgiving forge. Most people fuck about on the outside of the forge and then talk in pub after training about how hot it was. But you don't temper blades on the outside of a furnace. Those that have it most talk about it least. So it was down to the discipline, the repetitions, being out of your depth, scared to go to the gym because you knew how hard it was going to be before you even left your house. It was about living with adrenalin every day of your life, waking up with it, finding it in your cornflakes, cutting through it in your steak. You slept with it like an adrenalin whore until in the end it became as familiar to you as eating and pissing.

Most people go into the gym, do a bit of a warm up and then go on the bag or into the ring. They don't drill their techniques, they don't do the repetitions, they don't develop a steel lining and what Reg called 'beautiful technique'.

'Any arse with a pair of bandages and some mitts can thump the bag,' he told me. 'But it takes discipline to get in there and do the drilling till you're sick to the bones of it, and then come back the next session and do it all over again.'

And he was right. But after my dad died (and Reg was not long in following him) the urge to purge left me, and the training halls were swapped for curry houses. The lean whippet with the small bum and broad shoulders turned into a plump Labrador with wide sides and a saggy arse. But the lessons never left me and the knowledge was still there, even after years of neglect. When I let my right hand go, people were separated from their consciousness and the odd bodily part, and when I entered the grapple – even though my wind was unkind – I could still tug the biggest yoke into a submission within seconds. Reg said that once you got the feel, it never left you. And the steely will that you developed would take you the distance even when your natural instinct to run away or freeze and your stamina were enemies rather than allies.

But I wasn't too concerned at that time with fighting. My mind was filled with new life and new love and a change in direction that I had never foreseen. I wandered around my flat looking for things to take, realising that there was nothing of any real substance that I wanted. I was never one for new clothes and gadgets. When there is no one to impress – and in my life there had been many no ones – there was no need for a dress-to-kill lifestyle. I liked a pint in a quiet pub and real food in out-of-the-way cafés where the girls had flabby arms and builder's bums and a sense of humour. And they called you 'love'. I liked that. My money went right into the bank. I had enough in there to buy all the things that I never wanted. And nowhere near enough to buy the things I really did want. You can't buy a proper dad, you can't buy peace of mind and no amount of money would be enough to pay some psychotherapist dustbin-man to clear the shit from my head. What I wanted seemed elusive, beyond pound notes and buy-now-pay-later special offers that would fill your life with things but still leave your head like a shed. So the cash was there, a few grand in the bank, it soon mounts up when you don't spend much of what you earn because there is nothing to spend it on. I planned to spend a bit of it now though. On Ginger, on a new life.

In that flat, looking at those rooms, emptier than a rapist's conscience, I was saddened by what I had allowed my life to become. Meeting Ginger, the fights, the cells, thinking that I had ended another life; all of these things had opened my world and allowed me a glimpse of what I could lose. But also of what I could gain and what fantastic opportunities the world offered, even for a simple man like myself. I was excited to be getting another shot at life. Me and Ginger had even talked about leaving the city and starting again somewhere new, somewhere with fields and lanes and country pubs with log fires and warm locals. Maybe a slot by the sea where we could walk chocolate-brown Labradors along sandy beaches. We had talked a lot, me and Ginger. About life, about love, about forgiveness. She had convinced me that I could do anything I wanted with my future if I was prepared to forgive my past.

'The past is dead,' she had told me. 'Let it sleep.'

I could see that she was right, and already I could feel myself shedding the bad memories like an old skin. Making room for the new me. I was feeling lighter and, for the first time in a long time, happy. Actually, I was ecstatic. I had even talked about giving up the buildings and going into gym work, teaching, passing my skills as a boxer and a wrestler on to others, especially kids. It had been a secret ambition I had always carried but not shared. I never really believed that a builder could do anything other than build. Ginger said that if I wanted it enough I could move mountains and part rivers. It was weird really, because when she said that to me, when she told me that I had the potential to do anything I put my mind to, I knew she was right. And in my mind's eye I saw myself there, in my own gym, ring in the corner, kids at the bags, people skipping, folks wrestling. I was there; in my mind it had already happened. She made me feel like I could be a good person. I'd always wanted more. Always. As far back as I could remember, but my dreams of a better life had seemed doomed from the start. Whenever I mentioned bettering myself there was always someone ready to smack my ambitions in the mouth with a heavy 'you should be grateful for what you've got' put-down. Right from school when Conc, my careers advisor-cum-maths teacher, told me that if I worked *really hard* I might one day make a factory foreman. Even the other lads on the building site scoffed whenever I mentioned a better life. Ginger had re-ignited dreams that I had long forgotten, she was the catalyst that I had been waiting for my whole life.

As I picked through my old life and placed the things I did not want into a black dustbin bag I came across an old photo in the drawer of me with my mum and my older brother David. Mum was dead. Had been for a long time. Dead and missed like a severed limb. And Dave – crikey, he was the walking image of my dad: tall, broad, hands like spades and a shock of blond hair – he had taken his bricklaying apprenticeship to America where the life offered style and the Atlantic Ocean offered distance from his past. Poor old Dave. He'd had it as bad as me. He never quite came to terms with Dad's death because, like me, he still carried the guilt. Guilt because we were fucking glad he died.

You shouldn't feel relief when your father dies. We both grew up thinking we were to blame for the abuse. We both spent our post-dad existence trying to figure out what it was we'd done so wrong to make him the way he was. And then Mum going so quickly after him. So Dave hid himself in a house with a pool and an American wife and kids and I hid myself in manual labour and an empty flat. We both hid; he just did it in luxury.

I looked at the photo and then looked at the ceiling. She was up there somewhere, my mum. I knew that much. I could feel her. Sometimes I'd see her in the street, in the distance. My body would break out in goose pimples and I'd shout after her. She'd never hear, of course.

I placed the photo in an old box with the other things that were worth keeping. The box was filling slowly, but the bin bag was already bursting at the seams. When I came upon my confirmation medal – a small memento from the Catholic Church of when I confirmed my communion with God at the age of eleven – I felt my anger rise. Images from my past flashed across my mind and I remembered kneeling on a hard pew at school, praying into an empty chapel. Tears bleeding from my eyes, the smell of polished wood in my nose. I begged God to quieten my fears. It was not long after my dad had first abused me. I was distraught and looking for an escape from what had happened. As if in answer to my prayers the kindly priest, Father Tarbuck, a fat jolly man with a veiny nose and fumbling fingers, appeared and asked me why I was crying. He led me into his private room, warm, surrounded by shelves and books. He gave me tea and chocolate biscuits. I thought that my prayers had been answered, but his fatherly hug lingered uncomfortably long and when the squeeze became a crush, despite the fact that my instinct was screaming out an alarm, I told myself that it would be all right. This was a man of the cloth. God's right-hand man. I could trust him. Couldn't I?

His arms were around me as I sobbed into his robes. His hand stroked my back. Then he reached under my T-shirt and began to stroke my skin, pushing his hand down the back of my jeans. I struggled but his grip was too tight. His breathing became heavier. When his fingers unbuttoned my jeans and crept towards the crack of my arse I knew that my trust had been cheaply bought and was about to be sold to the Devil. I froze in terror. It was only because the school cleaner walked in – the priest pushed me away with a start – that I was saved. I learned from that moment to hide my tears and bury my secrets. Fuck, if you couldn't trust a priest, who could you trust? Many years later I trusted Janie, but when I mustered up the courage to tell her she couldn't cope and it destroyed our relationship. And I never entered the church again unless I was forced, and even then I cursed under my breath.

Fat Father Tarbuck. He didn't hang around at the parish for much longer. He was promoted and moved north to Hyde. It was easy for me to remember because I kept thinking to myself, *When I grow up, you fat lardy cunt, there will be no place to hide, not even*

Hyde. I vowed that one day I would meet this man again and it would be on my terms.

Then I remembered what Ginger had said about letting go of the past. About forgiveness. I wasn't ready to take that leap of faith yet, so I compromised, suppressed my anger and slung the confirmation medal in the black bin liner with all the other rubbish.

By the time I left the flat, there were bin bags full of bad memories at the door, waiting for the Monday morning dustmen. I took with me a couple of small boxes that contained elements of the old me that I wanted to retain. I placed them in the back seat of my yellow Cortina. It was one of those real old Cortinas, the Mark Three, with enough legroom for a team of basketball players.

Dennis came down from the upstairs flat.

'Leaving?' He looked genuinely concerned.

'Yeah.' I couldn't keep a smile from my face.

He smiled with me, the first time that year. 'And what might her name be?' 'Ginger. Her name's Ginger.'

He proffered his hand. 'My dear boy, it has been a pleasure.'

We shook hands. 'You do realise,' he added as I walked to my car, 'that your leaving so soon has left me in rather a pickle?'

'How's that?'

'Well, good man, I have not finished my novel yet, and the main character is based on you.'

I laughed. 'Make it up, Dennis, make it up.'

I got into the car and wound down the window.

'But give us a happy ending, hey? Oh, and don't forget to give my best to Parky when you see him.' I drove away.

Chapter Twelve

No Smoke Without Fire

I could see smoke in the distance and heard the distant wail of fire engines but thought little of it. Smoke in the inner city is hardly unusual. It was only as I got closer to Ginger's and the sirens got louder that the alarm bells started to ring in my head. The adrenalin, fear and dread grew inside me. These last few days had been an Everest of highs and lows, culminating in a high that had left my guard down and my chin exposed. Paranoia was setting in, and I could already see flames and death and the destruction of my world at the hands of Mick and his low-life cohorts.

I firmly told myself that I was being paranoid and that my fears were unjustified, certainly unsubstantiated. Mick was a scum-fuck, there was no questioning that, but there was a line even he would not cross. That's what I thought anyway. And for a second or two I even believed myself. I convinced myself that it was true.

The traffic was unusually bad. Every traffic light gave me a red that had my nerves singing. Every time I was stopped, I could feel the tension build and the fear grow. I banged my hands hard on the steering wheel in frustration at every obstacle stopping me from getting to Ginger's quickly. I could feel steam coming out of my ears. The panic and anxiety grew into a flaming ball that pushed from my stomach to my throat and back down to my toes. I was trembling with trepidation. I calmed myself, talked to myself, told myself how stupid I was being. But my fear was multiplied because my enemy, fear, was vague, an intangible something that could not be punched or kicked, could not be choked or strangled or thrown to the floor with practised technique. My internal dialogue was in prayer mode: *Please let everything be OK, please let everything be OK.*

As I hit Ginger's street the smoke turned into flames and my fear turned into unadulterated panic. The street was packed with fire engines and police cars and busy ants moving backwards and forwards in a chaotic flurry. Spectators had already started gathering to watch the real-life soap on their doorstep, horrified and mesmerised at the same time.

Burned out, smoke-covered flat owners stood helplessly outside watching their homes turn to toast. Some sat trembling in blankets, comforted by neighbours, friends and paramedics. Bodies gently rocked and shook as shock set in.

I pulled up and jumped out in a blind panic – keys still in the ignition – and ran into the crowds looking for Ginger. Even as I ran I knew she was dead. I knew it in my heart.

I ran for all I was worth. I felt like I was ploughing through a tunnel where sounds and voices merged into one big background hum. My chest was a symphony of fast drumbeats. My stomach full of churning stress hormones looking for a way out. My mind was racing around, a spin-dryer, and the internal dialogue was asking questions that I could find no answers to: where is she? Is she all right? What am I going to do? Where is she? Where is she? Where the *fuck* is she?

Then I thought I saw her in the distance, a mop of ginger hair disappearing behind a wall of police and firemen. I raced through the dozens of people stood helplessly staring into the flames. I could see her in front of me now, from the back, bent over, a blanket wrapped around her shoulders. I was filled with relief as I grabbed her, turned her round and … fuck, it wasn't her. Nothing like her apart from her ginger hair. I apologised and asked frantically if she had seen my girl. She shook her head, too wrapped up in her own woe. I looked back to the flats. I could already see that the block was being licked into submission by flames that leapt out from the building with an intensity that pushed all but the brave back.

The firemen were rushing around in breathing apparatus. Some were high on ladders that extended from the engine, shooting the flames down with water cannons, others were talking urgently into walkie-talkies. My temples were pulsating. I was full of indecision; which way to go? My eyes scanned every person in the expanding crowd, through old and young, tall and small, standing, sitting and prostrate. My eyes searched through the mayhem and the choking black smoke. I was looking for a shock of ginger hair, a freckled, pretty face. I was looking for my girl. She wasn't there.

Without even thinking, I ran straight to the flats only to be stopped by a heavy-set policeman.

'Hey, hey, steady chap. Where do you think you're going?' There was a firm authority in his voice. It sounded familiar. I stopped and looked at him fleetingly, scared to take my eyes from the scene for too long in case I missed her. It was Sarge from the station.

There was panic in my voice as I tried to push past him. 'I've got to get in there! My lady's in there! You got to let –'

He interrupted me, his voice was concerned and kind. 'What's her name? What flat was she in?'

'Sixty-three, sixty-three. She's in flat sixty-three, third floor.'

He gripped my shoulders, as though holding me in place. 'Stay there. Don't move. I'll find out.'

With that, he dashed off to one of the firemen with a walkie-talkie. They spoke urgently for a couple of seconds. My eyes turned back to the building, belching smoke. My eyes locked on to the third floor. I knew that Ginger's kitchen window would be visible from where I stood. I counted up the three floors, third window across. My heart felt like it had stopped beating. Fire was thrashing out of the window with small burnt parts of her world, of my world, on the end of the flames. I watched as the ash floated to the ground like black confetti and my world died. In the back of my mind, right back, so far back that it was almost lost there was still a little hope. She could have escaped. Just because the flat was ablaze didn't necessarily mean that she didn't get out. All these people around me had escaped. All these people being helped by the police and paramedics and fire-crew had managed to fight free. So why not Ginger?

The fireman talked quickly into his walkie-talkie, while Sarge looked over at me. He nodded his head. 'It's all in hand' he seemed to be saying. I was helpless. Frozen by my terror. A shop-window dummy. Sarge came back over to me.

'The lads seem to think that they might have seen her.' He saw the hope in my eyes and quickly added, 'They can't be sure, but they think –'

I interrupted him. 'Where, where did they see her? Was she all right? Was she injured? Did they say where she went?'

My voice suddenly dried up mid-flow as if someone had switched the electricity off. I saw her.

I ran past Sarge even though he tried to stop me. 'Hold on!'

I didn't even let him finish. Two firemen coming out of the building carried a smoke-blackened stretcher. On it lay a dead body. Even from where I was standing, I could see the lifelessness of the small form covered from head to toe by a blanket. Hanging over the end of the stretcher, as though trying to escape its own demise, was a shock of long and curling ginger hair. I leapt over the tape put up by the police to keep back all but the professionals and ran to the stretcher. I heard the distant voice of Sarge shouting for me to stop. My heart was pounding, I had tunnel vision, everything moved in slow motion. Sounds were relegated to a dull and dreamy echo. My mouth felt dry and pasty. My mind was already preparing for the inevitable. As I approached, the firemen with the stretcher stopped. They knew. No one had to tell them that she was mine. They just knew. My face started to twitch and contort. Tears streamed down my face. I stared at the beautiful red hair. My hand moved forward to lift the blanket from her face. One of the firemen shook his head, putting out his hand to stop me. He peeled off his breathing mask, eyes full of sympathy. He must have done this a thousand times and yet he still looked appallingly unprepared. Words that wanted to come from my mouth were trapped by lumps of emotion. I knew that I could not get one out without the other. If they came out together the words would be incoherent. But I needed to know. The second fireman bowed his head but remained anonymous behind his mask. I guess it was easier to deal with death when you were anonymous, one step removed from its brutality. I understood that. I managed to get the two words out that would end my misery.

'Number sixty three?' I asked, knowing the answer already but praying that I was wrong. They both looked at each other sorrowfully. The one without the mask nodded. 'Sorry.'

He opened his mouth to say more. Sorry that this has happened to you. Sorry I couldn't do more. Sorry for your hurt. Sorry that you will probably never get over this tragedy. Sorry that life is so shit. Sorry, sorry, fucking sorry.

Nothing came out.

He knew even as he was forming the apologies in his mouth that no words or sentiments or condolences were going to bring her back. Solace was not on sale today. She was dead. That was all.

Chapter Thirteen

Human Traffic

'You've got some enemies you, son.' It was Sarge.

I was sat trembling against the side of my car, surrounded by the sights and the sounds and the smells of disaster. I was oblivious to it all. Lost in my own world of loss and guilt. I had lost my soulmate, and it was my own fault because I had stepped into a world that did not belong to me. As a consequence that world had been devastated. I looked up at the burly, meaty-faced policeman. His black smoky cheeks were wet with sweat.

'This was no accident,' he continued. 'No accident. Two six-inch builders' nails through the top and bottom of the front door, right into the frame. Petrol through the letterbox, a lit match. Whoever started this fire knew exactly what they were doing. And they knew who they were doing it to.'

Another pause. None of it mattered, none of it. It wasn't going to bring her back.

'You got some big enemies, son,' he said again. 'It's no coincidence that you were somehow involved in the two ugliest crimes this week, is it?' I looked up. Shook my head. I knew that much. There was nothing to say. Nothing to fix. It was all beyond fixing. All I could do at this point was level the score by paying a visit to the bastard with death on his hands.

'If I was you, I'd want to know exactly who my enemies were. Not just that, I'd want to know *where* they were.'

I looked up at him. He took a small notepad from his pocket and wrote on the first page. He ripped the page from the pad and placed the pad back into his tunic pocket. He crunched the page up in his big hand without looking at it. It shook with rage as he squeezed, as though all his anger was being transferred into that small scrap of paper.

I still didn't say anything. No words were going to ease my pain. None of it was going to replace my loss. I just wanted to be left alone. I wanted darkness and a quiet room and time to disappear into myself.

'You see, the thing is,' Sarge continued, 'we know who did this.'

My eyes focused on him properly for the first time. He had got my attention. I knew who did it too, but confirmation would be nice.

'Oh yeah, we know him, every little thing about him: where he lives, where he socialises, his habits, mates, peculiarities, likes, dislikes; we've got files thicker than doorsteps. But we still can't convict. We know who the scroaty fucker is all right, we just can't prove it.'

He was not even looking at me any more. He was staring at the fire, still billowing plumes of black smoke. He was deep inside himself. I guessed that he was looking at the red tape and rulebooks that had allowed so many criminals to make their living from the suffering of others and get away with it. He was looking at the morality and justice and truth-will-prevail ethos that had kept him in the police for twenty years. The futility, heartache, and soul-searching that it had brought him. He was probably contemplating the fact that he had more dirty ulcers to his name than he had clean convictions. More sleepless nights than settled scores.

He shook his head in dismay. Twenty years in that bastard trade and nothing to show for it other than a long line of grudges against the scroats that successfully evaded the law, and they were many. The shade of light you lived under when your job was protecting good souls from arseholes. The promise of a pension had probably kept him tied to the job, even when his other 'police friends' (like he had any other type of friend), had left the force and found contentment in a life less fraught with aggression and negativity. A life where you were not dealing with the shit on the shoe of humanity, the violent minority. I imagined that even when his wife had begged him to look for pastures greener, the distant promise of a promotion, a pay rise and a job with an office held him there like a lottery dream. He looked like a man on the edge of a moral dilemma, ready to jump into the abyss but still not sure.

Then he smiled. A forced smile lined with sympathy. He turned to walk away. He had made his decision. As he did so, he dropped the ball of paper from his hand like it was scorching his palm. I picked it up, the feelings of revenge and anger and evil already burning inside me. I carefully unfolded it to see if it contained the information I thought it might.

It did.

I don't know if Sarge looked back. I was long gone. On my way to a house call.

I hardly remember the journey through the city streets. My mind was lost in a thousand thoughts of Ginger. She was gone and I was devastated. I felt numb. A part of me had been severed, like a limb from the body. I felt as if I was looking down on myself from a great height. I knew I had to avenge Ginger's death, but I felt that it wasn't really me driving the car, more that I was my own guardian angel, looking down on myself, willing me to succeed in this mission.

I was going to visit the man with petrol fingers and the lit match. And when I found him I was going to break those fingers off and stick the fuckers up his nose.

Funny, I had just escaped a police cell for nearly killing a man by accident; now I was about to try and do it on purpose. I no longer gave a flying fuck. I valued my liberty at nothing. I no longer feared my own death. I was at my most dangerous, not because I was angry – though an angry and scared man can be a fearsome enemy – rather, I was dangerous because I had nothing to lose.

The Japanese samurai faced their fear of death as a morning ritual because it liberated them. I had always felt a fear of something in my life. In fact I could not remember a single day that was not lined with fear, from mild anticipation right through to unadulterated terror apart from those precious few days of bliss with Ginger. But that day I felt nothing but a cold chill, a focus that could be read by even the hard of thinking. It said 'Get in my way and I'll fucking bury you'.

I headed to Delray Road, on the outskirts of the city. It was on a smart new estate, full of four- and five-bedroom detached houses, separate double garages and hefty price tags. It was full of lower league professional football players, senior police officers and middle management. And criminals. It was a social culture dish where ordinary people with good jobs got to live near minor celebrities and villains. Where there's money there will always be crime and criminals.

The majority of the estate was inhabited by the polo neck and Volvo brigade, the men and women who bored you with conversations about the rising price of their investment house and their next planned move to a place with its own land. People who were always so busy with their contingency plans for the future that they never quite got to enjoy the present.

I stopped at a red light, lost in thought. Ginger's sweet face floated in front of my eyes. I couldn't take my gaze away from her. My body started to ache just thinking about what we could have had. A car horn suddenly shocked me from my reverie. It made me jump and I stalled the car. I sat there, unable to move, my mind filled with sadness and loss and pain. And such profound love, beyond my ability to describe. I had felt its measure only once in my life, when cancer took my mum. She entered hospital on the Friday and was taken from me on the Tuesday. Weak and ravaged by the illness, a skeleton in a skin suit. I stood over her dead body in the hospital bed and smiled. I felt love in its purest form. I smiled and smiled and smiled. There would be no more pain for her.

'Oh my mum,' I kept saying. 'Oh my lovely mum.'

I felt it then as I felt it now. The heart-rending blend of love and loss.

The car horn was still beeping somewhere in the background. I was on a narrow piece of road where it was difficult for anyone to pass and the people in the cars behind were naturally anxious for me to move so they could continue rushing through their busy lives, unaware that I was dying in the tattered seat of my old Cortina.

Suddenly there was a bang on my driver's window. I looked out at a raging red face and a shaking fist. The veins were bulging out of the bloke's neck like scaffolding poles. His eyes were bulbous and fixed. Fists knotted. He was experiencing classical fight or flight symptoms where the body prepares for a life and death battle. It prepares the body to run short distances at great speed; it gets ready to fight the sabre-toothed tiger. His mid-brain, the part of the brain associated with survival, had been fooled. It was filling this man with enough liquid dynamite to run a marathon or fight an elephant. But there was no such threat, just an important deadline and a wanker in a yellow Cortina stopping him from making it. So I was getting the overflow of his stress and all I had done was daydream at the lights and stall my car. He didn't know that my girl had died. He could not have known that my life was over. He just wanted to get past me because I was holding up his very fucking busy life.

I tried to turn the keys in the ignition, but I fumbled and the car failed to start. My car door was yanked open and the red-faced man with pulsating worms in his temples grabbed me by the shirt and pulled me out of the car. Everyone was staring through their windscreens to see what the hold-up was, some getting out of their cars.

'A real fight,' I heard a young man whisper to his lady.

'You fucking cunt!' the bloke shouted in my face. 'You fucking stupid piece of shit! Get your fucking car out of my way before I –'

Bang!

I couldn't help myself. Honestly. It was an involuntary act. I put my head into his nose and he dropped as if an invisible trap door had opened up beneath him. The contact was solid and full of pent-up emotion that was meant for someone else.

I got back into the car and drove away. The pool of blood filled a yard of tarmac in my rear-view mirror. The man's wife knelt beside him, trying to collect what was left of his nose in a hanky. It turned red the moment it touched his face.

I pulled into the estate, still trembling with adrenalin and shock. It was a neat, quiet estate with a big superstore at the entrance like its own personal shop. I had worked on estates like this as a builder. The houses were what we in the trade called 'thrown up'. Built in a hurry. Nice places, generous plots, porches and double garages and en-suites. But thrown up by good workmen on a bad price using cheap materials. Within two years the paint would be flaking and the wooden window frames would be rotting at the sills. But they looked nice and for those on the way up they would last the course and justify the investment.

I cruised along, took a left and then first right into a cul-de-sac. I pulled up at the kerb and unfolded the piece of paper; my present from Sarge. Michael Wall, 12 Delray Road.

The house was large, with a small open porch at the front and a double garage and driveway at the side. Inside was a body that was wasting good oxygen.

I reversed into the drive and then pulled the car back to the kerb so that I was ready for a quick exit. I climbed out of the car, leaving the driver's door unlocked, and approached the house. My breathing was heavy and laboured. I breathed deeply though my nose to slow the flow. No need to control the internal dialogue today, it was in order and focused on the task ahead. I hadn't planned the job: my intention was to allow spontaneity, grief and rage to mix into a heady cocktail of violence. My body would do the bidding of those masters.

I banged on the door, ignoring the fact that there was a bell with a fancy chime ready to be pushed. I wanted the hammering on the door to start the proceedings, get the lad full of fear so that by the time he reached the front door he would already be primed. He was probably expecting a pull from plod. Mick probably thought that I had been in the flat with Ginger, the threat wiped out. No answer. I knocked again, louder this time. I stood back to survey the house for twitching curtains and peeping eyes. Nothing. The bedroom window on my right was slightly open so I was sure that someone was in.

I walked through the side gate to the back of the house. I entered the spacious back garden. It was all grey rock and shale that crunched beneath my feet, dotted with statues and water features. Probably ten grand's worth of design but no taste. A scum-fuck using money to buy class. It don't work. Scum is scum no matter how much coin he brings in.

On the decking was a sun lounger and a green plastic table with four matching chairs. Two unfinished bottles of beer sat on the table. The back door was open, and I could hear a radio playing somewhere in the house. The decking creaked as I crossed it to enter the house. I walked through a small amenity room and into a spacious, white designer kitchen. Expensive brass lids shone from the silver pans hanging on a rack by the Aga. The Aga looked pristine, as though it had never been used other than to stand plates on when the take-away curry was being dished out. I walked into the hall and climbed the stairs. The house was all expense and no taste, just the same as the man who owned it.

I could hear a shower running in one of the rooms. The sounds of splashing and the movement of feet on the shower floor were music to my ears. I followed the noises. The beating of my heart and the thumping in my head drowned them out as I got closer. I eased open the bedroom door to my left, where the sounds of showering and life multiplied.

'Who the fuck are you?'

I nearly jumped out of my skin. I turned to see a large beast of a man taking up most of the doorway of the bedroom opposite where the radio was playing. He was wearing a Lacoste T-shirt that was straining with his bulk. He was half bodybuilder, half ape with RSJ shoulders and arms that hung almost to his knees.

He had a toby-jug face with a bum-fluff moustache that did little to hide his scarred upper lip. The scar was probably a glass wound; it was too jagged for a knife and too neat for a bite. It added to his scowl, giving him a permanent frown. He was a scary fucker. I guessed that he was hired help, a little imported muscle to beef up the protection around Mick. I knew as soon as I saw him that he was a league above Mick, that he was a proper threat, not just a wad with a mouth. But I was there to do a job and no musclebound clothes-horse of a boxer was about to stop me. He approached me across the landing.

'Who the fuck are you?' he asked again, using the dialogue, the question, to bridge the gap between us. He was already in fight mode, his back up and his hackles raised. By now my heart was beating in my mouth and nothing worth saying came to mind.

Bang! I was so taken aback by his presence that the first punch he threw caught me by surprise and sent me sprawling backwards into the bedroom behind. My face was hot with pain. Blood and a gobstopper growth appeared on my lower lip as if by magic. The backs of my legs hit the foot of the bed and I fell on to it. I panicked for a second and tried to regain my feet while the boxer raced into the room to take advantage of my prostrate position. Rule one: when they go down, they should stay down. For good. He obviously knew the rule by heart and was racing to the bed to finish what he had started.

I couldn't believe I'd allowed him the first shot. Sacrilege. My mates on the door would be ashamed. You never let them get the first shot. Ever. I cursed myself. I should have expected this. The two bottles of unfinished beer on the garden table were sign enough. I should have known. But I didn't and now I was paying.

My mouth was already oozing where the first punch had pushed a tooth through my bottom lip. It was a good punch too. Sent clouds straight to my head and shot me backwards through the door like I was on skates. He was a professional puncher. He was streamlined and quick. The punch was a straight right cross, delivered with body weight and projection. The first two knuckles delivered the blow and he snorted on impact. All the trademarks of a pugilist. But for the fact that I instinctively leaned back to ride the blow, I'd have been counting z's already.

I could tell by the way his guard instinctively jumped to attention after the first shot that he wasn't just a boxer but one of repute. The bent nose and the scarring over the eyebrows only served to confirm my belief. His face had seen more leather than a biker's arse. He was a heavyweight too. Maybe seventeen stone. Too heavy for me. When skills and fitness are equal, the bigger man will always win unless you fight him at a different game where his expertise is not quite so honed.

'Never box a boxer,' Reg had always warned me. He was right. And this fucker was about to give me the benefit of all his experience. I was in good company. I knew right away that I had to take the fight to the ground. He might be a champion on his feet, throwing them bombs, but how good was he in the grapple?

Most people think that because they can throw a punch they can take their skills to any range. Not so. A good puncher becomes a novice when you take his hands away from him and move the fight to the floor. That was my intention. All I had to do now was avoid another one of those very heavy bombs that were now thrashing at my head. If I could ever get off the fucking bed. I was fighting with the duvet to find my feet.

I was on my back trying to get up, the duvet wrapping around me like it was alive. I already knew where I wanted to go. The first punch had given me all the information I needed. I had made my assessment. I needed to be in close where those big paws could not club another dark cloud into my head. I needed to be around his neck in a hurry, before Mick came out of the shower and joined in.

There was a satisfied look on Boxer's face. This was all too easy, it seemed to say. He had taken the first shot, the initiative, and that guaranteed him the next three. The pre-emptive attack is the staple diet of every fighter who stays in the game long enough to become wizened and weathered. The ones that wait to be attacked or who hesitate or err forfeit the chance to finish the fight before it has even begun.

Whoosh! A big hooking right hand whipped past my head and I rolled onto the laminate floor by the bed. My elbow cracked on the wood; another injury that would be hot with pain the moment this encounter was over. It was the least of my worries. I was being pursued around a strange bedroom by Herman-fucking-Munster.

Boxer followed me to the side of the bed and, before I could find my feet, he was on me, stabbing his lumped fists at my head and body. Most of the blows landed on my arms and back. I curled up like a hedgehog to protect myself. As I fell off the bed, a large cuddly elephant had fallen with me. Instinctively I picked it up and, before I could stop myself, I flung it at his face. If I was embarrassed about trying to use a cuddly toy as a weapon he must have been doubly so, because he instinctively ducked. The absurdity of the moment was lost. I was crammed tightly between the side of the bed and the built-in wardrobes. If I turned onto my belly to get back to my feet I knew I'd get a heavy right fist in the back of the head that my ancestors would feel. If I stayed where I was I'd be open to the heavy kicks of this Neanderthal.

As if reading my mind, he punished my indecision with a kick that cracked against my shin, then a kick at my bollocks. I turned my shin across the front of my body and took it on my knee. I think it hurt him as much as it hurt me but it was better than taking it across the testicles. My shin throbbed like a porn star's hard-on. No pain yet. The adrenalin had switched that baby off. But it would be back on again later and every blow landed, every muscle stretched and bone cracked would come back on again – and all at once.

Frustrated that he could not get a clean shot at me, Boxer jumped in the air and tried to stamp on my legs. As he landed, I pulled back my feet, just in time. The floor shook with his weight. As his feet hit the floor, I dived forward in a double leg take-down like a rugger tackle. I rammed my right shoulder into his right shin, arms around his calves, and drove forward for all I was worth. I yelled with the effort. He fought to keep his balance and tried to grab the air to save himself from falling, but his legs were tied and he was going down. As soon as he hit the deck, cursing angrily and still throwing punches that bounced off the crown of my head like flies off a windscreen, I knew he was mine. He was a stand-up fighter, not comfortable on the floor.

Boxer's panic was tangible. He let out involuntary screams as he tumbled back, smashing a mirror off the wall behind him as he fell. His elbow cracked a hole in the plasterboard wall. There was a time – when they built houses of brick – that you could really do some damage when you hit a fellow off a wall. Nowadays all you did was cost them a couple of quid in Polyfilla.

He was on his back, trying to sit up. I was tightly wrapped around his ankles, stopping him and already starting to climb up his body to get at his neck. His punches still fired but they had nothing left in them but sting. Boxers rely on hip-twist and weight transference to get power. On the floor, that body weight, that transference of power through the hip, is no longer available. It was just the arm, which, on its own, was useless, like taking a bullet from a gun and throwing it at someone.

'Who's that? That you, Jimmy?' It was Mick, shouting from the shower in the en suite. The voice sounded as if it had caught a gulp of air as it tried to get out. There was a hint of hysteria, and rightly so. He had to get dressed and get armed fast, or else get a naked beating and a bloody shower cubicle.

Jimmy was too busy closing in on me to answer Mick. I heard the shower turn off and the door of the cubicle open. I figured I had maybe thirty seconds before Mick was out of the shower and clothed enough to attack me. Believe me when I tell you that no one enters a physical fight naked. Too vulnerable. All those bits dangling, ready to be gripped and grabbed and ripped and kicked and bitten. Doesn't bear thinking about. Thirty seconds and I would be fighting them both in a space that was smaller than a boxing ring.

Jimmy must have known that the ground was not his arena because his girly panic did not match his manly gait. He'd looked fearless stood up; cast from stone, square jaw, bolts through the neck – you know the type. He tried to sit up but as soon as he moved, I thrust my head into his belly to control his torso. My breathing was already coming through my arse. I was sucking in air like there was a shortage. But I'd been here a million times; in the ring, on the doors, outside the chip shop. I knew about pain and I knew that it would be relegated to a background noise the moment I ignored it. If you latch on to the pain, give it any attention at all, it intensifies. To acknowledge pain is to begin the end. I also knew where to find my rest spots. My head was getting sore and lumpy from all the punches that he was bouncing off my swede. But it was superficial. I could take it on the head all day long. His hands would be breaking at the knuckle with every blow. You don't hit bone on bone, certainly not knuckle on head. You never do that. If you do, the weakest bone is going to give out. The small bones of the hands and fingers snap like Twiglets. They don't even begin to compare with the power of the skull.

I took my rest, trying to find some breath so that when I got to the top of his body I could finish the job. He was a monster and I could feel his physical power. Every part of his body that I connected with was tarmac hard. But I wasn't scared by his power. You don't fight muscle with muscle. That's the amateur game. There is always a stronger man. I knew from experience that if you fell into the strength trap then every yoke with a barbell in his bedroom and a pack of protein powder would be in with a fighting chance. Better to bring technique to your game, then even the biggest heavyweight can turn to jelly.

I still had his legs tied and my head firmly placed in his belly. I was up on my toes so that all my weight bore down on his stomach, forcing him to breathe in short, sharp rasps. Every time he inhaled I applied more pressure with my head. Eventually it would stop him breathing altogether. My head was tucked in tightly so that my shoulders were up by my ears, protecting my face and jaw from blows and stopping him from headlocking me.

Jimmy was now gasping in short breaths, his frustration, fear and misuse of strength were depleting his energy at a fast rate. His battery was low, nearly empty. Mine wasn't much better. We'd only been fighting for a few seconds but when your life is at stake and your arse is on the line you invest every ounce of your reserves just to survive. I was calm enough now though, so what energy I did have was being carefully distributed. The more Jimmy panicked, the more energy he utilised. The big guys are usually only good for a few seconds, especially when they're muscle-bound. Too much lean body weight to feed with oxygen. Better to be slight and wiry and light on the beef, better to have tactile strength and technique than a mirror physique. The beach body is good for the pose, good for the mirror gymnastics, but it doesn't help much when you've got a fat fourteen-stoner who likes a wrestle climbing up your legs looking to wring your neck like a dirty dish-cloth. Jimmy was upturned, turtle-like.

I heard Mick shouting from the en suite, panicky. 'Jimmy! Jimmy? Is that you?'

'Yeah. Get out here, you cunt! Now!' There was a squeal in Jimmy the Boxer's voice. The ten-stone weakling under seventeen stone of armour and camouflage was starting to come out. Real character always comes through when the pressure is applied.

As soon as I heard Mick I knew that I only had seconds to finish this thing. If I didn't, Mick would be out, armed and dangerous and on my back. Plumes of steam raced from the bathroom into the bedroom. I could hear Mick panicking, looking for a towel, anything to cover himself. Muttering 'fuck, fuck, fuck' under his breath like he had Tourette's, his wet feet farting on the dry lino floor. The fear, the anger, the massive anticipation of a man taken by surprise. A boy in a man's game. Out of his league. It was what I expected. Home visits always do that. An intruder in your house looking to damage you. A fucking nut-case of an intruder at that.

I needed a psychological edge. Mick was already panicking (and so he should, I was going to fucking kill him). I wanted him to panic more. I needed hesitation because that would give me vital seconds.

'Hey cunt, remember me? The café?' I shouted, out of breath and still pinning the beast to the bedroom floor by his legs, sweat and blood dripping from my nose, head pulsating. 'When I've finished with your mate here, I'm gonna fuck you!' I spat the word 'fuck' out of my mouth as if it was on fire. I heard a towel drop to the floor and Mick's feet did a little dance as he slipped, trying to put on his underpants. In his panic he fell. I heard the clang as his head hit the toilet seat and the under-breath cursing as he tried to get back up. It was all I needed.

'You don't know who you're fucking with, cunt!' Mick replied, still in the bathroom. There was a tremor in his voice. It told me all I needed to know. His head was already a shed and his bottle was leaving via the back door. 'I've got fucking connections. You're dead!'

No need to answer. I got my vital seconds and the reaction I was looking for. I still had Jimmy's legs, my head in his belly, my feet now at the side of him, ready to take the pin and then the choke. In panicking Mick, I had also inadvertently fired a bit of energy back into Jimmy. As soon as the words had left my lips, he found a new lease of life and started bucking and bronking. I held him firmly. My forearms were starting to blow. My breathing became more laboured. I could feel the queasy, sickly feeling that always comes when your conditioning lets you down.

I managed to feed my left arm under Jimmy's right armpit and my right arm around his tree-root neck. I was looking for a pin, the controlling position before the submission. Reg had drilled it into me a million times: 'Position before submission.' He would always say it was a waste of time learning submission techniques if you did not know how to control the thrashing body weight of a maniac with hod-lifting legs and a road digger mentality. The first few seconds of the pin were pivotal. When the opponent knows that a pin leads to a win, he becomes a bucking bronco in his bid to escape. He would butt and bite and kick and spit his way to freedom, anything to break the hold. Most men have about fifteen seconds of fury in them, thirty seconds tops. And in that time they will be surprisingly strong. But after thirty seconds, if you still have them secured, they are spent. They are yours.

I knew from experience that Jimmy would either try to wrench me off with his Popeye arms when I secured the pin, or spin onto his belly to try and escape it. He would roll to his belly in the false belief that it would be the quickest, safest, perhaps the only way to get from horizontal to vertical by getting to his knees and then his feet. And if it wasn't for the fact that I was anticipating his every move and that I actually wanted him to turn and open himself up for my *coup de grâce*, the carotid strangle, it might have worked.

As soon as I touched the cables on his sinewy neck, he spun like a shark. I was on his back the second he moved. A leech. A strangling, choking, salivating limpet.

I have to say that he *was* the strongest bastard I had ever encountered. I felt like I was riding a bull. But strong men grow on trees. And they tire quickly. As soon as he hit his belly, he climbed to his hands and knees. The space was very tight. Elbows, heads and knees were knocking and bumping into walls and furniture edges. As he knelt, grunting and blowing and sweating, the veins in his neck standing to attention, his heart tattooing out of his chest, I was at his back, hooking my left foot between his legs, behind his left knee, and looking for the strangle. I punched my right arm around his neck, tight so that my armpit was tucked into the back of his shoulder. This ensured that my right bicep closed the right carotid artery at the base of Jimmy's neck. As my arm whipped around his neck, the bone of the forearm did the same with the left carotid. It was like a tourniquet around the neck, a barricade that stopped all blood and oxygen from getting to the brain. It usually has them sleeping in seconds. My foot was hooked tightly in place to secure me, to stop him from bucking me off. I always hook in one, if not two legs. We became as one. No amount of strength could separate us. The hook allowed me to get so close that his movements became my movements, and the more he struggled, the tighter my grip became.

Mick was still panicking in the background, trying to put dry clothes on a wet body. Not an easy task with a wave of fear lapping at his internals.

The strangle was on and I was feeling good. Once I had secured the hold, the grip tightening around his neck, I knew that I was seconds away from victory. Still kneeling, still trying to stand, gargling and choking, eyes wide in fright, Jimmy grabbed hold of my fingers and tried to peel my grip from his neck. I immediately changed my grip from hand-to-hand to right-hand to left bicep, cupping the palm of my left hand over the back of his head like a skullcap. All my fingers were now hidden, making my grip impregnable. He tried to scream in fear and frustration, but I was too tight on his throat to let his vocals work. He gargled and spluttered and went big eyed, as if his voice was trying to shout out of his eye sockets. Just when I thought the fight was over he found a new lease of life and with the very last bit of strength in his body he climbed to his feet, me still on his back and strangling. I tightened my grip by hugging my arms and chest into the strangle and forcing his neck forward by drilling my head into the back of his.

Blood ran from my throbbing teeth into his cropped scalp. I wrapped my legs tightly around his waist in a scissor, feet linked at the front and thighs tightening at the back, to enable me to stay on. It also helped to close off his breathing. His hands were still clawing, futilely trying to find my fingers. He lurched backwards, me riding on his back, just as Mick, half-dressed, still wet and dishevelled, hurried out of the en suite with wide eyes and arms splayed. The cowboy was back for another shoot-out.

Mick ran straight at me, then hesitated. He'd suddenly remembered something, like a man leaving for work without his suitcase. He raced around the bed, away from us, and headed for the bedside drawers. He was obviously looking for a weapon, an appendage. Jimmy smashed backwards into the mirrors on the wardrobe to try and release me. The doors cracked but I was still hanging on. To be honest it didn't really matter what he did. He could turn cartwheels for all I cared. It was over for him. Once the strangle is on, you are out of there. As he bounced off the wardrobe, his clawing turned to a kind of pleading tap, as if he was saying, 'You win, let me go now. I've had enough.' Let me be the judge of that.

Suddenly he slumped to the floor, semi-conscious, and snored a death rattle that told me he was all but gone. I would let go, but not until he was fast on and no longer a danger. Fucking maniac. You do not want to fight a colossus like this twice in one day.

Mick was scrambling and muttering at the drawers, trying to find a weapon. I held the strangle for a few more seconds, my eyes locked firmly on to Mick. Jimmy's thrashing and pleading had stopped. His arms fell limp by his sides. He was gone. I was still sitting with my back to the mirrors, wrapped around Jimmy like a shell. Mick had found his weapon: a heavy, five-batteried metal Maglite torch that could turn bone to dust in the right hands. Thank fuck for that. It could have been a blade, then I'd have really been in trouble.

Mick raced around the bed to get at me before I could rise, torch held high, ready to strike, eyes full of panic and fear. I quickly released my scissor grip from Jimmy's waist and forced him over on to his belly so that I could get back to my feet.

I was on my knees when the first blow caught me on the arm. A dull ache raced right across the muscle and bone. I'd raised it as a shield to protect my head. The second blow flew right over my head as I shot forward, smashing my head into Mick's bollocks, tackling him to the floor. In a second I was sat on top of him.

After Jimmy, Mick was all too easy. He was a relative lightweight. His trousers stank of petrol. As soon as I smelled it, I lost the plot and hammered a right fist into his nose, smashing it across his face.

'Been lighting fires, you fucking prick? Been lighting fucking fires?' I yelled as the second punch closed his eye. Then I smashed a heavy cutting elbow onto his face with each frenzied word that left my lips.

'Been *smash* lighting *smash* fucking *smash* fires?'

He was out on the second blow. Out, out, out. A pulp. A bloody rag. A ball of contusions and rips and red. I kept punching until I had nothing left in me. If he wasn't dead it was pure luck.

My chest heaved up and down. No breath. The smell of petrol in my nose. Loss on my mind. Ginger on my mind. And me, a shit sat across the chest of another shit. Refiguring a face. Venting some rage. But still full of it. I knew even as I smashed my hands into his skull, as they bled and pulped, as he bled and swelled, that this would not bring Ginger back. Neither would it purge the feeling I had in my chest. I climbed off the piece of shit, my face an angry distortion. He was lying prostrate, one arm over his head like a hideous taxi hail, the other by his side. His face was one big, red blob of leaking boils. He looked like a bomb victim.

As I climbed up, Jimmy started coming to. I was still breathing hard, looking for more breath than my lungs could find. Spittle drooled from my lips like I'd just run a marathon on a hot day. Jimmy opened his eyes. They looked around the room. Then at me. He was not sure yet who I was and what had occurred. It would probably take a few seconds before it all came flooding back to him. I had been strangled out myself at the gym. When I did come around, I didn't know where I was either. Thought I was in bed. Thought I'd just woken up late for work. It took me half a minute to find my memory. So I knew how he felt.

Bang! I hoofed him in the head. An angry hoof. A hoof that said 'Back to sleep, you cunt. Don't ever, ever fuck with me again.' Straight across the face. Blood splattered up my ankle. His head bounced off the mirrors.

I caught a glimpse of myself in the mirror on the chest of drawers. A knot of aggression. An ugly head. I didn't know myself.

'Fuck off!' I shouted, attacking my own reflection. 'Fuck off!'

I left knowing that the city was no longer big enough for me. It was no longer safe. It was no longer my home. I didn't have a home. I left. For good.

Chapter Fourteen

On the Road

I hit the road and drove. I drove and drove, oblivious to everything around me. Not caring about the direction as long as it was away. I just needed to be gone. It wouldn't take the police long to find the mess at Mick's. It would definitely be a hospital job.

I pulled off the motorway the moment my eyes started to close involuntarily and I found myself up the arse of an artic in the slow lane. I needed to sleep. I needed to grieve. I pulled into a small B&B, dishevelled, tired and bloodied, and booked myself into a room for the night. I had no cash on me so I used my credit card. All I carried was a bag of clean clothes that I had packed to move into Ginger's. A small cardboard box of mementoes was in the boot of the car.

The receptionist, an elderly lady with hard eyes and false teeth that clacked when she talked, looked me up and down suspiciously.

'Rugger,' I told her. She looked at me questioningly but gave me a key. I found my room, locked the door and put the security chain on. I just wanted to lie down and lose the world.

When I finally came around my first thought was one of excitement, of elation. Of Ginger. It took several seconds for the dreaded truth to hit me. When it did, I felt my heart sink. I shook my head from side to side.

'Oh no. Oh no, oh no.' The only words I could find. An involuntary sob left me and I cried. I cried into the musty pillow, pulling the candlewick bedspread over my head to hide my face. There is nothing like a slice of death to make you contemplate life.

'God moves in mysterious ways.' It's what my mum would have said. God moves in very fucking mysterious ways. Anything that defies description, anything without a definable answer, anything heinous, unexplainable, unmentionable or unfathomable – the uglier the better – it all falls under the 'God moves mysteriously' banner. Third World poverty? God moves mysteriously. Your heart furs up and stops on a family holiday when you're swimming in the sea with your kids. It's all OK. It's just God moving fucking mysteriously. Your sister gets HIV after a one-off, first-time, never-done-it-before one-night stand with a cunt who says 'I love you'. Old ladies beaten the colour of a storm cloud for their measly pension. Paedophiles holding positions of power in government and schools, perverted judges, bent coppers, killer nurses. It's all OK! O-fucking-K. Because God rules and He's just having one of those 'I'm moving mysteriously' days. Worked your whole life turning a lathe, dripping sweat only to kick the crypt three days after they strapped the gold watch to your wrist? No problem. Got a little solace for you. Three words is all the medicine you need. Three words:

God moves mysteriously. Feel better now? Knew you would. It's the unanswerable problem solver.

You don't realise what a fucking cop-out it is until you lie on a spunk-stained, stiff, cigarette-burned bedsheet, looking at a yellowing ceiling. It's easier, see, for the priest with his brilliant white dog-collar and the probing fingers of perversion, living his brilliant white life, to smile sardonically and tell you that God moves mysteriously than it is to say 'Shit happens, and I don't have a fucking clue why'.

I lay there for ages in that empty room, lonely, angry and looking for answers that were not there. My hands were broken from the violence, my heart was broken from my loss. My clothes were covered with the flaky dried crimson of my labours. Every muscle was locked in pain and mourning. I could feel my mind racing and hoping to wake up soon, but at the same time I knew that nightmares didn't get this bad. Only real life gives it to you this nasty.

Guilt was colonising my thoughts. A vulture was eating me, pecking at my conscience with its sharp beak, eating me alive. Why did I get involved? Why didn't I walk out of that fucking greasy spoon café the moment that greasy spoon man poked his rectum into my greasy spoon face and offered me a free sniff? Why didn't I get the fuck out before the whole scenario sucked me in like some great dark vortex? Why didn't I keep out, butt out, fuck off, mind my own business? I had to attach, didn't I? And when you attach things take over. I should have known that. Reg had told me about Lao-tzu's *The Book of the Way* and I read it when I was on the door. I understood the concept of non-attachment, I knew that attaching to things was futile, that all things come and go and that the art of living a long, healthy, happy life was to be like a mirror, reflect everything, good, bad, pretty, ugly; but do not try to hold anything. Let it come, let it go. 'Like a cork on the waves,' Reg would say; surrender and let it take you. But never attach, never try to fight it. To have but not to attach. A paradox. A mystery. A fuck-up. But what else could I have done? Too many people walk away from the pandemic abuse that society keeps sicking up. They smother their conscience with thick layers of weak rationalisation. They tell themselves that it was 'a domestic' (that's OK then, the girl needs a dig, a bashing, a purple, public flogging, a rape). Domestic! Some lady, some daughter, mother, sister, wife is being punched and ripped and torn at midday in the city centre, right in front of a hundred witnesses. And what do they do? They close their eyes, walk past, or nudge, point and whisper. Sometimes the men take a perfunctory step forward. Arms splayed, eyebrows dropped, knuckles bunched ready for action, knowing that the wife will pull them back if they move slowly enough. The wife will save them, give them a loop-hole ('I'd have done something, but the missus pulled me back'). A tug of the elbow, a turn of the head, a knowing 'keep out of it' glance and bulls are being led away by nose-rings. He might make a few feeble 'let me at him' attempts to step forward, perhaps flail his arms in the air, fire out the odd 'I'm not happy about this' expletive. A thousand eyes but no one sees a thing. Conscience off, empathy in neutral, bottle in another jacket.

So I lay in that shitty little sticky-carpet room, the pungent, lingering smell of strawberry Shake 'n' Vac and stale tobacco hanging in the air, and I asked myself: 'What else could I have done?'

For the thousandth time I put myself back in the café on that fateful day. I rewound the whole scenario and replayed it from every angle. Where did I go wrong? What could I have changed to bring about a more palatable outcome than the one I now lived and breathed? No matter how many times I looked at it, I saw the same thing. A girl being abused by a piece of snot. A shit, a low-life, a yellow-bellied cunt. I suppose I could have called the police. Perhaps it would have been more responsible of me to hand the whole mess over to the boys in blue. They'd have dealt with it.

Yeah, that'd be about right. The police. They'd have got there in a right hurry. One hour, two closed eyes, a chipped tooth later, and they would have arrived, lights flashing, sirens wailing, truncheons raised in the offensive. Horse bolted, gate closed. Need I say more? Left his knuckles and boots on her face and ribs.

Witnesses are questioned. No one saw anything. Truncheons away, notepad out, pencil poised in the firm hand on the strong arm of a disenchanted, overrun, understaffed, hands-tied, unappreciated, going-through-a-shitty-divorce, highly answerable, unpredictably volatile, tied-by-a-pension policeman who'd rather be anywhere in the world at that moment than where he is.

'Why didn't you intervene? Why didn't you get involved?'

'It was a domestic.' Lovers' tiff. Family fall-out. Marital dispute. None of our business. Too embarrassed. Too scared. Too English. Too fucking English.

She won't press charges. Tried before, too much trouble. Two years waiting to go to court. Covert threats that don't register at the 'we need something more concrete to act upon' police station. Worry, stress, fear. By the time it enters a polished courtroom before the seen-it-all-no-longer-shocked-by-it judge, the accused has bought a suit and found God (He'll be sacked after the case, whichever way it goes) and rehearsed his 'I was brought up in a rough neighbourhood' displacement defence (it'll impress the judge, it's a language he understands). The details have faded, the bruises and breaks healed, and the judge is in the right mood to swallow. Whilst domestic violence is a heinous, unjustifiable crime, he stipulates, under the circumstances he will give a probationary slap-on-the-wrist sentence and a few old ladies' gardens to dig.

Real justice. The kind that'll have career criminals quaking in their fucking Armani boots. Apparently it is not just God who moves the pawns of life in a mysterious manner.

I replayed the scene in the café every which way: backward, forward, third person, first person, omniscient, through the eyes of Mick, through the eyes of Ginger and the girls at the café. I gave it the full DVD treatment. I came to a conclusion. Of sorts.

I did what had to be done. I did what the masses had failed to do. And I had lost everything because of it. Then I figured that I had fuck-all before, so what was there to lose? A flat that you wouldn't put a horse in, a back-breaking, ball-busting job in construction that I hated. I lost and found emptiness. So nothing lost. And nothing gained.

But this last bit was not strictly true. I could have lain on that bed for a week feeling sorry for myself and looking at life through the dark glasses of mourning, but I could not hide the fact that I had tasted love. Fleetingly I'll admit, but I had felt it all the same. And it had touched me. It had changed me beyond measure. It had all been worth it just for that brief liaison.

It was hard at that time, darkened by my loss and sickened by my situation, not to attack God, society, the law, the room, the fucking ceiling. It was hard not to attack and displace my anger at everything and anything. Part of the grieving process, I guess.

There seemed no reason to move from the bed. Brain racing, body locked by lactic acid and mourning. I was repairing. But I was not really interested in being mended. Not yet. I needed to be with my grief for a little longer before I would be able and willing to peel myself from the sheets, wash the past from my pores and place some sustenance back into my hungry body.

As I was lying on that bed, Mick would have been in a hospital bed, broken jaw, smashed teeth, closed eyes, comatose and looking at the possibility of a permanent sleep. It was good enough; I was just sorry I hadn't managed to kill the fucker. After that, if he ever got his brain back together, he would have a little explaining to do about the fire at the flats, a dead body and millions of pounds' worth of damage. His smoky clothes and fingerprints on the nails in the door would all help to take him from a hospital bed to a remand cell at Winsome Green Prison for arson and murder. All together, it had not been a good week for him.

But the police were probably looking for me too.

Chapter Fifteen

Killing Machine

When I awoke, sunlight was streaming through the thin curtains. An image of the stretcher, ginger hair hanging over the edge, flashed into my mind, and I felt the dread of loss. I pushed it aside so that I didn't have to experience the jagged shock that exploded inside me every time I remembered her face.

I sat up on the bed. I was aching from top to toe. Even my eyeballs ached if I moved them too quickly. The golf ball in my mouth was a constant reminder that my body and my mind were in no shape for fighting. It would be days, perhaps even weeks, before I could negotiate the hot lip of a teacup.

I was still caked in blood; my hands were swollen and lacerated around the knuckles. My white Adidas shirt, still on from the previous night, was torn and stretched out of shape. It had an impromptu Pollock of blood splashed across the front – some mine and some Mick's and Jimmy's. I must have looked as though I had fallen into a giant blender.

I made my way into the shower room. A rusting tap was hooked onto the wall behind a bath that might have been around to see the first millennium. Old steel taps were on permanent drip with scale ingrained under the lip where the water had worn away the enamel over a long period. I pulled the shower curtain across. It was transparent but crusty and orange at the bottom with ingrained dirt. I switched the taps on and tried to mix myself some hot water. The taps bumped a little then fired into life. Steam fogged the mirror and clouded into the bedroom. I started to unbutton my shirt, torn and stretched and bloodied. My arms and ribs ached with every movement. My fingers felt giant and stiff, and I struggled with the buttons.

Three buttons down, there was a knock at the door. I frowned, trying to figure out who it might be. I looked at my Cartier watch. The face was covered in a dry layer of crimson. I scratched it away, leaving me a clear view of the time and a fingernail tight with dry blood. It was just after 8 a.m. I remembered PC Apple and wondered if the police had traced me to the hotel. Surely not. And it was a bit early for the maid. By the looks of the room I figured that there might not even be a maid. I walked to the door. Another knock – more insistent this time.

The door was painted with a white undercoat, as if someone had primed it but never actually got around to applying the gloss. It had a small peephole in the centre. The round doorknob was brass-plated with a little security knob in the centre. It was on lock. I leaned forward to look through the peephole whilst simultaneously reaching to release the safety chain and open the door. Before I could look the phone rang behind me. I stopped mid-action. Phone ringing, door knocking, shower running. Which should I attend to first? I hadn't eaten for an age so my blood sugar was all over the place. It was making it hard for me to think. Decisions that would normally be made automatically in a second were laboured and slow.

'Hold on a sec!' I shouted through the door.

The phone was by the bed, sat on a small table. I walked around the bed and picked it up.

'Hello?'

'This is reception. Two of your friends are on their way up. Make sure you're all out by ten because the cleaner's coming,' she snapped.

I put the phone down. I felt empty. My legs had gone spaghetti. My arse was as baggy as a wet woollen sleeve. I felt an almost uncontrollable urge to shit my pants. I had to think. Part of me wanted to believe – as ridiculous as it might sound – that the men had made a mistake and knocked on the wrong door. But they'd said they were my friends. My mind raced for any rational reason why two men would be knocking at my door at eight in the morning. Could it be the police? But the police wouldn't have called themselves friends. Why lie when the truth is enough?

I knew that there was no way out. My early-bird visitors were not there to socialise. This was a come-back on my dirty deed the day before. But why? And how had they found me so quickly? Sure, Mick's mates would be a little peeved that I had moulded the lad a new head, and perhaps they'd enact some kind of revenge if I ever dared to set foot in their gaff. But taking the trouble to search me out so quickly and professionally? It didn't make any sense to me at all.

They knocked on the door again. Hard. Insistent.

A shot of adrenalin dropped like a bomb and raced through my whole body like I was plugged into the mains. Even my feet were tingling. I quickly scanned the room looking for an appendage. Anything with the potential to injure. Anything that would help me to equalise a situation that was heavily out of balance.

'Hold on a second, I'm just getting dressed!' I shouted, trying to hide the tremor in my voice. I scanned the room fast. There was a wooden chair in the corner, too big to be swinging in such a small space, but it would do if I could find nothing else. The telly was an old Granada, heavy as a dead politician. Buttons the size of saucepans. If I could pick that up it might be useful for dropping on toes. No. Too Keystone Cops. I needed something that could cause damage short range and heart-beat fast. The kind of damage that left aggressors with more than a throbbing big toe and the threat of nail loss. There was a pen and paper on the desk by the door. Maybe I could write them a very nasty note. That'd really scare them. The pen would be OK if I rammed it in an unsuspecting eye. It worked in the James Bond films. In real life it was less likely. The eye is a minute target, heavily protected by the skull and cheekbones. I raced over and placed the pen in my pocket, just in case. You never knew.

There was nothing else. Nothing. I felt naked. The only thing in this room that might fight these guys off was the smell. I scanned the room for an escape route, desperate now. There was a window by the bed. I raced over to the door and peeped through the spy-hole. The men on the other side were definitely in a different league to Mick and Jimmy. Heavy set. Hard faced. Fat hands. Bulbous knuckles. The kind of don't-fuck look that buckled knees. Bad intention jumped from every pore. One of the men was holding a long sports bag. The zip was undone and the bag was gaping open. I could see the teak handle of what looked like a rifle or shotgun. His right hand hovered over the bag, ready to dig into it the second some unsuspecting bloke opened his hotel door expecting a maid. I felt the breath stop in my chest. My heart did a drum-roll. My arse twitched to the beat, threatening to dump its load at any second. My internal dialogue was stuck on 'Fuck, fuck, fuck'. I looked again at the window. Then through the peephole. Back to the window again.

It suddenly occurred to me that this was how Mick must have felt when I entered his house whilst he was in the shower. Instant karma.

I raced around the bed and tried to open the window. It was one of those old stainless-steel jobs, built in the seventies, meant to last forever. The metal on the sill was bubbled and rough. The windowpane was opaque and layered with dirt. The swivel lock in the middle wouldn't turn. I strained my fingers to make it open but it was stuck tight. It felt as though it had been welded. Closer inspection showed me that it had.

I was welded into a death cell. My own personal tomb. A duck in a fairground shooting alley.

Outside the window I could see the gravelled car park. A plush black Range Rover was parked right next to my heap. Smoked glass. Twelve-inch wheels. Wipers on the headlights. I tried to open the window lock again, as if the welding might miraculously disappear. It didn't budge. I tried to lift the window anyway, despite the fact that it was frozen shut. No joy.

Bang! The door behind me was kicked in with a stomach-churning crash. My heart and my mouth met.

The door yanked and rattled onto the security chain. I thanked fuck that I'd thought to put it on. The stubby black barrels of a shotgun poked through the small gap.

'I can't fucking see him,' I heard a disembodied voice shout from the other side of the door.

'Just fucking shoot,' said another.

The gun was aimed in my direction as though it had its own set of eyes and they had spotted me at the window. It hovered on me for a hesitating second that seemed to stretch on for ever. My life did not flash before me. I just froze to the spot, mouth open like a flycatcher. I put my hands above my head instinctively as though the gun might see that I had surrendered. If I had a white flag that would have gone up too.

The barrels hovered menacingly. I waited for the explosion and the death that it would bring. I felt hopelessly vulnerable. My life at that point was no longer in my own hands. Providence was in the driving seat. Poking through the door on the end of two barrels I could see an arm keeping the gun steady. The arm of the man that was trying to take my life. Strange feeling that, looking at an arm that could kill you. No features, no face. No eyes to look into or lock on to. Just impersonal killing fingers that could not be reckoned or bartered with. The arm, I suddenly realised, was my only chance of getting out of this thing alive. I had to attack the arm.

'Shoot the fucker, shoot it!' yelled the second bloke.

The door was kicked again in frustration, smashing the bottom panel. The security chain shuddered and rattled but held. I knew what I had to do to buy myself a little time. I didn't need much. These lads had to be in and out in a hurry. And with all the noise they were making they would be drawing attention to themselves. Attention meant witnesses, phone calls to the local police station and the ultimate threat of getting caught with red hands. I knew I had to run at the door and slam it hard into that disembodied arm before the other arm, the one straining on the trigger, started to get itchy. One blast from that baby and I'd have been pebbledash. I knew what I had to do, and I knew I had a second in which to do it but terror froze me. My hands were high in the defensive, my bottom lip was on the floor. I was an escaping convict caught in a spotlight. My instinct was screaming 'Run, run, run!' My intellect was saying 'Where the fuck to?' My training was demanding 'Step through the fear and charge at that fucking door. Now!'

I was hovering, my feet felt glued to the floor, stopping me from going either forward or back. My legs had gone hollow and were threatening to collapse under me. My mind was still stuck on 'fuck, fuck, fuck, fuck, fuck ...'

Suddenly a vision of Ginger flashed through my mind and I felt something click inside me.

'ARRGGGHHHH!' The scream erupted from my mouth all on its own. It broke the deadlock. Smashed the indecision. I ran at the door, demented. I was running at death. Along the line of fire, right into the barrel of the gun. Attacking death. Defying death. It was the only way I was actually going to avoid its clammy fingers. I let out another banshee scream as I ran.

On the other side of the door I could hear the panicky words, 'Shoot it! Shoot it, you cunt. Shoot it!'

Smash! Too late. I ran a fourteen-stone shoulder into the door just above the handle, smashing it into the arm and the gun. The arm took all of the impact. The fingers stretched into a taut claw of pain and the gun dropped to the floor. A scream of agony came from behind the door. Panic. Scuffling feet, a race for the gun as it hit the floor, half in and half out of the room. I reached for the gun: my life depended on it. The scream echoed off the walls. I heard the body stagger backwards and slump against the wall of the corridor with a whimper of pain. I grabbed at the barrel. At the same time, another hand, also life-dependent, grabbed the trigger end. I knew I had to own the gun if I was to stay alive. My new opponent probably felt exactly the same. Both of us grabbed the weapon at the same time and pulled. The gun was yanked back and forward, in and out of the room in a grotesque tug-of-war. A breathless cry came from my mouth, the kind of sound you made in a playground fight with an older, bigger boy. From somewhere – I'm not quite sure where – I found a little reserve courage, the kind that you keep for a rainy day, and rammed the door again with every ounce of my strength and body weight. I lunged just as the gun was more inside the room than out and his arm was most exposed. *Crash!* Another hand clawed in pain, another disembodied scream. He let go of the gun and I fell back with the sudden lightness of the weapon, a veritable feather now without all that body weight on the other end.

I quickly found my feet, braver now that I had two barrels full of shot as my back-up. Trembling, I rammed the barrel through the gap in the door and aimed it at the hapless pair. Both of them were holding on to their injured arms like they were going to fall off. The first guy was in agony, he had taken the biggest blow because I had run at the door. The second guy was more angry than hurt. He was hovering between his injured friend and the door, unsure whether to have another kick at the lock or help his mate who was rolling around trying to find a space without pain. When he saw the barrel of the gun pointing in his direction, his eyes and sockets separated. He dived to the floor, trying to get out of my firing range. Not much chance of that. A gun like this was capable of spraying wide-angle death. He backed against the wall, trying to become one with the wallpaper. One shot from this baby and he would be.

'Don't shoot! Don't shoot! Don't fucking shoot!' He was a record stuck on repeat. A child's voice escaping from a man's body. I knew the feeling, I was sharing it.

'Stay back, stay fucking back! Stay where you are!' I shouted.

'Don't shoot!'

'Stay back!'

'Don't shoot!'

'Stay fucking back!'

We were both breathless and simultaneously shouting in a cacophony of noise. His hands hovered pleadingly in front of him, trying to calm me down. We both went quiet, neither of us quite sure what to do next. A moan of agony came from the first bloke. He was curled in a foetal position and cradling his smashed limb.

'He's broke me fucking arm,' he moaned. Aggression lined the words, as if he was using the anger to dull the pain.

My arms were trembling. My finger felt heavy on the trigger. I had never held a gun before. Never. But I understood enough from watching the films to know about triggers and how to pull them and the bloody consequences I should expect. The guy at the wrong end of the barrel also understood enough to know that a shotgun in the hands of an angry amateur was unpredictable and very, very dangerous. I felt the urge to pull hard on that trigger and destroy them both. I couldn't believe that this was happening. I had never held a gun before, other then those in the amusement arcades. Now I was gunned up and seconds away from my first kill. I was out of my league. This was a big jump from the fisticuffs I knew, very different from fights outside chip shops with knuckledusters.

'Don't shoot, for fuck's sake! Put it down.'

Yeah, right.

His voice had become quieter now, pleading. He must have felt the weight of my finger on the trigger. He must have felt his own life in the balance. He was backed as far up the wall as he could possibly be without peeling off the paper and climbing into the plaster. His hands were raised in a shield, dialogue in begging mode. Now his arsehole was in charge.

Old Broken Arm had gone pale at the gills. His hand and wrist looked pumped up, raw sausage fingers looking disproportionately large. He was breathing fast and heavily, trying to lock out the pain. I kept my gun trained on the wallflower.

'Who the fuck are you?' I asked.

'Look, kid, lower the weapon ...' He slowly got to his feet as he spoke.

'Stay the fuck where you are or I'll make your head into a fucking colander!' He did as he was told, eyes locked on the gun.

'OK, OK. Steady, steady.' He was saying everything twice in case I didn't get it the first time. He was nervous, he didn't know what I was capable of. He had every right to be nervous; I didn't know what the fuck I was capable of either.

'Who the fuck are you?' This time I was louder, more insistent. I jammed the gun forward to underline the fact that I wanted an answer. I was ready to use it. As far as I could see, I had nothing to lose. These maniacs had given me no reason to try and keep on their good side. That made me the most dangerous man in the world.

'OK. OK,' he said. 'Calm down. Fuck's sake, calm down. We just want the gear.'

'Gear?'

'Look,' he explained, 'you did a job on Mick and Jimmy. Fair play. But the gear. You shouldn't have taken the fucking gear.'

I was confused. 'What fucking gear, you penis? What the fuck are you on about?'

'Jimmy told us the crack. William ain't happy.'

'What crack? And who the fuck is William? I haven't got a fucking clue what you're on about.'

He looked over at Broken Arm and shrugged his shoulders, face full of doubt.

'The gear under the floorboards. The brown.' He said it as if it would all make perfect sense to me. 'The drugs. You taxed Mick.

I mean, fair enough, the guy's a pleb, but it ain't his gear, it's William's. He ain't happy. You wouldn't be on top form if some cunt – no offence – if someone took three hundred grand's worth of your merchandise. Look, do yourself a huge favour, kid. Slide the gun away. Fuck's sake. Eh? We've come to sort it out.' He curved his mouth into an ironic smile because, obviously, the 'sorting out' part had fallen at the first hurdle.

I was stunned mute. Brown? Heroin? Drugs? Me?

'I've had no fucking drugs! I don't know nothing about no fucking drugs. Why the fuck would I want drugs?'

They looked at each other, as confused as I was.

'You'd better tell this William bloke to start looking a bit closer to home.' Three hundred grand? Still couldn't get my swede around that. 'Look, all I wanted from that cunt was nine pints. I took that, nothing more.'

'We believe you, we believe you, now lower the gun. Lower it.' It was the Wallflower. I deliberately lifted the gun and aimed it directly at him. I wasn't in a trusting mood. Wallflower moved towards his mate, gently so as not to trigger my finger. Arms still raised like he was praying to Allah, he leaned over and helped his mate off the floor, never once taking his hundred-yard stare from the business end of my gun and the gap in the door. I trained the barrels on him, just in case he found a sudden surge of courage and went for the title.

'We're going now,' he said slowly and quietly. 'Wind your neck in.'

They backed down the corridor, still breathing heavily, still pale and pained, until they were out of sight.

'I'll be fucking back!' I heard one of them shout from the stairwell.

Yeah, all right Arnie. I'll be waiting.

I waited at the crack of the door for a couple of minutes before I dared move away. It was only when I heard the screech of car tyres from the car park that I ran to the window and looked out. I saw the tail end of the Range Rover disappear into the morning traffic, leaving a cone of dust and exhaust smoke in its wake. I walked back over to the door and placed a chair under the handle to force it shut. The top of the chair didn't reach the handle like it does in all the films so I just propped it by the door as an extra precaution. I sat on the bed, still holding the shotgun, knuckles white from the grip. I rocked back and forward, body in shock, mind in limbo. The door banged. I jumped to attention, gun raised in the offensive.

'Who is it?' I called.

'Reception. We've had a complaint from a customer. Said there was shouting and arguing.'

My body filled with relief. I walked over to the door and moved the chair. I looked through the peephole, just in case. It was the lady from reception. I unlatched the chain and opened the door. I checked past her, both ways. She looked at the hole in the door, then at me. I held the gun behind the door so that she couldn't see it.

'Your door's broken,' she said, stating the obvious. 'It'll have to go on your bill.'

'OK,' I said, too tired to argue.

'And any other damage,' she added, eyes flicking past me to look into the room.

'OK,' I said in a firm don't-take-the-piss tone. She backed away from the door.

'All right then. As long as you know.'

Chapter Sixteen

Trigger Happy

I closed the door for the second time, propped the chair behind it again and put the security chain on. I sat back on the bed, still holding on to the weapon. I closed my eyes, breathed deeply through my nose and filled my body with oxygen. My heart was still racing, limbs trembling uncontrollably, endorphins racing through me. I had survived. I was aware, even as I felt relief, that luck would not be enough if I wanted to last in the world I was now being sucked into. I knew that this would not be the end of it, and that if I wanted to keep this heart beating until old age, I would have to get it back into shape and stop relying on providence.

My mind was already reliving, replaying frame by frightening frame, the last few moments. What if I had not placed the chain on the door? What if there had not been a chain? Many of the new hotels didn't have internal security chains on the doors. What if the chain had not held and that maniac and his two smoking barrels had gained entry to my room? I could have been in the shower, wet, naked, blasted into the decor. They would have had to get me out with a shovel, carry me to the morgue in a bucket. Dead.

I nearly died.

I sucked the air from the room, desperately trying to slow my galloping heart; it was up there with my tonsils. My lungs filled with strawberry Shake 'n' Vac. I stood up. I looked out of the window again. I needed to make sure that the threat was gone. My nerves were in the wind. I knew that this threat was never going to go. Some threats are for life. That would take a lot of accepting.

I was losing it. My mind, my courage, my sanity were slipping fast and I was struggling to hold on. But the more I panicked, the worse it got and the more I paced the room trying to run from my thoughts, the harder they chased. I looked out on to the desolate car park, checking again for threats. There was nothing but light rain and empty cars and sunlight bouncing from the tarmac.

I was losing the plot. My mind and emotions were spinning, stretched to a level beyond me, to a place that I had only ever imagined in my worst nightmares. I had seen violence. I had been involved in it since I was in nappies. Smashed the odd head at school when the word 'tramp' was thrown at me from the mouths of the ignorant bullies. The training, the doors, hundreds of fights. Even the buildings demanded off-the-peg violence when hardened and weathered men used intimidation and fear to get their muck and bricks faster. But I had never been stretched this far. My body had coped. A bit stiff, a little sluggish, but it had coped. It was my mind that was trailing behind like the fat kid on a school cross-country run. My internal dialogue, the voice that had kept me iron through some very demanding times had switched off. A voice that I did not recognise as my own – a scared and cowardly voice – had taken over. I needed to get a grip on it. And soon. This situation was far from over.

I didn't bother with a shower. Suddenly lost the need to be clean. The threat was still fresh. The room was no longer safe, my world was no longer safe. I needed to be away, and quickly. The shotgun was still hot in my hands. I pushed it up the leg of my spare trousers and tucked it under my arm. I would lose it the minute I found a drain or a ditch. Fuck, this wasn't subtle. I gathered my gear together and left my room. The sports bag the scroats had brought the gun in was abandoned outside my door. I shoved the gun, still wrapped in the trousers, back inside the bag and covered it with my clothes. I looked all around me as I made my way downstairs. There was no threat here any more.

The receptionist gave me a funny look as I left. I gave her a funny look back. She was not the only one who could make faces.

I walked across the car park to my Cortina. My body was a throbbing mass of aches and pains and hurt. Every movement sent spasms of pain through my body. The air was fresh and sharp in my throat. I took a deep breath, looking for a little sustenance. The rain had stopped. It was a fantastic morning, spoiled by the fact that my life was missing, presumed dead. I felt conspicuous, carrying a shotgun, even if it was hidden in the bag.

I opened the boot of my car and dumped the bag in the back. Walked around and placed the key in the driver's door, fingers fat from their impact on bony heads. Just as I slid into the seat, my mind in neutral, *bang!* Fuck!

It was me and the stars. I felt a heavy fist burst my eyebrow into an oozing mass. The hot blood ran into my eye and down my cheek. I instinctively ducked my head and lifted my shoulders to protect my face from the blows that I knew would follow. At the same time, mind in turmoil, I was trying to make sense of what was happening. I tried to climb back out of the car to give myself a fighting chance. I was stopped by another blow, this time a nauseating fist in my right ear. The punch was heavy and sent my head into a buzzing frenzy. I could hear the scuffle of feet on gravel as my attacker lined up each punch. The next shot landed on the top of my head. A bad shot for the man who owned the fist; it cracked at the knuckles as bone hit bone. Broken knuckles would not be enough to stop the lad from attacking me, in fact it would probably be fifteen minutes before he even felt the pain, but it would place his hand in plaster for a month afterwards.

The punches rained in on me, porridge-thick and greyhound-fast. I tried again to leave the car. Fuck me, here we go again. I had fallen for the oldest trick in the book. The samurai had a saying: 'After the battle, tighten your helmet straps.' Your most vulnerable time in a fight – apart from the first three seconds before it goes from verbal to physical – is after the fight when the body and mind try to find some kind of balance, some kind of normality. You are usually so relieved that the fight is over that you totally switch off to the possibility of a second strike, the double-tap. It catches many fighters on the hop. Their minds are already down the pub, celebrating the fact that they have survived and it leaves their awareness, their guard, unprepared for the second strike. I had made the same mistake this day for the first time. Switched off too early. Now I was paying for it.

I could feel the weight of the punches as they landed, but they didn't have a vulnerable target to hit; I took most of the blows on the shoulders and skull. I covered my face just in time to stop a boot that was aimed at my teeth. I felt the weight of the kick on my arms, the lace-knot kicking into my forearm, the waft of leather in my nostrils. Behind the blows I could hear the vague grunts and expletives of my attacker. He underlined each attack with a 'fuck' or a 'cunt' or a 'bastard', but my ear was still buzzing and throbbing from the previous blow, as if a family of bees had been punched into my eardrum. The noise became a cacophony of sounds that mixed into an unrecognisable mush. One thing I could hear was my aggressor puffing heavily. His wind had already deserted him, and every breath that he took was in real danger of bringing some breakfast up with it. He stood back, trying to catch his breath. He was like many big-hitter doorman types; they were KO merchants, used to knocking people out with one, maybe two blows. The very first time that the KO fails them and they're forced into an elongated match fight, they realise their lack of fitness. With the majority of men, even those who can have a fight, when their stamina runs out, their bottle does too; when one goes, the other quickly follows.

I was hurting everywhere, and my own fitness was not at its best, but I was no three-second fighter. I gritted my teeth and threw myself into him, pushing him away and managing to get out of the car at the same time, guard raised and ready for a rumble. Heart beating fast but no real fear this time. I was taken by surprise and that had forced me to react spontaneously without the crippling pre-fight build up. I stood facing my attacker. He had stumbled back; his guard was at half-mast, lead fists too heavy to keep up, his eyes wild, his breath laboured. It was Wallflower, the guy I had pointed the shotgun at outside the hotel room. He must've driven off to trick me but just parked around the corner. At least I didn't have to worry about back up: old Broken Arm was most definitely out of the game.

'You're fucking dead!' he said, and spat at me. He was too tired to attack with his fists any more so he was using words and bodily fluids instead.

It was not the worst thing I'd been attacked with. One guy outside a nightclub took his dick out and pissed on me because I had refused him entry to the club. Pissed all over my shoes and trouser turn-ups. I was fuming. Stank of piss for days. I left him in an unconscious heap on the pavement with his dick dangling out of his flies and about twenty customers looking on.

'Oh yeah?' I said, engaging Wallflower's brain just enough to give me the opening I was looking for.

Telling me that I was dead was probably the worst thing he could have done, especially considering the fact that he was fighting on fumes and would be in no position to defend such a bold statement. He was waiting for a second wind that would not come – not in time anyway. It was all the opening I needed. He had given me his best shot and I had taken it and more. Now it was my turn.

Bang! I screeched across the gravel with my leading left leg, a sprinter from the starting block. I travelled maybe five feet in less than a second with a right cross that might have been shot from a cannon. It landed on the front of his jaw, just below his teeth, and it smashed the fucking life out of him. As he spiralled backwards, the contents of his jacket pocket fell onto the gravel with a clatter. A wallet, a business card, a bit of coinage. My punch was perfect – but I had practised it in the gym tens of thousands of times until it came with its own navigation system. It might've been years since I'd trained properly, but you never forgot. My skills were a little rusty maybe, but not lost. All I had to do was take my right hand out of my pocket and it did the rest all by itself. I had worked on this punch for hundreds of hours in the gym, and when the others were in the shower and on their way to the pub I was still throwing punches and perfecting technique.

He was out before he fell. Eyes closed. His body abandoned him as soon as his brain was switched off, falling like a slaughtered cow. It was a weird sight. I literally punched him out of his shoes. It was like a cartoon. He went one way, his shoes flicked the other, as though they had a life of their own, like rats abandoning ship.

His body shot off like a rocket from a milk bottle, then collapsed mid-air: a spent firework. He folded, falling to the floor, head limp. A carcass. He hit the deck with a heavy clump and his skull whiplashed into the gravel. Little bits of stone embedded themselves into his face and scalp. It would be weeks before he would be able to tidy his hair without dragging acres of scab through the teeth of his comb.

I looked down on the sleeping lump of shit. I hated this faeces to pieces. I hated every ounce. In him I saw every antagonist that had ever forced themselves into my life, every cunt that had ever kicked me in a direction that I didn't want to go, hurt me more than was bearable, scared me into a mass of insecurity, a life of supplication, intimidated me and left my confidence for dead. He was every blow that my dad had landed on my mum. He was part of Mick's violent world, a world that had obliterated Ginger, that had stolen happiness from my world. I hated men of his ilk. I suddenly had a horrible realisation that I hated men like him because I was a man like him. A red mist enveloped my mind. I hoofed him in the mouth as hard as I could, as hard as I could kick. I even stepped forward to add a run-up, as if I was converting a ball. Every fibre of my body went behind that kick, smashing his front teeth out with one sickening crunch, the sound you hear when you break a leg off a cooked chicken. I kicked him so hard my foot hurt. It sent an explosion of blood up my sock and across my shoe and left a gaping, flapping hole in his lips that'd need a good plastic surgeon with a sharp needle and a yard of catgut.

I bent forward to adjust my sock. The blood was already penetrating through to my skin. I hated the wet feeling of someone else's blood seeping through my sock. It felt like he was still a threat. I adjusted the sock, stretched it at the instep to break the wet contact of blood and skin. The splash went right up the leg of my trousers; a stain that would stay long after the Persil had done its job. His body spun as I kicked him, a break-dancer on a gravel dancefloor. He let out an involuntary grunt as I booted the remaining air from his mouth. His eyes remained closed. It was like kicking a corpse. My face was contorted, girning, hateful. There was satisfaction in that kick. A feeling of retribution. A good feeling. It was quickly followed by a feeling of guilt; kicking teeth from heads should not make you feel good, no matter how deserved it might be.

I bent over and picked up the business card that had jumped from his pocket. The lettering lifted from the card in gold: *ECSTASY – Manchester's Premier Nightclub, 1-5 Baldwin Street*. At the bottom of the card I read *Proprietor: William Collins*. This must be the same William that had my name on his job sheet. I put the card into my pocket.

I looked down at my opponent. He didn't look such a threat now, no longer a big aggressive man. He was unconscious, and without his double-barrelled appendage he looked harmless. Like a baby. After I'd transmuted the hate from my boot to his face I felt kind of sorry for him. Unconscious, he had become re-humanised. I could see a man under the hard skin of gangsterdom. He was someone's love. He shared someone's heart. Under different circumstances he might have even been my friend. Had I met him down the gym or on the sites, under more cordial circumstances, who knows? In situations like this it was him or me: you can be either the hammer or the anvil. Your choice. I chose life, and that meant fighting for it with the only weapon I had.

'We're all fucking dead,' I said as I walked away towards my car.

About a mile down the road, just before the motorway, I noticed a small bridge over a canal. I parked the car on the side of the road. Checked to make sure that the traffic was quiet, then took the gun from the bag out of the boot – making sure to wipe it clean of fingerprints in case it was ever found – and lobbed it into the deep water. The gun had frightened me. I didn't want to keep it, didn't want reminding of how close I came to an early expiry. Didn't want reminding of how close I myself had come to investing in murder. The dark and seductive urge I felt to pull that trigger at the hotel was scary. How easy it would have been to kill in anger and lose myself to a different world. Guns were out of my league, a level above me, a step into a darkness that I did not want to make.

Chapter Seventeen

Body Fuel

The last two days were still stained on my body, etched into my mind. I couldn't get the drugs thing out of my head. I could not believe that Jimmy the boxer, Jimmy the cunt, had set me up so badly. I had never taken drugs, never, and now here I was being accused of stealing three hundred grand's worth. I knew that my demolition job on Jimmy would take me off his Christmas card list, that much was expected. You don't strangle a man unconscious and hope to stay mates; you expect the bad feeling that comes after a first meeting like that. But three hundred K. Fuck me, what was that all about? No wonder my door was kicked down by two men and their shotgun. No wonder this William fellow was so pissed off.

My mind raced. I knew enough to understand that this thing was not over. Not while three hundred K of high was missing, presumed stolen. What to do? How do you even begin to deal with a situation like this? These men had found me once, and in a hurry. Inside twelve hours. And I had left them plenty of reason to want to find me again, which meant that they *would* find me, and sooner rather than later. They wouldn't rest until they'd redressed the balance. I was tired, confused. I needed food, fuel, sustenance, even though the very thought of it sent waves of nausea pulsing through my body. My throat was locked with tension, my mouth lined with a dry, sticky paste. But I knew I had more battles ahead of me that would need fuelling.

The first thing that disappears when fear is on the agenda is appetite. The first thing most people do when the appetite goes is to stop eating. And when they stop eating, stop supplying the body with vital nutrients and fuel, the body stops functioning properly. I knew from experience that I had to eat, whether I wanted to or not.

Power is not about having the ability to control others, nor about making others do your bidding. It is about having the ability to control yourself, having the ability to make yourself do your own bidding. In this case it was having the ability to make myself eat, even though every single part of me didn't want to. Anyone can walk into a gym and push metal; the physical part is the easy bit. It's the cerebral stuff, working with your head, controlling your thoughts, forcing yourself to do the things you are afraid to do, stopping yourself from doing the things that you know you shouldn't do, that's what turns most men to mice. Like the car, I needed fuel if I was to take this vehicle any further.

Three miles down the road I pulled into a café. The toilets were round the back. I went into the Gents and looked at myself in the mirror. My eyebrow was split and gooey with blood, my eye swollen and bloodshot. I rinsed my face as best I could and wiped the blood off my trousers. Because they were black, the blood hardly showed on the material. I was as presentable as I was ever going to be.

The café was tidy and clean with laminated menus. Every meal served was displayed on the wipe-clean shiny piece of card. A chubby waiter met me at reception. A big spot on his chin dominated my attention. It was stretched and yellow and ready to burst. I tried to ignore it but it was difficult. My tired eyes were drawn to it, and when I spoke I found myself talking to his spot. I thought that perhaps he should have had one of those blue catering plasters across it to protect the customers from any fall-out should it Mount Etna halfway through his shift.

He looked me up and down warily.

'Rugby,' I lied again.

He looked relieved. 'Smoking or non?'

'Non,' I replied, looking at the floor. There was no way I was going to have a conversation with a spot.

He sat me at a table by the window, one that allowed me to see into the car park and at the same time keep an eye on the main entrance. It also allowed me to eat my meal unspoiled by the carcinogenic waft of someone else's addiction.

My personal security, though tired, was fully manned. I looked around the room. Six of the twenty tables were occupied, mostly by middle-aged middle-management types. I looked at the menu. The lad hovered over me, pen held over pad in anticipation.

'Drinks?' The pen dabbed rhythmically on the pad.

'A pot of coffee please.'

'C-o-f-f-e-e.' He spelled it out aloud as he wrote, and then looked back at me, as if he was expecting me to comment. I raised my eyebrows into a question mark.

'That all?' he asked.

'I'll look at the menu.' I buried my head behind the laminate to get away from the spot.

He wandered off and returned with my pot of coffee. I poured it quickly and took my first drink since the day before. I flinched as my swollen lips touched the hot rim of the cup. The liquid hit my parched throat and sent tingles of relief over every cell of my body. It was strong and sweet and welcome. The aroma was deep treacle. I sucked it in and felt my mood lift to the ceiling tiles. The first cup went down in one and I quickly poured the second. I allowed the caffeine to make its way to my brain. I took another deep breath. I remembered waking up in Ginger's flat to the smell of coffee wafting out of the kitchen. I scanned the room again looking for threats and seeing none, just overweight men with mouths full of fried food and minds full of deadlines and projects and a better life. I had every right to be paranoid. In the space of a few days, my life had become one gigantic threat with violence lurking in every corner.

The room was open-plan with a cooking grill on display, allowing you to see the chef at his work. It says to anyone remotely interested 'We're so confident about our standards we will even let you watch your food as it is being cooked.' The chef looked young, maybe twenty. Just out of catering college, his first job. Probably went into catering with his eye on cruise ships and London restaurants, cooking for royalty and celebrities and Egon Ronay recognition. No one goes to catering college to end up grilling and frying in a café on the side of a dual carriageway.

The food was good enough. Greasy spoon style with portions like your mum would serve. When the food eventually came – it took an age, the waiter had spelled the meal out as he wrote it in his pad – I began shovelling it down, oblivious to taste and texture. I just needed the fuel. Every mouthful was an effort. Every bite, every swallow took massive discipline. I felt as though my stomach was the size of a sixpence; it was like trying to swallow old carpet tiles. It would have been easy for me to leave the plate three-quarters full. My belly was not in the mood for a culinary work-out. My throat had closed early, gone home for the day. Every single mouthful was forced down.

It was hard not to allow myself to spiral into a pool of depression. My head was full of fog and dark cloud. My body was a mass of tightening knots. My resolve had gone jelly at the knees. You can usually handle violence when it happens, especially when your body is no stranger to the gym, and your mind has a history of enduring discomfort and threat. But it quickly wears you down afterwards. Empties you like a car battery being hammered but not recharged. That's how I felt. A flat battery sat in a restaurant, eating a meal that my body needed but my mind did not want. My body was stuck in fight or flight, nervous system in survival mode. An army of adrenalin had colonised me, taken over. I was on constant alert because I sensed constant threat. But there's a big problem with adrenalin when it comes in floods. In order to survive the fight or flight response, the brain draws all the energy reserves it can from all around the body, ready for a thirty-second blast of ferocious fighting or speedy fleeing. All resources are channelled to the front line, to the major working muscles like the thighs, the back, the chest, the arms. The immune system is temporarily closed down, peripheral vision is lost, the digestive system is suppressed. Every single function that is deemed unnecessary for fight or flight is put on stand-by. It is the sympathetic nervous system protecting the organism: the body. And that's a good thing in itself; a survival mechanism. It keeps you safe from external threat. Once the external threat has gone, the body looks for some kind of normality.

Problems begin to occur when the threat not only fails to go away, but increases. The body is on constant alert, hence the digestive system stays switched off and the body fills to the brim with stress hormones, all psyched up but with nowhere to go. If these rogue hormones don't find an exit, a behavioural release, they start to act caustically, damaging cells in the body.

I had to fool my body, make it think that the threat had gone. This destructive process was happening to me in a big way. I had days, maybe weeks, perhaps even months of adrenalin to come, but with little possibility of release or reprieve. With the enemy I faced now I might possibly have a whole lifetime of employing games that would trick my body to make it stop playing the same old tune so that I could lift the needle past the scratch in the record.

If I obeyed my feelings and decided that I couldn't eat a bean, the beans would lie on my plate like stones. So I deceived my body and ate everything. Every last mouthful. I even wiped the bread over the bean juice and cleaned the plate. The spot returned.

'That was a fantastic meal, I enjoyed every mouthful.' Though my voice was flat with depression I picked it up an octave. A blatant lie, but a lie in a good cause. The lad smiled, displaying a mouthful of crooked teeth. He smiled as though he had cooked the meal personally and the compliment was for him.

'I'll tell the chef,' he said excitedly. 'He'll be pleased, he's new.'

He scuttled off to pass on the good tidings. I watched him go behind the open grill and speak animatedly to the young lad in the chef's uniform. The chef flushed red and looked over at me with a shy smile.

The food lay in my stomach like a slab of concrete. When I burped I could taste it all over again. I sensed that if I burped too hard I might see it all over again as well. The fear was still thick inside me. I closed my eyes, breathed in deeply through my nose and filled my lungs with oxygen. It was uncomfortable with so much food and so much fear and so much sorrow in me. Breathe in and out slowly. Diaphragmatic breathing, Reg had called it.

He knew it all, did Reg. Not just the physical stuff, the punching, the strangling the kicking; he knew the head stuff too. His house was a library of books: fighting, psychology, biography, biology, spirituality; anything that related to man and his ability to use his body. He passed it on to us at the gym. He said that if you wanted to know about fighting, you had to know about yourself and how you would react physically and emotionally before, during and after an affray. You had to become a body, mind and spirit mechanic. Once you knew about yourself, you automatically knew about others because we are all made of the same stuff.

Diaphragmatic breathing, he'd told me, was what you did when you wanted to close down the sympathetic nervous system, shut off the fear, switch off the adrenalin. When you breathed in deeply through the nose and filled the lungs from the bottom to the top it fooled the brain into thinking that the threat had gone. It was a way of manually bringing the body back to normal functioning.

I closed my eyes. I breathed in deeply, held it for a couple of seconds and felt the calm slowly returning to my mind. After a couple of minutes, my stomach gurgled like an old boiler. I clicked my internal dialogue into the positive. I used soothing words in my mind as a mantra: *Calm, relaxed. I am very calm. I am very relaxed. Calm. Feeling good. Relaxed.* Sounds like bollocks, I know, but it works.

In seconds the slab of food and the anxious tightness above my solar plexus melted and my body started to slow right down. I was so tired. I could feel a calm coming over me. Sleep beckoned. My body was desperate for repair. Now that I had fed it with some protein, vitamins and carbohydrates it went to work. The best time for the body to repair is when you sleep. That's why my eyelids went heavy and my head started to nod.

'Can I get you anything else? Shall I get you the bill?'

I jumped to attention, startled from my sleep. 'Bill please,' I replied.

When I paid, I picked up half a dozen of the free sugar lollipops by the till and took them out to the car. I hoped the sugar would keep me awake. I was leaden with stress. It was killing me. I had to do something about it, and soon. I had made my mind up. I was going to have to find William Collins before he found me.

I was only on the road for an hour when my eyes started to abandon me again. The sugar hadn't worked. I was on the M1 north; road works and heavy traffic made progress slow. I knew that I needed to rest up and repair. If I didn't stop soon I'd find myself on an operating table having bits of glass and HGV bumper removed from my face. I pulled off at a service station and booked into a room. It was very different from the last-chance saloon I had stayed in the night before. The room was polished, shiny, new. A virgin room that looked as if it had just been built, never slept in before. You could have eaten off the carpet. Fuck, you could have eaten the carpet. It was one of those minimalist rooms, clean and tidy with sharp white blankets on the bed, folded invitingly at the pillow. The en suite was show-home new with little bottles of shampoo and conditioner and miniature soaps wrapped neatly in crispy paper. Too nice to open, too delicate to use. The toilet had a bum-friendly seat; curved not sharp, not one of those that left a red ring around your arse. On the table by the fitted wardrobe was a tray that contained a neat white kettle and a dish with individual portions of tea, coffee and hot chocolate, even a couple of complimentary shortcake biscuits.

It was starting to get chilly outside and the warmth of a new bed was welcoming. But I couldn't get into that beautiful bed while I was still so filthy. Most of the blood had flaked off and I'd managed a quick rinse in the café toilets, but I was still caked in sweat and dirt. I walked to the door. I checked that the room was locked. It was. I looked through the spy-hole. All was clear, just an empty corridor. I entered the bathroom, locked the door and soothed my aching muscles under the hot shower. I washed away all the dirt, and the traces of blood ingrained in the lines on my hands. The water stung my split eyebrow but I didn't care. I couldn't wait to get into bed.

I dried myself with the fluffy white towels and lay on the bed. My body was wasted. I got back up again and checked the windows. They were well and truly locked. I was as safe as I could be. Drew the curtains. I needed to know that I was secure. If I was going to abandon myself to sleep I needed to be sure that everything was locked and bolted.

Back on to the bed. Eyes closed. Sleep took me.

When I awoke, the room was in total darkness. I strained to look at my watch. It was too dark. I switched on the bedside lamp. The corner of the room lit up. Three in the morning and my eyes were full of grit. My body was locked stiff, it felt like rigor mortis had set in. I struggled off the bed and headed for the bathroom. Every step hurt, every muscle ached, my head was clanging. I took deep intakes of air through my nose, supplying my repairing muscles and tendons and ligaments with much-needed oxygen. In the mirror behind the toilet I watched a stranger with half-moon eyes and ten-pound eyelids piss into the loo. I wondered who the fuck he was and how he had come to this place in his life.

My mind was numb, tingling and fat like gums full of anaesthetic. I stared for a long time at a man who had aged ten years in three days. My body was thirty-five years old but I felt like a pensioner. More deep intakes of breath, a stream of piss that just seemed to keep coming.

I travelled to my dark tomorrows. A murky place with characters who might have walked straight off the set of a *Flintstones* film. I viewed the situation from every angle but only one outcome seemed realistic: a physical fight which would leave me either dead or damaged. It was unlikely that I would come away at all.

This was not the first time I had entered an affray with death as my wish. When you feel as though you have nothing to lose, death no longer holds any fear. The thought of being frightened, hurt, damaged, even killed, does not even enter into the equation. It is as though you're staring into a void, locking eyes with the Grim Reaper and saying 'Fuck you, let's have a bit then, let's get it on.' It's not brave. It's more crazy than it is brave. Looking at what I had to do through my tomorrow goggles all I could see was blood and an uncomfortable exit under a wool blanket and flashing blue lights.

I was wading up to my neck in shit and I had a choice: spend the rest of my days hiding from this William wanker, or find him and face him down. The latter was the only choice I could rationally make. It was going to happen sooner or later anyway, so by making it happen sooner at least I got to control my destiny. I no longer cared about life and death. I wasn't bothered if fronting William meant my demise. I was tired of running.

I would obviously be out-numbered for a start. Anyone who owns a nightclub has the loyalty of those whose wages they paid. And I would be dealing with honourless men who would take every advantage when I showed up at their club. I doubted very much if they would let me anywhere near William. But I would try, and anyone who got in my way would lose something. Focused intention is more deadly than a room full of weapons. A fifteen-year-old with a sharp pencil and a death wish is infinitely more dangerous than a colossus with a sawn-off and a hint of hesitation.

Back on the bed. Eyes closed. Room dark. Blocking out bullying thoughts, disturbing images, a frame-by-frame of the last three days. Pictures of Ginger kept appearing in my head. Each image sent beats of sadness through my body, each one stabbed me from the inside out. Images of beautiful ginger locks and freckled skin turned to charred and melted rope, hanging from a featureless face that was locked in a scream of death. Too tired to resist any longer, sleep took me once more and it was a blessing. Sleep was my only solace, the one sanctuary left until enough time had elapsed to heal. I wasn't sure that time could heal – it was more likely that time simply allowed layers of forgetfulness to dull and bury painful memories.

In my dreams she came to me, Ginger in all her splendour. Vivid dreams where I felt her touch and remembered our brief liaison almost verbatim. But each time, before I could wake, she turned into a thin, burnt frame with a mop of singed red mane.

When I awoke I felt a terrible melancholy. I just lay there like a corpse and allowed the negativity to envelop me. I stared at the ceiling. I remembered staring at the ceiling back in the cell when I thought I had killed Ponytail. All I wanted way back then in that other lifetime was freedom, liberty, life. Now that I had my liberty back I no longer wanted it. I didn't like the world I now inhabited. It was cold, uncaring, aggressive, pushy, clammy. Unfair.

'Un-fucking-fair?' Reg boomed into my consciousness.

It was that word. Unfair! It triggered a rage in me that I had not felt in a long time. I had used the word once at the gym after a particularly bad session that had me tapping like a typewriter. One of those sessions that was wrong from beginning to end. It happens sometimes. No matter what you do and no matter how hard you try, nothing works, and even the crap fighters tap you out and make you submit. I made the mistake of telling Reg that it was unfair, the other fighters were too good for me, too experienced, too fit. I had never seen him so angry.

'Un-fucking-fair?' he screamed.

Apparently – the other lads told me later – I'd hit on the one word in the English language that Reg was hypersensitive about. Even as I said it I could hear the sharp intakes of breath from the others. It was one of those moments where I knew I had said something bad, but wasn't quite sure what. It went so quiet in the gym that I almost expected tumbleweed to blow across the floor. Reg went red in the head and proceeded to give me what for. His lecture was filled with expletives – he liked an expletive did old Reg, he felt that it added a certain emphasis to his words. He went on to tell me over the next hour that in life there were winners and losers and he respected both because they tried. Then there were those he didn't respect, in fact, he despised them, the ones that whined and moaned and procrastinated instead of shutting their runaway mouths and dealing with it. Get your arse back off the canvas and try again, train harder, do more work, invest more time, learn, learn, fucking learn. It was never down to the fact that they might simply be having a bad day. It was because life was unfair.

'Fuck unfair!' he shouted. 'Unfair means you don't have the testicles to say "I lost and it was my own fault".' It means that you're no fighter at all because real fighters experience loss on a daily basis and they learn from it, they thrive on loss, they immerse themselves in fear and pain because that is where the growing happens. It's how they develop. They look for fighters that can beat them, training clubs that frightened the brown stuff out of them, opponents that bring blood and snot to the arena because that is exactly what enables them to grow, and if they lose they shake the other bloke's hand and thank him for the lesson. You stop losing, you stop growing.

Reg went on to explain that our power as a species was in our ability to captain our own fate; it was in our ability to mould life into any shape that suited us. He felt that life was not a sequence of random occurrences in which we had no say. Instead, the power is ours to do with as we please. But the moment we start to apportion blame, the moment we charge life with being unfair, we give away all our power.

So when I lay on that bed in the hotel room and brought blame into the equation his voice boomed in my head: 'Shut the fuck up and get off your lazy arse!'

Reg was in my head and he was barking orders. He told me to stop being such a whinging bastard and do something. Get on the floor, do some press-ups, sit-ups, burpees, Hindu squats, make a cup of tea, order a sandwich, go for a fucking run – anything other than lie there like a beached seal and complain about how unfair the world is.

I climbed off the bed. I knew he was right and I knew that despite all my woes I could do something about it. So I did. Press-ups. I struggled to do even a few but at least I was on the floor having a go. My body felt weak and injured; all the more reason to get back into shape and help the healing process. I made myself train and it took every ounce of my will-power to make it happen. Each press-up sent pulses of pain through my body. My negative internal voice screamed for rest. 'Why the fuck are you bothering?' it kept asking.

'Shut the fuck up,' I replied.

I was back in charge, firm again, solid in my thoughts, unsympathetic to any weakness that tried to take over. Pain? Bring it on. Suffering? I want more! Sadness? Did it. Handled it then, handling it now, no problem, the more the better, bring it on, bring it on, bring the fucker *on*. A little voice somewhere in the background threatened and blackmailed me.

'You can't handle it! There's more pain to come, more sadness, more depression. I'm coming, I'm coming, be ready because I'm coming'.

These snivelly little bastard voices rely entirely on panic and fear, that's their mainstay, that's their food, their sustenance. The moment you engage them, the second you listen in and allow yourself to be intimidated, they grow fat and multiply. Negative thoughts are like watermelon seeds: if planted firmly and fed they have the potential to grow to 350,000 times their own size.

You kill these little bastards by starving them of your attention and of your fear. This is where the discipline comes in. Thinking bad thoughts is really the easiest thing in the world. They enter your consciousness, seemingly uninvited, and even a second of attention is enough for them to plant roots. Then every subsequent meal that you feed them fattens them and makes them grow. If you give them no attention from the very beginning they can't establish roots. If you make a mistake and the seed takes root, the next thing is to starve it until it dies. It is a mental scrimmage that few ever get to grips with, not because it is a difficult fight (and let's be clear here, it *is* a fucking difficult fight) rather because people don't know their way around a mental wrestle.

So I switched the negative voice off and dominated it with my powerful positive voice. As I trained I separated myself from my physical body as though I was a bystander watching from the sideline. Pain – there was plenty of it. Each press-up gave me some until the blood had circulated around my tired veins and the three-day ache had started to lessen. On to my back; sit-ups, one, two, three, felt like giving up almost immediately. Four, five, six, seven, I wanted to throw in the towel and lie on the bed, lie down and die. Before I knew it I was up to fifty reps. I stood back up. Hindu squats. Hands out in front. I squatted until my arse was parallel with my knees then back up again.

If you want fitness in a hurry, if you want a fuck-off, take-no-shit sinewy physique then working the thighs is the quickest way there. Most people avoid training the legs because it is the hardest and most painful exercise on God's green earth. It is murderous. But it does the job and it works because squatting incorporates all the major muscle groups in one go, so you have to feed multiple working muscles with oxygen at the same time. That's why exhaustion comes quick and the weak of will buckle in the very early stages. Those that want supreme fitness and a hardy mentality go to the thighs first. Reg had taken the concept from the Eastern wrestlers who worked their thighs to unbelievable levels.

I trained.

I slept.

It was my first step back to the real world. Destiny was waiting for me in Manchester.

Chapter Eighteen

Parky

Initially the training on the hotel bedroom floor was a salvation; I needed it to keep me alive. I'd have died I'm sure if I had not dragged myself from that bed. I had come close to giving up. Letting myself be found and destroyed. Though many times I found myself – in my weaker moments – thinking 'Stay alive for what?' I expected to die in Manchester. But as long as I was fit, had breath left in my body and the memory of Ginger in my mind, I was in with a chance.

During those low moods my negative thoughts tried to bully and intimidate, as if I was in self-destruct mode. But I knew from experience and from Reg that the mind is like a garden. It can be made beautiful with a little care and attention or it can become wild and uncontrollable. The latter is easy; just don't do anything, sit on your arse and let it go. But I understood the nature of my positive thoughts, they needed guiding gently. Left alone they would quickly fall into decline. I also understood bullies – I was raised by one after all. And I knew that negative thoughts were no different to the playground thugs that haunted every soft kid too scared to fight for his lunch. And even when I was scared to the point of trembling I still stood my ground and refused to be forced. It was a stubborn habit that I had developed, even nurtured, to keep going when there seemed little point. Push me one way and you could be sure of one thing: I'd push the other. Every press-up in that small hotel room, every Hindu squat, every yoga stretch was fired by a stubborn internal voice that said 'I don't give a rat's arse how many times I get knocked down, I'll get right back up again.'

At times it seemed as if every single living part of me wanted to lie down and give up. But my will was a granite drill sergeant hovering in the background, urging me on. I kept seeing Ginger's face in front of me, smiling at me, encouraging me. I wasn't going to let her death be for nothing – and I wasn't going to wait and be killed. So I trained, I pushed my body to the point of exhaustion and then further. I was way outside my own limits, stretching, willing on the pain, almost loving the pain; I seemed to be punishing myself. I did more reps than I thought were in me. If nothing else it got my body tired enough to sleep, even if it was just for a short while. Every time that cowardly voice in my head cried and begged for a rest, when my muscles burned with the effort and my breath reached gasp-point I forced out one more repetition until I could taste the bile in the back of my throat.

You don't need fancy equipment and gyms and personal trainers and barking commands and big fees to get into shape. All you need is a bit of space – a small bedroom is enough – and a burning motivation. I had both. Not only did I need the training to give me a reason to live – the endorphins released in training help to bring a traumatised body back into balance – but I also needed the conditioning to fight an enemy that seemed intent on killing me. At the time my life didn't seem to be worth a gnat's nuts.

Not to me anyway. Even so, that stubborn part of me was not about to let anyone take it away without my permission.

The training wasn't the only thing that gave me the will to continue. The second catalyst was Who-the-fuck-is-Dennis.

I'd woken from a fitful sleep and flicked through the channels on the telly. I wasn't really watching, it was just background noise, a bit of company. *Parkinson* was on.

'My guest tonight is an esteemed and controversial novelist who has just spent a year living incognito in a run-down bedsit to research his next book. Ladies and gentlemen, please welcome my first guest, the charismatic millionaire novelist Mr Dennis Harper.'

The audience applauded and I watched, dumbfounded, as my old neighbour walked centre-stage to join the legendary chat-show host. Even though he was cleaned up, shaved, suited and poshly booted, I could still see my eccentric, dishevelled neighbour shining through – the only thing missing was his cat One Eye. And when he spoke I was transported back to my flat and my old, uncomplicated, beautiful life. I was thrilled. My face split into a joker smile, and I leaned closer into the telly to make sure that it was real and that I was not having some post-bang-on-the-head hallucination.

Over the next twenty or so minutes the man I had falsely branded a harmless Walter Mitty-type regaled the audience with stories of his time in the bedsit. He even mentioned me. Me on Parky! A plain old labourer being mentioned on telly. Parky told the audience of Dennis's prolific success – *New York Times* and *Sunday Times* bestseller several times over, forty million books sold worldwide, a multi-millionaire and friend to the stars.

Dennis chatted about the storyline of his book, though, he said, he didn't want to give too much away, as the story was still not finished. It was a tale of an ordinary working man who, tired of living under the dominion of local gangsters, went out to take on the drug lords of the north single-handed.

'My one big dilemma,' he said to Parky, but looking into the camera as if he was delivering a message directly to my room, 'is that the gentleman I have based my story on left before I could get my ending.'

I stared into the telly, fixed my gaze and I spoke to Dennis as if he was right there in the room with me.

'I'll give you a fucking ending,' I said.

And I knew then that I would.

After the programme ended, I made a cup of tea and I sat in that room and thought about Dennis, lovely Dennis. I just smiled and smiled and smiled. It wasn't just the fact that I was pleased for his success or even that I was amazed that he'd been telling the truth all along. It was more that I felt there was hope, that there was a chance for me to be better than I was, or certainly better than I thought I was. I knew Dennis; he was my neighbour, the bloke upstairs, an ordinary man. Like me. He was a simple bloke just like me. And it made me feel that, actually, if I really wanted to, I *could* do something with my life. People like me could make good, they could break out of their self-imposed, working-class, hand-me-down existence. For a few minutes it filled me with such hope, something that I had not felt in a long time.

And at the end of the interview Dennis said that he believed that poverty and discomfort, the kind he had lived in for research, could be overcome. He told of his own upbringing, on a council estate in Hackney, about how he'd kept his head down and worked hard at school, and eventually won a scholarship to Cambridge. He said that if people stopped clinging to what they were used to, if they got out there and faced their problems, there was nothing they could not achieve. He explained his belief that people were often held back by traumatic experiences from their past and that, until they could clear the backlog, what he called the 'kinks in the hose', it was very difficult for them to move forward.

'Sometimes,' he said, 'you have to move backwards before you can move forwards.'

Now if someone had thrown a paradox like that at me as little as a couple of months ago I would have parried it off, scoffed. But now I got it, I really did. When Ginger had told me that I needed to forgive before I could be free, it had made sense to me. But I'd filed it away to think about some other time. That time had come. I knew what I had to do. Before I could move forward into my future I had to get rid of a demon from my past. I knew in that moment that Dennis was right, that there was hope, even for me. So I made up my mind, there and then, right after Parky, right after seeing my mate Dennis. I was going to stop clinging to my own comfort zone, stop mourning for what had gone and for things that could not be changed. I was going to stop running and face my fears. I decided to find this William bloke and get the monkey off my back once and for all. But before that there was someone else I wanted to find, someone else that needed fronting, that had been on my mind and in my nightmares since school. A man that had hidden from his karmic debt for long enough. He would have to come first, and once he had been dealt with – and I did intend to deliver a heinous hurt upon him – I would go after William and end this thing, one way or another. It was as though a portal had opened in my mind to show me the way.

The mirror in the hotel bathroom was kinder to me the more I trained. The stress and the lack of food and the working out had stripped the fat from my bones like a butcher's blade. My appetite – as Don McLean might have said – had caught the last train for the coast. But I still ate, from room service, and every mouthful was a training session in itself. Every forkful was chewed and swallowed on manual. The fry-ups had gone now, the chips and pie things of the past. I was in training so I needed the best fuel my body could get. I placed myself on a regime of skinless chicken and rice, salmon and pasta, clear water, high protein and no carbohydrates after 7 p.m. Carbs late at night did nothing but sit on your sides like a skin-coloured bumbag and force your trouser measurement up two sizes.

So the mirror was kind. The muscles that had lain hidden beneath layers of bubble-wrap since I stopped training, since the old man had died, reasserted themselves on my body. Two nice biceps veins reappeared like old soldiers reporting for duty, one more campaign. Even my abs were peeping through. The belly that had hidden them for so long was on the hotel carpet. A shape from the past was re-emerging.

It was a shame that I didn't care. I was growing a physique that I could use to protect my right to this incarnation. It was my basic right, even if at that moment in time I didn't care too much for it.

What was there to want when all I ever desired was gone forever?

I saw myself back in Ginger's arms, the scent of her covering me like a warm blanket, her warm arms around my neck, her lips on mine. That touch, the tingle, the excitement of new love. I saw the beach at Lyme Regis – an old holiday haunt from my childhood – with its row of ice-cream parlours and seafront cafés, a chip shop on the corner that sold tea by the mug and chips in newspaper. My one great memory from way back, when Mum was happy and Dad was sober. I only had it the once and it was grand. I saw me and Ginger there, shoes and socks in our hands, pebbles under our feet, sea and sand between our toes, walking hand in hand. I could feel the bliss permeating every cell of my body.

My rational self was telling me 'she's dead, she's dead', and vivid images of scorched hair and paramedics and smoke kept trying to infiltrate my thoughts. This was where the real wrestle began. I reminded myself again that every thought was flesh, and every thought that I dwelled upon I fed, and that fed thoughts grew into fat realities. I let Reg's wise words come to my defence again.

'Do you want this thought in your head, do you choose it? Is it what you want to see?'

'No.'

'Then fuck it off out! Don't choose it, don't think it, don't feed it.'

My positive thoughts were starting to take over and every negative thought and image was neutralised. My safety mechanism was starting to click in. I smothered all the negative images with powerful, positive ones.

Ginger lingered in my mind throughout my waking hours. She was in my thoughts almost permanently. But I knew now that I couldn't have her back. That was one thing I was sure of. The thoughts of her in my arms and of me inside her were too much to bear. I had to stop thinking about her. Force my thoughts onto anything but her. It was hard, but necessary. Felt like I was betraying her memory if I didn't mourn. I had to starve the thoughts that filled me with such sadness and try to nurture thoughts that at the very least left me neutral. So I tried to fill my mind with my mission, with healthy eating, with press-ups and sit-ups and Hindu squats.

When the depression was too great to ignore, I immersed myself in it. I challenged it, invited it in. 'Come on in,' I'd tell it. 'Have a sit down, want a drink? Bit of telly, something to eat?'

Once I faced it, accepted it, I realised that actually it wasn't so bad. It was only tough when you tried to run away from it, as if you can run from what is inside you; it's like trying to run from your own shadow. You can run as fast as you can but it will always be right behind you. I stopped running. I lay on the bed, breathed deeply, channelled my mind. I was swallowed by the feelings. I let the melancholy envelop me but didn't latch on to it; it was just a wave that washed through me. Reg had always told me that when you stopped fighting evil it disappeared all by itself because it had nothing to feed off. What we resist, he had said, would persist. Mind calm, meditative, into a dream.

Mum walked into my bedroom. It was Christmas morning, the birthday, she said, of Christ, a time when you are supposed to be happy. So why was I crying? I couldn't tell her. She was full of concern and love. She hugged my wet face into her wool cardigan. 'I prayed that you wouldn't inherit my nerves,' she said.

This was years before I even knew what nerves were. A long time before I was able to come to terms with the fact that whatever they were and despite her prayers, inherit them I did. A blight on my life I thought, a birthmark beyond removal. Reg had taught me better. He showed me that my nerves were my power, they would give me superhuman energy if I could learn to control and harness their latent potential.

It took time. Training taught me the art of transmutation. Changing raw energy into form. My inheritance was an infinite geyser of potential power that got me to the gym before everyone else and kept me there long after the showers had stopped and the other fighters were pushing a second beer past their dry tonsils. What Mum had labelled the blight of her life, Reg had called a gift. But he warned me then – as I warned myself in that hotel room – that what can heal can also harm, and creative forces in the wrong hands also have the capacity to destroy. This power, this geyser, can overwhelm those that do not circulate the energy correctly. I had learned to keep the energy flowing: when it wasn't in the gym it was on the building sites and the doors. Now it was in a small hotel room in the north of nowhere. I was finding my old self again, only now with the added wisdom that I had learned from my short time with Ginger. It was as if she had tempered what had been a rough and rusty blade. Deep breathing, positive internal dialogue, body relaxed. I let go.

I went fifteen years back in time, to the Ring Gym and my old wrestling teacher. He was as craggy and weathered and wizened in my mind's eye, as vivid and as charismatic in my imagination as he was way back then. I loved the guy, proper loved him, and to my aching mind he was a balm. When Reg walked into a room he dragged stories, history, colour and character with him. He had an aura that lit the small bar at the Ring like it was on fire. The respect was such that when he entered a room people would instinctively stand or nod or raise a hand to shake as he passed. Free drinks lined his table like winners' cups. He'd stroll through the room slowly but erect, a slight limp from injuries still alive on his old body. Every movement carried a history. His face – full of scars and wounds like badges of battle – unfolded a thousand tales. When he spoke, ears pricked up and heads turned and crowds gathered. Every word that left his lips was full of philosophy, insight, warmth and truth. The man had integrity writ large right through his centre. And though I heard the stories more than once they got richer and more profound with each telling.

'Is that what you want to see?' Reg's voice rang in my ears. I was fifteen and impressionable when he first spoke those words and they had stuck with me all these years. I was halfway through telling him how black my future was going to be – at the time it was what I believed – it must be true, I told him, because my father had told me so.

'You'll come to nothing,' my dad had said after a gallon of strong ale and a dozen whisky chasers. Dad's face was just as craggy as

Reg's, weathered auburn by the elements. His mind was hardened and callused like a labourer's hands. But he brought no inspiration into the room for me, just a whole load of pain and guilt that hung beneath my heart like a rusty dumb-bell.

'So?' Reg waited for me to answer. He wanted to know if that was what I wanted to see with my life. His voice was full of concern, but firm, with a harsh edge.

'No, but ...' I replied, looking at the floor and kicking imaginary stones.

Reg interrupted me before I could take the 'but' any further. 'Then stop seeing it,' he said, like it was the most natural thing in the world. He pointed to the gym door. 'You think the fight is in there, lad, but you're wrong; the real fight is in here.' He tapped his head to indicate what he meant. I sensed that he'd had this conversation with many would-be fighters before me. Probably three generations of young people who, like me, saw nothing but a bleak future.

He pointed to the gym door again. 'That,' he said, then pointed to his head again, 'just helps you to access this.'

I didn't get it at the time. I was too young, my brain was stuck on throws, hooks and punches, and it was hard for me to conceive of anything beyond that. What he showed me – and it didn't sink in properly for another decade – was that the real power was on the inside, not on the outside. You didn't have to leave your own front room to get it. Fuck, you didn't even have to leave your own head. He taught me the power of my thoughts. He told me: 'Your thoughts create your reality; they create your world.'

'Thoughts can be so real they are flesh,' he was fond of saying. 'They act like magnets, drawing you towards the reality of all the things you think about. It's like a self-fulfilling prophecy. So don't think it if you don't want it.'

He rolled up his sleeve and flexed his biceps, a sinewy little apple with a neat vein at the front, the arm of a twenty-year-old. 'That's not where it's at kid.' He tapped my head again, gently, parentally. 'This is where big is. Exercise this. The rest is just games.'

His voice and his message were still clear, as if he was sat in the hotel with me. And he was right: what you saw was what you got, so don't see it if you don't want it; start seeing what you do want.

So in my meditative state I started seeing the conclusion that I wanted to see. The real wrestle never leaves the confines of your own head. Reg was definitely on-the-ball right. It had been a long time since I had heard that sage voice. It was welcome and inspiring. After my dad had died and the inclination to tear holes in the wrestling mat had abandoned me, Reg's voice and my conditioning had died with it. It's funny. It takes months to become a sinewy Adonis, yet you lose it almost the moment you stop using it. Having said that, it wasn't taking me long to get it back again. The hotel mirror was being truthful; in fact the mirror is probably the best friend you'll ever have. It tells it how it sees it. Fat is fat from any angle and under any shade of light.

The internal wrestle was on, and the only real training – the one that goes on inside your head – was back on the agenda. I started to see what I really wanted. Even if it meant seeing what others might call the impossible. In my mind's eye I saw a life without pain and strife. I saw it vividly and in colour and in six dimensions. My problems with the Manchester crew were gone, resolved, and, in my mind's eye, I was back home with Ginger. The feeling was ecstatic.

'Think it strong enough,' Reg had insisted, 'and you will make it a reality.'

I was back again in that small bar with Reg. Wise, older now, failing slightly but as charismatic as ever. He believed that our ability to have whatever we wanted was only a strong thought away.

'If that's true, Reg, then why do so many people have fuck-all?' I needed convincing.

He smiled knowingly. 'Because they ask for fuck-all, kid.' He said it as though it was the most obvious thing in the world. 'They are living proof that it works. They get what they ask for.'

He pointed to Tony, a fat guy sat close to the bar with a full pint of Guinness and a heavy frown. 'He ain't happy because that's what he sees. It's what he talks about, it's what he hears. Ask him why he ain't happy and he'll tell you all right.'

Tony spoke in my mind, a conversation that I'd overheard many times: 'I'll never be fucking right in this city. If it weren't for her at home I'd be off, I'm telling you, I wouldn't be hanging round here. The trouble with this city ...' He went on and on, blaming his wife, the city, the council, the schools, his slow metabolic rate, his poor eyesight, the politicians, the beer, the Pope, fucking God. Once he started there was no end to it, though I never once heard him apportion any of the blame to himself.

'He's a shit magnet,' said Reg. 'He attracts shit because all he can think about is shit. He gets what he asks for. He is proof that the law is working, a well-oiled machine, clunking beautifully.'

'What about Sam?' I wanted more proof.

Sam was a hard-working, diligent trainer who never seemed to move forward in his life or his training. He attracted bad luck like shit attracts flies. Every business venture he entered failed, and every woman he attracted – and he did attract some nice ones – he lost within weeks. He was full of bad luck.

Reg answered. 'What about him?'

'Well, he works hard, harder than anyone I know. If anyone deserves success he does.'

'He don't deserve it.' Reg was blunt. He had a way with bluntness. If you had a fat face he told you so; if you didn't train hard enough he was straight. He believed that the best way to avoid a base man was to be honest with him. 'He's a nice kid,' Reg said.

I raised my eyebrows, looking for an explanation. Reg sipped on his beer, his eyelids baggy, a slight tremble in his old hand. 'He gets what he asks for.'

'He does?' I couldn't quite see how. No one asks for crap and failure and misery. Do they?

'He does, kid.'

Sam appeared in my mind's eye. Early twenties, built like an Olympic swimmer, big schnozzle. He was staring into a beer as though searching for good fortune and finding only froth.

'I'm jinxed. Every business I start is doomed before I even begin. I can't hold a good woman for more than two minutes; fuck me, I can get them, no worries, just can't hold the fuckers. My women are like soap in the bath; slipping through my grasp and disappearing into the suds.'

Reg was back. 'You should never mistake hard work for progress, kid. The factories are full of men who work bollock-breaking hours, but it don't get them any further forward in life: they're still there thirty years on and just as unhappy. Hard workers grow on trees. It's hard thinkers that make winners, kid.'

A hard thinker. Reg had always said that. Think hard, wrestle with your thoughts. And if you get thoughts in your head that you don't want, then stop thinking about them, stop feeding them, stop attracting them. He was right. I knew that. I just needed to hear it again.

'Don't take my word for it, kid. Don't take anyone's word for it. Try it yourself and see.'

I did. I put my thoughts to work on one thing. Hard and practised thought. I was young. All I could see at the time was one thing and I made it appear so real that it convinced me forever of the potency of my own mind. For good and for bad. It scared the crap out of me. Reg had warned me to be careful about what I thought because thoughts created realities that had consequences. These also needed to be foreseen. Thoughts were like children that went out into the world and had more children, and those children had children and so on and so on. Cause and effect, action and consequence, karma. My thoughts at that time were one-dimensional and undisciplined. They were also very short-sighted: all I could see in my young mind was me facing down my dad, facing him down, knocking him down and keeping him down. And I naively thought that it would solve all my problems. It would stop him from harming my mum, from abusing me. If he was out of the way, I thought, all would be well. I really believed that. I saw it day and night. It took me through every training session. It pushed reps out of me that I didn't know were there.

I saw it in detail. Dad grabbing my mum, violently pushing her up the cooker like he always did, his little Sunday ritual, spitting and swearing and salivating with the beer. Me watching on. Him warning me to fuck off and shoving me with those Popeye arms that sent me sprawling across the floor. Only this time I was strong. I didn't fall back, I didn't cry, I didn't run. I stood my ground and I faced my fear. In my mind's eye I prised him from my mum like I was pulling a child from a climbing frame. He swings at me, one of those blows that knock cowboys over tables, only I see it and slip underneath and take a trapped arm strangle, just like Reg had taught me, and hold it on until he splutters and coughs and falls like someone has unplugged him from the mains.

And that was where I always stopped the visualisation. Not realising at the time that there would inevitably be more to come, that my actions would have consequences that I had not envisioned. But one day I did have to live with the consequences. One day my thoughts became reality, just as Reg had told me. I did all those things to my dad that I had imagined. I beat him. I conquered him. But after the knockout – my father on the floor snoring fitfully, my mother by the cooker weeping and dripping blood – there was a terrible rush of sadness and grief that I had never expected. I felt sorry for him, for my father. I thought I would be uplifted by my deed. Instead I was crushed, a tremendous sadness and regret fell over me as I looked down at this man mountain, asleep like a baby. Yellow. Already in the latter stages of alcoholism, drowning in ale. Then my mum – I expected her to be happy – pushing me out of the house like an unwelcome intruder, driving me away. Through the kitchen window I watched her as she tended to my father and I saw the love she still held for him. And I felt the love that I still had for him, despite it all.

Don't see it if you don't want it. That is what Reg had told me so many times, over and over, don't see it, don't think it, don't say it. Discipline your mind. And if you do want to see it, make sure that you take in the full picture, the full perspective – the aftermath and all. See the consequences of your actions, and the consequences of those consequences. Follow each ripple that your action makes and be sure that you want it all before you make the action a tangible reality. See a happy ending. That was Reg's favourite piece of advice. The clearer you made the pictures, the quicker you would make them a reality. Believe it and you will have it.

I failed to see that when I finally confronted my dad, when I took him over with a brutal and practised strangle, that it would kill him. Dead.

'I killed my dad.'

I was naked, ready for a shower, my body rippling with muscle as I threw the statement into the mirror of an empty bathroom. Then I smiled, an involuntary smile, the type that appears when your mind does not know how to deal with what it has done.

I killed him.

Until that moment, alone in a hotel bedroom, I had never allowed myself to admit responsibility for the death of my father, let alone say it out loud. I had buried it like a family secret, never to be revealed. But over the years it had eaten away at me and acted like a cancer. Now, having lost Ginger and any chance of a normal life, there seemed little reason to keep it hidden any longer, certainly not from myself.

I had killed him, and I was sorry. That was all.

It had been easy for my mum to cover up. When she called the ambulance and they saw the state of her – beaten black and blue – it wasn't hard to believe her when she told them that he had passed out and choked on a throat full of vomit. That part was true: after I'd left, he had thrown up and choked. What she didn't tell them was that I made him pass out.

When he lay in that hospital bed and I watched him die it was hard to be kind to myself.

'The drink would have killed him anyway,' my mum had assured me.

It didn't take away the fact that the alcohol had not killed him. I had.

Chapter Nineteen

Rock Star

My mind and body were refreshed, re-energised. I'd been in this hotel for a week now. It was long enough; it was time to make a move. At reception I paid the balance for the room and asked to look at a motorway map. I flicked the pages to find Hyde. It was surprisingly close. Just a few junctions up the motorway.

It had been raining outside and the early morning sun reflected off the wet tarmac as I walked to my car. I could smell bacon cooking in the nearby café. I noticed a black Merc in the corner. I wasn't going to make the same mistake that I'd made with Wallflower and let my guard down. I was on red alert. Nothing was going to take me by surprise. A black Merc surrounded by middle-range cars was a bit of an anomaly. The windows were drug-dealer smoked glass so it was hard to tell how many people occupied the car. I knew one thing: it was unlikely to be less than two and, if the last visit was any indication, they would be carrying. They'd probably been sitting outside the hotel for a week while I was training, hoping I'd eventually lead them to the drugs. I made a point of not looking directly at the car; the last thing I wanted to do was let them know that I knew they were there. And anyway, there was a small part of me that thought 'You're just being paranoid.' Fear does that to a man. It could have been just a coincidence. I had no proof after all, just an intuitive itch.

I looked across at the Merc as I pulled out and headed for the motorway. North. My destiny. If it followed, I told myself, then I knew my intuition was serving me well. I prayed that I was wrong.

The Merc started its engine and followed me out, and not even at a respectable distance. Fuck. I hadn't expected this. I desperately hoped that I'd be able to just drive up to Manchester, plop myself into the Ecstasy Club and do the job I had decided to do. No chance. William must have been tracing my credit card transactions somehow. He was determined to find me before I found him.

I was on the motorway in seconds, the Merc three cars back in my rear view mirror. I had no idea of what I should do next. I wanted to go straight to Hyde to face down my past but I couldn't while I had a tail. How was I going to get rid of them? I didn't know the area well enough to try and lose them down a back street, and a high speed chase between my Cortina and a Merc? I couldn't see it somehow.

When I passed the Huddersfield turn-off I noticed a sign for services and an idea came to me. It was not much of an idea. This was real life, not James Bond, so no explosions or complicated traps. Just a simple idea that would give me enough getaway time to create some space between me and them. I would draw them into a trap. I figured that they were on my trail for one of two reasons: either to hurt me, perhaps end me, or because they were hoping I'd lead them to the drugs. There was only one option. I wasn't going to lead them to the drugs so a beating was definitely in order. If I stopped at the services, they would stop with me.

I pulled into the service station, Merc at my tail, parked and made my way into the shopping area. Once inside the doors and with the glare of the glass offering a little secrecy, I looked out at the Merc to make sure that I was definitely being followed.

I was. Two men exited the car from the front seats. Scary fuckers, big, no strangers to the gym or the nightclub door. To my right was the Gents, to my left a small shop offering sweets, books and magazines. Ahead was a cafeteria. I walked into the shop and ducked behind a bookshelf. It allowed me a vantage point. From where I squatted I could see the doors to the service station without being seen. Other customers hovered around me, looking at the books and mags. A guy in a crinkled suit with a comb-over that looked as though it might have started at his arse had his head buried in a top-shelf erotica novel. I could see him skimming through the text looking for the juicy lesbian bits. Just enough to get his head right for a wank in the toilet before he headed back home.

The automatic doors to the service station opened and the blokes walked in. My adrenalin shot into overdrive. I breathed deeply and evenly through my nose to slow the flow. My internal dialogue was in shape, I knew what to do. Now it was just a matter of doing it. And as quickly as possible.

One of the scroats was wearing sunglasses and a trashy tracksuit about ten years out of date. His long blond hair was lank and unwashed; a great appendage if it came to the grapple. He looked like a failed rock star. His shoulders were broad and he had thick, dirty hands, and a belly that hung over his trousers like a balcony. His mate was smaller in height but wide, with splayed arms that looked as though they were carrying invisible rolls of carpet. Unshaven, unkempt, there was a hardness in his face that scared me. Both these men were in their late thirties and had seen some life. They were not like the last fellows I had encountered, the ones with the gun. They were smart, minder types. These two goons were hired help, street lads out to earn a quick wad for a kneecapping or more.

They hovered at the door of the services, just outside the shop and looked around them. I ducked lower behind the bookshelf. I hoped that they would split up to find me, that way I would only have to deal with one of them at a time, or just one of them full stop. That was the extent of my plan. The services was the best place to do that, not only because I could hide and they'd probably separate to find me, but also because I knew that they were very unlikely to bring any hardware into a public place.

The small one nodded to Rock Star and they separated. Rock Star came my way, into the shop, and Shorty made his way into the Gents. *Whoosh*. Adrenalin rushed through me, causing a tremble in my thighs and bats in my stomach. I knew what to do now. I was focused. Someone was going to get a dig and I'd be fucked if it was going to be me. I had to act quickly, no time to waste. I needed to be in and out in a hurry before Shorty came back from the bog to help his mate, who I was about to beat a new head. The good thing for me was the fact that I had no decisions to make, no 'Should I, shouldn't I? Does he deserve a dig, doesn't he deserve a dig?' I knew it needed to be done: it was life and death. All I had to decide now was when and how to neutralise this piece of shit. The when would present itself quickly enough, the how would be spontaneously decided the moment I stood face to face with him. I already hated him. I had to, it's in the job description. It is the natural precursor to separating a man from his consciousness – or at the very least his teeth. It's hard to hit them with everything but a tax bill if you don't dehumanise them first. I watched Rock Star walk through the shop, the swagger of a cunt with the confidence of ten men. He slipped his sunglasses off and hung them from the top of his tracksuit bottoms. He was getting ready for a fight.

Fighting is a bit like conkers. The more conkers you break, the bigger your confidence grows until it bloats and manifests itself in a cocky I-don't-give-a-fuck walk that says to anyone in the vicinity 'I can fight'. This man had obviously beaten a few heads in his time because his walk had a smarmy bounce that made me want to hoof the head off him and do a riverdance across his face.

Rock Star walked past the chiller cabinets at the far end of the shop. He was heading towards the crisps and magazines. His eyes were busy, looking this way and that, trying to find me. I had the urge then to leg it, make a run for it. A little bit of negativity found its way into my head and advised me of how ludicrous this was and how I should fuck off out of it while I still had a chance. The whole thing was crazy, I knew that much, but it was not one of my choosing. I reminded myself that I had to make the best of a bad situation.

I stood up and walked across the shop behind Rock Star, like following the trail of a slug. I walked past the till, crouching slightly, trying to keep my head below the displays so as to stay hidden. I must have looked absurd, like Groucho Marx doing his funny walk. I pretended that I was scratching my shin to try and make myself appear less strange to those who might glance my way. My heart was beating faster now, and doubts were trying to race into my brain. I beat them back with my practised internal voice.

Closer now. Rock Star stopped by the crisps and picked up a bag. Fucking amateur. It was all the distraction I needed. There were only a smattering of faces around me now, most were lost in decisions of food choice, blissfully unaware of what was about to occur. I was right behind Rock Star, and I shouldn't have been – he should never have allowed it. I tapped his shoulder. He turned.

Bang! I dropped a heavy right on his jaw and followed with a left hook that hit nothing but fresh air. The first one had done its job, he'd dropped like a shit sack, like he'd been shot behind the ear. The second punch, the hook, went right over his head.

I had learned the art of knock-out from Reg. Actually I'd learned just about everything to do with the fighting arts from him. He taught me young and he taught me well. Hit the jawline he always told me – anywhere from the ear to the chin – with anything from an open-hand shot to a closed fist, even an elbow, though the latter lacked the accuracy of the hands. When you hit the jaw it shakes the brain and even the biggest yokes go out like the gas. It works best if you have the element of surprise because it leaves no time for the recipient to tense their neck and shoulder muscles to lessen the impact. And you get the element of surprise by either hitting them when they're not looking or by engaging the brain with a question before you strike. Anything that temporarily distracts their mind from your punch. Real fighting is all about deception and the master always looks for it to initiate his attack. I just do what works. I'm with the great martial artist Miyamoto Musashi: every advantage fair or foul should be employed once you know that war is inevitable and unavoidable. There is no room for ethics when survival is on the cards.

The second thing you need for the KO is accuracy. You need to hit the target like a sniper, not an inch below or an inch above or either way to the side. An inch out and the knock-out would be missed, and you'd end up hitting the cheek bone, which would smash your knuckles on impact, or the teeth, which would leave you with fingers full of molar and a messy finish to what should have been a clinical job. As obvious as it might seem, to get accuracy you have to look directly at the target before you hit it, not an easy thing to do when the adrenalin whippet is racing around your veins. People unused to violence tend to hit out in the general direction of the head whilst perhaps looking at the opponent's feet, chest or even eyes. A bit like a sniper focusing his sights a foot above their target and then wondering why they missed.

Once you have the accuracy, you need speed and power. Deception gives you a window of opportunity, but that window only stays open for a split-second. Hesitate, throw the punch too slowly or with not enough power or accuracy, and the chance will be lost.

Last, and certainly not least, you need gonads. Reading it in a book or watching it on the TV is one thing, doing it when the arena is the pavement is an entirely different matter. Even with an experienced fighter, a man with a history of doing it for real, there is still the danger of adrenal overload causing hesitation, even abortion.

Your natural instinct is to turn and run, and when you can you *should* run. What moron wants to scrap around in the dirt with some Neanderthal, risking life, limbs and liberty, when he has the choice of doing anything else? Me, I'd rather be sat in a pub somewhere having a pint and a bag of peanuts and watching the barmaid juggling her assets by the glass washer any day of the week. When you face violence, when it's there, in your face, close enough to smell, there is not a single part of you that doesn't want to fuck off and make for the hills. In those few seconds before lift-off you doubt every technique that you ever practised, you feel that they will never work, even though they have worked many times before. This is where courage comes in, when you can't run, and your only options are to be the hammer or the anvil. When you know that hesitation might get you a dent in the head, it is hard not to tremble in anticipation.

As soon as I dropped the right on Rock Star's jaw he spun grotesquely on the spot. The crisps left his hand like they had somewhere better to go. He hit the deck with a loud thud and his head whiplashed into the crisp stand, scattering the packets in every direction. The clatter woke the whole shop and everyone froze, then turned and stared like startled cattle.

'Ambulance!' I shouted before they had a chance to make their own assessment. 'Someone's collapsed.'

Everyone looked at me for a shocked second. 'Can someone call a paramedic? This bloke's just fallen over. He's ill.'

I took advantage of the fact that everyone was in shock and the real details of what had just taken place would not register until I was long gone.

An elderly gent approached me with an excited, confused look on his face – he knew I'd dropped Rock Star but my plea of innocence had baffled him. He looked like a shop doorway dosser on a day trip to the service station. He smelt of piss. He pointed at me. The skin of his hand was gathered and shiny like it had grown too big for the bone.

'He just fell,' I said, shrugging my shoulders in my best 'I'm innocent, guv' pose.

'Is he all right?' His question, like his pointing finger, was full of accusation.

I looked at him dumbfounded. I wanted to say, *Oh yeah, the lad's a hundred per cent, as right as ninepence. He's always collapsing and bleeding in public places*. I didn't think it would help, so I opted for the more conservative and innocent, 'He just fell.'

Someone else rushed forward, a fat, crimson-faced shop assistant fresh from her first-aid course and in a hurry to see if it might work.

'First-aider,' she announced with a slight tremor in her voice.

'He just fell,' I said for the third time as she pushed me out of the way and knelt by Rock Star's side. Her service uniform stretched at the thigh, defying the laws of expansion. Within seconds there was a circle of do-gooders all trying to help Rock Star find his consciousness and stop the blood spurting from his head like a burst dam. He was gurgling and snoring as I quietly backed away. The old gent was still looking at me through the crowd, his finger still hovering in the air, pressing an unseen button. He was obviously still unsure about whether he'd actually seen me punch the guy a new head or if he was at the beginning of some brain-altering disease that hits the over-seventies. I didn't wait for him to make his decision. The confusion was my best window of exit.

As I left, I took a can of Lucozade from the chiller cabinet and made my way back into the car park. No one noticed; they were too busy watching the first-aider tipping Rock Star onto his side into the recovery position with a shove of her meaty knee.

A can of Lucozade is great little device for disabling cars. Forget the bag of sugar in the fuel tank or the pliers to cut brake cables. I needed something more immediate. One can of Lucozade was quick, efficient and guaranteed to do the job in a heartbeat.

I quickly paced towards the Merc, which was standing four cars down from mine, waiting for its owners. I lifted the can of Lucozade high in the air like a hammer and dashed it straight into the windscreen. It imploded instantly, a slush of glass littering the seats and the bonnet. The alarm went off immediately as I knew it would.

I walked past as if nothing had happened. One or two people in the car park stopped to stare in amazement but I was already in my car and heading north.

Two more enemies were made this day. But I didn't care. I was safe. For a short while anyway.

It was obvious that these guys were tracing me through the places that I was staying in. It was also obvious that they were not going to give up and that the next time I stopped at a hotel they would be right on my trail again. And I couldn't expect them to keep sending amateurs; eventually they would send someone who knew what they were doing, and then I would be in shit street.

I headed back down the motorway, south, towards the next services. I stopped there to get petrol and cash. My cash card would only allow me two hundred and fifty pounds in any one day, but that would be enough. By the end of the day I intended to be in Manchester; by the morning this thing would be over. One way or another. My idea was to make them think that I was going south by going back on myself. It wouldn't take them long to trace the fact that I had been at the services and conclude that I had made a change of direction to get away from them. Instead I would load up to the brim with fuel, get the money out, and book myself into the services hotel, as though I intended to stay the night. But I intended to fulfil the promise I'd made to myself, to confront one of the demons from my past.

I had to do this. Had to. I could go no further in my life until this was done. I had run away from this for too long. Now was the time to end it once and for all. That kid, that eleven-year-old, needed to be released, and I knew that until I had faced this man down, the cell doors would still be locked. And whilst he was still trapped inside me I would never be complete, my energy would always be fighting on two fronts. To face my final frontier I would need all my energy to be focused in one direction. Once I had done my dirty deed I would take a slow and deliberate drive into 'mad for it' Manchester, the land of the Happy Mondays, Oasis and attitude. There I would finish my business with William.

I'd be there before nightfall.

In the services I bought a notepad, a biro and a packet of envelopes. In the car I wrote a basic will, slipped it into one of the envelopes and wrote 'Last Will and Testament' neatly on the front. There were two good reasons for doing this. The first was obvious: the possibility that I might die in the next twenty-four hours was fast becoming a probability. I still had money left in the bank, and I wanted it to go to my brother in America. The second reason? That would come later. It was the slimmest chance, a hair's breadth. I didn't set any store by it. But it was just a pinprick of hope at the end of a very dark tunnel.

Finding Father Tarbuck was frighteningly easy. After I arrived in the market town of Hyde I parked close to the town hall and found a small Internet café. I banged 'Hyde' into the search engine – several pages of options appeared on my screen in seconds – then 'priests' and hey presto. There was the fat fucker as large and as ugly as life.

Father Tarbuck, the blurb beneath his portrait said proudly, *has been the parish priest at Meadow Church for over twenty years*. I'll spare you the rest. It was all lies about what a marvellous man of God he was and how fortunate the townspeople were to have him as their representative. I took down the address of the church, got into my car and made my way along the Manchester Road for a couple of miles.

I was trembling as I pulled up outside the church. From a distance this had been a great idea; I would find the church where he served and give him what I had been holding in for all these years. I knew that I needed the catharsis before making my way to Manchester and William. But now that I was here, actually outside the church, it did not seem like such a great idea.

Why was I so scared? I realised the fear I felt was not that of a fighting man with thousands of ring matches under his belt and hundreds of blood-and-snot street fights, it was the fear of a young, vulnerable lad who had gone to God for help and got a perverted priest with a penchant for young boys instead. I breathed in deeply.

This really was scary. I didn't want to continue. But I had to, I had to clear my past before my future would open up. There is an old Kabbalic saying that all our power is locked into our fears, and when we kill the fears our power is released back to us. I knew I had to face this man down now, once and for all.

I climbed out of the car. Before me was a meandering path that led through ancient graves up to the vestry door. I straightened my back and pushed open the tiny rusting gate. I walked past the graves of people long gone, men and women who would have walked along this same path a thousand times. The huge oak door to the church was open, and I walked in. The place was empty. Memories of my youth wafted out to meet me like old enemies. I nodded respectfully to a life-sized Jesus on the cross.

I have no argument with you, I thought as I walked towards His watchful eyes.

My footsteps echoed in the empty church. Wooden benches acted as my gauntlet and I walked toward the front. I was trembling again. I felt strangely emotional, my bottom lip quivered. It was unnerving. I was more frightened of what I was about to do now than I was of going to Manchester and facing down a known gangster.

Halfway down the aisle I stopped. My nerve had left me and I didn't feel that I could finish what I had started. I decided to leave then, to make my exit. No one would know. Only me.

I froze to the spot.

I would know.

I forced myself forward again, then stopped just as quickly. My mouth was quivering now. What was wrong with me? I felt so weak and vulnerable, totally unprepared. I shook my head, disappointed at my inability to move another step. I looked up at Jesus, hanging above me.

'Give us a hand, eh, mate?' I said to the kind-eyed man nailed to the cross.

'What can I do for you?'

Fuck me, I nearly jumped out of my skin. My neck lurched forward and my eyes peeled. Was that Jesus talking to me?

A heavy shadow emerged from behind the altar.

Thank fuck for that. Asking Jesus for guidance and help is all well and good, but actually having him talk to you from a crucifix in Hyde was a little too surreal.

The shadow approached.

'I'm looking for the ...'

I hesitated to use the word 'priest', to me he was no priest, but asking for the church pervert was unlikely to buy me any favours.

'I'm looking for Father Tarbuck,' I said finally.

The shadow got closer.

'You'll have to come back in the morning,' he said. 'The church will be open then. We're just about to close the doors.'

'Oh,' I said, obediently turning to leave. 'OK then.'

I had forgotten the power that these places held and the awe that you felt when surrounded by the walls of God. And the priest was next to God after all. Above reproach. Even the adults, the hard men and the fighters, never answered back to the priest. He was always held in the highest esteem.

I had started walking towards the door when I stopped and reminded myself that I was no longer a spotty, frightened lad of eleven, no longer a lackey to the church or frightened of men that hid their perversions behind the dog collar of faith. I was a man who no longer gave a fuck about his place in the here let alone the hereafter. And I'd be fucked if I was going to walk away and wait another night to do something that should have been done years before.

I turned around resolutely. The figure was right behind me now, obviously in a hurry to close the doors after me.

It was him. It was fat Father-fucking-Tarbuck. Older now, and ravaged by age and drink, his face a map of blue, red and purple veins that stretched from his nose to his ears. His lips were blue and his belly was distended, causing him to waddle rather than walk.

I smiled, an involuntary smile to hide my fear. I was here. This was real.

'You don't remember me,' I said, knowing that he wouldn't. I was sure that I was not his only victim.

He looked at me, squinted his eyes, made a sneering shape with his mouth that said 'Why should I?'

'Who are you?' he asked.

There was an arrogance in his tone that angered me. I wanted to punch him out there and then. Smash him, beat him, bury him.

'I'm the kid that came to you, crying, when I was eleven because my dad had sexually abused me,' I said. 'Remember?'

His face went pale. He opened his mouth to speak, lifted his hands as if to push me from the church.

'You remember?' I said again with mock kindness. The arrogance was all mine now. 'I came to you because I was in bits, and you tried to stick your fat finger up my arse.' Then I shouted: 'I was eleven!'

My words were tremulous, angry, vengeful. I was close to tears. It was all I could do to stop myself from losing it completely and flooring him with a practised right hook. I had waited a long time for this. I had dreamed of facing this man down, of laying him out cold. I wanted to hurt him. But when I looked at him, savaged by age and the burden of guilt, I saw that he was already fucked.

Again he made to interrupt me. 'Leave. Leave now,' he said, 'before I call the police.' He tried to push me out, but I was firm and his arms collapsed against my chest.

'Call 'em,' I said. 'Wouldn't mind talking with them myself.'

His bluff called and his panicky chest rasping, he stepped away from me. It was then that I knew what I had to do. It came to me like a message from the sky. I knew how to hurt this man beyond repair and heal myself at the same time. It was Ginger who gave me the answer. She came to me, her freckled face full of smiles and love. She whispered into my ear and the conversations shared in her warm bed raced back to my mind. She was right. I knew she was right. So I did as she said.

'I'm here to tell you two things,' I said, looking directly into Father Tarbuck's eyes and forcing him to avert his stare.

'Firstly, you destroyed me when I was a baby. Destroyed me. But I'm not a baby any more.'

I breathed deeply, desperately trying to take the tremble from my lips.

'Secondly,' I said, watching him step away from me in horror, expecting a dig any minute, 'I forgive you.'

He took another step back, detaching himself from my words, from his past, from the truth. He opened his mouth angrily to protest. This time I did not try to stop him. I just stood and waited to hear what he would – what he could – say in defence of his actions. Nothing came out. He was struck dumb.

'I forgive you,' I said again to make sure that he got it.

Father Tarbuck trembled, then exploded. 'Get out, get out, get out!' he screamed at me.

I smiled. I could see that he was powerless. That his position as a man of God no longer protected him, not even in the church. He was finished. Wherever he went in the world he would not be able to hide from his conscience. He could scream into an empty church for as long as he wanted to. It would not take away what he had done. Now he had another burden to contend with. My forgiveness. It would probably crush him.

'I forgive you.' I said it one last time. I wanted to make sure he got it. He lifted his hands in the air as though holding a huge rock. Like he wanted to strike me but didn't know how. He shook with rage and, I hoped, shame. I turned and walked away. I left the church and floated back to my car.

Ginger's voice was still with me. 'Forgiveness is setting yourself free.' And I did feel free. I felt lighter, looser.

When I drove away from Hyde I left a part of me there that I would never have to visit again.

Chapter Twenty

Mad for It

It was late when I arrived in Manchester. After my encounter with Father Tarbuck I had sat in the car and stared out of the window for an age. Strange feeling. Strange. I felt kind of free. And it had been so easy. I had seen this dark part of my past as an insurmountable obstacle for many years. I had made it so big that I felt it was beyond me. And yet here I was, in Manchester, and it was already behind me. My mum always used to tell me not to worry when things seemed dark in my life. 'You can't stop time,' she'd say. 'It will pass.' Situations would come and they would go. And no matter how bad they appeared to be they would be swept away with time. She was right. It was over and I was free and in a way it seemed as if it had never happened. I could still see his fat face. So angry. Livid. Fuming. And powerless. Like he couldn't believe that I had actually turned up on his doorstep, like he was saying 'Don't you know who I am?' And me there saying 'Actually, I don't give a flying fuck who you are. I'm your fucking past and you can't run from it any more, you pervy fucker.'

Only, if I am being honest, that wasn't quite how I felt. Sure, there was a good feeling when I left that church and that man in my wake, but there was also a feeling of compassion. Compassion for a man that had abused his position, a man who used his ability to heal to harm. Fucking wasted. A life wasted. I thought about him with his fat body and his ravaged mind and his sad, sad life. And the karmic debt that he would still have to pay. I felt sorry for him. Even after all he'd done to me I still felt dead sorry for the sad bastard.

It was raining as I drove into the city centre, the yellow of the street lamps bouncing off the wet road bringing melancholy into my lonely mind. It was a hard thing facing the unknown, knowing that it might be my last day on this spinning planet. The samurai believed that contemplating death liberated the soul. But as I played with the possibility of my own demise in a foreign, faceless city, the home of my enemy, all I felt was fucking miserable. Maybe, I thought – trying hard to be philosophical – I was doing it wrong. Or maybe the 'liberation' bit was still to come.

My belly rumbled; a concoction of hunger and adrenalin mixed with a bit of excitement and sheer terror. I had hardly eaten all day. My appetite was still as dead as dungarees. But I knew that I had to get a bit of sustenance into me if I was going to have a fighting chance at the Ecstasy Club. The lack of carbs was giving me a headache and a tremble in my limbs that made me feel kitten-weak. I noticed a takeaway on the side of the road and pulled across the traffic to get a feed. A couple of pieces of chicken and some fries would give me a bit of energy. Not the best grub I have to say, and if I was sticking strictly to my regime of healthy eating I would have by-passed it for some pasta or rice, but getting healthy food in a hurry is not easy in a fast-food, fast-lane city. Anyway, what's a few extra calories on your last day? This was like a death row prisoner's last meal before the noose. I remembered reading about an old woman of ninety-five in a tabloid newspaper. When asked what she would do if she had her life over again, she said, 'Eat more cake.' Sounded good to me. Fuck healthy, let's go out with a belly full of chicken and chips.

The shop was as dirty as you could get without some yoke pinning a 'closed due to contamination' poster across the front door and ringing a leper's bell. The proprietor stood behind the counter waiting for my custom. Dressed in a dirty white pinny, he looked like he might have just escaped from a mental institution for the criminally insane. He was dark, hairy and large with a black moustache that covered most of his lower face. His left eye was half closed. A scar ran through the eyebrow, eyelid and cheekbone. He picked at his nose as I entered.

I noticed that there were rat traps on open display behind the food counter and wondered if I should really be eating here. The Moustache lifted his good eye to ask for my order. Obviously a man of few words. I looked at the menu, which was hovering above the till in neon. The meal I wanted was listed on the board as Meal Two. The 'M' was missing from the word 'Meal' so it read 'eal two'. In normal circumstances I might have made a funny, perhaps laughed at the absurdity of 'eel' on the menu of a chicken-only restaurant. I decided not to. Nothing seemed funny today. I pointed to the menu; the Moustache's eyes followed my finger. I was as eager to avoid conversation as the Moustache. He nodded, and I think he might have moved his mouth but it was lost under yards of facial hair. He dished my food out into a paper box without a word. I paid, he tried to pass me the change, I shook my head indicating that he should keep it, he nodded his gratitude.

Before I'd even left the premises, the box of chicken and fries was already dripping with grease. I stood outside the shop and picked at the chips. I watched the traffic go by. It was nearly midnight but still busy. Cars, trucks, bikes and people flooded the streets and the roads, all on their way home after a night out. I envied them. They were probably heading back to their loved ones, some warm semi with two kids and a Labrador and a warm mate in bed. How I envied them. I wondered if they knew just how blessed they were.

I picked a chip from the box, my fingers trembling slightly with fear, my stomach a spaghetti junction of nerves and hormones, all racing around inside me. The skin slithered off the chicken. I held it up; it looked alive. It might as well have been. I slung it in the bin by my side, where it wrapped itself around a discarded Coke can. I tossed the rest of the food after it. It was about as appetising as eating it while it was still clucking.

I leaned against the window. Closed my eyes, breathed in deeply through my nostrils, then gave a deep sigh, that kind of pissed off what-the-fuck-is-this-all-about sigh you give when life no longer seems worth the effort. I leaned over the bin to take out the serviette to wipe the grease from my fingers. I caught sight of myself in the window. I was unshaven, uncouth, scruffy; I looked like I had been on the streets sleeping in shop doorways. Although I had been training hard in that hotel room I had let my whiskers grow and put on the bloodstained clothes from my past fights. It felt good going into a showdown with the badges of battle emblazoned across my shirt. Like notches on a gun. It would add to the psych-out when I finally made the club: turning up looking mean, mad and dirty. I needed every edge I could get. No wonder the Moustache had looked me up and down when I'd entered his place for food: probably thought I was about to steal the tills.

Crash! The smashing of glass made me jump out of my skin. I had hardly noticed two young blokes in tracksuits and baseball caps swagger drunkenly into the takeaway. When I looked through the window into the small shop I saw the Moustache behind the counter, arms aloft in surrender, shouting in what sounded like

Arabic. The two youths were shouting back at him and throwing things over the counter, smashing the perspex menu and the glass display case that held the chicken.

'Money, money, come on, cunt!' It was the thinner of the two scroats. He looked like a scarecrow in a tracksuit: pale, bony face, vascular, angry neck. Scroat Two was ballooning from left to right, building up for the attack, a cheetah hunting a gazelle. He was black with large eyes and flaring nostrils that snorted as he postured. To the uninitiated the posturing might have seemed frightening – and that's the response it is meant to elicit – but to me it just said scared. When they posture, splay their arms, big themselves up, make loads of noise, snort, dribble, verbally attack, you know that they are trying to get the booty through intimidation, without a fight. And it usually works because it triggers the flight or freeze response and turns the majority of us into quivering wrecks.

It was working. The Moustache was falling apart at the seams, screaming and cowering. The scroats piled the intimidation higher by hitting him with verbal from both sides so that he had nowhere to hide; whichever way he turned there was a spitting, attacking expletive. It's how these scroats work. Come in, smash something to elicit the adrenal dump, and once the recipient is full to the brim with fear and shock, they employ the pincer movement. One comes in from the left with demands and verbal attacks, the other duplicates it from the right. They pile it on until their victim breaks and hands over the cash. The only thing that they didn't count on was me. I suppose it was the fact that I looked like I'd fallen asleep in a skip that made them underestimate me, or perhaps the fact that I had my hand in the bin getting the serviette when they walked past. Whatever it was, it was a mistake. I was already full of adrenalin and feeling pretty fucking shit anyway, and these two pieces of nob-cheese were the final straw.

•

I rushed into the shop just as the black guy was moving forward to hurl a punch. *Whoosh!* I raced in and kicked both of his legs from under him with a back-leg sweep, a technique Reg had taken from Shotokan karate and passed on to me. The scroat must have gone three feet off the ground, and when he hit the greasy tiles head first he was already out of it. The stamp that I followed up with came spontaneously and bounced his already unconscious head off the floor like a basketball. His eyes were closed, his foot twitched involuntarily, and I followed the physical attack with a growling battle scream. There was so much adrenalin in me ready for the showdown at the Ecstasy Club, I couldn't help but bleed a little of it now. The scream to underline my stamp was a psychological attack, ideal when you are dealing with more than one opponent. It scares the shit out of them in five colours and ten barrels, and tells anyone in the vicinity that might be thinking of getting involved 'Keep away or I'll make your head into a canoe.' The Native Americans used screams, chants and war paint to scare enemies from afar; the ancient Chinese general Sun Tzu recommended the use of drums, whistles and bells to scare the enemy whilst they tried to sleep; even Scottish clans in the time of Rob Roy and William Wallace used drums and bagpipes to get the enemy shitting their kilts before the battle.

The other scroat fell for the oldest psychological ploy in the book and froze to the spot. He looked down at his mate, who had a hat of bloody treacle already forming around his head, then he looked at me, eyes climbing out of their sockets. He obviously didn't want any of that 'sweep, stamp, scream' shit.

'Fuck off!' I said, indicating the door with a nod of my head.

'Who the fuck are you?' he asked.

Whoosh! I don't like having to ask twice. Once is more than adequate with men of this ilk. I used the same technique, the double-leg sweep, with the same result. He was ripe for it, his feet were close together and his mind was on his mate.

Bang! He hit the deck hard but he wasn't out. He instinctively climbed back to his knees with the obvious intention of getting back up for a second round. *Bang!* I hoofed him full force across his face and he was eclipsed. Out there with Pluto.

I looked over at the counter and the Moustache made a smile and nodded several times. 'Thank you, thank you, thank you.'

Behind him appeared a young man of about eighteen, an older lady and a couple of young kids. They all smiled and nodded their appreciation. As I made my way to the door, the lady approached me with a box of chicken pieces and a huge bag of chips. I lifted my hands and tried to decline the offer but she would have none of it. I had helped them and she wanted to repay me.

'Best chicken, best pieces,' she told me in broken English, as if reading my mind and knowing that my last order was more grease than it was chicken. I took it from her and smiled.

As I drove past the shop, I could see the whole of the Moustache's family dragging the two prostrate bodies out of the door and onto the pavement. What a crazy fucking world we live in.

I parked up and scoffed my dinner. When the lady in the shop said 'best pieces' she wasn't kidding, though having to destroy two scroats to get the right service is asking a bit much. Or it might have been the fact that I had emptied my body of the very corrosive adrenalin and my appetite had returned, even if it was only temporarily. I sat in a car park eating my dinner and patiently waiting until closing time for the clubs. Not long; a couple of hours and I would be on my way.

I must have dozed off because I suddenly came to with a start. I still felt shaky and hyped up after the encounter in the takeaway.

Looked at my watch. It was 2.33 a.m. Time to go. I wanted to get the whole thing with William out of the way. A thought suddenly jumped into my mind. Maybe I should wait a bit longer, make sure that the club was well and truly empty before I went in. Maybe I should even reconsider. Perhaps I could wait until the next morning when the light of day offered a little protection. I was hesitating. My nap had weakened me, allowed a little hesitation to find its way through my resolve. I suddenly felt very lonely, very sad.

Fuck it, enough of this! Let's get down there and get it done. I was so angry, so very angry at the situation I was in. I didn't want to be there, I didn't want this shit in my life, I didn't want this grief any more. I needed it to end, and if that meant me losing the beat in my heart at the end of a stubby nozzle, so be it. I was fucked off with this shit and crap and muck.

I needed to act and act soon. If I didn't, I feared that I might never do it, and that would be a tragedy, because running is painful. It was not a life I wanted to live any more. I wasn't even sure at this point that I wanted to live at all. I was so angry that nothing scared me.

I started the car and headed for Baldwin Street, the address on the gold-lettered business card I had tucked in my jacket pocket. I knew that I was on my way to a messy encounter, and there was little doubt in my mind that this would not end without some grievous hurt. But at least there was solace in knowing that the end was nigh. I now knew why the samurai believed that embracing death empowered you. It did, it really did. The feeling was almost epiphanic. I felt high. I was facing my nemesis and I felt great: I had held my bottle and made myself do it. In that moment I was impervious to fear. I had faced death in my mind, accepted it without demurring and my reward was this grand moment of clarity.

The Ecstasy was a glorious club with huge silver doors and a neon sign as big as a double-decker bus: *The Ecstasy Club – Manchester's Premier Nightclub*. I was greeted by a pyramid of steps up to the front door. I walked up them and hammered at the doors. I waited.

I had worked in plenty of clubs, so I knew that the staff and management would be there until at least four in the morning. I also knew that after a night of tension and a club full of raving punters, the majority of them E'd up, they would all be relaxed, switched off; an ideal time for me to make my move.

The door opened just enough to reveal a black-haired doorman. He was lean and neat, his bow-tie undone and hanging around his neck, cigarette dangling from his lips.

'What's up, kid?' His manner was polite.

'I'm after William.'

He looked me up and down. I'd had a lot of similar looks today, and I was getting a bit fed up with it.

'Tell him the bloke from the Midlands has come for a one on one.' I smiled as I said it.

His face became vacant, as if he did not quite comprehend what I'd said.

'How you gonna get past me?' he asked with the confidence of a veteran doorman.

I shrugged. I got straight to the point. 'I'll choke you out until you piss your pants.'

He was taken aback. 'You got a fucking death wish?' he asked, sure that I must have.

'Yeah. I have,' I replied flatly, equally sure.

There was a moment of unreal tension. He just didn't know how to respond. His eyebrows lifted in confusion. He looked behind him, as if checking that no one had overheard us.

'You'd better come in then.'

I followed him into the club. He locked the doors behind us. I could sense that disturbing quiet that you always get in a nightclub after the music has been switched off, the memory of it still in the air. The carpet was beer-sticky under my feet, the air stale with cigarette smoke and alcohol fumes. In the distance I could hear the sounds of laughter and chat, obviously the staff having a late one. I followed the doorman through the foyer, through two glass doors and past the huge downstairs bar. Grand stairwells stood at each corner of the main dancefloor, leading to bars and smaller dancefloors on different levels. There were cigarette butts all over the floor. A young lad walked around the club with a dustbin bag, collecting the rubbish left from the night and hunting for any money that might have been dropped inadvertently. The lad caught my eye as I passed him. I nodded. He smiled.

As we got to the end of the dancefloor my companion stopped in front of three tables full of large men, about ten in all. A couple of other tables close by were filled with pretty barmaids and glass collectors. The laughter and chat stopped as I approached and everyone looked at me. The first face I recognised was that of Jimmy, the boxer who I had beaten a new head at Mick's, the one who'd accused me of stealing the brown, the cunt who had lied. He rose from his chair and stood to attention like someone had rung a corner bell for the first round. His face was a mask of hate. His arms splayed aggressively. He couldn't believe I was there.

The next to stand was Wallflower, the guy who had tried to kill me at the B&B. Ugly scabs over his face, his smile on the floor, his teeth missing at the front. The doorman accompanying me looked towards a smart man sat with the barmaids and the glass collectors.

'He reckons he's come for a one on one with you, William,' he said, mockingly.

There was a sudden chill in the room. No one spoke. William stood up and everyone looked to him. This was obviously not a man to fuck with. He was the leader here, and they all wanted to see what he was about to do with me, the challenger to his throne.

Jimmy the boxer moved forward first and fast.

'Stop!' It was William. His voice had that 'don't fuck' quality that I'd heard only a few times in my life. Jimmy froze to the spot as though he was on remote control. His face remained angry, ready for the fight. William stepped forward. I glanced to my side and noticed an empty beer jug. That would be my first line of attack. If things went all team-handed on me some fucker would be wearing it, whether the colour suited them or not. William noticed that I had noticed the jug. And I noticed that he had noticed me noticing. But that was my game and not his. I'd deliberately lingered on the jug so he would notice. The art of saying without saying 'Get too close, you dog's doings, and I'll turn your mug into a chandelier.'

I'd also made a mental note of a heavy wooden stool and a small copper-topped table. It looked light enough to swing, heavy enough to crush a couple of skulls and dense enough to act as a makeshift shield should glasses, knives and bats find their way into the fight.

The game was already on. Fast assessments were ping-ponging back and forth. Two old pros in the pre-posture to war, two dogs circling, waiting for a tear up.

The game begins with the assessment, looking for strengths in your opponent that you can avoid and weaknesses that you can exploit. William's gait was confident and authoritative. His back was so straight that it looked as if he had a plumb line going through his arse and out of the top of his head. He was fucking Clint Eastwood. I half expected him to mutter in that southern

Josey Wales drawl, 'Are you gonna use that glass or are you gonna whistle Dixie?' He was not what I had expected.

What had I expected? A monster, I suppose, like Jimmy, like Mick the prick, like the gangsters who tried to shoot me. I expected a mass of muscles and expletives, tattoos and the perfunctory bald 'gangster' head. I expected a monosyllabic thug who could throw a combination of punches with ease but struggled to make a full sentence without the aid of a picture book. Or perhaps I expected a Kray type with big shoulders and a bigger attitude. I got neither.

At first glance the man before me looked more like a bank manager than a gangster. He was tall, maybe six foot, grey, thinning on top and athletic. He was meticulously dressed; his suit looked like it was worth more than my car, and his shoes were polished and pointed at the end. If you want to judge a man, look at his shoes: polished shoes usually mean a history of discipline, possibly military. Most people let themselves down with their footwear; they dress to the nines but then wear scuffed shoes that spoil the whole ensemble. I checked out his hands as he approached, to see if he was carrying. If they are carrying weapons they make a point of hiding the weapon hand in a pocket or turning their palm into the side of their leg. This man did neither. His hands were open and in plain view. A good start.

A weapon changes everything. If he was carrying I would have ploughed a projectile right into his teeth, preferably the beer jug sat on the table by my side. But he would have known that. He'd seen me check it out, and he would have been doing the same assessment of me. So it wouldn't have been in his interest to come straight into the affray tooled up. That would have told me all that I needed to know, leaving no room for negotiation. Everyone wants to negotiate a little, even if it is just as part of the assessment. Especially when some maniac turns up on their turf looking for a bit of contact. A weapon on open display would have left no room for him to get inside my guard and take me out before the physical game had properly begun.

I checked out his knuckles. They were disjointed, the right fist in particular looked like a knot at the end of an ugly-club, his middle knuckle was way up in the back of his hand. This told me that he was a big banger and that he had smacked a few heads in his time, not all of them accurately. Any veteran of the dark arts of the street wears their broken hands like badges of battle. The scars offer a visual pedigree to anyone who cares to look. If you fought and fought often you broke hands, simple as that. And if I ever faced anyone without broken hands, or without some kind of battle scar I knew that I was in for an easy time.

William offered no such promise. I knew I was facing a master. His fingers were bent and fat, the fingers of a jacketed wrestler, a judoka. His wrists were sinewy and vascular; he was no stranger to heavy weights and extreme fitness.

His face was healthy, sharp, with no sign of fat around the cheekbones or jawline. This guy was conditioned. His left ear was slightly scarred, the definition around the lobe was flat and smooth, a 'designer cauliflower'. Not completely busted up, but enough to show that he had done some scrimmage, enough to cause his ears to bust, bleed and congeal internally.

His eyes were what got my arse twitching the most. He had that hundred-yard stare, the white of his eyes visible above his lower lid, telling anyone with even a modicum of sense that this was a man of experience. I was desperately looking for any sign of weakness. I could see none.

William threw the first subliminal attack when he slipped off his jacket gracefully and deliberately. Phase one of the threat, which says 'I'm preparing to fight'. It is a part of the pre-fight psych-out, either priming the opponent and weakening them to open a window for the first attack, or triggering their adrenalin into overload. And on most fighters this would have done the trick. But I was not most fighters. I was a veteran with thousands of hard wrestles under my belt and enough fights in chip-shop doorways and pub toilets to know my way around the rituals. To return the unspoken challenge I slipped off my Cartier watch – it still had a film of blood across most of the face from my previous battles – placing it on the table next to me.

I moved slowly and deliberately, letting my hand hover in the air slightly, controlling the tremor that was trying to run through my fingers. This was my way of blagging William that I was not scared. Of course I was scared, but you know what they say, when ignorance is mutual, confidence is king.

William walked forward and rolled up his sleeves, his way of saying 'I'm serious here, I'm ready to fight'. That's what it was meant to say, but to me it simply said 'I'm posturing because I want to avoid a physical fight if I can'.

It was the first weakness that he had shown, and inside I gave a small smile. He spoke to me for the first time as he rolled up his sleeves.

'So, what's the story?' he asked. It was a way of bridging the gap between us, a bid at engaging my brain and creating his window of opportunity. This guy knew his stuff. I raised my hand to stop him, to let him know that I knew the game and was not about to play.

He paused and splayed his hands. Again he asked, 'What's the story?' He was getting impatient.

Everyone looked on silently. William should not have been talking at all, he should have been fighting. Letting someone, anyone, walk into your place and throw down a challenge was sacrilege. I should have been unconscious, on the way to dead by now. And yet he was talking. I decided to gain the upper hand.

He was looking for a verbal spar, a bit of round-the-table negotiation. I decided to go for the kill.

'No story, William,' I replied flatly, being very careful not to allow any emotion that he might read as weakness into my voice. 'I've come here to fight.'

This was a bold move on my part because it left him nowhere to go but the fight. It could have backfired on me if he'd turned out to be a monster ready to tear me a new arsehole. He stopped dead, already aware that his tactics were not working. He splayed his arms again and smiled, then looked behind him at the others, his crowd, his followers, who were all waiting for a response. They were silent as statues.

'What kind of a cunt are you?' William asked, turning back to face me. Before I could answer, he continued talking, building himself up into a frenzy, another ploy to try and psych me out. I could have told him that it wasn't going to work. I'd made my mind up to fight, come what may, and no pre-fight games were about to change it.

He nodded to Jimmy. 'First you fuck my man here when he ain't looking, then you trot off with three hundred K of my brown. Now, now –' He was starting to stutter and salivate and go red in the head. This immaculate catalogue gangster was starting to crack. I had admired him so much before. He was building up an anger that might take him into a battle that his cool had already backed down from. 'Now you come into my club, *my* fucking gaff, *mine*, you come in here and challenge *me* to a fight! You're a cunt.'

'I never touched your gear.' I said it evenly, no emotion, still playing the game. I looked at Jimmy and continued, 'You want to look a bit closer to home.'

Jimmy started to foam at the mouth. 'I'll fucking kill you!' he said, moving forward. All the other lumps, as if waiting for permission, leapt forward at the same time. I dragged the beer jug off the table, wrapped my fingers around the handle and smashed it on the edge of the table, leaving me with a jagged razor knuckleduster. William stopped them from moving forward with a wave of his hand. They did their master's bidding and stopped dead, but hovered on the periphery, just waiting for the forward command.

I didn't need to speak. My action said more than a ream of words. William looked at me, tilting his head as though he couldn't quite believe I was actually there.

'Have you got a fucking death wish?' he asked me incredulously.

It was the second time that night I had been asked that question. I played my ace. I took a creased envelope from my pocket, skimming it across the floor. It landed at William's feet like a fencer's challenging glove. He bent over and picked it up, mouth ajar, and read the front. *Last Will and Testament.* He shook his head as if he couldn't believe what he was reading.

'I never had your gear,' I said, deciding to offer him a window. Most people will take an honourable exit from a fight if you let them have one. I felt that William might just take it if it was offered in the right way and at the right time.

'I've got no quarrel with you,' I said firmly. 'I don't do drugs. I know fuck-all about yours. I wouldn't know what they looked like if they fell out of the sky and hit me on the head.' The room was deathly quiet. I waited for the response.

William looked long and hard at the envelope. He walked back to the bar and placed the envelope on top of it. He looked at it again, nodding to himself as if his mind had been made up. Suddenly he pulled a long metal baseball bat from behind the counter.

Fuck, I didn't expect that. I felt my limbs go to jelly as he walked back, his eyes never leaving me, not for a second. I was about to die. I was sure of it. William stopped at Jimmy, still looking at me. Jimmy looked at the bat, light from the ceiling glinting off it like a light sabre. Jimmy then looked at me and smiled.

Bang! Without warning, William put the full force of his body weight, plus momentum, plus projection behind a heavy, sickly swing and smashed the bat right across Jimmy's teeth.

It sounded like a hammer hitting a girder. The girls closest caught most of the blood. All the other doormen – as shocked as me – took two steps backwards as if separating themselves from the violence just in case the second swing was aimed in their direction. Jimmy let out a primitive scream, one of those involuntary types that you don't think are in you until someone separates you from your teeth with the heavy swing of a steel bat. Everyone, including me, 'oohed' in unison, as if it was our teeth on the bat and on the way to the floor. I saw a single tooth fly through the air on the end of a spit of blood. Jimmy went over immediately, on to his knees. His fingers dabbed hesitantly at his lips, trembling, hoping perhaps that the damage was not as bad as he knew it was. Pathetically he tried to collect what was left of his mouth in his hands. An impossible task. What was left just seeped through his fingers and dripped to the carpet. Jimmy looked up at William, his eyes full of bewilderment.

The second volley from the bat, full of menace and anger, smashed across Jimmy's fingers so hard that the bones snapped and poked through the skin. Another pathetic yelp escaped from Jimmy, one that seemed too high-pitched to come from the mouth of a grown man. The girls screamed and the men took two more steps back, transfixed in morbid horror and fascination.

The third strike took Jimmy out of the game. His blood dripped from lumps of torn mouth into the carpet. William was red. Seething. Blood had splashed up his trouser legs and the bat had all but changed its colour to crimson. William held the bat in strike pose for a second, maniacally rocking it back and forward as though awaiting a fast ball, his lips pulled tightly and viciously over his teeth. His eyes bulged. He hissed as he looked at the other men.

'Any other cunt want a bit?'

He walked towards them as he said it to underline his threat. This post-assault was standard text for men of his ilk. William was using this chicken slaughter to train the other monkeys. His question was just a way of making sure that they were all reading from the same script. Everyone shook their heads in unison. Then he looked over at me. His breathing was heavy, he was salivating, his face a conflicting concoction of hate and admiration. I felt that part of him wanted to decapitate me with the flat end of his bat and the other part wanted to pat me on the back and offer me a job.

'You,' he panted, pointing the bloody bat in my direction, 'are one brave bastard.'

The bat was still hovering there, as if William was trying to make up his mind whether or not he should give it to me just for my temerity. He was working out whether letting me walk would damage his credibility amongst his criminal underlings. I knew in my heart that William wouldn't attack, he just needed an honourable exit. I was too dangerous: the envelope with my last will and testament in it told him that much. I was prepared to die in that club. He knew that this made me the most dangerous man in his world. A man who does not fear death – and at that moment in time not only did I not fear it, I actually embraced it – fears nothing; he has nothing to lose.

Jimmy's groan of pain broke the deadlock. It took William's attention away from me for a second. William turned to look at him just as Jimmy vomited up a porridge of sick, teeth and blood.

'Get that piece of shit off my carpet,' William commanded.

Three of the heavies moved over and dragged the bleeding lump to the exit doors, kicked them open and threw him outside like yesterday's rubbish.

William flung the bat across the dancefloor. It clattered noisily before coming to rest in the corner. His action looked aggressive, and everyone jumped in fright, but I knew what it really meant. It was over. He had discarded his weapon, made his choice. I would walk.

William sauntered over to the long bar that only two hours before would have been six deep with customers looking for a liquid high. He went behind the bar, all eyes following his every step. He served himself a drink. Breakfast with Jack Daniels.

One of the barmaids, a beautiful twenty-something with a catwalk body, walked past me towards the bat. She smiled shyly. I stood there like a dick, not sure what to do. I had never expected to leave this place other than on a stretcher or in a box. I had not planned this far ahead and now that I was here, miraculously unharmed, I didn't know what to do.

I needed to get rid of the jug. It was so tight in my grip that my hand was starting to ache. I unravelled my fingers and placed it back onto the table, my stiff joints locked in place. I clenched and unclenched my fist to get the blood back into the fingers.

The barmaid picked up the bat from the corner of the room and walked back to me. She looked at me and then at my glass weapon, discarded on the table, asking for permission to take it away. I nodded. She took it behind the bar. William was gulping his drink. She gently rubbed his shoulder. He flinched and turned, but when he saw her his face broke out into a smile and I saw the bank manager return. The barmaid smiled back and walked to the end of the bar where she put the bat in the glass washer and switched it on. Another barmaid appeared with a bucket of hot water and disinfectant. She knelt on the carpet and started to wash away the blood and vomit. The water in the bucket quickly turned a muddy red. These girls were well trained and certainly used to the blood and snot of nightclub life. By the time the police came – if they ever did – all they would find would be deaf and dumb witnesses and the smell of Dettol.

Everyone else in the room stood to attention: no one seemed ready to sit, unsure as to whether the situation was over or not. William looked over at me. He held my gaze for a minute, then nodded his head and winked. He beckoned me to the bar with a wave of his hand. I couldn't be sure that the threat was over either, but I took the chance. What did I have to lose?

I picked up my watch from the table, pocketed it and walked over. I sat on one of the tall bar stools and looked at William. As soon as I sat down, the others in the room followed suit as if on cue. The room filled with hushed excited chatter.

'How did you know I was telling the truth?' I asked William, breaking the silence between the two of us.

He shrugged. 'I'm not a cunt,' he said. 'Some people might think I am, and that's OK as far as it goes. But I'm not. And when someone I trusted –' I could feel the hurt in him as he said the word 'trusted' – 'goes from driving a beat up old Jag to a new XKR, you've got to start asking yourself a few questions.'

He took a drink from the glass and filled another for me. I was never into shorts but this was not the time to be refusing hospitality. I sipped the bitter whisky, grimacing at the taste.

'I suppose I knew right from the off,' he continued. 'But, well, it's easier to turn a blind eye and believe some stranger had your stuff away than it is to believe that your own brother has fucked you over for three hundred K.'

I nearly choked on my drink. 'Your brother? The boxer is your brother?'

He looked at me quizzically. 'Who's the boxer?' he asked.

'Boxer,' I repeated. 'Your brother.'

'My brother?' he said, confused. 'My brother's name is Jimmy.'

'Yeah, Jimmy the boxer.' Oh fuck, here we go again.

It took me a couple of seconds to explain and when I did William cracked his ribs laughing. It broke the tension.

William refilled his glass and necked another mouthful of whisky, then filled it again from the optic.

'I'm really sorry,' I said. 'About, you know, your brother.'

'It happens,' he said. 'It happens.' He paused for a second as if my apology had taken him by surprise and he had to find an apology of his own to match it. 'I'm sorry too. About the lad.'

I frowned. Now it was my turn to be confused. 'Lad?' What the fuck was he talking about?

'Bad form that,' he continued. 'A shit trick. Still, you evened that baby right up: I heard Mick is still breathing through a machine. His brain thinks it's a cabbage.' He laughed.

I paused for a second, trying to make sense of what he was saying. I didn't have a clue.

'What lad?' I asked again.

'In the flat. Shit trick that. None of my doing.' He could see that I was still confused. 'The fire in the flat. I'm just saying it's bad form about the lad dying and that. I don't blame you for raring up. I'd have done the same myself.'

My head was spinning now. 'I'm not sure what you mean. Lad? You mean girl? You mean Ginger?'

My mind raced back to that fateful day, to the fire, to the stretcher, to the firemen with their mournful looks, to the long locks of ginger hair hanging lankly from under the smoke-blackened blankets.

'Was definitely a lad. Mick's a psycho. Obssessed with his ex. It was her flat, he was trying to kill her, couldn't bear her being with anyone else. But that's the irony – she'd popped out, it was her brother who got it in the neck. Shit trick.'

What? Ginger wasn't dead, she wasn't killed in that fire? I dared not accept what I'd hoped beyond my wildest dreams, that Ginger was actually alive. My mind was racing. It couldn't be true, it couldn't be.

'I had the law down here the next day trying to tie me in on it. Fuck all to do with me. They couldn't interview Mick could they? The cunt's been asleep for a week.' He laughed again.

My head was gone, it was back there again, at that burning flat. It hadn't been Ginger on the stretcher. It'd been Cap, Steve, her brother who had the same hair. I stood up from the stool. My head was in the clouds, I couldn't believe it. I had to leave, there and then. I had to get back to see her. What the fuck must she be thinking of me? I had been missing for over a week, thinking that my lady was dead. What must she be thinking? That I had fucked off, abandoned her, run away? I was already leaving, heading for the door, heading for my car.

'You OK?' William asked.

'There's someone I need to see,' I said.

Just as I was about to leave something occurred to me. I turned back to William.

'How did you keep finding me?' I asked. 'At the hotels? Who told you where I was?'

'An old friend of yours.' He smiled.

'Who?'

He shook his head. He wasn't about to give me that kind of information. But he did tell me how. This 'friend' had an official line to my credit-card company's head office, and they had informed him of where I was the moment I used my card. I had guessed that William was tracing my credit-card transactions but I respected the fact that he couldn't break a confidence.

'Let's just say,' he concluded, 'that for the price of a nice Cartier watch you can buy just about anyone.'

The smile dropped from my face. He'd told me exactly what I needed to know.

That left me one more score to settle.

In minutes I was back on the road and heading home as fast as my wheels would take me. Home. To Ginger. I was elated, fucking elated. Things would be different when I got back. I wouldn't fuck up this time. I would find my lady, hold her and never let her go again. I was two hours away and it felt like twenty. The motorway was orange and quiet, empty and beautiful. The car stank of chips but that was lovely too. I was on my way home. On that journey I thought about all that had happened in my life since meeting Ginger in the café. About the first look we had shared, and her smile and her love. How I had lost her in the flames and how, after facing my greatest fears, I had found her again. I thought about Mick. I'd destroyed him, and in the process nearly destroyed myself. I thought about how I had very nearly walked out and left him to his dirty deed when he first walked into my life and laid his ugly mitts on Ginger. And how, when I lay on that candlewick bedspread in the B&B I'd wished I had walked out. I felt so glad that I didn't. What if I had? What if I had walked away, left the café, minded my own business? I'd have had none of this. No Ginger, no freedom, I'd still be stuck with my shitty mentality and a job shovelling shit and a flat that you wouldn't keep Lassie in, with two back-monkeys, my dad and Father Tarbuck, growing fat from my fears. I felt so grateful that

I didn't walk out that day, so grateful that I'd got involved. The journey to Manchester, the training, the healing, the self-honesty, the conviction that I should stop running and face my fears. Getting back into training, remembering Reg and all his wise advice. It would all have been a dream but for that one meeting. I was so glad that it had all happened. Even with all the pain, the fear and the dread I was still grateful. Because now I was really free. I wouldn't be working even a single day more on that building site. I knew I could do better. I knew that the world was open to me and that I could do anything, I could be anything. I had found my promised land behind the walls and guards of my deepest fears. I would never look back.

It was dawn and I was nearly home when the flashing blue lights of a police car pulled me over. No problem, I'd done nothing wrong, I wasn't speeding. I got out of the car to meet the policeman halfway.

How naive I was. It was only when I saw that shiny apple head walking towards me that I realised what a twat I'd been. What about Mick? The lad was in a permanent sleep, being kept alive by a plug in the wall.

Apple approached me, a big fuck-off smile on his face like he'd just won the lottery.

'I think there's a warrant out for you, ain't there?' he said. I hated him to pieces.

Chapter Twenty-One

Full Circle

So here we are, back at the beginning of my story, in the prison cell looking at a nine. And if Mick died, it'd be an eighteen. I was cabbaged. Destroyed. I felt that there was no justice.

Fuck it. Of course there was justice. And this was it. I was facing it. I couldn't lie to myself any longer. Not after all I had gone through. I was in that cell because of my own actions. Imprisonment was the consequence of taking the law into my own hands. I had nothing to complain about. At least Ginger was alive, even if I hadn't seen her, and might never see her again. She didn't even know where I was. But what does all that mean when measured against the life of the girl you love?

I had good reason to attack Mick. I had smashed him because of the crimes he'd committed against Ginger and her brother, both innocents. There might be a little reprieve in the courts if I could claim mitigating circumstances. I might have been looking at a nine but at least I was alive and Ginger was alive. No sense in complaining. I would take what came. No more running, no more hiding, no more grudges or secrets, especially from myself. I had learned a few things, faced my shadows and brought them into the light. If nothing else, I had freedom from my deepest fears. I had come to terms with the abuse I suffered from the two men that should have deserved my trust the most, but who had both betrayed me. I felt that when I did get out I would still be young enough to do a few things with my life. And maybe, I hoped, Ginger might wait around for me. I wasn't sure if I dared expect that much; it was a lot to ask.

I lay on the cell bed, hands behind my head, trying to come to terms with what had happened. The cell door opened. Apple stood in the doorway like an executioner. His face was full of anger and hate.

'Suppose you think you're a clever cunt?' he asked.

I didn't reply. I didn't have the slightest inkling of what he was talking about and I didn't want to give him the pleasure of seeing my confusion.

'Out.' I squinted my eyes. What the fuck was he on about?

'Out.' He said it again but this time he raised his voice an octave to try and sound commanding. Not easy for a weak man like him. I stood up and looked at him. He stepped back from the doorway to let me through. I walked past him. I was probably being transferred to a remand prison whilst I awaited trial.

I found myself facing Sarge again at the front desk, the kindly chap who had given me Mick's address at the scene of the fire. He had just started work. It was six in the morning, the shift change.

Fuck, it seemed like so long ago since I last saw him. Another lifetime. Another person. He looked up from his desk and held my gaze for a second. I gave him one of those 'ah, well' smiles and shrugged my shoulders. I liked the man and wanted him to know that I didn't hold any grudges against him. Apple was at my back like a limpet.

'Just out of curiosity, who gave you Mick's address?' asked Apple. The question was full of contempt. Sarge looked at me, worry in his eyes, then shot an angry glance at Apple.

I smiled again. 'I don't know what you're talking about,' I said, turning to look at Apple. I held the stare and smiled until Apple was so uncomfortable that he started to cringe. I turned back to Sarge. We both smiled. Then Sarge looked at his watch and glared past me at Apple.

'It's six,' he said. 'The prisoners need breakfast.' I looked to see Apple's reaction; he was a picture.

'Two sugars for me,' I said. Apple took a sharp breath, and it must have taken everything he had not to explode there and then. He backed away slightly, still looking at me and Sarge, then turned and stomped out of the room to the cells. I turned back to Sarge. We both grinned. He handed me a pen.

'Just sign here for your stuff,' he said. I took the pen and signed. I guessed I was being transferred and needed to sign to make sure that my belongings, a Cartier watch and my shoelaces, were all accounted for. I handed Sarge his pen. He handed me my watch and shoelaces.

'You're free to go.' His ruddy face was full of smiles.

'Pardon?' How could I be? What about Mick? Still plugged into the wall and eating through a hypodermic.

'You are free to go. You're a free man.'

I couldn't believe what I was hearing. Free? How so? He must have read my thoughts.

'You had two witnesses to say that you were at the scene of the fire when Michael Wall was attacked in his home.'

'What about your man?' I asked, indicating Apple.

Sarge winked. 'He's bent from his top to his toes,' he said. 'We all know it, we're just waiting for the lad to fuck up. And he will, they always do. Then I'll be down on him so hard he'll wish he never joined the police force.'

But the witnesses? What witnesses? I didn't know anyone that liked me enough to lie for me in a police statement. Unless …

'Who?' I needed to know. Sarge smiled again. Cool air hit my back as the door on to the street opened behind me.

'I was one of them,' said Sarge.

I leaned back, startled, needing distance to take the full impact of what he had said. I wanted to speak, to thank him, to ask him why, to beg an explanation. Sarge looked right past me and his whole face lifted into a huge affectionate smile.

'And she was the other,' he said.

I turned to see who was standing behind me, who this mystery second witness might be, who was responsible for switching a light on in Sarge's face.

I turned. She was stood there in all her freckly splendour, a beautiful vision. My heart exploded. It was Ginger. My girl. She was smiling and crying at the same time and in a second I was in her arms and doing the same. I was home and happy.

Before we left the station I took the Cartier off my wrist. 'You'd better keep this,' I said, handing it over to Sarge. 'It don't belong to me. It's your man's there.' I nodded towards the cells, indicating Apple. I turned the watch over and showed Sarge the inscription on the back. 'Fell off his wrist when he arrested me a couple of weeks ago,' I said. 'I was just keeping it warm for him. I meant to give it back then, but, well, you know how it is. It slipped my mind. Can you make sure he gets it?'

Sarge looked at the watch, a huge grin across his face. 'Oh, he'll get it all right.' I didn't doubt that he would.

I turned back to Ginger and hugged her. We walked down the steps of the station to freedom and all I kept thinking was *This God fellow, He really does move fucking mysteriously*.

⋆ END ⋆

Read on for sample extracts from Geoff Thompson's bestselling autobiography, *Watch My Back.*

Praise for *Watch My Back*:

'A brilliant insight!'
Reggie Kray

'This man is very, very hard. Buy his book if you know what's good for you.'
Maxim

'This is as real as it gets.'
Dave Courtney

'The psyche-outs, the stabbings, glassings, incidents involving the camaraderie of the door . . . Thompson's 300 fights – never losing, not once – are recorded in this excellent book.'
Loaded

'Surviving 300 bloody confrontations and earning the fearsome reputation as a knockout specialist, Thompson takes you as close to real-life street fights as you'll ever want to get.'
Bizarre Magazine

'A compelling insight.'
Arena

'Utterly compelling . . . read it.'
Men's Fitness

'Grabs you by the throat and doesn't put you down.'
Front

'. . . a stimulating read.'
Sky News

Watch My Back is available in hardback and paperback from all good bookshops, or via Geoff Thompson's own website www.geoffthompson.com, or via the Summersdale website, www.summersdale.com.

PREFACE (FROM *WATCH MY BACK*)

. . . he'd underestimated me. I would make sure he paid for his mistake. Whenever anyone underestimates me I always know the fight is mine. Their weakness makes them unprepared and gives me a window for the first shot. I train for the first shot – it's all I need. He was still holding the bottle of champagne by the neck. I made a mental note – I didn't want to be wearing it, it just wasn't my colour. We stood close together as I talked, too close really, so I tucked my chin down as a defence against a possible head-butt, forcing me to roll my eyes upwards to see his face. I got right to the point.

'Look, I've never met you before and you come into my club when I'm working and talk to me like I'm a piece of shit. If you do it again we're gonna be fighting.'

He was square on and badly positioned to launch an attack.

'Oh yeah,' he said, lining me up. 'Sure.'

He moved his left leg slightly back and prepared me for the champagne supernova. But he was a fucking amateur and hid his line-up badly. I noticed immediately, it stood out like a hard-on. It might have worked on the part-timers, the lads that liked a fight at the weekend, but I was a veteran in these matters: seven days a week, it was my job to notice when maniacs were trying to hit me with a bottle. I had maybe two seconds in which to make my move before he made his. No decisions to be made, too late for that. Hesitation is the biggest killer in nightclub fighting. The decision had been made for me ten minutes earlier when he told me that I sucked cocks, it was just a matter of putting my game plan into action. Not too detailed a plan, no complications, no equations, no grapple with morality or peer pressure, just bang him. That's it. All this bollocks about karate or kung-fu, about this range or that range, bridging the gap, setting up, weakening them with a kick – there's no need, just hit the fuckers . . . very hard! Time was tight and a single mistake could mean drip-food or worse. I played the game right back and simultaneously moved my right leg, giving myself a small, compact forty-five degree stance, hiding the movement with,

'That's all I'm saying.'

Bang!

A right cross, slightly hooked, hit just above his jawbone as his left hand lifted the champagne bottle towards me. The contact was high so he didn't go right out. Sometimes that's how it works, when the adrenalin is racing, targeting is often off, and you only have to be millimetres out to miss the KO. It did catch him hard though; he reeled back like he'd been run over. His body hit a forty-five degree angle going backwards and for a second I thought he was in sleepsville, but no, he back-peddled rapidly, trying to regain his composure. He was a hardy fucker. Usually when you hit them that hard they have themselves a little hibernation. Not this fella. He tried to stay up and fight but it was too late, he was mine. Like I said, I only need one shot.

I followed with a rapid-fire five-punch combination, slicing open both eyebrows and breaking his nose. Oozes of blood flicked through the air and splattered my white shirt. And me with no condom, too. He covered his bloodied face trying to capture what was left of his nose. As he cowered over I grabbed his white, stained shirt by the shoulders and pulled him face first into the carpet – he was gone. His sugar pedestal melted all around him by the rain of my attack. He kept his face covered, so I axe-kicked his back, many times. Too many. He was a big man to take over, but I had no intentions of letting him back up again, not this night. Kevin, who had been close by watching my back, stepped in and stopped me.

A small crowd of onlookers had gathered. They whispered excitedly. I liked this bit, especially at a new club. Suddenly I was not the soft 'what's he doing here' doorman they all mistook me for. I was a man to be feared. I felt good about the adulation, the back-pats and the line of free Buds on the bar like winner cups. I felt good as the endorphins raced around my blood in a celebratory lap of honour. I felt good that I had survived. The blood on my shirt was my badge; I was proud to wear it for the rest of the night. Deep down though, right in the very bowels of my mind, there was an aching realisation that with every blow I threw in anger and fear I was becoming more and more like the bastard on the floor in front of me swimming in his own blood and snot.

Mr T's girlfriend was running around him like a headless chicken. Collecting her man's blood and what was left of his face in a small cotton hanky that seemed inadequate amidst such mayhem, screaming at me, shouting at the other doorman, wailing for an ambulance and the police: it was all so undignified. I didn't give a monkey's fuck. I was on a high. The worm had turned – control of my fear was my greatest ally, his overconfidence my greatest asset. He'd trodden on a small, insignificant mound of earth and was blown to pieces. It was a fucking landmine. He should have known.

Later, many years on, I shared a beer with the guy. He still had the scars to prove I'd been there and we laughed about our first meeting. He admitted it was his fault and as the second beer passed his tonsils he said, 'I just picked on the wrong guy, that's all'.

Chapter 9 – It's a Knockout

(From *Watch My Back*)

So I was hardening up a little. All the exposure I was getting to violence, dealing with the police and having to face monsters as a way of life was starting to have its effect. At the time I felt good about it. I had learned, mostly through the tuition of John, how to adapt the physical skills of karate so that they worked in the pavement arena. I was no longer scared and could handle just about any situation that came into my life, something I had always struggled to do before the door. I was even starting to take control of situations that, in the beginning, I was happy to let John or the other lads deal with. I had gone from need to being needed. I felt good about the fact that not only was I controlling and looking after myself, but I could also – when needed – control, and look after others. That's the main reason doormen exist, so that they can look after the customers, the property, and not forgetting the staff of course. On one particular occasion it was the cloakroom girl that I came to the aid of.

'What's the problem lads?' My question was direct and hard.

'She won't fucking give us our coats, I've pointed them out to her. They're there, look, there.'

He pointed at two jackets in the middle of a hundred more hanging from coat racks in the tiny cloakroom in the tight reception area of the nightclub. I looked at the girl. Blonde and gorgeous but thicker than a whale omelette.

'They haven't got a ticket, Geoff.' Her voice was scared and I gave her a wink to let her know that I would deal with it. That was my game, what I was paid to do. I felt the ever-so-familiar tingle of adrenalin as it got in place for fight or flight, only in this game there was no flight, you either stayed or you didn't work. Runners got blackballed from every club in the city the very first time they listened to natural instinct and broke the minute mile. Bottling it even once could be a career-ending event, it also crushed hard-earned kudos and self-belief flatter than a shadow; it did for your confidence and reputation what syphilis does for your social standing. They say that you are only as good as your last fight and it's true; you could be the bravest man on earth a hundred times and become a coward by bottling it once. Not fair, methinks, but that, as you might say, is life.

This particular night had been a little slow. I'd just come back from the toilet, where the big nobs hang out, to find these two guys arguing with the cloakroom girl. I have to say that she was a nice little thing, though a bit thick; thought fellatio was an Italian opera, you know the type. The guys arguing with her were in their mid-twenties, scruffy looking, hard-eyed men with barbed attitudes and scowls. They'd come to pick up their jackets from the cloakroom but unfortunately they had both lost their tickets. They couldn't prove that they'd placed jackets in the care of the club. The girl explained that they'd have to wait until the end of the night if they couldn't produce a ticket. That's the club rules, it was nothing personal. The lads were not happy and told the lovely lady that she was 'fucking useless' and intimated that she might get a slap if they didn't get their coats. This is where I came in.

I splayed my arms in front, blocking the gap between the two men and me. This was my fence. Verbal dissuasion – the 'interview' started.

'Lads, you know the crack. You need a ticket. No ticket, no jacket.'

'Yeah, I know, but look,' he pointed at the jackets again, scruffy looking cleaning-chamois leathers, 'they're there.'

'So give me your tickets and you can take them.'

'She fucking told you, didn't she? We've lost the tickets.' He raised his voice challengingly, and moved towards me as he spoke. He was testing me out. It had worked with the young girl, now he was trying it with me. This was a subliminal challenge. As he moved towards me I stopped him with my lead hand fence. I was controlling the play. I picked up the aggression to meet the challenge. It was a game and I was used to playing it.

'Yeah, and she also told you that you don't get the fucking jackets without the fucking tickets. All right?' I deliberately included expletives to raise the play and speak the speak. I stared both of them down as I said it. The bird with the mouth became submissive, my aggression had out-leagued him.

'Come on man, just let us have the jackets. They're ours, honestly.'

I'll be honest, I didn't like the guys – they were big-mouthed bullies. If I hadn't arrived when I did they'd have already taken the jackets and hurt the girl if she'd stepped in their way, I was in no mood to do them any favours.

'No. You'll have to either wait till the end of the night or leave the club and come back for them later.'

They looked at each other hesitantly. Should they go for it or not? They stormed out of the nightclub mumbling something about coming back. The little girl in the cloakroom smiled, I was her hero, I smiled back. To be honest, I never really thought any more about the incident until about 2.30 in the morning when the guys returned. Everyone else had gone home bar John, Simon (the manager) and me.

'What are these two after?' Simon asked, looking at the CCTV screen in the corner of his small, cluttered office. Two men were walking menacingly towards the doors of the club.

'Probably after their jackets, I wouldn't give 'em them earlier because they didn't have a ticket.'

John drew on his cigarette.

'They don't look too happy Geoff.' There was no emotion in his voice.

'Well,' I continued, 'they had a go at the cloakroom girl earlier and they weren't happy when I wouldn't give them their coats.'

The doors to the club banged violently. We watched the lads, on screen, as they kicked and punched the doors. They were unaware that we could see them. At the time the cameras were a secret known only to the club staff.

'Looks like they want some!' John commented.

'Yeah, I think you're right,' I replied, still watching them on screen. A burst of adrenalin hit my belly and ran through my veins. I sniffed heavily, as though I had a cold, to hide the natural inhalation that comes with fight or flight. My legs began their pre-fight shake. I tapped my foot to the sound of an imaginary beat to hide it.

'Well they've certainly come to the right place,' added the manager with a grin. He was our biggest fan. We liked him too. He had stuck with us through thick and thin over the years and had lied to the police, on our account, enough times to warrant an honours degree in perjury.

John and I walked out of the office to the entrance doors. A violent encounter awaited us. It felt no different than going into a sparring session with your mates at the gym. But that was only because our training sessions were more brutal than the real thing – well, we wanted to get it right, no sense in taking the word of some ancient whose last fight, honourable as it might have been, was against a samurai on horseback. The enemy had changed; the environment had changed too, so logically the 'arts' had to change with them. Only, when you try and tell many of today's traditionalists this, they don't hear you because they've got their sycophantic heads stuck up the arse of some Eastern master.

John opened the front doors of the club, the sound of the metal locks echoing into the night. He stood in the doorway, filling the space ominously. He stared at the two men. That should have been enough really, they should have read the 'don't fuck' sign emblazoned across his face like a Christmas banner but they were blind to what was patently obvious to us: they were way out of their league.

'Wot d'ya want?' John was blunt. He frit the shit out of me and I knew him. Someone once said to me, 'What do you reckon you could do against a man like John Anderson, Geoff?' 'Oh' I replied, 'about sixty mile an hour!'

The smaller one got straight to the point. He'd had a long night, he was pissed up and pissed off. He obviously hadn't done his homework on street speak, he didn't know that he was already in quicksand up to his scrawny little neck, otherwise he would have shut his big mouth and called a taxi. 'We've come for our fucking jackets,' said Number One.

'Yeah,' Number Two echoed like a parrot, 'you're fucking out of order.'

I popped my head out of the door over John's shoulder. As soon as they saw me they lit up like luminous nodders, which was appropriate because they were a pair of nobs.

'Yeah, he's the one, he's the wanker that wouldn't give us them earlier on. Out of order.' He stabbed the air aggressively with his finger.

Wanker? Me?

'You didn't get the coats earlier on because you didn't have the tickets and if you don't watch your mouth you won't fucking get them now. All right?'

John grabbed the coats from the cloakroom and held them at arm's length out of the door. As the lads went to take them off him, sure that they had already won because they were getting what they'd come for, he dropped them on the floor at their feet. Grudgingly, amidst a few inaudible mumbles they picked the coats up and dusted them down, like they were polishing a turd. As they walked away, slipping their arms into the leathers, Number One said, hammering the nails into his own coffin,

'We'll be back for you two. You've got a big problem.'

As one, John and myself stepped out of the door towards them.

'Don't bother coming back, do it now!' I challenged.

'Yeah! Yeah! Why not? Lets do it!' Number One said, accepting the challenge. His chest heaved and his arms splayed, his speak became fast and erratic – he was ready to go. Number Two's face dropped like a bollock, his chin nearly hit the floor. He looked at his mate, 'Shouldn't we have talked about this?' he seemed to be saying. He was obviously in no hurry to get his face punched in. He put on his best pleading look, raised his arms submissively and retreated away from us quicker than a video rewind.

It was nearly 3.00 a.m., pitch-black but for the fluorescent lights at the entrance of the club that lit our arena. The air was thick with quiet, less the galloping hearts and frightened bowel movements of our opponents. The manager stood at the doorway, a pugilistic timekeeper about to witness the mismatch of the century. He shook his head knowingly as John and I squared up for the match fight with the two unhappy campers. He had seen John and myself in action more times than he cared to remember and felt sorry for the lads in front of us, one of whom foolishly thought he was in with a fighting chance. He had more chance of getting an elephant through a cat flap.

I must admit, though, that he did have me a little worried – I was scared I might kill him.

John raised his guard like a boxer, mine was at half mast like a karateka. My man raised his own guard high and ready, covering his face in an amateurish boxing guard, heavily exposing his midriff. His stance was short and off balance. His ribs looked mighty suspect.

Adrenal deafness clicked in and tunnel vision locked onto my opponent as he moved in a circle, to my left and around me.

John's opponent took one look at him and lost the fight in Birmingham. He said,

'You're a boxer, aren't you? Fuck that. I don't want to fight you.'

I started to move in for the kill.

Many people lose the fight before it even begins, in Birmingham, as I'm fond of saying, because they mistake the natural feelings associated with combat for sheer terror and allow their inner opponent the run of their head. There is a story of a wonderful old wrestler from London called Bert Asarati. In his day he was a monster of a wrestler with a fearsome reputation for hurting his opponents, even when it was a show match. He was seventeen stone at only five-foot-six and a fearsome fighter. Another wrestler of repute was travelling down by train from Glasgow to fight Mr Asarati in a London arena. All the way down on the train journey the Glaswegian ring fighter kept thinking about the arduous task that lay ahead, and every time the train stopped at a station his inner opponent would tempt him to get off the train and go back to Glasgow. Every time he thought about the forthcoming battle with Mr Asarati, his adrenalin went into overdrive. He was more scared than he could ever remember being. His fear ran riot and started to cause massive self doubt, he began to wonder whether he was even fit to be in the same ring as the great man. Every time the train stopped at a station the self-doubt grew, propagated by his inner opponent who kept telling him to get off the train and go back to Glasgow. At every station the inner opponent got louder and the adrenalin stronger. The wrestler's bottle gradually slipped out of his grasp until, in the end, he could take no more. At Birmingham station he got off and caught the next available train back to Glasgow. He sent a note to Bert Asarati, which read, 'Gone back to Glasgow, you beat me in Birmingham.' His inner opponent had beaten him a hundred miles before he even got to the fight venue.

This is what often happens to people in street situations. This is what happened to John's opponent on this night. He didn't lose the fight to John; he lost it to himself. John, not one to hit a man that didn't want to fight, let him off.

I buried a low roundhouse kick, as an opener to see what my opponent had got, into his ribs. As I had surmised, they were indeed suspect. He doubled over in pain and I swept his feet from under him. He lay on the floor like an upturned turtle. I didn't have the heart to go in for the finish, he was no match at all so I let him back up again and played for a while, shooting kicks to his head – something I would not have tried had the man been a threat. Every time he got back up I swept him back again.

In the end I felt sorry for him and told him to 'fuck off home' before I really did hurt him. He got angry and ran at me, arms flailing. I dropped him with a low sidekick in the belly and followed with a heavy punch to his jaw.

Bang!

He hit the deck heavily and I heard the familiar sickly crack of bone on pavement. He lay before me like an unconscious thing. I wondered whether he was badly hurt. For a second he looked all right, then, to my horror, a huge pool of blood appeared like a purple lake around his head. I thought I'd killed him. The pool got bigger and darker by the second. His face was deathly pale.

He didn't wake.

I felt panic in the pit of my stomach. My life passed before me. John walked over and looked down at the bloodied heap.

'Good punch,' he said, as though I'd just performed a nice technique on the bag in the gym.

I felt terrible. He looked dead and the blood intimated that perhaps I had cracked his skull. I waited for the brains to seep through with the blood, then realised that the guy probably didn't have any. His mate looked on, shaking his head.

'Is he dead?' he asked, adding to my misery. At the word 'dead' my stomach exploded. The adrenalin of aftermath shot through me, I couldn't stay any longer. Thinking that I had killed him was killing me so I wandered back into the club to grab a drink and a bit of calm. This was my worst KO on the door thus far and it scared the shit out of me. At the bar I trembled with fear. I made a promise to God that I would never hit anyone again if only he would let this one live, a promise I made every time some unfortunate with an eye for my title hit the deck, and broke every time they recovered.

Erasmus (no, he didn't work at Buster's) said that 'war is delightful to those who have had no experience of it'. He was right; fighting doesn't look so nice when it's basted in blood.

Outside, John lifted the unconscious man's head out of the blood with his foot to see the extent of the damage. Blood was still pouring out, leaving an explosion transfer across the whole of one paving slab.

'Is he dead?' his mate asked again, almost as though he wanted him to be – something to talk about on a Sunday afternoon in the pub. John gave him one of those looks and he shut his mouth.

Inside the club, already contemplating the big house and life in a cell with a right forearm like Popeye – or a very close cell mate – I made my way to the manager's office and watched the fight on the CCTV recording, just to see how bad I would look should the police get their hands on the tape. My shaky hand pressed Play and I watched the silent re-run on the small screen. It looked bad enough, though it lacked the sounds and smells of what had just occurred. I'm ashamed to say that I almost admired the action as I watched myself battering this non-entity, even using the 'slow mo' to highlight the meaty parts and check out my fighting technique. Sadly I, like most, had become desensitised to screen scraps from a lifetime of watching empty vignettes of violence crafted by screen technicians to stir inspiration. It makes me smile when I see how great directors creatively weave the sow's ear of real violence into the silk purse of celluloid. It would seem that the hypocrisy of people knows no bounds. Millions who abhor brutality, flock to view justified killings and glorious Oscar winning deaths, enacted by handsome thespians with carved features and rehearsed pros. The wowed, entranced audience visualise their finger on the killing trigger.

Someone once said that if they could put smell into cinema every war film ever made would flop at the box office. They were right. The recording did little more in replay than make me smile at how easy it all looked.

I was sickened, and at once enthralled, by what I saw. I quickly rewound the video and scrubbed the tape, then rewound it again and gave it a second scrub, just to be sure. In court, tackle like that could hang a fella. Back up to the bar in the empty club, I helped myself to another drink.

I felt sick with worry. I felt confused by the feelings that ran through my body. I was scared by what I had done and yet, in part, I felt exhilarated by the victory. It was probably due to the fact that, after adversity, the body releases endorphins, a natural morphine, into the blood. These give you a pick-up, a natural high, I guess that's where the confusion begins. Happy and sad at the same time; what a paradox. Years later, after many more KOs, sleepless nights and talks with God, I would develop a tighter control over this panic and learn better to live with fear. For now, I had to contend with the ignorance that came with still being new to it all.

Back outside, my unconscious opponent finally came round, his head in a blood-pillow. He looked like he'd been machine-gunned.

'We thought you were a goner,' his mate smiled.

John shot him another angry glance.

'Well *I* did.'

John looked on the floor at the three broken teeth lying forlorn on the concrete. They looked a little bizarre without the attachment of gums. He'd obviously landed on his face when he fell; that's where all the blood came from. He followed John's glance to the floor and his eyes squinted as though struggling to focus on the fact that he was looking at his own teeth. It was the first time he had ever seen them out of a mirror. He quickly felt his mouth and the numb, bloodied gap where the same teeth used to reside.

'Your mate's knocked my teeth out,' he said.

'There's no hiding anything from you is there, you fucking genius?'

John found me at the bar looking pale and very worried. I was still thinking about prison and wondering whether this job was really for me. I didn't like the feeling of losing my liberty to a wanker like the one outside collecting his teeth for the tooth fairy. The picture of unconsciousness and a blood splattered pavement stuck in my head like a freeze frame. In that moment of wonderment, Napoleon Bonaparte came to mind – doesn't Napoleon always do that to ya? – when he said (not to me personally of course, the man's been dead for ages) that 'there is nothing like the sight of a battlefield after the fight to inspire princes with a love of peace and a horror of war'. I had just seen the battlefield and felt that inspiration. Unfortunately I was to experience it a lot more, and far worse than this, before I learned the lesson and dumped the door in a transitional leap for a better, less violent existence.

John broke my daydream and ended my agony.

'Don't worry, he's all right, you just knocked his teeth out. Nothing bad.'

A sigh of relief raced through my body, a Death Row reprieve.

'Thank fuck for that!'

I was thanking fuck when I should have been thanking God; sadly, I'm ashamed to say, he had already been forgotten.

'Don't get too complacent, though, Geoff. He's a wanker, he'll go to the police. I know the type.'

'That's OK,' I thought. 'I can live with that. As long as he isn't brown bread.'

We were pretty sure that the police would get involved because it was an 18, a wounding. Broken bones and blood meant a probable charge of GBH with intent, which carries a possible five years in prison. So, as always, me John and Simon got our stories sorted out ready, just in case. The video had already been doctored, twice, so that wasn't a problem either. Simon agreed to say that he had switched the video off at 2.30 a.m. John and I agreed to say that the men did turn up at 2.45 a.m. and that we gave them their coats and sent them on their jolly way. A bit belligerent, but unhurt.

John was right. Within two days of the incident we'd had a visit from plod and were both taken in for a statement. As planned, we recited to our stories like lines from a bad play. 'No. I didn't hit the man, officer. That would be breaking the law. Must have fallen down the stairs' – that sort of scenario. And why not? The police are always covering themselves with accidents and stairs, even when they happen to reside in a station that has no stairs.

'He fell down the stairs m'Lud!'

'What, ten times, officer?'

This was one of the things we always did at Buster's, and did it well; whenever there was an altercation that we thought might attract attention from plod we would immediately work out our story so that, if we were arrested, there would be no confusion or contradiction. Our aim was to get the charges thrown out at station level, if not, next best was to get it thrown out by the CPS (Crown Prosecution Service). If the evidence was 50/50 the CPS had a habit of not proceeding with charges because it would be a waste of taxpayers' money, dragging a case through the courts when there was little chance of a conviction or prosecution. Why waste it on us when they could waste it on so many other things? It was a system that always worked well for us.

Sometimes we would have to tailor our stories so that they fitted a law that is unkind to those whose job it was to stop others from breaking it.

'John, my good man, the story is a little fat and won't fit into this blasted law thing. What I propose we do, me fella, is slim the blighter down with a diet of half truths so that it does fit!'

Genghis Khan said that the British were uncivilised because the law of the land did not protect the people. We made it protect us by lying; it was either that or become a victim of its often archaic precept.

We always kept the story simple, leaving very little to remember. We never allowed the police, the little devils, to draw anything from us that we didn't want to say. They play the game very deviously, as John and I were about to find out.

As luck would have it, 'Broken Teeth' was hated by plod because he had previous convictions for police assault; they had no intention of doing him any favours. In the old days the lad would definitely have been exposed to the 'accident with stairs' scenario that was almost the perfunctory penalty for 'beating copper', but with things the way they were at that time this was no longer an option, not if an officer valued his pension and wanted to remain in employment.

Robin Williams said that in New York a policeman will shout to a robber, 'Stop or I'll blow your fucking head off!' In Britain, a bobby is more likely to shout, 'Stop . . . or I'll be forced to shout STOP again!'

Thankfully this disease had not yet spread to the door – though it won't be long I think – you hit a doorman and, if the team is worth its salt, you'll pay in blood. That's the unwritten law.

In the interview room the atmosphere was tense, and I practised the 'duck syndrome' to hide the fact that I was experiencing adrenalin. If the plain clothes DC interviewing me could see my fear, she might rightly assume that I was lying through my teeth. I was, of course. I had become a master of the lie.

Let the games begin!

'This guy was a bit of a wanker, wasn't he, Geoff?' WDC was trying to get into my confidence. I wished she was trying to get into my pants – she was gorgeous.

'Absolutely.' I knew the game, I'd played it with better players too, though none so delicious as this one.

'That's why you gave him some pain?'

'Pain? I don't remember giving him any of that.' I was convincing, even I believed me.

'I told you already, Jane,' (we were on first name terms but only because she wanted to hang me), 'I didn't touch him. I had no reason to. He was just a mouthy youth with a fetish for abuse. Nothing more. Probably got dropped by someone less tolerant than me on his way home.'

'Yeah I know, you said. But we both know that you did it. And I don't blame you. He's a pleb, a lemon. Deserved all the pain that you gave him. Off the record Geoff, why did you hit him?'

Ah, the old 'off the record hook', the old 'we don't blame you' trick, the 'let's pretend that we're on his side and then fuck him' ploy. It'll be flattery next, mark my words. I wondered if I might get a cup of coffee and a date out of this?

'Any chance of a cup of coffee, Jane?'

Worth a try.

'Yeah, sure. I'll just fetch one. White with sugar?'

'Thanks.'

Yippee! One down. The coffee was machine-made but welcome. Actually it could have been soup, you can never tell, can you? I thanked her effusively.

'So. You were going to tell me why you hit him.'

I was?

'I just told you, Jane, I didn't hit him.' I was going to tell her that he looked better without teeth but thought better of it.

'You're a bit of a karate man, aren't you Geoff? Was it a karate kick that you hit him with?'

Yawn – flattery! I tried not to smile but I couldn't help myself, a small grin formed on my lips. I felt a belly chuckle rousing down below but held onto it for dear life. This was a serious business.

'I never laid a glove on the guy.'

'Geoff, we know what happened, your mate's already told us. This is off the record. I'm just interested in what happened out there.'

Jane was a beautiful woman, a cracker. I fell in love instantly. She was tall, curvaceous, with dark brown hair and a figure to die for. I liked her a lot. She looked tough in a womanly kind of way, and I couldn't help examining the curves so delicately pronounced through her dark blue skirt and white nylon blouse.

There was a faint hint of nipple peeping through, it wasn't cold so I pretentiously surmised that it must have been me. I'd heard of this DC before and by all accounts she was a good girl with loads of bottle. Apparently she could have a fight as well. I liked that in a woman.

As we sat in the tiny interview room at the police station Jane gently questioned me about my statement, trying to trick and trip me. I did my best to answer her as untruthfully as I could. That wasn't too hard.

John wasn't so lucky, all he got was a bald beat cop with a bad attitude and halitosis – his breath could strip paint. His head shone like a polished apple and hair hung out of his nose like spiders' legs. He tried to talk the talk with John but he was swapping speak with the wrong guy. John told him,

'Don't waste your time.'

Damn, back to the drawing board.

As Jane walked me out of the station, after two hours of questioning, she gave it one last go, her parting shot.

'Must have been a really good kick to do that much damage, Geoff. What was it that started it all, anyway?'

I stopped and looked at her. I have to say that I was disappointed. She was insulting my intelligence. I thought she might have had a little more respect.

'What are you trying to say, Jane?' I said in a disappointed tone.

For a second she was silent.

'Nothing,' she said quietly, 'it doesn't matter.'

I made my way out of the station and home. We weren't charged. When I told John that Jane had tried to trick me he laughed his nuts off. In a way everyone was happy, except Broken Teeth who now talks with a whistle. The police were happy because a known police attacker had caught some karma and we were happy because we got away with it, once again. I did get to meet Jane later in a personal capacity: we laughed about the incident and became friends, she was a beautiful woman.

www.summersdale.com

www.geoffthompson.com